JEFF VANDERMEER is an award-winning novelist, most recently the author of the *New York Times*-bestselling Southern Reach Trilogy – the first volume of which, *Annihilation*, is now a major motion picture released in 2018 – and the co-editor with his wife, Ann VanderMeer, of *The Big Book of Science Fiction*. His non-fiction about storytelling and climate change has appeared widely, and he has lectured on the topic at Vanderbilt, MIT, DePaul, the University of Florida, the Arthur C. Clarke Center for the Human Imagination and many other institutions. He grew up in the Fiji Islands and now lives in Tallahassee, Florida.

Praise for *Borne*:

'No one writes a post-apocalyptic landscape like VanderMeer, so detailed and strange in all its lineaments and topography'

NEEL MUKHERJEE, *Guardian*

'As Borne grows and evolves, so develops a weird family dynamic in a novel that is as much of a fascinating hybrid as its title character, both an enthralling fantasy adventure and a bleak eco-dystopic admonition'   JAMES LOVEGROVE, *Financial Times*

'From being a very successful science fiction writer, VanderMeer will become mainstream – and *Borne* is full of signs that he is already thinking ahead of that easy transition, and perhaps subverting it'   TOBY LITT, *New Statesman*

'Jeff VanderMeer's Southern Reach Trilogy was an ever-creeping map of the apocalypse; with *Borne* he continues his investigation into the malevolent grace of the world'   ...SON WHITEHEAD

'*Borne* is a fantastic read, a vivid vision of an apocalyptic future that defies expectations and challenges any preconceptions as to how events are going to unfold. It can be disturbing at times – there are some chilling moments that wouldn't be out of place in a horror novel – but it's a book that ultimately transcends genre, offering its reader a range of emotions and a finale that provides more than one twist, all of which should be applauded. Rachel's story is one that will stay in the memory for a long time'

Starburst

ALSO BY JEFF VANDERMEER

FICTION

The Strange Bird
Annihilation
Authority
Acceptance
Area X
The Book of Frog (stories)
Dradin, in Love
The Book of Lost Places (stories)
Veniss Underground
City of Saints and Madmen
Secret Life (stories)
Shriek: An Afterword
The Situation
Finch
The Third Bear (stories)

NONFICTION

Why Should I Cut Your Throat?
Booklife: Strategies and Survival Tips for the 21st-Century Writer
Monstrous Creatures
The Steampunk Bible (with S. J. Chambers)
Wonderbook: The Illustrated Guide to Creating Imaginative Fiction
The Steampunk User's Manual (with Desirina Boskovich)

BORNE

JEFF VANDERMEER

4th ESTATE • London

BORNE

4th Estate
An imprint of HarperCollins*Publishers*
1 London Bridge Street
London SE1 9GF

www.4thEstate.co.uk

First published in Great Britain in 2017 by 4th Estate
First published in the United States by Farrar, Straus and Giroux in 2017
This 4th Estate paperback edition published in 2018

1

Page design by Abby Kagan
Bestiary illustrations by Eric Nyquist

Printed and bound in Great Britain by
CPI Group (UK) Ltd, Croydon CR0 4YY

FOR ANN

PART ONE

WHAT I FOUND AND HOW I FOUND IT

I found Borne on a sunny gunmetal day when the giant bear Mord came roving near our home. To me, Borne was just salvage at first. I didn't know what Borne would mean to us. I couldn't know that he would change everything.

Borne was not much to look at that first time: dark purple and about the size of my fist, clinging to Mord's fur like a half-closed stranded sea anemone. I found him only because, beacon-like, he strobed emerald green across the purple every half minute or so.

Come close, I could smell the brine, rising in a wave, and for a moment there was no ruined city around me, no search for food and water, no roving gangs and escaped, altered creatures of unknown origin or intent. No mutilated, burned bodies dangling from broken streetlamps.

Instead, for a dangerous moment, this thing I'd found was from the tidal pools of my youth, before I'd come to the city. I could smell the pressed-flower twist of the salt and feel the wind, knew the chill of the water rippling over my feet. The long hunt for seashells, the gruff sound of my father's voice, the upward lilt of my mother's. The honey warmth of the sand engulfing my feet as I looked toward the horizon and the white sails of ships that told of visitors from beyond our island. If I had ever lived on an island. If that had ever been true.

The sun above the carious yellow of one of Mord's eyes.

To find Borne, I had tracked Mord all morning, from the moment he had woken in the shadow of the Company building far to the south. The de facto ruler of our city had risen into the sky and come close to where I lay hidden, to slake his thirst by opening his great maw and scraping his muzzle across the polluted riverbed to the north. No one but Mord could drink from that river and live; the Company had made him that way. Then he sprang up into the blue again, a murderer light as a dandelion seed. When he found prey, a ways off to the east, under the scowl of rainless clouds, Mord dove from on high and relieved some screaming pieces of meat of their breath. Reduced them to a red mist, a roiling wave of the foulest breath imaginable. Sometimes the blood made him sneeze.

No one, not even Wick, knew why the Company hadn't seen the day coming when Mord would transform from their watchdog to their doom—why they hadn't tried to destroy Mord while they still held that power. Now it was too late, for not only had Mord become a behemoth, but, by some magic of engineering extorted from the Company, he had learned to levitate, to fly.

By the time I had reached Mord's resting place, he shuddered in earthquake-like belches of uneasy sleep, his nearest haunch rising high above me. Even on his side, Mord rose three stories. He was drowsy from sated bloodlust; his thoughtless sprawl had leveled a building, and pieces of soft-brick rubble had mashed out to the sides, repurposed as Mord's bed in slumber.

Mord had claws and fangs that could eviscerate, extinguish, quick as thought. His eyes, sometimes open even in dream, were vast, fly-encrusted beacons, spies for a mind that some believed worked on cosmic scales. But to me at his flanks, human flea, all he stood for was good scavenging. Mord destroyed and reimagined our broken city for reasons known only to him, yet he also replenished it in his thoughtless way.

When Mord wandered seething from the lair he had hollowed out in the wounded side of the Company building, all kinds of treasures became tangled in that ropy, dirt-bathed fur, foul with carrion and chemicals. He gifted us with packets of anonymous meat, surplus from the Company, and sometimes I would find the corpses of unrecognizable animals, their skulls burst from internal pressure, eyes bright and bulging. If we were lucky, some of these treasures would fall from him in a steady rain during his shambling walks or his glides high above, and then we did not have to clamber onto him. On the best yet worst days, we found the beetles you could put in your ear, like the ones made by my partner Wick. As with life generally, you never knew, and so you followed, head down in genuflection, hoping Mord would provide.

Some of these things may have been placed there on purpose, as Wick always warned me. They could be traps. They could be misdirection. But I knew traps. I set traps myself. Wick's "Be careful" I ignored as he knew I would when I set out each morning. The risk I took, for my own survival, was to bring back what I found to Wick, so he could go through them like an oracle through entrails. Sometimes I thought Mord brought these things to us out of a broken sense of responsibility to us, his playthings, his torture dolls; other times that the Company had put him up to it.

Many a scavenger, surveying that very flank I now contemplated, had misjudged the depth of Mord's sleep and found themselves lifted up and, unable to hold on, fallen to their death . . . Mord unaware as he glided like a boulder over his hunting preserve, this city that has not yet earned back its name. For these reasons, I did not risk much more than exploratory missions along Mord's flank. *Seether. Theeber. Mord.* His names were many and often miraculous to those who uttered them aloud.

So did Mord truly sleep, or had he concocted a ruse in the spiraling toxic waste dump of his mind? Nothing that simple this time. Emboldened by Mord's snores, which manifested as titanic tremors across the atlas of his body, I crept up farther on his haunch, while down below other scavengers used me as their canary. And there, entangled in the brown, coarse seaweed of Mord's pelt, I stumbled upon Borne.

Borne lay softly humming to itself, the half-closed aperture at the top like a constantly dilating mouth, the spirals of flesh contracting, then expanding. "It" had not yet become "he."

The closer I approached, the more Borne rose up through Mord's fur, became more like a hybrid of sea anemone and squid: a sleek vase with rippling colors that strayed from purple toward deep blues and sea greens. Four vertical ridges slid up the sides of its warm and pulsating skin. The texture was as smooth as waterworn stone, if a bit rubbery. It smelled of beach reeds on lazy summer afternoons and, beneath the sea salt, of passionflowers. Much later, I realized it would have smelled different to someone else, might even have appeared in a different form.

It didn't really look like food and it wasn't a memory beetle, but it wasn't trash, either, and so I picked it up anyway. I don't think I could have stopped myself.

Around me, Mord's body rose and fell with the tremors of his breathing, and I bent at the knees to keep my balance. Snoring and palsying in sleep, acting out a psychotic dreamsong. Those fascinating eyes—so wide and yellow-black, as pitted as meteors or the cracked dome of the observatory to the west—were tight-closed, his massive head extended without care for any danger well to the east.

And there was Borne, defenseless.

The other scavengers, many the friends of an uneasy truce, now advanced up the side of Mord, emboldened, risking the forest of his dirty, his holy fur. I hid my find under my baggy shirt rather than in my satchel so that as they overtook me they could not see it or easily steal it.

Borne beat against my chest like a second heart.

"Borne."

Names of people, of places, meant so little, and so we had stopped burdening others by seeking them. The map of the old horizon was like being haunted by a grotesque fairy tale, something that when voiced came out not as words but as sounds in the aftermath of an atrocity. Anonymity amongst all the wreckage of the Earth, this was what I sought. And a good pair of boots for when it got cold. And an old tin of soup half hidden in rubble. These things became blissful; how could names have power next to that?

Yet still, I named him Borne.

WHO I BROUGHT BORNE TO

There is no other way to say this: Wick, my partner and lover both, was a drug dealer, and the drug he pushed was as terrible and beautiful and sad and sweet as life itself. The beetles Wick altered, or made from materials he'd stolen from the Company, didn't just teach when shoved in your ear; they could also rid you of memories and add memories. People who couldn't face the present shoved them into their ears so they could experience someone else's happier memories from long ago, from places that didn't exist anymore.

The drug was the first thing Wick offered me when I met him, and the first thing I refused, sensing a trap even when it seemed like an escape. Within the explosion of mint or lime from putting the beetle in your ear would form marvelous visions of places I hoped did not exist. It would be too cruel, thinking that sanctuary might be real. Such an idea could make you stupid, careless.

Only the stricken look on Wick's face in response to my revulsion at the idea made me stay, keep talking to him. I wish I had known the source of his discomfort then and not so much later.

I set the sea anemone on a rickety table between our chairs. We were sitting on one of the rotting balconies jutting out from a sheer rock face that had inspired me to name our refuge the Balcony Cliffs. The original name of the place, on the rusted placard in the subterranean lobby, was unreadable.

Behind us lay the warren we lived in and in front of us, way down below, veiled by a protective skein Wick had made to shield us from unwelcome eyes, the writhings of the poisonous river that ringed most of the city. A stew of heavy metals and oil and waste that generated a toxic mist, reminding us that we would likely die from cancer or worse. Beyond the river lay a wasteland of scrub. Nothing good or wholesome there, yet on rare occasions people still appeared out of that horizon.

I had come out of that horizon.

"What is this thing?" I asked Wick, who was taking a good long look at what I'd brought. The thing pulsed, as harmless and functional as a lamp. Yet one of the terrors the Company had visited on the city in the past was to test its biotech on the streets. The city turned into a vast laboratory and now half destroyed, just like the Company.

Wick smiled the thin smile of a thin man, which looked more like a wince. With one arm on the table and left leg crossed over the right, in loose-fitting linen pants he'd found a week before and a white button-down shirt he'd worn so long it was yellowing, Wick looked almost relaxed. But I knew it was a pose, struck as much for the city's benefit as mine. Slashes in the pants. Holes in the shirt. The details you tried to unsee that told a more accurate story.

"What isn't it? That's the first question," he said.

"Then *what* isn't it?"

He shrugged, unwilling to commit. A wall sometimes formed between us when discussing finds, a guardedness I didn't like.

"Should I come back at some other time? When you're feeling more talkative?" I asked.

I'd grown less patient with him over time, which was unkind as he needed my patience more now. The raw materials for his creations were running out, and he had other pressures. His rivals— in particular, the Magician, who had taken over the entire western reaches of the city—encroached on his thoughts and territory, made demands on him now. His handsome face beneath wispy blond hair, the lantern chin and high cheekbones, had begun to eat themselves the way a candle is eaten by flame.

"Can it fly?" he asked, finally.

"No," I said, smiling. "It has no wings." Although we both knew that was no guarantee.

"Does it bite?"

"It hasn't bitten me," I said. "Why, should I bite it?"

"Should we eat it?"

Of course he didn't mean it. Wick was always cautious, even

when reckless. But he was opening up after all; I could never predict it. Maybe that was the point.

"No, we shouldn't," I said.

"We could play catch with it."

"You mean, help it fly?"

"If we're not going to eat it."

"It's not really a ball anymore."

Which was the truth. For a time, the creature I called Borne had retreated into itself but had now, with a strangely endearing tentative grace, become vase-shaped again. The thing just lay there on the table, pulsing and strobing in a way I found comforting. The strobing made it look bigger, or perhaps it had already started growing.

Wick's hazel-green eyes had grown larger, more empathic in that shrunken face as he pondered the puzzle of what I had brought to him. Those eyes saw everything, except, perhaps, how I saw him.

"I know what it isn't," Wick said, serious again. "It isn't Mord-made. I doubt Mord knew he carried it. But it isn't necessarily from the Company, either."

Mord could be devious, and Mord's relationship with the Company was in flux. Sometimes we wondered if a civil war raged in the remnants of the Company building, between those who supported Mord and those who regretted creating him.

"Where did Mord pick it up from if not the Company?"

A tremor at Wick's mouth made the purity of his features more arresting and intense. "Whispers come back to me. Of things roaming the city that owe no allegiance to Mord, the Company, or the Magician. I see these *things* at the fringes, in the desert at night, and I wonder . . ."

Foxes and other small mammals had shadowed me that morning. Was that what Wick meant? Their proliferation was a mystery—

was the Company making them, or was the desert encroaching on the city?

I didn't tell him about the animals, wanted his own testimony, prompted, "Things?"

But he ignored my question, changed course: "Well, it's easy enough to learn more." Wick passed his hand over Borne. The crimson worms living in his wrist leapt out briefly to analyze it, before retreating into his skin.

"Surprising. It is from the Company. At least, created *inside* the Company." He'd worked for the Company in its heyday, a decade ago, before being "cast out, thrown away," as he put it in a rare unguarded moment.

"But not by the Company?"

"It has the economy of design usually only achieved by committees of one."

When Wick danced around a subject, it made me nervous. The world was already too uncertain, and if I looked to Wick for anything besides security, it was for knowledge.

"Do you think it's a mistake?" I asked. "An afterthought? Something put out in the trash?"

Wick shook his head, but his tight frown didn't reassure me. Wick was self-sufficient and self-contained. So was I. Or so we both thought. But now I felt he was withholding some crucial piece of information.

"Then what?"

"It could be almost anything. It could be a beacon. It could be a cry for help. It could be a bomb." Did Wick really not know?

"So maybe we *should* eat it?"

He laughed, shattering the architectural lines of his face. The laughter didn't bother me. Not then, at least.

"I wouldn't. Much worse to eat a bomb than a beacon." He leaned forward, and I took such pleasure from staring at his face that

I thought he had to notice. "But we should know its purpose. If you give it to me, I can at least break it down into its parts, cycle it through my beetles. Discover more that way. Make use of it."

We were, in our way, equals by now. Partners. I sometimes called him my boss because I scavenged for him, but I didn't have to give him the sea anemone. Nothing in our agreement said I had to. True, he could take it while I slept . . . but this was always the test of our relationship. Were we symbiotic or parasitic?

I looked at the creature lying there on the table, and I felt possessive. The feeling rose out of me unexpected, but true—and not just because I'd risked Mord to find Borne.

"I think I'll keep it for a while," I said.

Wick gave me a long look, shrugged, and said, too casually, "Suit yourself." The creature might be unusual, but we'd seen similar things before; perhaps he believed there was little harm.

Then he took a golden beetle from his pocket, put it in his ear, and his eyes no longer saw me. He always did that after something reminded him of the Company in the wrong way, unleashing a kind of self-despising rage and melancholy. I had told him confessing whatever had happened there might bring him peace, but he always ignored me. He told me he was shielding me. I did not believe him. Not really.

Perhaps he was trying to forget the details of some personal failure he could not forgive, something he'd brought on himself or actions he'd taken toward the end. Yet the job he'd chosen—or been forced into—after leaving could only remind him of the Company hour by hour, day by day. It was hard to guess because I didn't know much about biotech, and I felt the answers I wanted from him might be technical, that maybe he thought I wouldn't understand the details.

If I'd had his full attention, if Wick had argued with me over

Borne, the future might have been different. If he'd insisted on taking Borne from me. But he didn't. Couldn't.

WHERE I LIVED, AND WHY

By the time I found Borne, I was entangled with Wick in so many ways. We were bound by our mutual safe place: the Balcony Cliffs, which existed on the northeast fringe of the city, overlooking the poisoned river. To the west as the city sloped toward sea level lay the territory of the Magician. To the south, across desolation and oases both, the remnants of the Company, protected by Mord. Much of all of this sprawled across a vast dry seabed that extended into the semiarid plain beyond the city.

Wick had found the Balcony Cliffs and held them for a time without me. But only by inviting me in had he held *on* to that place. He provided his dwindling supply of biotech and chemical deceptions and I provided a talent for building traps both physical and psychological. Using Wick's blueprints, I'd reinforced or hollowed out the most stable corridors and the rest now ended in hidden pits or floors strewn with broken glass or worse. I used a terrifying nostalgia: book covers with death's-heads drawn on them, a bloody cradle never meant to break, a few dozen pairs of shoes (some with mummified feet still in them). The brittle remains of a doglike animal that had wandered in and gotten lost hung from one ceiling, while the graffiti added to the wall opposite would haunt an intruder's nightmares. If they knew how to read. A horror show linked to Wick's pheromones and hallucinogens, activated by trip wire. Attacks had come and squatters tried their luck, and always we had fended them off.

One route we'd made led to Wick's rooms, another to the stairs in the former lobby that granted access to a blind hidden near the top mulch. Another route came after subterfuge to the converted swimming pool where Wick stirred a vat of seething biotech creations like a mad scientist—and then from there to the cliff where lay the balconies that had given the place its name.

From the center, near Wick's workplace, the lines in my head were drawn most urgently to the southern edge of the mound, which faced the Company across the great broken divide of the city's southwest flank, the confusion deliberately multiplied, my purpose to create a maze for any unexpected visitors . . . before simplifying again at the exit to three passageways, only one of which led anywhere safe, and before that the door, which from the outside appeared to just be a part of the mound, obliterated by an inspiration of moss and vines. A strong smell of carrion, one of Wick's most inspired distortion pheromones, grew unbearable closest to the door. Even I had trouble leaving by that entrance.

Throughout the warren we had made of the Balcony Cliffs there now existed allegiances that felt intimate—more intimate even than our sleeping arrangements. Corridors? Tunnels? Even those kinds of distinctions had been lost under our excavating rule and Wick's addition of special spiders and other insects. I kept track of my traps with a map, but Wick, Company-savvy, used a flounder-creature in a shallow pan of water as his command and control, an ever-changing blueprint traced delicate across its back.

At some point, just as our systems of defense had become entwined, so too had our infertile bodies, and that had wrought an unexpected synergy. What had been created from extremes of loneliness, of need, had moved beyond mutual comfort into friendship and then toward some amorphous frontier or feeling that could not be love—that I refused to call love.

In weak moments, I would run my hand across his wiry chest and tease him about his pale, almost translucent skin against the deep brown of my thighs, and for a time I would be happy at the hidden center of our Balcony Cliffs. It suited me that we could be lovers there and retreat to being mere allies in the aftermath.

But the truth is, when we were together on those nights, I knew that Wick lost every part of himself and let himself be vulnerable. I felt this quite strongly, even if I might be wrong. And if I held back something from Wick because of it, still I let the Balcony Cliffs in, connected by something almost like lasers. These lines that radiated out from both of us surged from body and brain and through the rooms our talents kept safe. Sensors, trip wires, sensitive to touch and vibration, as if we lay always at the center of something important. Even lying there, beneath me, Wick could not be free of that connection.

There was also the thrill of secrecy, for to preserve our security, we could not be seen outside together—left by different pathways, at different times—and some of that thrill entered into our relationship. Anyone passing furtive far above us would have thought that underfoot, beneath the copse of sickly pines, lay only a vast midden, an old garbage dump with dozens of layers of crumbled girders, human remains, abandoned refrigerators, firebombed cars—crushed into a mulch that had a springy, almost jaunty feel.

But beneath that weight lay us, lay the stalwart roof of the Balcony Cliffs and the cross-section of body that served as our home—the lines that connected a woman named Rachel to a man named Wick. There was a secret shape to it all that lived inside us, a map that slowly circled within our minds like a personal cosmology.

This, then, is where I had brought my sea anemone named Borne—into this cocoon, this safe haven, this vast trap that took time and precious resources to maintain, while somewhere a ticking clock kept track of the time we had left. Wick and I both knew that no matter how much raw biotech material he created or bartered for, the beetle parts and other essentials he had taken from the Company so long ago would run out. My physical traps without

Wick's almost uncanny reinforcement would not keep scavengers out for long.

Every day brought us closer to a point where we would have to redefine our relationship to the Balcony Cliffs, and to each other. And, in the middle of all routes, my apartment, where, pulled taut by our connections, we fucked, we screwed, we made love, equidistant from any border that might encroach, any enemy that might try to enter. We could be greedy there and selfish there, and there we saw each other fully. Or at least thought we did, because whatever we had, it was the enemy of the world outside.

That first night after I had brought Borne into our home, we lay there in my apartment and listened to the remote, hollow sound of heavy rain smashing into the mossy surface far above. We both knew it was not real rain; real rain in this city came to us ethereal and brief, and thus we did not venture out. Even real rain was often poison.

We did not speak much. We didn't have sex. We just lay there in a comfortable tangle, with Borne on a chair as far from us as possible, in the corner of the bedroom. Wick had strong hands with fingertips worn almost smooth from his years of handling the materials that went into his vats of proto-life, and I liked to hold his hands.

This is how far we had come, that we could be silent and we could be still together. But even then, that first night, the presence of Borne changed things and I didn't know if part of the silence was because of that.

In the morning, we peeked out through one of our secret doors to find the cracked earth writhing with the death throes of thousands of tiny red salamanders. So intricate, their slow-questing limbs, their obsidian eyes. So much like a mirage. A mosaic of living question marks that had rained down from the darkened sky without meaning. And already to the west we could hear the rage of Mord and feel the tremor of his passage. Rage against this illogical rain or against someone or something else?

Once, comets had appeared in the heavens and people mistook them for celestial creatures. Now we had Mord, and salamanders. What did they portend? What fate was the city working toward? Within minutes of the sun hitting their bodies the salamanders dissolved into liquid, absorbed by the earth so that only an off-red sheen like an oil slick remained behind, dotted with the tiny tracks of investigating animals.

Wick did not seem much concerned about the salamanders despite his need to replenish the supplies in his swimming pool.

"Contaminated," he said, which I had known already from the look on his face.

WHY I CALLED HIM BORNE AND HOW HE CHANGED

I called the creature Borne because of one of the few things Wick had told me about his time working for the Company. Remembering a creature he'd created, Wick had said, "He was *born*, but I had *borne* him."

When I wasn't scavenging for myself or Wick, I took care of Borne. This required some experimenting, in part because I had never taken care of anyone or anything before—except some hermit crabs as a child and a stray dog for a day that I had to give up. I had no family, and my parents had died before I had arrived in the city.

I knew nothing about Borne and treated him like a plant at first. It seemed logical, from my initial observations. The first time Borne felt comfortable enough to relax and open up, I was sitting down to a quiet dinner of old Company food packets I'd found buried in a half-collapsed basement. He was sitting on the table in front of me, as enigmatic as ever. Then, mid-chew, I heard a whining noise and a distinctly wet pucker. As I set down the packet, the aperture on top of Borne widened, releasing a scent like roses and tapioca. The sides of Borne peeled back in segments to reveal delicate dark-green tendrils that even in their writhing protected the still-hidden core.

Without thinking, I said, "Borne, you're not a sea anemone at all—you're a plant!"

I'd already gotten into the habit of talking to him, but at the sound of my voice Borne snapped back into what I thought of as his "defensive mode" and didn't relax again for a full day. So I put him on a plate in the bathroom, on a shelf beneath a slanted hole in the ceiling that let in improbable sunlight from far above. I savored that green-tinged, musty light in the mornings before I went out to do Wick's work.

By the end of the second day, Borne had taken on a yellow-pink hue and the tenacity of his defensive posture hinted at either sickness or religious ecstasy, both of which I had seen too often out in the city. He smelled overcooked. I removed Borne from the shelf and returned him to the kitchen table. However, by then I noticed that the worms that composted my bathroom waste and excreted the nutrients Wick used in his vat had "disappeared."

Now I knew a few useful things. Borne could overdose on sunlight. Borne was a glutton for compost worms. Borne could move around by himself but wouldn't while I was there. So Borne chose to overdose on sunlight. Nothing now indicated that Borne was malformed or in any way a mistake.

I upgraded Borne from plant to animal, but still did not reclassify him as "purposeful." I should have, though, because following his bathroom adventures, Borne made no attempt to disguise his movements. I would come home to find him in the bedroom when he had been in the kitchen when I'd left—or back in the hallway when he'd been on the living-room floor. Upon my approach, Borne always remained silent and unmoving, and I could never catch him in the act. I sensed amusement from Borne over this, but I was probably projecting. This made me smile. It became a kind of game, to guess where he might be when I returned. I looked forward to coming home more than usual.

When I mentioned this to Wick, while giving him a half-dead azure slug I'd found near the Company, he didn't find it funny.

"You're not worried?"

"Why should I be worried?"

"Because it is concealing its capabilities from you. Already. You have no idea what it might do next. You're telling me it's organized and possibly as intelligent as a dog, and we still don't know its purpose."

"You said Borne didn't have to have a purpose."

"I might have been wrong. Give it to me. I can find out what it is."

That made me shudder. "Only by taking Borne apart."

"Maybe. Yes, of course. I don't have any sophisticated equipment here. I don't have the time or the ability for anything noninvasive." The Magician encroached, the supplies wouldn't last forever—the rhythm that ruled our lives.

To Wick, Borne was just another variable, something he needed to control to manage his own stress. I understood that, but perhaps the lie created by life inside the Balcony Cliffs was that at some point we might think beyond the next day or the next week. That was the sliver of doubt that had crept into me along with the laughter at Borne's antics.

On impulse, I hugged Wick, held him close, even though he tried to pull away. *This was business, this was survival*, that resistance told me, and I shouldn't mix our personal relationship with business. But I couldn't help it.

And I still couldn't give him Borne—not out of pity or concern or anything else false. And because I couldn't give him Borne, I stopped talking about Borne with him. When he asked about Borne, I kept my answers brief and casual. *He's fine. He's really nothing more than some kind of vegetable. A potted plant that walks.* Wick would look at me like he saw right through me, but he didn't take Borne away from me.

It was all a test as to whether trust could still exist between us, and every time I extended that trust a little further I expected it would be unable to take the weight, or the pressure of my weight on it, and snap.

WHAT I FOUND IN WICK'S APARTMENT

Trust, though, required certain betrayals. Long before the arrival of Borne, I had searched Wick's quarters while he was out selling his drugs. I assumed he had done the same to me, but who knew? This aspect of trust you don't talk about with the recipient.

My betrayal required skill—to un-puzzle locks, to bypass traps, to snuff optics—but in the end it wasn't worth the effort. Wick's three rooms did not reveal much about the man. The sum of his existence in that cramped space came to so very little. No family photographs or portraits, few personal items.

Perhaps, I thought, he chose to live so small to keep whatever secrets he hid out of his mind? I imagined that somewhere buried deep in our Balcony Cliffs midden lay a warehouse full of artifacts Wick kept locked away so he could not be compromised by them. But if that was true, I never found that place.

I had only the stark evidence at hand, coerced gently from a desk drawer with a little creative lock-picking: a diagram of a fish curled inside the outer tube of a broken telescope and a metal box filled with tiny vermilion nautilus shells, curled up and dry.

I pocketed one nautilus shell for later, examined the fish diagram. I held the diagram unfolded beneath the dim light of the fireflies Wick had embedded in the ceiling. I knew it was a relic from Wick's final project at the Company, the one he would only talk about when he was drunk. Certainly nothing like this had ever arisen from Wick's makeshift swimming-pool vat. Yet.

Whatever purpose the schematic had served, in the end it depicted an ugly fish, like a huge grouper or carp. A sideways, cutaway view, with lines radiating out from the brain, but also other parts, with numbers and random letters at the end of the spikes. That the fish had a wistful face of a woman with pale skin and blue eyes did not help, the effect ghoulish. It made me wary, as if some mad scientist had decided to make real a figurehead from an old sailing ship.

Wariness was not the term for the scrawling on the back. The more recent notes around the edges I could tell were in Wick's handwriting, and amounted to nostalgia: little nudges about how he might re-create the fish project, which had clearly petered out over time. But there was also a second writer, dominating the center space, with what looked like older marks, whose clear passion had increased into madness. The handwriting devolved into sweeping or stabbing marks, less and less legible, and then became gouged dark clouds of scribbles. The damage obscured meaning or told me too much. And what words that did peer through the mess were less than useful. Near the end of legibility, the scrawled words, *No more company*.

I put the empty telescope on the bed, continued my rummaging, worried Wick might catch me in the act. But I quickly realized there was nothing left to riffle through. So some scavenger's sixth sense made me return to the telescope. A patina like mother-ofpearl covered the surface. I held the telescope up to the firefly lights to admire it.

Then frowned. Something seemed etched on the surface. In fact, up close, the "metal" surface revealed itself as hundreds of tiny hard fish scales forming a pattern so integrated you almost couldn't see the joins. The surface was still silver shiny, blank, but when I adjusted my grip I discovered that the heat of my fingers had done something to the scales: miniature photographs had formed there. Sneaky, sneaky Wick—although I couldn't understand the purpose of concealment. The photographs appeared to date from before the city's ruination, reproduced from old books, but hardly seemed worth keeping secret.

Curious, I made quick work of the telescope's surface, heating up every scale with my touch, almost as if playing a musical instrument, and then squinting at the results.

Most that weren't photographs of places now destroyed held a record of impressions of the city. There were lists of places under titles like "Reclaim" and asked/answereds like "How do you kill a building? Do nothing." Some of it appeared to be the equivalent of microfiche containing a rich history of the city before the Company's appearance. Other fragments were so microscopic I could only guess at their importance, and wondered how Wick could read them, unless he had some viewing device hidden away, too. None of this seemed like the Wick I knew—who was a loner, who had never mentioned the city as it had existed before the Company, and who seemed to have blocked the hope of any future for the city from his mind.

But I finally understood the need for secrecy when I realized it wasn't just old photographs and older data. Some scales held monstrous visions of projects never completed that scared me because they made Mord seem mundane. Most important, other scales included a fair number of technical specifications for biotech that I knew Wick had created. None of our enemies needed that information.

Sometimes I wondered whether I would still find Wick fascinating if I uncovered all of his secrets, if I would even know who he was without them.

Back in my apartment, I dropped the nautilus I had stolen into a glass of water and watched as it reanimated, turned a brilliant shade of crimson, began to uncoil as it stared at me, almost defiant, and then disintegrated into nothing as if it had never existed. A disappearing trick. An illusion.

Drinking that elixir of Wick mysteries was impossible for me. I poured the water out, cleaned the glass, tossed the glass onto a pile of dirty old clothes out in the corridor.

◘

My other betrayal was simple: I liked Borne too much. I knew this in my bones, knew I really should give him up. But I also knew it would take something catastrophic for me to do so. The more personality Borne showed, the more I felt attached to him.

Borne also made it easy to keep him because I discovered he would eat just about anything—any crumb, lowly pebble, or scrap of wood. Any worm of any description that came within reach would disappear, never to be seen again. Borne ate a lot of what I would have discarded as trash and in a sense made a compost pile redundant. I think he would've eaten a garbage can if he'd been hungry enough.

This ease of life with Borne didn't stop him from continuing to puzzle me. The most basic and troubling puzzle? Even though so much went into Borne, nothing ever came out of Borne. This fact struck me as absurd, even humorously sinister. It actually made me giggle. *No pellets. No dung. No little puddles. Nothing.*

Borne was also growing. Yes, growing. I hadn't wanted to admit it at first, because the idea of growth carried with it the idea of a more radical change, the thought of a child becoming an adult. In how many species did the transformation become radical, the parent so different from the juvenile? So yes, by the end of the first month, although the process had been gradual, I could no longer deny that Borne had tripled in size.

I also could not deny that I was actively hiding Borne from Wick. I no longer let Wick into my apartment, or if I did I made sure to put Borne in the back room, out of sight. I ignored Wick's attempts to engage me on the subject of Borne as a threat or a creature that required caution.

Since Borne never displayed any kind of threatening behavior, I never thought to take him as a threat. Even calling Borne a "he" began to feel faintly ridiculous as he didn't exhibit the aggression or self-absorption I expected from most males. Instead, during those early days Borne had become a blank slate on which I had decided to write only useful words.

WHAT WICK HAD TOLD ME ABOUT THE FISH PROJECT AND THE COMPANY

Most of what I knew about the fish project, and the Company, came to me from Wick like fragments of a dark tale I had to put together myself. I couldn't tell if he held those memories close to ward off the world or to let in something of the world. The Company had come to the city unbidden, when the city was already failing and had no defenses against the intruder. For a time, the Company must have seemed a savior to the city and its people. For a time, the prospect of jobs alone must have been enough. I tried to imagine a young Wick being drawn into the Company, working his way from apprentice to making creatures on his own. Yet the vision always blurred, fell away. I could only ever see him in my imagination, fully formed, Wick as I knew him now.

The fish project had been his undoing, the cause of his being cast out from the Company after many years of service. But although the fish had led to despair, memories of the creature filled him with nostalgia, too.

"A tank of a fish," Wick told me one night more than a year before I found Borne.

We were on our balcony, looking up at the black sky and ignoring the slap and rush of river poison below. Sometimes, through the protective veil Wick had created to disguise us, we would see others on the balconies to the north, beyond the area we controlled. They looked like manikins or statues, something hopelessly remote, even though we knew they could be dangerous.

It was early in that year, far into a chilly evening. The wind gushed up out of the dark, broke against the balcony stone to bring the faint sting of river smells, and I heard the reassuring hut-hut-hooting of owls and the sounds of stealthy things moving through the underbrush below. I remember thinking that the creatures we couldn't see had no use for us, went about their business without the need to figure us into their plans. I had no use for me, either. We were both drunk on alcohol minnows and exhausted from a long day of work. I had blood on the bottom of my boots from a scavenging mission gone wrong, but not too wrong.

The sky and its blurred stars, seeking something, wheeled and roved and quivered despite how little I moved as I stared up from my chair. But still I listened to Wick beside me. Still I was awake. My sadness gave me a clarity, a kind of sobriety I hadn't earned, Wick much drunker.

"A wonderful fish! With a wide and mournful mouth—like you see in certain kinds of dogs. Beautiful and ugly and it moved like a leviathan. On land, no less! It could breathe air. I loved that it could breathe air. I gave it wonderful eyes, too: veined with emerald and gold."

I had heard this part before, but as much as Wick went on about the fish, the depths of his feelings weren't about the fish. Not really. As time passed and the stars above began to slow, to reorganize along familiar constellations, most of his emotions were focused on people from the Company: the old friend who had abandoned him, or whom he had abandoned, and the new employee who had betrayed him. The supervisor who had overseen the fish project. All of these people he had let into his life, and who had turned against him. Or had changed. Or had simply been acting to their nature, and Wick had come into focus for them for a time and then drifted out of focus again.

I didn't know them, and Wick never gave enough context to make me care. But also I couldn't remember as an adult when I had trusted three people at the same time. That Wick had once trusted so many seemed silly and irresponsible: an old-world indulgence. That he might have trusted them more than he trusted me I didn't want to think about.

I wondered, too, if Wick's view of the Company, his willingness to forgive, could ever be reconciled with my own view. To me, the Company was the white engorged tick on the city's flank, the place that had robbed us of resources and created chaos. The place that, it was rumored, had sent its finished products out by underground tunnels to far-distant places and left us with the dregs at the holding ponds.

Sometimes I met rare older scavengers who would spin me tales of the richness of the city before the Company's appearance, and their faces would shine with an inner light that almost made me change my mind about memory beetles. Almost. What they told me could not be the whole truth, the same as when we speak of the recently deceased and tell only the good stories. That was the beauty of the Company—how it won no matter what. How it had attached itself to the history of our city, even when it no longer existed here except as a husk, a ghost, or a giant, murderous bear.

"Someone killed it, showed it to me through a camera embedded in one of my spy beetles." Except, later on Wick said that another person had killed it.

Yet another version: that it had been wounded and lingered on for a time in the holding ponds outside the Company building. In this version, the fish had survived for almost a year—longer than it should have, in part because Wick had fed it. The creature had become a terror of that place: the monster with the human face that rose from the depths to devour. Although the human face was dead almost from the start, nibbled at and gnawed on by lesser creatures in the water, became waterlogged and misshapen in its decay, and no one would have recognized who it once was, nor could the rest of the fish ever recover from the death it carried atop its head.

In a fourth version, Wick hinted that the fish might linger there still, deep under the water. Wick telling versions. Wick hurt. Wick falling back into angst—Wick recounting how he had been forced out of the Company when his fish project was sabotaged, the Company sliding into anarchy, out of contact with its headquarters, and he having to live his life without the protection to which he'd grown accustomed. Turned him into a drug dealer, a survivalist, a man so thin and translucent he wouldn't have looked out of place in a row of creatures from a cave or the deep ocean.

In my darker moments, when I doubted my own true self and betrayed that self by framing my attraction to Wick as a kind of antidote, I knew that what Wick was really admitting was that in his past he had helped to create a weapon so deadly that not even its extreme beauty could justify its use.

The truth that Wick conveniently left out of most of his memories but was explicit in the notes on the diagram in his apartment: The purpose of his monstrous fish had been to serve as enforcer and crowd control, to instill fear, and perhaps to kill. In some remote place, a government still had had, at the time, the authority or the stability to restore order, was invested in restoring it.

And then, that night on the balcony, for the first and only time, another monster entered Wick's rambling discourse about the Company. "Mord knew about the fish project. Mord showed me what I was."

I didn't know how to take that. Had Wick coexisted with Mord in the Company? When Mord was smaller, when Mord couldn't fly? But whenever I sensed Wick had let slip something important, he would stop abruptly, as if reading my sudden interest, and fall silent. That silence was no natural end.

It was more like a cutting-off point, the border beyond which Wick could not venture.

WHAT I DID TO OTHERS AND WHAT OTHERS DID TO ME

In the city, the line between nightmare and reality was fluid, just as the context of the words *killer* and *death* had shifted over time. Perhaps Mord was responsible. Perhaps we all were.

A killer was someone who killed for reasons other than survival. A killer was a madman or madwoman, not a person just trying to get through another day. Once, I hit a woman with a rock. We encountered each other while out scavenging on the same deserted street on the west side of the city. I had found a smooth piece of metal being absorbed by a glistening red piece of fleshlike plant. I didn't know if Wick would find it useful, but I had never seen anything like it before.

As I turned a corner holding my prize, I came upon a woman walking. She was about fifty, wiry in the way survivors often are, gray hair hanging in a sheet, clothing a patchwork of gray and black.

She saw me and smiled. Then she saw what I held and her smile went away. "Give me that. That's mine." Maybe she meant "That's going to be mine."

I didn't wait for her to get close enough to grapple with me. I knelt and picked up a rock with my free hand. As she rushed toward me from the middle of the street, I threw it at her, catching her in the forehead. She went limp, fell onto her side, breathing heavily. Then she got up and I threw another rock, catching her in the head again.

This time she staggered back, put her hands on her knees as she hunched down. I could see the bright red pooling from her head to the ground. She sat heavily in the rubble and put a hand to her head, stared at me as I dropped the third rock I'd picked up.

"I just wanted to look at it," she said, puzzled as she kept putting a hand to her wound and taking it away again. Her eyes began to glaze over. "Just a look is all I wanted."

I didn't stay to help her or hurt her. I left.

Did she die? Did I kill her, and if I did, am I a murderer?

What happened between the woman and me wasn't new, no matter how much amnesia we've suffered; it was as old as the old world and older still. The first rule, the only rule, is that you carry your safety with you the best you can—you protect yourself the best you can, and you have that right.

But one evening, three weeks after I found Borne, I let down my guard. A gang of children creeping through the moss and detritus caught the door behind me before it shut. Followed me silent down the corridors to my apartment, keeping to my same path to avoid the traps and pheromones and attack spiders. I didn't notice because I was already thinking about Borne and wondering where I would find him this time.

Wick had left to tend to the farthest reach of his crumbling drug empire. None of my personal defenses—predator cockroaches in the hallway, the crab spiders embedded in the door, a good old-fashioned knife blade—could stop them.

Other than Mord, the poison rains, and the odd discarded biotech that could cause death or discomfort, the young were often the most terrible force in the city. Nothing in their gaze could tell you they were human. They had no memories of the old world to anchor them or humble them or inspire them. Their parents were probably dead or worse, and the most terrible and transformative violence had been visited upon them from the earliest of ages.

There were five of them, and four had traded their eyes for green-gold wasps that curled into their sockets and compounded their vision. Claws graced their hands like sharp commas. Scales at their throats burned red when they breathed. One wing sighed bellows-like out of the naked back of the shortest, the one who still had slate-gray human eyes. After a while, I wished he'd had wasps instead.

They smelled of brine and sweat and dust. They licked their lips and flexed their biceps like little conquerors. At that time, we did not know how they had become so changed, unless it was from contamination from the Company, and could not identify the new impulse rising nor where it came from.

I fought, but sometimes fighting isn't enough. Showing aggression and resistance isn't enough. You can't blame yourself for being outnumbered, if you want to stay sane.

It was useless. I was useless. They tortured me in various unimaginative ways for hours. The shortest mostly just watched, stood beside the bed with his slate-gray gaze shining dull from huge eyes, the whites not as white as his pale skin. They were on drugs they'd probably found on a toxic waste heap.

Between my whimpers and screams and thrashing, as the sheets grew red and the other three howled their dominance, I kept saying to the gray-eyed child, "Don't watch. Don't watch." I wanted to believe I was trying to spare him, but I was really trying to spare myself. It was too late for him.

When they began to tire of their games, they broke everything not of value, stood on one another's shoulders to snuff out my fireflies.

Then they found Borne—he must have moved or somehow attracted their attention. Soon their interest in me faded. On their way out, they decided to take Borne with them—through one bleary, blood-encrusted eye I saw them snatch him up.

That was the first time I pleaded with them, when they took Borne. That was the first time I truly knew Borne was important to me. But it didn't matter. They took Borne and left me in the dark, cheek laid open, face and arms and legs bleeding, some of the wounds deep. My skin burned. My skin was numb. My open flesh felt cold against the heat. I didn't have the strength to get up.

The city had visited me, to remind me that I meant less than nothing to it, that even the Balcony Cliffs wasn't safe. That every wire in my head connected to our defenses could be snapped, just like that.

✿

Time passed, and I existed in a quivering, exposed, horrible state. I was howling and shrieking, and there was nothing of restraint left in me; the pain took care of that. When I came to for the third or fourth time, my head lay upon Wick's lap and he was looking down at me with a curious expression on his face. His body flickered a light green with his stress, a side effect of giving a home to the diagnostic worms. My body felt soft and warm as he tended to me, with an ache behind it that threatened to become all-consuming.

"I'm so sorry," Wick said in a quiet voice as if talking to a corpse. The concern I hadn't seen in him came through in his voice, so thick and heartfelt, as if he had been crying, that it transfixed me, became something horrifying. I didn't need his devastation but his strength. "Just lie still. You shouldn't feel pain for a while."

I did feel pain, muted yes, but I felt it. But I nodded to give us both comfort, my vision blurring as I stared up at him. I could still make out the precise and beautiful architecture of his face, god help me. That still mattered to me.

He ran a diagnostic beetle over my body. It was old and worn, its carapace scratched, but its legs felt smooth, glossy. Everywhere it touched me, I felt an immediate, fast-fading glowing sensation. Wick had already closed up my wounds with the help of surgical slugs. I remembered the cool-cold sensation of their progress from the last time I had suffered an injury. My attackers had been creative, had cut me in patterns, writing words that had no meaning to anyone, least of all them. And so the movement of the slugs had retraced those paths, those words, given them a meaning by accident.

"I would hold you," Wick said from far away, "but I'm afraid I would hurt you."

Then I remembered they had taken Borne and wanted to ask Wick . . . what? To go after them? But Wick told me not to speak, said, "I'm sorry I wasn't here. I'm sorry they got through." He was in a different place than me, worried about different things.

"How badly did they hurt you?" he asked then, with a particular emphasis, and I knew what he was really asking. The question was medical but not medical. He had been re-creating my attack in his imagination and seeing the worst—and he needed to know just how invasive to be with his diagnostics.

"Just what you see," I said, and there was a noticeable relaxation of Wick's taut stance that somehow agitated me.

My attackers had been too single-minded or too inhuman to rape me. The one with the gray eyes, the oldest, had been about eleven years old. With sandy blond hair and delicate hands. I might not have told Wick the truth even if they had, but they hadn't. Two of the wasp-eyes had shoved their tongues in my mouth as they cut me, but it had been as if trying to contaminate me with something. A metallic aftertaste still lingered on my tongue.

Now I was crying—just a steady stream of tears without the expression on my face changing at all. There is only so much you can take before you begin to feel that the effort to survive is too much to endure. It would have been better if I had been attacked in the street. It would have been better if I lay out there now in a heap than to lie in the middle of the Balcony Cliffs and have to absorb Wick's guilt, his concern, his regard. To be *seen*, when all I wanted was to crawl away into a dark hole to die or recover from my wounds.

But I let Wick do his work and also told him how it had happened, so he would know how to bolster our defenses. I was alive, and from past experience I knew in time I would forget enough to again pretend that we could someday be free. Of the city, of Mord, of all of it. I don't know if that was hope. Maybe it was just stubborn inertia.

"And they took Borne, too," I said a little later, not sure my words were coming out right. Borne being gone was a concept I had to think around or I wouldn't make it.

Wick frowned from the chair next to my bed. "But they didn't take Borne." He nodded toward the living room. "He's right in there."

Even through my numb discomfort, the beetle crawling across my torso, I felt an overwhelming confusion and relief.

"Did they bring him back?"

"I don't think so. He was in the hallway by the door. Your attackers got away. I brought him back in."

"Thank you," I said, knowing that might not have been an easy decision.

"He's bigger," Wick said.

I said nothing. I didn't dare. For the first time I realized Wick looked worried or preoccupied for reasons that might have nothing to do with me. I'd managed to keep Wick away from Borne for two straight weeks.

The beetle had finished its work.

Wick got to his feet. "You need to rest. I've brought food for the kitchen. I've put up better defenses. I have to go out for a while, but I'll be back soon."

I understood. He needed to make sure my attackers were really gone. He had to change the locks, make sure no one else could enter the same way. All of which meant eating up more resources we didn't have, putting us both at risk much sooner.

The burn, the sting—the screaming agony—of what had happened would not return for hours, as if it was coming toward me from light-years distant. I extended my arm to touch Wick's cheek, the edge of his mouth, but he was too far away.

"I should have been here," he said.

"If you hadn't come back, I might be dead," I said, but this was no comfort. If the city had really wanted to kill me, it would have killed me, as it had so many others.

"I should take Borne with me," Wick said, trying to sound casual.

I winced. "No. Please. Don't."

It would have been better for Wick's peace of mind if I had shouted it out or said it just as casual. But I didn't. I said those three words in a small, broken voice, and Wick couldn't push back against them.

¤

At some point after Wick left, I realized I couldn't sleep and decided to get up. It hurt but I was already restless, unused to bed rest. I wanted to go see Borne. In my altered state I worried my attackers might have injured him as well. Or maybe I just wanted to be sure Wick hadn't taken him away.

He sat on a chair at the kitchen table, pulsing a faint green-gold. Wick had restored a few of my fireflies, but not many, so all I could really see was the glow of Borne.

Borne stood at least half a foot taller than that afternoon, his base thicker and more robust. On the chair, he came up to my shoulders. I couldn't see that any harm had come to him—he still had that perfect symmetry. He was beautiful in that darkness. He was powerful.

"It's just me," Borne said.

I screamed. I stumbled back, looking for a weapon—a stick, a knife, anything. His voice sounded just like the rasp of the boy with the gray eyes.

"Just me," Borne said. "Borne."

Just me.

The worms Wick had left inside me struggled to release the drugs that would calm me. I was shaking. I was making an uncontrollable sound.

"It's just me," Borne said again, as if testing out the words.

I flinched again, stayed up against the far wall. This time he sounded less like my attacker, warmer and more lyrical. What I would come to know as his normal voice, although he could assume many.

"Rachel," Borne said. "Don't need to be. Afraid." The gray-eyed boy's voice was completely gone now.

"Don't tell me what I need to be!" I shouted at him. "What *are* you?"

He began to shamble off the chair.

"Don't come closer. Stay the fuck away!"

I struggled for more words, to fill the space between us.

Into that gap, Borne said, "Go rest. Please rest. Don't worry. Sleep." I could tell Borne had to consider each word carefully before choosing one, unsure how they fit together.

"Sleep?" I laughed bitterly. "I'm not going to sleep now. You're *talking* to me."

"I am Borne," said the thing in front of me. "I talking talking talking."

Those words came out in a kind of mellifluous burble that reminded me of how much he had amused me those past weeks. But where did those words come from? Borne still had no face, no real mouth.

"Is this a dream?"

"Dream?" Borne said.

"How did you escape them?"

"Them?" Borne said.

"Yes, them—the children who attacked me."

"Children," Borne said. "Attacked me."

I was drifting then, drifting against my will, swaying as the medical creatures inside worked on me. I staggered, knew I was sliding down the wall onto my butt. The worms must have decided I needed sleep. Everything became fuzzy, indistinct.

After a time, I had a sense of Borne's shape looming over me, of things crawling around inside my veins. I was in my bed. I was on the floor. I was in the living room. Awake. Asleep. Suspended between. Delirious, raving, wondering if I was in a nightmare or just now entering one. All the things in my past that I tried not to think about rose to the surface, spilled out of my mouth, and Borne stood there, listening, I told him everything about me. Things I hadn't admitted to myself, that had been bottled up for so long I had no control over them.

I couldn't know it then, but what I offered up to Borne probably saved my life.

WHERE I CAME FROM AND WHO I WAS

Once, it was different. Once, people had homes and parents and went to schools. Cities existed within countries and those countries had leaders. Travel could be for adventure or recreation, not survival. But by the time I was grown up, the wider context was a sick joke. Incredible, how a slip could become a freefall and a freefall could become a hell where we lived on as ghosts in a haunted world.

Once, at the age of eight or nine, I had still wanted to be a writer, or at least something other than a refugee. Not a trap-maker. Not a scavenger. Not a killer. I filled my notebooks full of scribbles.

Poetry about how I loved the sea. Retellings of fables. Even scenes from novels I never finished and will never finish. Borne could have been a creature out of those childhood fictions. Borne could have been my imaginary friend.

I rationalized later that this is why I told Borne about my past, why I told him what I could never tell Wick, just as he could not tell me about a diagram, a hidden history of the city, the nautilus biotech. But maybe it could have been anyone, in that moment.

✿

I was born on an island that fell not to war or disease but to rising seas. My father was a politician of sorts—a member of the council that ruled the largest island of the archipelago. He liked to fish and build things in his spare time. He collected old nautical maps and liked to find the errors. He had a boat that he built himself called *The Turtle Shell*. He used to take my mother out for "floating picnics" while he courted her, land just a dot on the horizon.

"I must have trusted him," my mother said when he told the story. "I must have really trusted him, to go so far out at sea."

My mother had been born on the island, too, but her people came from far away, from the mainland, and it was a scandal when the two of them married because it wasn't ever done. That scandal gave me my name, Rachel, because it came from neither family but from outsiders. A compromise.

My mother was a doctor who took care of infants. She was quick to smile and laugh, perhaps too quick because she would laugh when nervous or distressed, too. I could see my father observe her carefully, perhaps to make sure of the difference. She liked the spicy food of her family's homeland and took up making little models of ships. She would playfully mock my father's fascination with boats using her models. Scale versions with toothpicks. Like my father, she loved to read and books surrounded me growing up.

We had what we wanted and more. We knew who we were. But that could not stop the rising seas, and one by one the smaller islands around us winked out of existence. We could see their lights at night with our telescope, standing on the shore. And then came the nights when we could no longer see those lights. We had known before that, but after that we put away the telescope.

I was only six when we left, boarding a ship as refugees. I remember because my parents told me the stories as I grew up. They told me the stories even as we continued to be refugees, moving from camp to camp, country to country, thinking that we could outrun the unraveling of the world. But the world was unraveling most places.

I still have vague memories of the camps. The ever-present mud churned to muck by overcrowding, of mosquitoes so thick you had to keep your mouth shut, of extreme heat balanced later by extreme cold. The fences and guard dogs that always seemed better tended to than the tents. The new papers we needed to apply for, the old ones that were never good enough. The cast-off biotech they shoveled into troughs for us and the way phones and other devices became extinct over time. The feeling of always being hollowed-out and hungry. Sickness, and always having a cold or being feverish. The people on the outside, the guards, were the same as us, and I didn't understand why they should be on the outside and we should be on the inside.

But also I remember my parents laughing and sharing things about our home as I became old enough to appreciate them. Photographs, a ceremonial bowl my father insisted on lugging with us, my mother's handmade jewelry, a photo album. Every time we moved and started over, my father would build things: tents or enclosures or vegetable gardens. My mother would pitch in and tend the sick, even though the countries we lived in didn't recognize her medical license. Was it selfless? They were fighting for their lives, their identities. So, no, it was not selfless, but it helped people.

My father must have been cheery for my sake, for my mother's sake. She might one day be able to return to a homeland. He could not, and it was rare we met anyone who had lived on the island. The stories he told became boring to me through repetition, but I understand now that he was just trying to fix that place with the compass of his memories.

Throughout all of this, my parents did not forget my education. Not a formal education but the education that mattered. What to value. What to hold on to. What to let go of. What to fight for and what to discard. Where the traps were.

Once, we found a kind of peace. My father led us to another island: not the same, not at all, but whether from an impulse futile or courageous or both, he meant to re-create what he had known. We had a good life there for almost two years. A city to live in, a beach to walk on, a botanical garden, a school, playing with children who looked like me. We lived in a little two-room apartment and my dad built in the backyard an outrigger canoe with a cannibalized motor. My mother became a doctor again, working in return for goods.

Every so often information came from the mainland that whatever might have been bad was getting worse, but my parents withheld any news from me for as long as they could, as best as they were able. Until, one day, shock: We were herded by soldiers via a crowded, diesel-spewing ferry to the mainland and another camp. The green-blue water and my father's boat and our apartment were gone.

It got worse after that, not better. It got worse and kept getting worse until we didn't even have the camps. It was just us, trudging across a land that held pockets of sanity and insanity both. Kindness and cruelty, sometimes from the same source. My father carried a knife in his boot and took turns with my mother holding on to a small revolver. We were as likely to come across burned and half-buried bodies in a ditch as a farmer and his sons armed with shotguns. Once, a grinning man invited us into his house and tried to rape my mother. My father had a scar across his left arm after that and we would stay off the main roads.

We starved at times rather than join the ranks of those marching toward an illusion, that slow, tired trudge. The back roads we took would become reduced to gray snakes against the blackness of forest or scrubland. In the distance, lights of a cabin or of a town would invoke in us dread and then caution, followed by avoidance.

Months after we had stopped believing in refuge, there appeared on a distant hill a city so miraculous it looked at dusk like a huge crystal chandelier that had fallen to Earth or a stranded ocean liner listing on its side. I could not keep my eyes off of it and pleaded with my parents to go there. They ignored me. They were right to. It lay on our horizon for several days, and during the night of the ninth day, having rounded its eastern side, still fighting our way through forest and plain, it caught fire, all of those sparkling lights taken up in a huge conflagration that burned the darkness away for miles around.

There came the blinking red hazard lights of bombers flying away from the city, and we so far down below marveled at the sight because it had been years since we had seen a plane of any kind. Something so old and so new. We wondered if airplanes might mean some resurgence, that some resurrection of a normal life might be upon us. But it was just an illusion. It meant nothing.

We made our way quickly more eastward still, fearing the exodus of the survivors as if it were a wave that might drown us, and yet they were no different than us. Then came the thick, powdery black smoke during the days, gathered up in the sooty rain that fell, and out of the ground came writhing worms and rabbits and other dying things.

Soon we would think back kindly on those days. But throughout it all, my parents held on to hope, kept trying to find a safe place. They would not give up. They never gave up. I knew that, even now that they were gone.

There was more that I told Borne, but I can't bring myself to write it, because it is too terrible to put into words. And it pushes up against the one thing I couldn't remember: how I came to this city, what had happened to my parents. My last memories from before the city were of floods and makeshift rafts and the expanding silence of people dead or dying in the water—and a hint of land on the horizon. My last memories were of going down for a second, third time, my lungs full of silt.

But when I came to, I was in the city, walking. I was walking by the river as if I had always been there.

Alone.

WHAT I DID NEXT, EVEN THOUGH IT MIGHT HAVE BEEN WRONG

For every clear-eyed view of my room that took in the lack of running water, the mold that had begun its war against the constellations of fireflies embedded in my ceiling, the half-collapsing wall with the window that looked out on a mountain of dirt . . . for all of that, and the scenes out on the streets of one tired and dirty person fighting another person who was just as tired and dirty over a scrap the old world would have found useless or disgusting . . . for all of that, I still could imagine a time when the small things we used to love might be returned to us.

"It's just me," Borne said and for a long time huddled on my bed, trying to recover, I didn't answer. Not really. I just spewed words at him, lost and rambling. Wick appeared next to him from time to time and winked out again. Sometimes I would feel Wick's arms around me. Sometimes I would see him staring at me with an expression of guilt and, I thought, of suspicion.

Was the suspicion because of Borne? Since the attack, Borne had changed again. He had abandoned the sea-anemone shape in favor of resembling a large vase or a squid balanced on a flattened mantel. The aperture at the top had curled out and up on what I chose to interpret as a long neck, sprouting feathery filaments, which almost seemed like an affectation. The filaments, with a prolonged soft sigh, would crowd together and then pull apart again like bizarre synchronized dancers. He was tall enough now that the top of him loomed a good two feet above the bed. Colors still flitted across his body, or lazily floated in shapes like storm clouds, ragged and layered and dark. Azure. Lavender. Emerald. He frequently smelled like vanilla.

As I lay on my side and stared at him—half curious, half afraid—I could see that Borne had developed a startling collection of eyes that encircled his body. Each eye was small and completely different from the others around it. Some were human—blue, black, brown, green pupils—and some were animal eyes, but he could see through all of them. They perplexed me because I didn't know what they meant. I decided to think of it as a kind of odd adornment, Borne's equivalent of a belt.

When Borne saw me staring at him, he would make a sound like the startled clearing of a throat, and his flesh would absorb all of the eyes except two, which would migrate higher on his body and away from each other. Sometimes they would slip back down to his hips, but once in position on his torso they became larger, took on a sea-blue color, and grew long, dark lashes; they moved independent of each other.

He must have thought he looked more normal that way.

On the sixth day, I felt more lucid, woke with only a slight fuzziness. Wick had gone out again, reluctant, to conduct business. He hadn't found my attackers, and I knew he probably never would. We hadn't talked again about what had happened, or about much of anything. I even pretended to be asleep when he came in. I had energy only for Borne.

From my bed I asked Borne a question. It was really the only question—a dangerous question to match a dangerous mood. I was still on the worm-drugs and I wanted to be of use, to do anything but just lie there.

"What are you?" My heart beat faster, but I wasn't afraid. Not really.

"I don't know," Borne said in a rough yet sweet tone. For a confused moment I thought he'd spoken in the voices of both my parents at once. Then, sincere and eager: "Do you know what *you* are?"

I ignored him. "Let's play a game to figure out what you are."

Borne went quiet for a second and his colors dimmed. Then he flared up.

"Okay," he said. "Okay!"

"Then you have to be honest with me."

"Honest." Turning the word over in his head.

"Tell the truth."

A ripple of vibrant purple traveled across his skin.

"Honest. I can be honest. I am honest. Honest."

Had I upset him or triggered some other emotion, or was he just testing out the word?

"You know a lot about me," I ventured. "But I know nothing about you. The game is about questions. Will you answer some questions?"

"I will answer questions," Borne said, uncertain. Did he understand the word *question*?

"Are you a machine?" I asked.

"What is a machine?"

"A made thing. A thing made by people."

This puzzled Borne, and it was a long while before he said, "You are a made thing. Two people made you."

"I mean something made of either metal or of flesh. But not through natural biological means."

"Two people made you. You are made of flesh," Borne said. He seemed agitated.

"Why didn't you save me from those boys?"

"Save?"

"Rescue. Help. Stop them from hurting me."

There came a long pause and everything about Borne shut down until he was just a gray shape. Even the eyes went away.

Then the colors came back in an explosion of reds and pinks and a roiling, turbulent green. The eyes popped up as a rotating halo embedded in the skin near the top of his aperture. "But I did help! I helped! I helped Rachel. I *helped*." This said in an anguished tone.

I tried to control the trembling of my voice. The spirit of Mord filled me up.

"Those boys hurt me for hours." I spat out the words. "Those boys did that and you did nothing. They hurt me badly. And you could have *done something*."

Silence again, then, in a whisper, "I could not. I did not. Help. Until."

"Until what?"

"Until I knew them."

I realized *knew* wasn't the word he meant. That the word he sought might not exist, that he was trying, perhaps, to tell me two or three things at once.

"Knew them how?"

"I am not complete," Borne said. "I was not complete. I am not complete." He tried "put together," which didn't help, finished his sentence with a kind of frustration for words that caused the feathery pseudopods to straighten like spikes.

"Now you are complete? Aware?" I didn't want to use the word *activated*, because it scared me.

"More complete," Borne said.

"You killed them," I said, calm. *But not before they hurt me,* came the raging, screaming thought behind the words.

"Kill?"

"Cease to be. No longer alive. Dead. Not here."

Confusion shuddered through Borne. "I know them now. I know them."

"Killing is bad," I said. "Killing should never happen. Don't kill." Unless someone attacks you. Unless you have to. But I didn't think to make the distinction to Borne, because I didn't have the strength.

Those eyes no longer seemed beautiful. They looked ever more trapped and horrible. Was it my imagination, or was one of them a familiar gray? I turned away from Borne then, and drifted into unconsciousness for a while. It was easier than facing what he'd said.

And yet why would I turn away unless I felt safe?

The seventh night, I slept in Wick's quarters, and Mord, far above, slept over us, sprawled across the sea of loam and debris that covered the Balcony Cliffs. We experienced his breathing as a haunted depth charge that tumbled down through the layers, the beams, and the drywall, the supporting columns and the cracking archways. The sound of it permeated the atoms of a dozen ceilings, vibrated through our bodies. We felt it in our flesh after we heard it in our ears, and it lingered longer under the skin.

The stench came to us, too, faint, carried by the ducts and the thousand imperfections in the sediment above us, carried by the subterranean tunnels of worms and beetles. Like the thunder after lightning, it came to us late, but then wrapped around our throats. It was the stench of every living thing Mord had killed in the last week. Could Mord smell us down here? Could he smell us mice? Us little human mice?

Wick lay frozen, unable to move, terrified that somehow this was not random, that Mord knew he was there, that come morning Mord might start to root us out. And so, for a time, we whispered and moved in slow motion and in all ways acted as if we were submarines and Mord a destroyer above, seeking us. Even to whisper, Wick would put his mouth right up against my ear. He could not stop talking about rumors of Mord proxies being seen, searching in the city and the hinterlands beyond. Searching for what? Wick wouldn't say, but I had the sense he knew.

Then we didn't even whisper, as Mord began to moan in his sleep. His moans sounded like gnashed, crushed words, filtered through the dirt, and we could not understand them. I knew only that they felt like anguish.

Some hours later we felt his weight leave us, the Balcony Cliffs almost seeming to spring back up around us with relief. When we examined the spot above in the morning there was a deep depression from Mord's weight. If he had spent the whole night there, would he have fallen through, smashing down level by level until, still sleeping, his body bulged through our ceiling? The stench remained for a day or two, and whenever I smelled it I felt a pressure pushing down on my head.

I had come to Wick's place so he wouldn't come to mine and be reminded of Borne, but Borne is the subject he raised as soon as Mord had left. I almost wished Mord was still there to silence him.

"I could still take him," Wick said.

"Who?" I asked, although I knew.

"Borne. It's time. I should just take him and figure him out. While you recover."

"You don't need to."

He hesitated, about to say more, thought better of it, and seemed to accept what I had said. He hugged me close and, as if I were his shield against Mord, soon enough snored quietly against my shoulder. I let him, even though it hurt; the price of peace. Because it was simple. Because it helped us both.

But I could not sleep. I was thinking about the silly conversations Borne and I were having because Borne didn't seem to know much about the world, had only fragments that didn't quite fit together.

Borne: "Why is water wet?"

Me: "I don't know. Because it's not dry?"

Borne: "If something is dry, does that mean it's not wit."

Me: "Wit or wet?"

Borne: "Wit."

Me: "Wit is in the eye of the beholder."

Borne: "What?"

I tried to explain *wit* to him.

Borne: "Like grit in the eye? Is wit like dust?"

Me: "Yes, dry."

Borne: "I'm thirsty. And I need a snack. I'm hungry. I'm hungry. I'm hungry."

Conversation would fall away again while I tried to find a snack for Borne, which, again, wasn't hard. He especially liked what you might call "junk food," even though that concept had become obsolete long ago.

Maybe, too, I liked Borne so much because Wick by then was almost always serious. For the longest time, Borne didn't know what serious was.

In the morning, with Mord and the weight of Mord just a bad dream, Wick tried again.

"I can do it in a gentle way," he said, but that didn't reassure me. "I can return him the way he is now."

"No."

His weight went taut against my back.

"I shouldn't have to ask. You should know it's the best thing."

"It's not."

"You know something's not right, Rachel." Now he was almost shouting.

Like most men, Wick could not help terror about one thing erupting as anger about something else. So I said nothing.

But he wouldn't let up. "Give me Borne," he said.

I refused to turn to look at him.

"You need to give him to me, so we know what he is. He lives here, among us, and you protect him in a way that's unnatural. This thing you know nothing about."

"No."

"He may be influencing you using biochemicals," Wick said. "You may not know your own mind."

I laughed at that, even though it could be true.

"You have no right, Rachel," he said, and there was a wounded quality to the word *right*.

"Tell me about your time at the Company." I was tired of talking, just tired period. "Tell me all about your weird telescope."

But he had nothing to say about his telescope. He had nothing else to say at all, and neither did I. We both knew that one word more and either I would leave his bed or he would ask me to leave.

Wick. Wick and Rachel. Portrait of us. Wick and I, at opposite ends of the frame, half out of the picture. Oddly wary of each other now, for all that he took care of me, perhaps because he expected more blame from me, to bolster the guilt he had decided to keep. And perhaps I did blame him—for making me weak, for making me rely on his surveillance, his beetles and spiders, rather than my own traps.

Was that fair? No, it wasn't fair. But I had my own guilt: I now kept an even bigger secret from him.

Borne can talk. Borne killed my attackers and hid their bodies. Borne is intelligent. Borne makes me happy.

WHAT I TAUGHT BORNE AND WHAT HE TAUGHT ME

Borne made me happy, but happiness never made anyone less stupid. During my recovery, I had such trouble remembering what waited for me outside, as if I had to learn it all over again, despite having been taught so many lessons.

All kinds of dangerous ideas entered my head while groggy. It was as if the little foxes and other animals out in the desert ran in circles around my mind, barking and kicking up dust, stopping only to stare at me from afar and encourage me to wander. I kept fantasizing that I lived in a real *apartment* in one of the stable sanctuaries from my past. Everything would be fine—I just *had the flu* or a cold and was *out sick* until I got better. And when I was better, what would I do? When I was better, I would *go back to university* and to *some part-time job*. I would complete my *studies* so I could become a *writer*. Because the ruined city was just a bad dream and my life as a scavenger was a bad dream, and soon I would wake up, and the visions of almost drowning, of losing my parents and with them all connection with the past, would prove to be an illusion, too.

The longer Wick expended time and energy protecting me, the more ideas like this took hold of me. They had only a vague relationship to my memories of flight, of trying to find refuge, of all the dangers before the city.

But minds find ways to protect themselves, build fortifications, and some of those walls become traps. Even as I started to walk around my rooms with Borne, even as I ventured out into the corridors. It was so sad a fantasy that I brushed by without recognition the revenants that told me it was a lie. The chair stuck in the wall. The filing cabinet rusted beyond use, now just a barricade at the mouth of a tunnel. The lack of libraries or other people.

Yet those sequestered weeks also contain some of my best memories because of Borne. Wick was gone a lot, spying on the Magician's movements, providing beetles to his small band of dealers . . . and possibly because of our argument.

Which left Borne and me ever more time to explore. He'd gotten tired of being cooped up in the apartment. On days when I knew Wick would be out for hours, I'd take Borne into the hallways, prickly with the fear of discovery and stiff from my slow-healing wounds.

It was all a construct by then, this game of not telling Wick that Borne could talk. He had to know. But because I never admitted it and Wick never brought it up, Borne became an open secret that existed between us like a monster all its own. It made me reckless, as if I wanted Wick to confront me. That somehow our relationship would be a total lie if Wick didn't confront me.

Ignoring the strain on my own body, Borne and I would race down dim-lit, dust-covered corridors, Borne afraid of colliding/ congealing with the wall and tripping over his own pseudopods, wailing as he laughed: "You're going toooooo fast!" Or, "Why is this fuuuuuuuuun?" Which just made me laugh, too. When you don't *have* to run and you have the chance to run for the hell of it, it becomes a strange luxury.

Then we'd collapse at the end of the hall and Borne, in addition to his usual observation that he was hungry and needed a snack—I now let him hunt lizards and rats to blunt his appetite— would ask some of his questions. He never stopped asking them, as if he were really ravenous for the answers.

"This dust is so dry. Why is dust so dry? Doesn't it need some wet for balance?"

"Then it's mud."

"What's mud?"

"Wet dirt."

"I haven't seen mud yet."

"No, you haven't. Not yet."

I would show Borne a photo of a weasel in an old encyclopedia and he'd point with an extended tentacle and say, "Ooooh! Long mouse!" Which brought me quickly to the idea of teaching Borne to read, except he picked that up on his own. When we played hide-and-seek, I'd sometimes find him hunched up on the edge of a midden of discarded books, two tentacles extending out from his sides to hold a book and a single tentacle tipped with light curling down from the top of his head.

He would study any number of topics and had no real preferences, his many eyes enthusiastically moving back and forth as he read the pages at a steady clip. I don't believe he needed light, or eyes, to read, but I know he liked to mimic what he saw me doing. Perhaps he even thought it was polite to seem to need light, to seem to need eyes.

But the truth is, I don't really know what he thought or how he thought it, because most of the time I just had his questions.

Eventually, I took him to Wick's swimming pool, which was Wick's laboratory. I loved the swimming pool, and perhaps that meant I loved Wick, too, in a way. The swimming pool had originally had a skylight above it, extending to the top of the Balcony Cliffs, and a divot of open space remained all the way to the top, with Wick contriving to camouflage it from above with his illusions.

When the light from the hole in the ceiling was right, it formed green-and-gold waves, as if the moss and lichen on the surface had mingled with the sun's rays and been transformed in some fundamental way. The light would glisten against the living filaments Wick had placed there as part of his work, and you could see dust motes floating and the occasional water bug or glider and, rising off the water, a mist that curled back on itself like certain kinds of ferns.

It could take a while to get used to the mélange of chemicals, which gave off a dank smell, cut through with something spicy. That spice could be sweet or sour, but was always sharp. Wick needed the light in the mornings to feed the rich, revolting, shimmering stew-brew to finish his beetles and other creations. But our shit and piss fed it, too, although the harsh smell was more of algae and peat and some bitter chemical. I'd long ago gotten used to it, even found it pleasant.

Eellike things wriggled in the mire and the fins of weird fish broke the surface only to submerge again.

"What's a swimming pool?" Borne asked.

"A place people go into to . . . swim."

"But it's full of *disgusting* things! Disgusting things live in there. Just disgusting. Really disgusting." Disgusting was a word Borne had just picked up and used often.

"Well, just leave those disgusting things alone, Borne, even if you are hungry." I gently slapped away a tentacle he'd begun to inch toward the water. I had no idea what effect those chemicals would have on him. Nor did I want Borne eating Wick's supplies, which would only endear him further.

Borne summarized for me: "A swimming pool is a place where people like to swim in *disgusting* things."

"Close enough," I said, chuckling. "You won't be encountering many of those when you're out in the real world."

And then I wished I hadn't said it, because I'd acknowledged that this wasn't the real world. That we lived in a bubble, of space and time, that just couldn't, wouldn't last.

I took him to the balcony out on the cliffs, too, but that was a little harder because I felt Borne needed a disguise, to be safe. I found a flower hat with just one bullet hole and a brown bloodstain to match. I found a pair of large designer sunglasses. I had the choice of putting him in a blue sheet or a black evening dress that I'd salvaged from a half-buried apartment. The evening dress was moth-eaten and had faded to more of a deep gray, but I chose it because I had nowhere to wear it and it was several sizes too big for me now.

So Borne reconfigured himself to be a little longer and less wide than usual, sucked in his "stomach" more or less, and put on this ridiculous outfit. Only, on Borne it looked good, and it wasn't until later that I realized he'd drawn himself up into an approximation of my own body, that I was looking at a crude faux version of myself with green skin.

But it wasn't complete enough for him.

"What about shoes?" he asked me, and I regretted having gone off on a rant about the value of a good pair of shoes a couple of days before.

"You don't need shoes. No one will see your feet." Probably no one would see him, period.

"Everyone wears shoes," he said, quoting me. "Simply everyone. You even wear them to bed."

It was true. I'd never gotten over having to sleep in the open so often. When you slept in the open in dangerous places, you never took off your shoes.

Borne really wanted shoes. He wanted the full ensemble. So I gave him shoes. I gave him my one extra pair, which were really boots, the ones I'd come to the city in.

He made a great show of growing foot-legs and with his hand-arms reached down to put on his new shoes. He'd muted his skin to a shade that mimicked my own. From the aperture at the top of his head, muffled by the hat, came the words, "We can go now."

But if Borne wanted the full ensemble, I wanted the full human.

"Not until you grow a mouth," I said, "and a real face."

"Uh-oh," he said, because he'd forgotten. In those days, he always said "uh-oh" when he felt he'd made a mistake. Maybe he also was trying to be a little "difficult," a concept he'd been field-testing, usually in charming ways.

The transformation only took a second. All of his eyes went

away, then two popped up where appropriate—never, ever gray anymore—and a nose protrusion that looked more like the head of the lizard he had eaten a few hours earlier, and a kind of crazy grinning mouth. In that hat. In the black evening dress. In the boots.

He looked so earnest that I wanted to hug him; I never for a second understood the gift I'd given Borne. Never realized what other uses disguises could be put to.

We went out on the balcony. Borne pretended he couldn't see through his sunglasses and took them off. His new mouth formed a genuinely surprised "O."

"It's beautiful," he exclaimed. "It's beautiful beautiful beautiful . . ." Another new word.

The killing thing, the thing I couldn't ever get over, is that it *was* beautiful. It was so incredibly beautiful, and I'd never seen that before. In the strange dark sea-blue of late afternoon, the river below splashing in lavender, gold, and orange up against the numerous rock islands and their outcroppings of trees . . . the river looked amazing. The Balcony Cliffs in that light took on a luminous deep color that was almost black but not, almost blue but not, the jutting shadows solid and cool.

Borne didn't know it was all deadly, poisonous, truly disgusting. Maybe it wasn't, to him. Maybe he could have swum in that river and come out unscathed. Maybe, too, I realized right then in that moment that I'd begun to love him. Because he didn't see the world like I saw the world. He didn't see the traps. Because he made me rethink even simple words like *disgusting* or *beautiful*.

That was the moment I knew I'd decided to trade my safety for something else. That was the moment. And no matter what happened next, I had crossed over into another place, and the question wasn't who I should trust but who should trust me.

PART TWO

HOW IT HAD BEEN, AND WHAT CAME NEXT

The first time I saw Mord it was twilight six years before I found Borne, on a day when I'd found nothing much except some autonomous meat quivering foul in a ditch next to a half-open storm grate. I knew a trap when I saw one. I marked the area with chalk to remember and made my way far to the west, to the remains of an abandoned highway covered over with lichen and rust and bone fragments. They formed a green-red-white pattern that almost looked purposeful. Not the good kind of lichen, or I would've harvested some for later.

The high level of chemicals in the city's air has always made sunset a stirring sight, even if you were jaded, had become fatally distracted, or just had no room left for poetry. Orange and yellow melted in layers into blue and purple. I checked to the north and south, saw no one. I found a faded deck chair somewhere and sat in it, eating some stale crackers from the week before. My stomach was a tight, aching ball as I watched the sun go down.

I was filthy from climbing through tunnels all day in the semi-abandoned factory district. I stank. I was exhausted. Despite my precautions, anyone could have seen me. Anyone could have attacked me. I didn't care. You had to let your guard down sometimes or you forgot what that felt like, and I'd reached my limit for the week. That meat going to waste to bait a trap set by a crazy person, a cannibal, a pervert—it had gotten to me.

Mord rose from the cluster of buildings directly ahead of me. At first he was a large, irregular globe of dark brown against the orange edge of the sun. For one terrified moment I thought he was an eclipse or a chemical cloud or my death. But then the "eclipse" began to move toward me effortlessly, blocking out the sun, destroying the sky, and I could see the great furred head in every detail.

I couldn't run. I should have run, but I didn't. I should have leapt out of my deck chair and made for a drainage tunnel. But I didn't. I just sat in my deck chair with a cracker half in, half out of my mouth, and watched as the shadow of the behemoth stole over me.

Back then, Mord wasn't as large, and he still lived in the Company building. As he rose over me like a living dreadnought, his pelt was golden brown, pristine, and clean-smelling, as if an army of Company employees had done nothing but groom him for hours.

His enormous eyes were bright and curious and curiously human, not as bloodshot and curved as they would later become. The smooth white of his fangs seemed less a bloody threat than the promise of a swift, clean execution. He luxuriated in the feel of the wind against his fur.

I cannot fully explain the effect of Mord on me in that moment. As that silky, gorgeous head glided toward me, as his gaze slid over me and past, with what seemed almost a secret amusement, as that pelt hovered mere feet overhead and the smell of jasmine came to me from his fur . . . and as I watched that whole vast body pass over me, I fought the urge to raise an arm to touch him.

Some part of me could not decide if I was witness to the passage of a god or, perhaps, out of hunger, a hallucination. But in that moment I wanted to hug Mord. I wanted to bury myself in his fur. I wanted to hold on to him as if he were the last sane thing in the world, even if it meant the end of me.

After Mord had passed me, I didn't dare look over my shoulder. I was afraid. Afraid he would be staring back with a ravenous look. Afraid I had conjured him up out of some dark need and he didn't really exist. How could Mord possibly fly? By what miracle or what damnation? I didn't know, and Wick had never offered up a theory. That Mord might once have been human, then, seemed like some distant, remote truth that lived on a mountaintop far from here. But it was this ability that made some in the city believe we had died and now existed in the afterlife. Some purgatory or hell. And some portion of all of those who believed sacrificed themselves to Mord—and not by gaping at him from a lawn chair, munching on a cracker. Because if you were already dead, what did it matter?

I sat there with the last of my crackers, as dusk settled over me and the stars made themselves known. Only after some time did I begin to shiver and take note of strange sounds coming closer, and seek safety for the night.

I had only been in the city a short time. Soon enough, I would meet Wick, and then, after some caution, move into the Balcony Cliffs with him.

◻

Even knowing that Borne had killed my attackers—even though I still knew too little about Borne—I could not give in to Wick's judgment. Wasn't there so much that was good and decent in Borne that I could bring out, no matter what I discovered about his purpose? This was the essential question that kept coming to me out of the darkness, even if I already had Wick's answer.

I worked so very hard at accepting Borne in the weeks that followed that I no longer saw him as odd. Even as he grew larger and larger, until he was taller than Wick, even as he kept trying out new shapes—changing from cone to square to globe, and then back again into his inverted squid pose.

Wick was there almost all the time now, still taking care of me. I should have been more appreciative, but I resented his presence more and more. When he was around Borne had to be motionless, voiceless, eyeless—sitting there in the far corner while Wick and I talked. He resembled a giant question mark, and the way in which Wick never looked at Borne made me know just how aware Wick was of my new friend.

But even when Wick left, my conversations with Borne continued to be halting and stilted at first. I had avoided the questions I had to ask at first, but then returned to them because I had no choice. I thought of myself as a shield against Wick, that Wick's questions would be more invasive, his conclusions harsher.

I returned to the idea of Borne as a machine. I found an old book amongst the wreckage and showed him a photo of a robot and then of a bioengineered cow. How we would long today to find a cow wandering the city!

"See? Like this?"

He reared up, exuding pseudopods as if they were coming out of his pores. "I am not a machine. I am a person. Just like you, Rachel. Just like you."

It was the first time I had ever done anything to offend him. I'd perplexed him, yes, but not offended him.

"I'm sorry, Borne," I said, and I was sorry. I changed the subject, a little. "Do you know how you came to the city, then?"

"I don't remember. There was water, a lot of water, and then I was walking. Just walking."

"No," I said patiently. "That's my memory. That's something I told you." This kind of confusion happened more often than it should have.

Borne considered that for a second, then said, "I know things about things that are not mine. But it's mixed up. I mix it up. I am supposed to mix it up. In the white light."

I thought of the white light common to tales of death, of dying. *I was in a tunnel. I saw a white light.*

"What do you remember about the light?"

But he wouldn't answer that question, defaulted to a common response that he thought pleased me.

"I found myself when you picked me up! I was found by *you*. You plucked me. You plucked me."

The word *pluck* was new, but always and forever amused him; he could not tire of "to pluck" or "plucked." He would make a sound like a chicken saying it, something I had taught him—"pluck pluck pluck"—and go running down the halls like a demented schoolboy.

But this time when he said it, Borne's voice got lower and lower and he flattened himself across the floor next to my bed, as he did when talking about things that scared him.

"Do you know your purpose?" I asked.

Borne's eyestalks, newly budded and continually extending and then retracting into his body, all looked at me quizzically.

"The reason," I said. "You know—the point of being alive. Were you made for a purpose?"

"Does everything have a purpose, Rachel?"

His words got to me, sitting in the living room, looking up at the mold-stained ceiling.

What was *my* purpose? To scavenge for myself and for Wick, and now for Borne? To just survive . . . and *wait*? For what.

But I was trying to be a good parent, a good friend, to Borne, so I said, "Yes, everything has a purpose. And every person has a purpose, or finds a purpose." Or a reason.

"Am I a person?" Borne said, and his eyestalks perked up and took special attention.

I didn't hesitate. "Yes, Borne, you are a person."

He was a person to me, but one already pushing on past to other concepts.

"Am I a person in my right mind?"

"I don't know what you mean," I said, my standard ploy when I wanted time to think. With my right mind.

"If there's a right mind, then there's a wrong mind."

"I suppose so. Yes."

"How do you get a wrong mind? Is it borned into you?"

"That's a tough question," I said. Usually I would have responded with something like "Do you want a wrong mind?" or told him it could happen either way: borned into you, or through trauma. But I was too tired from repairing traps all day.

"Is it tough because I already have a wrong mind?"

"No. Do you like to be silent sometimes?" Borne might be a person, but he was a difficult person, because he probed everything.

"Is silence because of a wrong mind?" Borne asked.

"Silence is golden."

"You mean because it's made of light?"

"How do you even speak with no mouth?" I asked, but not without affection.

"Because I'm not in my right mind?"

"Right mind. Wrong mouth."

"Is no mouth a wrong mouth?"

"No mouth is . . ." But I couldn't stop from erupting into giggles.

I saw these conversations as Borne playful. But really it was a youthful, still-forming mind that couldn't yet communicate complex concepts through language. Part of why Borne couldn't is that his senses worked differently than mine. He had to learn what that meant, at the same time he had to navigate the human world through me. The confusion of that, of finding unity in that, of basically becoming trilingual while living in the world of human beings, was very difficult. Always, as long as we knew each other, Borne was offering up so many *approximations*, so many near misses on what he meant that might have meant other things.

Much later, when I realized this, I went back over our conversations in my memory, to see if I could translate them into some other meaning. But it was too late. They are what they are. They mean what they meant, and I know I misremember some of them anyway—and that pains me.

✿

The last night before I would have to go out scavenging again, Wick came to check on me. It was perfunctory during this phase of our relationship, a duty and an obligation. Borne went into what he would later call, jokingly, "dumb mode" or "sucking in your gut." He drew in his eyes, got small, waddled to a corner, and sat there, immobile and mute.

"How are you?" Wick asked from the doorway. The intensity of shadow hollowed out his cheekbones, and I felt as if I were being approached by a concept, an abstraction.

"Good, thanks," I said.

"You'll be okay tomorrow."

"Yes," I replied although he'd not asked a question.

Wick lingered there for a moment, eyes glinting like mineral chips, holding himself apart, distant. I didn't like to see him hurt by me, but I was stuck. He didn't have to be so adamant about Borne—that was his fault—and I said nothing more. So he receded from me, back into the corridor, perhaps to go shove a memory beetle in his ear.

Wick receded; Borne blossomed. That was the way of it in those days—and in those days, too, the situation in the city had changed, and strange things were flourishing and familiar ones withering.

Since I'd last been outside, the Magician had become a major force in the city. She now held an area in the northwest starting roughly in a line extending out from where the Company building's jurisdiction ended on the city's southern edge. A growing army of acolytes helped make her drugs and protected her territory against Mord and others; Wick had only his peculiar swimming pool, the bastion of the Balcony Cliffs, a scavenger-woman who could make traps but kept secrets from him, and a creature of unknown potential that he desired to cast out.

Worse, the rumored Mord proxies had finally made their presence known and seemed more bloodthirsty than their progenitor. They knew no rule of law, not even the natural law of sleep. Upon their appearance, as if there were some collusion between the proxies and the Company, Mord spent several days huffing and puffing in front of the Company building. Under his uncertain aegis, the Company building was becoming more and more unstable and unsafe. Mord would sleep in front of it, and then other times he would forget his seeming role as protector and absent-mindedly butt into the walls with his broad head. We could see that people still lived in the top levels, under siege in a way as they were reduced to serving Mord's whims—while rumors came to us that beneath them, in the Company's deepest levels, no one ruled at all.

Despite these dangers, Wick had given me no refuge. We had an agreement and I had to begin to honor my side of it again. I would go forth and scavenge. I didn't know if that was a mercy or a cruelty, or where that impulse came from in Wick. I didn't care. It was time to get out of bed.

When Wick had gone, Borne extended a tendril of an arm, to take one of my hands in his own "hand." A reasonable facsimile, if a little damp.

"Rachel?"

"What, Borne?"

"Do you remember what I said about the white light?"

"Yes."

"Part of me had a nightmare about it while your friend was here."

I checked myself from asking all of the questions I could have asked.

Part of me?

Just now you were asleep?

You have dreams?

I had learned that when Borne used this tone of voice he was about to trust me, was sharing something important.

"What kind of nightmare?" I asked. How did he know the word *nightmare*? I hadn't taught it to him; he hadn't used it before.

"I was in a dark place. Only it was filled with light. I was alone. Only there were others like me. I was dead. We were all . . . dead."

"Not alive?" Sometimes Borne said that something was dead if it didn't move, like a chair. Or a hat.

"Not alive."

"Like a heaven or a hell?"

"Rachel." Said with soft admonishment. "Rachel, I don't know what those things are."

I didn't know, either. How could I know, talking to a cheery monster, living in a hole in the ground, among too many broken things? I laughed as much to dispel that thought as because anything was funny.

"Never mind. It's 'religion,' which I can teach you . . . never." My parents hadn't been religious, and I'd learned from the Mord cults that religion in the city wasn't about hope or redemption but about tempting death.

"Okay," Borne said, and his eyes formed a kind of reproachful smile. "I don't always understand, Rachel. I love you, but I don't understand."

Love? He'd just admitted he didn't know about heaven and hell. What could he know from love? I pushed forward, past it.

"And what happened next?"

"I tried to wake up. I tried to wake us all up. But I couldn't. I couldn't because I was dead. That's the word: dead. And I needed to wake up because a door was opening."

"Door" to Borne could, again, mean many things that were not doors.

"What happened when the door opened?" I asked.

"They would make me go through the door. I don't want to go through the door, and not just because I am dead."

"What's on the other side of the door?" I asked.

All of Borne's many eyes turned toward me, like rows of distant, glittering stars against the deep purple earth tones of his skin. For the first time in a long time I felt as if I didn't know him.

"Because I am dead, I do not know what is on the other side of the door."

That is all that he would say.

WHAT HAPPENED WHEN I WENT OUTSIDE AGAIN

My plan had been to try to take up with Mord, shadow him as before. This was still the best way to find useful things—and because the truest test of my recovery was to go right back to his shuddering flank, to risk it all now rather than find out later that I no longer had the nerve, or the skill. But now, that was too dangerous. Instead, I would travel to an area controlled by the Magician.

I delayed. I woke leisurely, pretended it was just another day in my recovery. But by early afternoon, I was all out of play-pretend and all out of excuses. It was a good time to go. Wick slept very late after having been out longer than he'd planned, to make sure neither the Magician nor Mord's proxies followed him.

I prepared my pack, with a small cache of weapons and supplies. Two of our last neuro-spiders that, like bio-grenades, would freeze an assailant's nervous system. Two memory beetles to negotiate my way out of trouble. A lump of something aged that might've been meat or bread but Wick reassured me was edible. A good old-fashioned long knife, a bit rusty, I'd found in the tunnels. A canteen of water, gleaned from condensation from the hole above the bathroom.

I felt surly and dangerous and powerful.

Borne discovered me as I was putting the water in my pack. "Do you make do with dew or do you dew with dew or dew ewe make dew with do?"

It had taken me a while to know what words he was using in which places in that question. "Ewe" had come from an animal-husbandry book.

"We all make do with dew," I said, even though it wasn't strictly true. But by now it wasn't a question, just a call-and-response.

"Are you going somewhere?" Borne asked. "People with packs are always going somewhere. People with packs are people with purpose."

I'd avoided looking at him and all of those eyes, but now I turned, pack packed, and said, "I'm going outside. I'm going on a scavenging run. I'll be back before dark."

"What's a 'scavenging run'?"

"Doing dew," I said. "Doing dew for you."

"I want to go," Borne said, as if the city were just another tunnel. "I should go. It's settled. I'll go." He liked to settle things before I could decide.

"You can't go, Borne," I said.

All the dangers had come back to me, and I didn't think Borne was ready to encounter them. It wasn't just the Magician or Mord. My own kind, too, were dangerous: scavengers who hid under trapdoors like spiders to leap out; ones who repurposed what they found in factories and sold it for food; ones who found a good hoard and defended it; ones (few) who had learned to grow a form of food off of their bodies and cannibalized themselves, with ever smaller returns; ones who had half wasted away, because they weren't smart enough or lucky enough, and whose bones would salt the plain of broken buildings, leave no memory or imprint to worry the rest of us who lived. I didn't want to end up like any of them, and I didn't want them claiming Borne as salvage, either.

But Borne was undaunted by my resistance.

"I have an idea," he said. "Don't say no yet." Another favorite gambit. *Don't say no yet.* When had I ever really said no to him? The number of discarded lizard heads gathered in a wastebasket in a far corner of the Balcony Cliffs was testament to that.

"No."

"But I *said* you *can't* say no!" In a flurry and fury, he expanded in all directions and covered the walls like a rough, green-tinged surreal sea with what now became two huge glowing red eyes, staring down at me from the ceiling. I smelled something burning. He knew I didn't like that smell. (Unfortunately, he didn't mind the smell of me farting in retaliation.)

I was wise to this form of tantrum, and it did not startle me. I had grown accustomed to so many things while recovering.

"Next time, maybe." My own favorite gambit.

He contracted to something the size and shape of a large, green dog, his two red eyes becoming one large, brown affectionate one, and he blobbed down from the ceiling onto the floor. A doglike tongue extended to pant ferociously as he stared up at me.

"Next time! Next time. Next time?"

"We'll see," I said.

He went into the bathroom and sulked. He was getting impatient and moody, in part because the food I gave him had become boring but also because he had explored every inch of the Balcony Cliffs, even with the constraint of having to avoid Wick. I'm sure, too, that even though he could become small for a period of time, the tunnels and corridors were becoming claustrophobic. But I didn't want Borne going outside.

Sometimes, when my parents had looked at me in an adoring way, I felt the weight of their love and stuck my tongue out like a brat. Now I looked at Borne in the same way.

✿

The brightness of the outside surprised me, shafts of light cutting through at odd angles. I'd taken three or four different shake-off routes and crawled the last hundred feet through a tunnel that bruised my sides just to make sure no one could figure out my point of origin. Emerging, the light made me squint, but I welcomed the blunt heat after so long inside. This might be the Magician's territory, but unlike the Mord proxies, the Magician did sleep, and her control was more like an insurgency, since she could not combat Mord direct.

It was a residential neighborhood but looked like it had been bombed or held by an army before the end. Anyone squatting since had left no mark, because to leave a sign was to invite predators. Blackened supporting walls punched full of ragged holes. Doors gone, hinges gone, too. Few roofs. Brittle old telephone poles cracked at the stem leaned up against the walls of rows of dead houses with tiny dust squares for lawns. The poles could have been felled by Mord, all crooked at the same angle. Where the dust and sand had taken the street, the poles helped orient me.

As I moved across that stillness, I would be vulnerable, even if I stuck to the shadows of those useless walls, kept the sun to my back when I could. I deliberately chose paths where I saw no one, except from afar. A few souls resting on a stoop, the house behind them a litter of fallen beams. Two people running away, looking over their shoulders. A powerfully built man in black robes casually chopping at something with an ax—firewood, flesh? I didn't linger to find out.

It was never that the city in those days lay still or seemed quiet because no one lived there; only that you could not always see them or evidence of their movements. Few lived well, few lived happily or long. But we did exist, and when beyond the sanctuary of the Balcony Cliffs I always tried to remember that people slept there, hid there, had burrowed down deep, or were waiting for me or someone like me to venture past—trigger a trap or snare, or shadow me to see if I had hidden food or biotech somewhere.

I crossed an intersection, running low, bent over, to the next place of concealment. I entered through door-size holes blasted in walls that must have been made to allow safe passage under threat of long-ago sniper fire. Lizards scuttled away from me, and there was just my quickened breath and the smell of sweat and the scuff of shoe against dusty gravel. Just the yellowing remains of someone's attempt at a vegetable garden, a few clotheslines strung up out of sight of the road that in their tautness seemed new, not old.

I came to the edge of a courtyard and a peculiar sight. For anywhere but here. Three dead astronauts had fallen to Earth and been planted like tulips, buried to their rib cages, then flopped over in their suits, faceplates cracked open and curled into the dirt. Lichen or mold spilled from those helmets. Bones, too. My heart lurched, trapped between hope and despair. Someone had come to the city from far, far away—even, perhaps, from space! Which meant there were people *up there*. But they'd died here, like everything died here.

Then I realized they were not astronauts but only looked like astronauts because the sun had bleached the contamination suits white, and I felt perversely less sad. I couldn't tell what had happened. Perhaps they'd been doctors sent to fight some epidemic in the last days before chaos and then the Company. Perhaps they'd been something else entirely. But they were planted here now and grew strangeness from their faces, and I didn't trust them. I didn't trust that they'd been here a month ago. I didn't trust who had planted them like that, even though they might be long dead or just long gone. Who or what might be lurking down below, in the dirt and sand.

Approaching was a foolish idea, what created carrion, so I took in the details with my binoculars. So posed. So little like life. The gloves over the bones of their hands were store-plundered and didn't go with the suits. I thought I saw movement in a faceplate, a reflection of someone behind me, turned, saw nothing. But the feeling remained, and I always trusted that feeling.

There are tricks to flushing out a watcher. The most obvious is to stop, half-turn, and bend to tie up your bootlaces—enough to catch out an innocent or inexperienced or just incompetent watcher. Or, if they mean you harm, it will flush them out because they think you're vulnerable, distracted.

Another hint of movement behind me, coming from the corner I'd just peered around to get to the courtyard. But it stopped immediately or became something else. A strange thought, but I was beginning to trust my strange thoughts again.

Behind me and to the left lay rows of houses smashed to hell, more single-story houses on the right, the dust road in the middle.

I took a spider out of my pack, shoved it in my pocket, then, avoiding the courtyard of dead astronauts, quick-turned down the next side road with houses that were still intact, then used a hill of rubble to clamber up onto a gently steepled roof. I needed a bird's-eye view, even if there was a twinge in my knee and a weakness in my shoulder to tell me climbing was a bad idea.

I lay on my stomach atop rough tile and splintered wood, a faded, tired heat rising from the roof into my body. The roof was damaged but stable. The sky beyond was a burnt blue, dissolving into almost-dusk. A mirage of delicate fracture lines in the distance promised mountains. But there were no mountains as far as we knew. That was just the sky lying to us.

Below I could see down the stacked rows of tombstone houses, which along with the roads conspired to form a ragged intersection or X in front of me. At the fringe, I could even see the pupa heads of the dead astronauts in their freakish courtyard.

I felt exposed despite my vantage, transfixed by a sense of triangulation and old scores to settle—an exhilarating sense of spying, of being a spy, or even a sniper that made me uncomfortable. A height, too, on a roof, that in this city wasn't what it might have been. Mord could swoop down to pluck me up before I had a chance to pluck something below—or, less poetic, Mord's proxies clamber up for a frolicking dismemberment.

So many minutes passed with me as a pretend horizontal statue that there was relief when I saw something I didn't understand at first: a shape coming up the street. I tensed and made myself smaller against the angle of the roof, staring into the light and shadows.

Someone tall in dark robes was walking toward me. Someone with a pointy, wide-brimmed hat pulled down very low. The floppy hat spun and glittered, and the gait was oddly fluid and disjoined; later I realized it resembled a baby's clumsy walk but in a man's body. The arms of the man hung out at his sides and the hands flopped as he walked. The too-pale hands seemed unimportant, as if the torso and legs were real but the arms were just there to complete the illusion.

Trailing this figure at a distance: a small animal, peering and peeking from the corners like I was peering and peeking from the roof. It had outsize tall ears and a rasping pink tongue, and my binoculars confirmed it for a kind of fox, but with strange eyes. A curious creature out wandering? Seeking carrion? Or a spy, a watcher? For whom or what? Whatever it was, it had instincts like mine, and all of a sudden looked up and spotted me, and then it was gone as if it had never been there.

A few more steps of the figure it had been following, and the fear in my gut turned into a wordless chuckle, and then irritation and concern. I knew I was looking at Borne in a disguise. Except he wasn't wearing clothes—he'd taken it one step further and just grown clothes from his skin. The hat was his head and the stars were his eyes, transformed into a pattern.

I leaned over the roof when he was one house away. I still wasn't going to stand up and give anyone a silhouette to target.

"Borne," I said.

Borne, startled, looked up.

"Oh my!" he exclaimed. "Oh my!"

Then he made himself large, larger, spun like a corkscrew, brought himself springlike up to roof level, so the magic hat could stare at me as if nearsighted. I almost lost my purchase on the roof.

"Borne!"

"Rachel!" He sproinged back to street level, looking up at me.

"Borne." I felt dizzy in the aftermath. He had grown more since the morning, clearly.

"Rachel. You weren't supposed to see me."

"You aren't supposed to be here! It's not safe."

A twinge of irritation from Borne, a new thing, from just the past week. "If it's not safe, why did you go?"

"That's my business. You disobeyed me. You followed me like someone not nice. *Not nice!*" Even though Borne still waffled between childlike and adult states, he'd never grown out of "not nice." Never not wanted to be nice.

"I know."

Downcast. But was he really? There was still something too *elated* about him. He'd become elated, and no punishment could un-elate him if the whole wide, horrible world hadn't. And under my gruffness, there was something too elated about me, out in the world again. Maybe he sensed that.

Borne's clothes fell away, and he was again a six-foot hybrid of squid and sea anemone, with that ring of circling eyes. I was rattled, drew back, reached for a beetle, stopped myself. He never looked so alien as he did in that moment, naked and alone on the street, even though it was how I knew him back at the Balcony Cliffs. Nothing and nobody has ever looked more like it didn't belong.

I had the impulse to leave him there, on that dusty street, leap across as many rooftops as possible to get away from him. That my life would be simpler, better, if I let him become someone else's problem. But the sense of loss that swept in behind almost made me stagger, there on the roof. I couldn't do it.

The air had a sudden weight to it, which made me think, irrational, that Mord must be drawing near, so I came down swiftly from the roof. And I didn't want to be out there after dark, either.

"What were you disguised as?" I asked.

"Nothing much," Borne said, not looking me in the eye with his eyes, which was quite a feat.

"What?"

"A wizard," he said grudging, bashful. "From one of the old books in the Balcony Cliffs."

"Which one?"

"I don't know. A lot of them have wizards. They all seem the same."

"They all cast different spells, though," I said.

"Do they? Is Wick a wizard? Does he know spells?"

"I'm a wizard," I said. "The spell I know is how to get you back to the Balcony Cliffs."

"That's not a spell," Borne said, but he didn't sound certain.

Wizards were not magicians, at least. If he ever fell under the spell of a magician, we were all lost.

"What am I going to do with you, Borne?"

I asked him because I didn't know. I'd been stupid to think I could keep him safe from contamination by the city. If there had been time, I would have given him a lecture right then on the dangers all around us. I would have told him what I hadn't up to that point: That most scavengers would see him as the ultimate scrap. That no one who saw him would think of him as a *person* but as a *thing*.

On the way back, we passed the dead people in their contamination suits one last time, and Borne waved to them and said goodbye.

As if he'd known them, as if they'd been his good friends.

A little later, I felt a prickling on my neck, the sensation of eyes upon us. Soon enough I identified the source, hanging back, shadowlike, padding on soft paws.

"That fox keeps following you, Borne. Should I be worried?"

"He's my pet," Borne said.

"That fox is not your pet. Do you pet him?"

"No, because he won't let me."

"Do you know why he follows you?"

"I told him to."

"You *told* him?"

"No, of course, I didn't tell him. That would be preposterous. Unholy. Stupid. Not cool."

"Why not sneak up on him and eat him like a lizard?"

"No, he won't let me," Borne said.

"Even if you lie in wait?" I had nothing personal against the fox, but it and its brethren had begun to bother me.

"He's always on," Borne said.

"What does that mean?"

"He's always on, like a lightbulb. He's not dim like most things."

"What does that mean?" I asked again. No one had lightbulbs anymore. How did Borne know about them?

Borne didn't reply, and the next time I looked back, the fox wasn't there.

But I still took evasive maneuvers, doubled back, and made sure by the time we took the secret door into the Balcony Cliffs that no living creature could be observing us.

✿

Back in my apartment, I woke with a start in the middle of the night, realizing that Borne might have been talking for a while. He was curled up next to my bed, a self-contained sprawl of short green-glowing tentacles, the myriad eyes darting across his body. Half of them watched me. Half watched the door. I had the fading impression he'd been peering at me from much closer just moments before.

". . . but I don't know why they were following me and I didn't know it would be so dusty out there and so big. It was so big out there. There was even sky. A huge sky. Such a huge sky it was like it was going to fall down on me. And all of those . . . walls. All of the walls. And the little things following me and it was hot. Hotter. It was hotter. Definitely hotter. I wasn't thirsty, but I could've been thirsty. Because it was hot. And wide and big. That's a city. That's what a city looks like in person. Like that. Like that.

"And there were astronauts. Buried in the ground."

He would remember the dead astronauts for a long time. In the next few weeks he even took three dolls and pretended to have conversations with them. They'd just come back from the moon and were helping to replant the Earth, or some such nonsense. Borne had so many tentacles, he could've put on a complicated play if he'd wanted to.

I rolled over and tried to ignore his ceaseless patter. Of course it had been sensory overload for him. Of course it had been something new. I'd have to get used to that or Borne's surprise would always be surprising me. Yet when I did get used to it, I would miss sharing that with him, even as it would be a relief. To be dulled to someone else's perpetual sense of awe was a kind of gift.

Then a thought occurred, and I reached over and tapped Borne on what I assumed was the top of his head.

"Huh? What? Rachel?"

"Borne, how did you even get out of the apartment? When you followed me."

A sluggish, slow response. I had a sense even in answering my questions he was devoting only a little bit of his self, while parts of his body popped and quaked, and continued to be somewhere else.

"The door was open. It was all the way open and it seemed like that meant you want me to—"

Propping myself up to one elbow, I cut him off. "No it wasn't and no I didn't." I had locked the door with several kinds of locks, mostly so that Wick could not get in.

"The space at the bottom of the door was open."

I took a moment to digest that. So Borne had made himself pancake-thin and, boneless, then gotten out under the door. Great.

I let Borne drift back into whatever boundary between watchfulness and sleep allowed him to dream.

But I was awake now, and so I went to Wick's apartment, thinking he might be back from his nocturnal wanderings. I wanted to sleep with Wick. Whether I meant sleep or *sleep*, I didn't know. But for an hour or a morning, I wanted some kind of oblivion that didn't mean anything for a while.

Raising Borne all by myself was exhausting.

I found Wick next to his beloved swimming pool full of "disgusting" biotech, and I took him right there, on the floor—unexpected and with complete surprise, even stealth, and found him willing.

After being outside, after having to be so alert, so in control, I was the opposite of those things—and fully recovered from the attack. I could move in all sorts of ways without pain.

I'd been outside and nothing bad had happened to me. Or, at least, nothing bad had had a chance to happen to me. And nothing bad was happening to me back inside, either.

"Not now," he said, "I'm working!" As per our old rituals, our codes and procedures.

"Now," I said.

"But I'm trying to work," and the joy in him, to voice the old complaint that meant he'd like nothing better than to be taken from work. To be taken by me, as hadn't happened for weeks.

So I took him and kept taking him until he had nothing left and we glistened with each other's sweat. Our bodies still knew each other, and the Balcony Cliffs still *knew* that we belonged together. I could still feel those lines of power extending outward, my traps and his surprises intertwined, and here we were at the absolute center of our creation.

Even if we hadn't spoken after, whispered those endearments so personal no one else would have known what they meant, it would have been good. It would have felt good, would have let me know that whatever had come between us that was wrong could be put right. But that led to me letting down my guard, perhaps because Wick in those moments after we had sex always seemed more playful than usual.

Wick got up, put on some ragged shorts and an old T-shirt, and went to the edge of the pool. He leaned on one knee, fishing something scaly and metal-gray out of the pool's fetid depths while, around one pale, thin, but muscular haunch, he looked back at me with those magnetic eyes.

"You're putting us both in danger, Rachel," he said cheerily. Wick looked naked from that angle, exposed and rangy. There was an almost insect-like humming and buzzing to the way he moved. That's when I knew for sure he'd taken something to make himself feel calm, or taken one of his own beetles and part of him was now far away from this place.

"With sex?"

Wick laughed, a higher-pitched sound than usual given the acoustics of that cavern, and padded around to the other side of the pool, some glint or glimmer driving him to use a stick to stir up the goop.

"Borne followed you out today," Wick said. "Because of him, you came back early. Borne continues to grow at a ridiculous rate, Rachel."

So there it was, said out loud. I opened my mouth to protest that he'd been spying on me, but what was the point? I'd snuck into his apartment and gone through his things.

"Shouldn't you be more concerned about Mord—and the Magician?"

"Borne is not your friend, Rachel."

"I never said that, Wick." Although he was now.

"You stood right here and told me that, told me to accept it."

I sidestepped that. "I never said that to you. Not that way."

"You told me I had to accept Borne."

One step more and all we'd be doing is denying, denying, denying. *I never said that, I never did that*, the way couples do.

"But why can't you accept him?"

"Because you're wrong. Because I can't go against the facts. I can only work around them." He was telling me that belief in Borne was like a religion. "Like the fact nothing ever comes out of Borne."

That again, as if it meant anything.

"Him not shitting or pissing doesn't seem to be dangerous. Him not *shitting* or *pissing* hardly seems a threat to our security."

"Maybe he hides it somewhere."

"Who cares if he hides his shit or not?" These were the conversations I loathed, the ones that made us sound dumb, distracted, petty.

"Because if not, then Borne is the most efficient creature I've ever seen."

"It's too late to break him down into parts, Wick. He's more valuable to us alive." There were some facts for him.

"Yes, it is too late, but not for that reason," Wick said. "I should've been stronger in the beginning. I shouldn't have listened to you."

"If you hadn't listened to me *then*, we might not be together *now*."

Wick gave me a quick, darting look. "Are we together now? Are we really together or do we just share a roof?"

I didn't answer right away. The ease with which I'd slipped into his bed now struck me as a problem. Not because I was returning to him but because he'd asked no questions first, hadn't resisted, had saved them for the aftermath despite our difficulties. I knew it meant I had a power over him I'd only guessed at before. Although perhaps I'd known it ever since he'd let me keep Borne.

"Only if we have no secrets," I said. Which wasn't fair. But it was also true. Wick still kept secrets from me.

Wick stood, stared back at me, still holding the handle to the pole, at the end of which he'd attached a strainer to separate out the smallest inhabitants of the green-orange pool. The water popped and hissed as half-grown fetal things broke the surface and submerged again. In the greenish light, Wick looked a lot stranger than Borne.

"I know he talks," Wick said. "Borne talks. I've heard him. I heard him once saying he might be a weapon."

Anger gathered, and I tried to tamp it down. "You were listening. You were eavesdropping in my apartment."

That feeling again, of this one issue rising up to destroy us. I hated the idea that someday we would be like some estranged couple forced to share the same apartment because neither could afford to move out and pay full rent.

Wick shook his head. "No, I wasn't. I heard him talking in the corridor. He was talking to a couple of lizards he'd killed. Before he ate them. He didn't see me."

Of course Borne talked to himself a lot. He was alone a lot more now, or alone together with me. Somehow that burned more than anything else. The sense that I might not be enough.

"He's not a weapon. You misheard. He doesn't know what he's talking about."

Wick shrugged. "Maybe."

I could see the hurt in Wick's eyes, at the way I hadn't even acknowledged the betrayal of him finding out Borne could talk that way.

And so I relented, in a kind of full surrender that covered his hurt with kisses, covered that hurt with sex. Because I still wanted him, but also so I wouldn't have to talk. Talking was the problem. Talking was the enemy. No more talking.

What drew me to Wick? What kept drawing me to Wick? I don't want to soften him for you, or give excuses, or hand over to you things that are too personal or ammunition for like or dislike.

But maybe in the beginning it was similar to what I liked about Borne. In the beginning, I could remember the childlike delight he took in so many simple things that subsumed or put aside his dread, his fear, his stress. The most hackneyed, clichéd, sentimental things. Like a ray of sunlight or a butterfly. Because that was such a contrast to the brittle quality of his suspicion. The wariness he wore like an exoskeleton, to disguise the shy boy underneath.

Even in those difficult times, stressful and uncertain, this sensibility could return to him. Just a couple of days after our conversation I observed him mirthful, not knowing I watched: running and skipping down a corridor of the Balcony Cliffs, saying over and over to himself, "I can do this. I can do this."

I wondered if Wick's diagnostic worms had eaten into his brain, for him to become so happy. I could remember this mood in Wick early on, but not now, so surely he must be drunk. Then, a little later, I went to his apartment and he was serious again. Could he only show that side of himself when he was alone?

I've brought you in late. I can only recite what were hauntings. He could be kind. He could be thoughtful. He could be idealistic. That's what I know. But I also know Wick put words in my mouth. I had never flat-out told Wick he had to accept Borne, never told him Borne was my friend.

HOW BORNE LET ME KNOW HE NEEDED PRIVACY

A few days after I'd caught Borne following me in the city, he shocked me with a formal announcement: He was moving out of my apartment. To tell me this, Borne had made himself small and "respectable" as he called it, almost human except for too many eyes. But, really, "respectable" meant he looked like a human undergoing some painful and sludgy transformation into a terrestrial octopus with four legs instead of tentacles. This is how he presented himself to ask a favor. Anyone else confronted with Favor Borne would have run screaming.

"Moving out, huh? That's something," I said, inane. My hands were shaking at the thought. My heart was up near my throat, everything in my head like a fluster of wings. Was he serious? He couldn't do it. I wouldn't let him do it.

"Yes, Rachel," he said, releasing a smell like honeysuckle and sea salt, which was his way of pushing. "It was bound to happen."

Really? Bound to happen? Because I truly had never thought it would happen. For all that I could see every branching tunnel of the Balcony Cliffs when I shut my eyes, this future had been dark to me. Borne existed in one particular place, existed at the heart of all the lines I had drawn here. I would raise him in my apartment and we would live here together and that was that.

But all I said was, "Where are you moving out to?"

"To another apartment in the Balcony Cliffs."

"Why?" Such a naked word, looking at him.

"I need my space," he said, and said it so adorably that I melted even in the midst of my panic. "I need privacy. I need to be private."

"Do I make you feel like you don't have enough space?"

"No," Borne said. "I just want some of my own. I promise I'll come visit. You can come over after I get settled, after it's all better in there." Which meant he must have chosen a real dump, requiring a lot of work. Or that a Borne-friendly apartment looked very different from mine, which hurt, too.

I couldn't help but think he'd read a scene like this in a book and was acting out one of the roles. Perhaps the role I was playing had gone to someone in the book who shouted at him or told him no or led him into a long, circular dead end of an argument about why he was wrong. But I couldn't be like that to Borne.

So many bad and not-so-bad thoughts, unworthy of either of us. Castigating myself already, cursing how I didn't know how to be a good mother. How of course if I forbid him to go outside, if I offered up slights, I might not even recognize that he'd leave me. And also: Wasn't this the natural progress of a child growing up so fast? To become an adult. To move out. To be on their own. But it wasn't the way in the city, where to hold fast, to be as one, was safer, even if I'd been filling him with the idea of a normal life, with commonplace ideas.

"I have conditions," I said, after a pause. "There are rules. Break them and you'll be living back with me again." As if that was such a bad thing, such a horrible thing, and me still not quite sure where this impulse, this urge for separation, had originated. Had it come from some outside source? I kept seeing the little fox as if the fox were a question mark behind everything.

"What are the rules?" Borne asked.

"You come visit me every day."

"Of course I will!" He seemed sad I'd thought he might not, or maybe I projected that onto him.

"You don't go outside, into the city, unless I'm along with you. For now, that means you don't go outside. You can sneak out of your own apartment under the door all you want, but you *do not* leave the Balcony Cliffs."

"That's fine, Rachel," Borne said. "I will be busy decorating my apartment anyway."

"And you still help me around here whenever I need you. And Wick, too, now."

It was inevitable that Wick and Borne would exchange more than suspicious glances soon enough. Each knew the other existed. Each acted a role around the other. Someday soon they'd be formally introduced. I'd taken pains to only talk about Wick in positive ways while around Borne, although I'd slipped up a couple of times.

"I can do that," Borne said. "Do we have an agreement?"

"Yes, we have an agreement," I said, bending to Borne's wording, as if we had signed a treaty.

A treaty that hurt my heart, but the great lurch within me, the thought I was losing him, had receded. He would be close by. He would still be with us.

"Thank you! Thank you! Thank you thank you thank you thank you thank you."

Borne became huge, spreading almost manta ray–like wings, and bore down on me to give me an enormous, all-enrapturing hug—and I withstood it, standing there buffeted and wondered why I was so sad. He was so strong now even this well-meaning gesture would leave bruises.

"You need to get off me." But I clung to him a little longer.

Borne's new apartment was only a corridor and a corner away, and the first night it didn't even feel permanent, as Borne dropped by to talk, mostly about the tragic lack of lizards in the Balcony Cliffs. Then we played a game from when he was younger, scant weeks ago. He was too old for it, but it served as a happy memory, something we shared now to show affection.

"Rachel, Rachel—what am I?" The strobe of colors felt like a smile or a flash of relief.

"That's a tough one, Borne. I don't know what you are."

"Am I a squirrel?"

"I don't think so."

"Am I a fish?"

"Definitely not!"

"Am I a . . . fox?! Secretly raised as a common animal. But really a royal fox. Most royal of foxes. First among fox-kind."

I shook my head. "No, not a fox." Again, Borne was telling tales out of a children's book. I resolved to give Borne some tomes on economics and politics in the morning. If I could find any. Maybe an airport thriller, except then I'd have to explain "airport" to him. Perhaps that was my subconscious revenge: If he wanted to be an adult, I'd make him become an adult all the way.

"Then . . . am I a . . . Borne?"

"Yes," I said. "You are a . . . Borne!"

"Oh, good," Borne said, "because that's the name you gave me." I couldn't tell if he was being sarcastic or not.

"And I'm a Rachel."

"No, you're not. You're a human being."

"Maybe I'm a ham bone connected to a finger bone." Something my mother used to say.

"Does a ham bone have a finger bone? I can see all your bones but I don't know what they mean."

Biting my lip to suppress a kind of nervous giggle, I said, "Stop thinking for a while, Borne. All that thinking can hurt your brain. Do you want to hurt your brain?"

"I don't know," Borne said. "If I hurt my brain, will I get a bigger one? One that isn't in my fingertips?"

Too silly for me, so I quit on him, which meant it was time to move on to the part where Borne used a newly formed arm to create the silhouette of an animal and I tried to guess what it was. Then I would do the same with my human hands, so slablike next to his adroit tentacles.

For a long time, even though he didn't yet invite me over, I guess I thought he was still just playacting, figuring out what it meant to be a person. And I still had the consolation that I was Borne's confidante—that Wick was still the intruder who had to sneak up on Borne and listen to him talk to imaginary lizards.

That Wick might know more than me about Borne was laughable.

WHAT HAPPENED WHEN I TOOK BORNE OUTSIDE ON PURPOSE

Soon enough, Wick would find out Borne occupied another apartment, and find in that fact further proof of threat. But a more immediate problem was that around Borne I had to be careful not to mention the outside, because the concept of the city, of anything beyond the Balcony Cliffs, now captivated him to a worrying extent. In time, whether we lived apart or together, I would have no control—no matter how he might want to keep his word, Borne would be tempted to go out.

"What rhymes with *crappy?*" Borne would ask.

"*Happy?*"

"No, *shitty.*"

"No, that word doesn't rhyme with *crappy.*"

"But it rhymes with *city,* and that rhymes with *happy.*"

"None of that is true."

"*True* rhymes with *fact.*"

"In a way, I guess."

"*Fact* rhymes with *city* and *happy.*"

"No, in this case *city* and *happy* put together rhyme with *opinion.*"

"You don't share my opinion?"

"Borne . . ." His asymmetrical rhymes were like bad puns in three dimensions—tiring, often scatological, or, as he put it, "only natural, which rhymes with *cultural*"—but always coming to a point. And the point he would generally arrive at was that he wanted me to take him out into the city.

But I exhibited discipline, did not rush to bring Borne along with me, even though that was the only remedy. I ventured out twice more first, although not in the exhilarating, dangerous sense of climbing up onto a sleeping Mord. I bought this time by promising Borne that the third time I went out into the world, he would go with me. I would be his teacher, even though I was still being taught.

Twice, then, I took to the streets alone, and twice I thought of myself as bait. I would not believe in my traps or my ability to see traps. I would see myself as bait, like the dead astronauts, who had never fallen to Earth but looked like they had. To be bait was to think of what or who I was bait for, and what might entice those who might want to take the particular bait that was me.

I was twenty-eight years old and from another country. Someone who scavenged for a living and who, when not searching for spare bits of biotech, took care of a child who wasn't human. I was good at using weapons. I could sniff out a trap from a distance. I had no formal education, but had been home-taught well and could read at an advanced level. I could, with Wick's guidance, grow things in my bathroom that I could eat. That was the treasure that was me, and every time I went out I would need to gauge who would ignore the résumé to gather the protein or want the skill set, or want the skill set snuffed out.

When I came back from those expeditions with enough salvage for Wick to take it as a sign that I had fully recovered, and that perhaps our relationship might recover, too . . . I had no excuse not to take Borne with me.

✿

Because Borne was coming with me, I would have to forage much closer to home, which was against the rules, but I didn't have much choice. I had been circling closer to home anyway, on my own. Mord was a mighty weight that could not disguise itself, but the Magician was the blade slipped between the ribs that you don't sense until too late. Her signs and symbols were everywhere, and certain neighborhoods had become unsafe swiftly, overrun by a mix of her true believers and her converts in the flesh. A scrawled M on the side of a building might mean Mord or it might not.

I had decided to hazard the factory district to the northwest of the Balcony Cliffs. In that tangled mass of warehouses and rusted industry lay every excuse and promise of a death foretold—inert, empty, silent, vast. Those were the smokestacks that had killed off this part of the world. Those were the assembly lines that had choked us with products we did not need and had to be told we wanted—before the Company had snuck in and shown us our truest, deepest desires.

The district had a deceptive feel to it of dark and calm and quiet. Most of these buildings had structural damage, some even ripped open by the missiles of an ancient war. The route was easy to find but physically difficult—a lot of climbing over stacked and cracked girders. You could trap a foot and twist your ankle, and I was soon sore in all the places where I had been wounded. I was armed this time with a metal bat and a beat-up pair of binoculars. No more spiders to spare, so I had one of Wick's poison beetles in the pouch on my belt. The beetles burrowed into flesh, opened their carapaces, and twirled around once inside you. The shock alone would be enough to kill.

The way became less arduous once we were in the middle of the warren; there were narrow streets and pathways, and not always blocked by broken machinery or the remains of trucks, tires long gone. Torrents of rocks and concrete girders to the left, the highway of dust through it, and the factories on the right. Rocks, rocks, rocks. Pillars, pillars, pillars. All smashed to hell. I always felt small in that place, amongst the cathedrals of that age.

Trailing a little behind me, Borne was a large rock that bumbled to a stop, soundless, when I looked back. Almost stealthy.

I kept walking, with a quick glance back every once in a while, since I couldn't persuade Borne to walk beside me.

Soon I was no longer being followed by a rock but by a giant undulating worm, very similar to the ones that broke down waste in my apartment.

Then, for a brief time, an enormous fly nervously buzzed forward—most unlikely of all!—but my stalker soon realized that such an organism stood out like a sore thumb. Given what I knew about Borne's sense of humor, I would not have been surprised by then if the next time I had looked back and *seen* a sore thumb. Instead, the next incarnation just confirmed what I already knew about Borne: that he loved lizards, even though they did not love him.

A giant lizard, roughly human-size, clambered across the terrain behind me. An apologetic lizard. An embarrassed and socially awkward lizard, with huge bulging eyes and protruding tongue, a reptile that progressed in stops and starts, peeking out from behind boulders. Checking to make sure I hadn't gotten too far ahead of him. It was hideous and amazing all at once, and that bothered me. I was continually being taught by Borne how to "read" him, and yet what did this mean except that I was supposed to accept the impossible?

It was then I stopped and, bat balanced over my shoulder, faced down the lizard.

The lizard morphed back into a rock, close enough now I didn't have to shout to talk to it.

"Borne. I can see you. You came out here with me. I *know* that it's you."

Silence.

"Borne. You've been a rock, a worm, a fly, and now a lizard. Do you think I'm stupid? Even if I hadn't brought you out here?"

The rock moved from side to side a little.

"You are the wrong size to be a fly or a lizard. And you look disgusting. Like a swimming pool."

"I am a rock," Borne said, muffled, as if from some orifice now underneath him. "I am a rock?"

"Oh, you're a rock all right. You're a great big fucking rock. You're a boulder. Change back right this instant!"

I was seething. Was this a joke to him? It wasn't a joke to me. I did not like his style of camouflage—crude and almost comic, but not on purpose. Or, if on purpose, even worse. Amazing, maybe, but the opposite of camouflage. A changed context could kill. And maybe I was paranoid, but I thought I'd caught another glimpse of that fox following us.

"Borne, I need you serious," I said to the boulder.

The boulder mumbled something to itself. I wasn't sure if he knew I meant it or not.

"I raised you from a pod. You know I did." We shared this myth because it was simple and easy, even though he'd not really been a pod and the "raising" had been all of four months, not exactly a lifetime. But maybe it felt like a lifetime to him.

"Yes," the boulder admitted. "You raised me from a pod."

"And you know I want only the best for you?"

The boulder became a lizard again, but its skin matched the dull dust color everywhere around us. From a distance, I had no doubt that it looked like I was arguing with no one, with nothing.

"The very best," Borne said, "or the best you know how. How do you do, Know How?"

I ignored that rebellion, sidestepped it as my mom always had raising me. "Out here, Borne, you cannot be playful. You can be clever, watchful, resourceful, but you *cannot* be playful." All words he knew, that I'd taught him. "You can only be *playful* inside the Balcony Cliffs."

Borne became Borne again, which still managed to startle me.

"I'm sorry, Rachel," Borne said.

"Can you please try to look like a person?" I asked. "Please?"

"Yes," Borne said, and became as person-like as he could, without a wizard hat but instead a "normal" one, even though it was made of his own flesh and skin. That meant cowboy-style, something he'd discovered in a tattered comic book, a Western.

I wish he hadn't—it was foreign to me and meant less than nothing.

We'd agreed on robes as his camouflage because that meant he didn't have to grow feet. He hated feet more and more as he grew up, maybe because his architecture, his physicality, made it uncomfortable. God forbid he couldn't have a thousand cilia propelling him forward over that rocky ground!

More than anything, though, Borne's antics had thrown me off, cut the connection between me and my surroundings, and I was having a hard time getting that awareness back. I should have marched him right back to the Balcony Cliffs. But instead I decided to press forward.

Seeing an open doorway ahead, I ducked into a building at random: a large, four-story place with a buckling steel frame and not a window unbroken. Maybe someone had tried to live here once, but what we called Company moss grew along the sides. You could eat Company moss if you were starving, and its presence usually meant an abandoned place.

Inside, spread out across the vast floor of the factory: the corroded remains of machinery, enough dust to choke ten of me, pools of liquid rust, a series of ladders and stairs along the side wall leading to the roof, and nothing worth scavenging. We needed what could be burned or bled or transformed.

Borne, once inside, couldn't stay still. In an instant, he reverted to a kind of converted "travel" mode: shorter, about five feet tall, with an expanded base for support. At the top the aperture had also widened out, the tentacles multiplying in number, but shorter and thicker, except for one that slowly rose like a periscope for a better vantage. The eyes that appeared occurred at the end of the tentacles and peered out in all directions like sentinels. He called this mode being "layered thick."

"What do you think you're doing?" I asked.

"Exploring with you?"

"Just because we're inside doesn't mean you can be Borne again. You have to *stay* Person Borne as long as we're outside the Balcony Cliffs." I had told him this plenty of times before we'd left.

None of the eye-tentacles would look at me, but I didn't get the sense he was embarrassed or concerned. More that his attention was elsewhere.

"Yes, Rachel. You're right. But they're coming. They're coming soon and you want to be ready. I think. I think you do?"

They're coming soon.

That put the fear into me, quick. That and the sound of running feet. Many running feet.

They were coming *right then*—the sound close and fast and I couldn't tell from where. I just knew someone or something was coming. The only way out was up. So I ran with Borne—up the ladders, the stairs, to the roof, Borne once more a lizard so he could scuttle faster.

Me and my lizard-monster, lunging up the stairs to the roof.

WHAT HAPPENED UP ON THE ROOF

We didn't see the intruders at first because they were seething up from the underground. I couldn't figure out where they were coming from for this reason, too: The inside of the factory threw the sounds off. But soon enough from our vantage on the roof, looking down to the factory floor through a couple of loose slats, I saw who it was: more poisoned half-changed children, like the ones who had attacked me. Spilling out of a culvert. An explosion of colors and textures and such a variety of limbs. Some had iridescent carapaces. Some had gossamer wings. Some had fangs like cleavers that half destroyed their mouths. Soft and exposed and pink or hardened and helmeted, they spilled out. A carnivalesque parade of killers. Some, if I were looking through Wick's eyes, would've registered as "mods" and others as "homegrowns."

Borne's intake of breath matched mine. He didn't need binoculars, apparently, to zero in on them. He'd gone rough and prickly beside me, and a faint snuffed-match/grain-alcohol smell wafted over.

"More," he whispered. "More. Many more. Of the same."

"Hush," I said. "Hush."

Yes, more, and they looked like they had purpose, like they were on patrol. They had spears and bats and knives and machetes and a smattering of shotguns that might have been loaded or, from the way carried, used as clubs. They spread out across the factory floor, searching for something. A coldness colonized me seeing them so small, from above, their footprints and paw prints and hoofprints and boot prints leaving such a dance of marks in the dust, and our own not betraying us only because the children had frothed up like flames to obscure all that had come before, so that seeking, they had only the evidence of their own lives all around. The stairs to the roof didn't leave such traces. Yet they clearly sought us, had heard us or been tracking us from below.

The patterns of those footprints are what I focused on for a moment, unable to look directly at the children. I let the splinters of wood and tar pebbles from the roof cut into my palm. I wanted to be so still and so silent and so not-there that those children would never think to come up to where we were. Never even think to look up and perhaps catch a glint off my binoculars. Every scar on my body seemed to pulse, to burn. But pulsing there too was a need for revenge, and that I had to tamp down. I was with Borne. I knew he'd killed four of them, but this was more than twenty.

But Borne had no intention of going down there. Something else was coming in across his superior senses—senses that might outnumber mine. Borne became hard, rigid, and his eyes became blowholes that pushed out curls of pink mist.

"Other creatures are coming, Rachel," he hissed at me like steam. "Other *things* are coming—now!"

Other things?

"Not nice," Borne was breathing, "not nice not nice," and what scared me was Borne being scared.

Borne turned the drab color of the roof and went pancake-flat and spread out, and tried to curl over me like a carpet was rolling me inside of it. Or like he was a giant harsh tongue.

"Stop it!" I whispered, losing my grip, binoculars jangling at my throat. "Stop it, I don't need your help," pushing back, pulling back the edge of Borne. "I need to see this. I need to see this."

I managed to free myself from enough Borne to lie half in and half out of his protective embrace, put the binoculars to my eyes once more.

Down below, the roaring and screaming and bleeding had already begun, the wet, flopping sounds of people being taken apart. Mord proxies. Pouring in from the doorway where Borne and I had entered. Smashing through the windows.

"Don't look," I told Borne. "Don't look."

But how could I stop him? His entire skin was full of eyes, full of other receptors I couldn't even name.

How to describe what I saw? It was a terrible, swift slaughter, possessed of an awful precision that made it hard to look away. Worse, the Mord proxies were enacting a revenge I'd played out in my mind a thousand times—sped up and preternatural.

The speed shocked me the most. For they were all golden bears, all huge in their hideous beauty, much taller than a man, with thick muscles that, in their stride and bounding, came at times to the surface of their fur like the hardness of a vine-wreathed tree trunk wrung and stretched taut. Yet they moved so lithe and sinuous they could've been snakes or otters or flowing water pushed along in a strong current.

Monstrous gold-brown blurs, they took apart the feral children with a gruff, ballet-like ease, the footprints on that dusty floor splattered with blood and offal. The arterial spray. Heads swatted from necks. Gouts of dark blood from deep gouges in thighs. A kind of communal baying or shrieking from the ferals as a last half dozen formed a semicircle soon rendered down into a chaos of viscera and exposed bone, the Mord proxies lunging forward from either side in hugs that burst, through fang and claw, the flesh that separated them.

The sharp, bitter smell of blood carried even to the roof. The smell of piss and shit, too.

There were pleadings and rough refusals to submit, although the Mord proxies never asked for surrender. You could not surrender to a proxy except through your death.

When they were done, the factory floor had been transformed into a violent canvas of body parts and fluids. A rough raw circle that pushed a broom or mop of reds and yellows and darker tones across its surface to create swaths and paths that almost had meaning. Here too were swirls and outcroppings of thicker paint that had not been smoothed out. I felt as if I were looking at a crosssection of Mord's brain.

When they were done, the hummingbird quality to their movements, the blurring effect, faded, and the Mord proxies became just bears again—bears who, unlike Mord, could not fly. Fur matted with blood, the bears examined the evidence of their own battle lust, waded through it, and all the while huffed and bellowed and coughed deep in their throats, went from all fours to standing on two legs, to all fours again. Sniffing the air and finding it smelled good. Batted into the center the heads that hadn't been crushed flat. As they panted and hummed and mumbled their contentment.

Now that the Mord proxies had come to rest, I could count their numbers. Five had slaughtered twenty-five ferals, with hardly any effort.

Yet, even with no proxy casualties, I could calculate the cost, for once the initial battle lust faded, some animating impulse fled with it, and these bears moved not in normal time but much slower, and shakes rippled through their fur and at times amongst the roaring and snarling came a whimper or a moan. Something about their speed before had been unnatural. Something about it cost them now, almost like the human body coming down from amphetamines. Which meant they might be vulnerable, if only you could catch them after a slaughter.

"Drkkkkk," one gutteralized to another.

"Drrkkkkkkkrush," said a third.

"Drrrkkkkssssiiiiiiii."

With that, the fifth Mord proxy, now ponderous and slow but still dangerous, began to head up the stairs to the roof where we hid. Through a trail of blood.

Half wrapped in Borne, it had made no difference when he'd extended a pseudopod to my ear and talked to me in a whispered way while the carnage took place. If it helped him from panicking, if it stopped him from intervening, all the better. I was like a dreamer half asleep who responds when someone talks but is not really awake yet. I was too captured by the carnage, too aware of the vulnerability of my own flesh.

"Not nice not nice," was still in Borne's vocabulary as the ferals died. And, less usual, "A waste. What a waste. They *wasted* it."

"They're dying, Borne," I said as I watched it. "They're being killed."

"Not here anymore. Not there, either."

Where was *there*? Did I want to know?

"When are they doing this?"

Another strange question. "*Now*, Borne, they're doing it *now*. Right in front of you." But I had the idea that his gaze was seeing more than mine.

"*Why* are they doing this, though? Why?"

I didn't have a good answer for that one. I didn't at all. Or for why Borne no longer seemed frightened.

But now a Mord proxy was pawing up the stairs to investigate the roof, and the tremors of that passage left no doubt what would happen on the roof. To me. To Borne.

"Borne," I said, "can you hide us?"

"Hide?! Hide from what?" Something in my urgency had triggered urgency in his reply.

"From the bear."

"Bear?"

"The thing coming up the stairs!"

"Hide." At a critical moment, I seemed to have hit a communication glitch. A translation problem.

"*Like a rock*. Can you pretend to be a rock, with me inside— with room for me to breathe inside?" I already knew he could be a rock. So, why not? We had no other choice.

"You told me not to be a rock," Borne pointed out.

"*Forget that!* Forget it! *You can be a rock now.* Can you be a rock?"

"Yes, I can be a rock!" Borne said, enthusiastic. "I can put you in a rock."

"And can you stay a rock no matter what happens? Can you stay a rock? Be quiet as a rock?"

The bear bounded up the stairs at a blistering pace now, recovering. The bear would be out on the roof in a moment. Just a moment more.

"I can stay a rock."

"Can you smell like a rock too? You must *smell like a rock*."

"I can!"

"Then do it—*now!*"

"Yes, Rachel!"

Borne unfurled, uncurled, and rose high and came down like a crashing wave, and me tumbling in the middle of it all, bent over and half crushed by cilia and rubbery flesh.

I could see nothing.

I could do nothing.

I was trapped within Borne, hoping that on the outside he looked like a rock.

I did not do well in truly dark places. They reminded me of other times I'd had to hide, as a child, with my parents. Confined. In a pit. In a tunnel. In a closet. Waiting to be discovered, uncovered, given away. Staying silent, still, until the danger had passed. My panic in such situations had gotten worse when I reached the city, not better.

The huffing of the bear came close, closer, a rabid snarl of pure animal bloodlust, but still the strangled words behind that, the muffled lunge of language forming: "Drrrkkkkkkk. Drrrrrrk. Drrrrrk."

I was having trouble breathing, trouble controlling my breath. I was in a situation no human being had ever been in and a situation that human beings had experienced for thousands of years. In one world, I was cocooned inside a living organism that still defied explanation, that was, no matter how I loved it, a mystery to me. In the other world, I was inside a cave trying to hide from a wild animal. Disoriented, I saw again the fox's strange eye. I saw again the dead astronauts. I saw the odd bit of meat left as a trap for me. I saw Mord's shuddering flank.

I wanted Wick then. I wanted Wick to be there on the rooftop, to tell me what to do beyond what I had done already. I wanted Wick to make things easy and to make the Mord proxy go away. Surely there was something he would know how to do. Borne was just a child. Borne was just a rock.

A moment more, as the bear circled the Borne-rock, and the claustrophobia would have sent me over the edge.

But Borne sensed this, Borne knew what was happening within and without. The space widened and a dull green light came from the flesh walls all around to let me see and a flesh book extended out of the wall and on a shelf that formed I saw a flesh telephone.

The telephone shook like it was ringing. I picked up the receiver.

"Hello," I whispered.

"This is Borne. This is Borne calling you."

"I know," I said. I felt like a child on a pretend phone, having a chat with an imaginary friend.

"You don't even need to make sound. I'll hear you if you mouth the words," Borne told me.

"What is going on outside," I mouthed, even as Borne lurched a bit from some *push* off to the left of me.

"The bear is circling me. The bear just pushed me and I rolled a bit like a rock. But only a bit. Because I'm a rock, not Borne."

"Good. Maybe the bear will go away."

"Should I be afraid, Rachel?"

"Are you afraid, Borne?"

"I worry the bear might eat part of me."

"Bears don't eat rocks."

"I worry that if I worry too much about the bear eating part of me that I will stop being a rock and then the bear might eat me."

"You. Must. Be. A. Rock." I willed Borne with all the force of every secret thought to continue to behave like a rock.

"I am going to end this call," Borne said. "I think the bear is about to do something else. Goodbye."

"Goodbye, Borne," I mouthed.

Goodbye Borne, and hello Borne all around me.

Borne lurched dangerously and I put out my arms to keep my balance. I was terrified that no matter the illusion, the bear would eat through Borne to the center, to me, and we would both die here, on the rooftop, for Wick to eventually find.

A shudder, a recoil, a head-over-heels moment, and again Borne was tight and close, leaving only a globe of air around my head. The light was gone along with all of the fake things he'd created to put me at ease, and I lay there, panting, as the skin of Borne around me, the flesh of Borne, went prickly and rigid again and the cilia that rubbed up against me turned into tiny mouths that screamed into my clothes, arms and legs and hair. Borne was screaming silently into his own body because he could not scream on the outside.

I had a horrible panicking moment where I realized that the

bear might be able to smell *me*, inside the rock, and I kicked out, flailed out, then went still because each movement made Borne constrict on me more, and it hurt to breathe.

I could feel the vibration of Mord proxy paws and Mord proxy jaws biting into Borne. I could sense the bear *hugging* and *squeezing* and *mauling* the top of Borne. Excavating the rock. Savaging the rock. And me a dead person in a coffin, preparing to be revealed as alive, to be face-to-face with the enormous broad furry head of a bear. To meet Mord's emissary. To meet death.

Came the prying snarl. Came the toothsome growl, so thick and loud it permeated every surface, seemed to shake my bones out of alignment. Came the huffing after.

But then the bear sounds receded and I felt through the floorboards the padding away of a great weight.

When that weight transferred to the stairs, when I could feel nothing, hear nothing, I whispered, "Borne. Borne are you there! Are you all right?"

The cilia had stopped screaming. The flesh had stopped responding. Nothing about the Borne around me seemed alive. I could as easily have been in something inert—in an emergency space capsule ejected from an exploding starship far from Earth or in a one-person submarine deep beneath our deadly river, surviving within a pocket of air that would soon exhaust itself. There was that sense in my lungs of having plunged underground, of being so far from the surface of anything that I had no idea how I might emerge. If I would have the sick, terrible task of digging my way out of Borne.

"Borne!" I risked a louder voice.

There came an accumulated reply, a voice from everywhere and nowhere: "I am here, Rachel. I am here. I am still a rock."

"Are you hurt?" I mouthed.

"Parts of me I cannot feel," Borne said. "Parts of me are gone."

"Keep still," I said. "Keep still until they've left."

"It is easier to keep still now," Borne said, "when there is less of me to move."

He sounded odd, not just damaged but puzzled. His own wounding puzzled him.

✺

In the old world, when I emerged with my parents from secret rooms or tunnels or caves or closets, we knew what we were returning to—the same place we had left, as dangerous or as safe as before. We had hidden so we could remain in that world, were saying we believed in that world no matter what. Because we had no choice. Because there was no better or worse world, there was just the place we came out into.

But when I emerged from Borne, out onto the rooftop again, I did not feel the same way. We had waited until Borne told me the Mord proxies had truly gone and all that remained below were the kinds of scavengers that would scatter at our approach. The cast-off biotech that could move, well or not so well, that came out nocturnal.

We had waited until nightfall, even then, and so when I stood outside of Borne the world had changed in more than one sense. It was not just that Borne had shielded me rather than the other way around. It was not the change in the sky.

Pieces of Borne had been torn from him by the Mord proxy in its suspicion. These pieces had bounced like rock, settled on the rooftop like rock, but now quivered and flexed like hands opening and closing, reformed as Borne flesh.

The Borne that faced me was, even in that dim light, scarred and misshapen. He had returned to his normal size and shape, the one that looked like an upside-down vase, that combined attributes of a squid and a sea anemone, but he had a slumped, subdued quality that I'd never seen in him before.

I winced to see that his left side was fissured and purpling-black and the ring of eyes, darkly luminous, circled his body in a haphazard way, like a rotting carnival ride one loose bolt away from spinning off into the crowd. He had a smell like turpentine and rotting fish sticks and moldy bandages.

"I'm sorry, Borne," I said, feeling shaky. "I shouldn't have brought you out here."

Somehow they had known. Somehow they had known where we would be—but which ones? The ferals or the proxies? I was unwilling to accept that this had just been coincidence or bad luck. And also tumbling through my mind, an awful sense of responsibility: that if Borne hadn't moved out, if Borne hadn't pretended to be more like an adult, I might not have taken the chance.

"It's okay, Rachel," Borne said. "It's okay."

"No, it's not okay."

Borne's eyes flashed up at me, and another new thing: anger, and not over me saying no to him. This was a real thing, an adult emotion that had never been there before. It expressed itself through an orange-red glow just visible at the core of him. Who knew if red meant caution to Borne, but he knew it meant that to me.

"It is okay," Borne said. "I need to learn. I need to know."

"But not by being hurt."

"It's not being hurt that hurts," Borne said.

Borne might be alien to me, he might have more senses, he might do things no human could do . . . but I thought I understood what he was saying. (Although, did I, really?) He knew now that he could be harmed. He knew now that he was vulnerable. No joy would be the same for Borne. No playfulness, either.

Because behind it would be this certain knowledge: that he could die.

"I'm tired, Rachel," Borne said. "I need not to move for a while."

"That's okay," I said, and it was. If we had to make this rooftop our home for a few hours, I was prepared to do it.

It had cooled as the sun disappeared and the stars came out across an unusually cloudless sky. We were silent for a long time, and I made no move to go downstairs to recon. Borne needed my attention, but I also think we both dreaded going downstairs. Neither of us wanted to experience the aftermath up close, even in the dark. But Borne was also looking up at the stars, all of his attention drawn there.

Borne was reaching out a tentative tentacle, as if to touch the stars.

He must have known he couldn't, but I still said, "You can't touch them!"

"Why not? Are they hot?"

"Yes, they are. But that's not why. They're very, very far away."

"But my arms are so long, Rachel. My arms can be as long as I want."

"That might be so, but . . ." I trailed off when I realized Borne was joking. He had a little tell when he joked—or it was actually a big tell. Some of his eyes would drift to the left, a particular cluster. He couldn't control that.

"Diabolical," he said, still captivated by what lay above. "Diabolical. Deadly. Delirious. Deep." Four new words he'd been trying out. Except he had not learned "diabolical" from me, and I felt a twinge. Some book, some other source.

A normal night sky, but I was attuned to Borne in that moment and I saw it from his eyes—like a rush or an onslaught. Because as far as I knew, he had never seen the night sky so unguarded before—glimpses, maybe, from the Balcony Cliffs at dusk or in his books. So many stars, so little light from the city to disguise them. It was just like I remembered it from our island sanctuary so long ago. Walking down the beach and not needing a flashlight because the stars were so strong.

A glittering reef of stars, spread out phosphorescent, and each one might have life on it, planets revolving around them. There might even be people like us, looking up at the night sky. It was what my mother said sometimes—to be mindful that the universe beyond still existed, that we did not know what lived there, and it might be terrible to reconcile ourselves to knowing so little of it, but that didn't mean it stopped existing. There was something else beyond all of this, that would never know us or our struggles, never care, and that it would go on without us. My mother had found that idea comforting.

Borne's many eyes became stars as he watched them, and his skin turned the color of velvety night, until he was just a Borne-shaped reflection. So many eyestalks arose from him that his body flattened away to nothing, into an irregular pool of flesh across most of the roof, the edge lapping up against my boots. I could still see how he had been injured, because he looked like a circle that had had a bite taken out of it. Each eyestalk ended in a three-dimensional representation of a star, and the stars clustered until he was a field of stars rising from the rooftop, forming nebulae and galaxies, and a few fireflies like meteorites across the depth and breadth of him.

"It's beautiful," he said, from across the star field of his body. "It's beautiful."

For once what he thought of as beautiful really was beautiful. It was as if we had become closer even as he exhibited more alien attributes, but I quashed that with an instant of wariness. Was he truly without guile? Wasn't this repetition because of my reaction about the polluted river? But even if I suspected "beautiful" was just him making conversation or in some other way for my benefit, I knew that he'd taken this form to begin to heal, that there was something comforting about it, something that helped him.

"What are they?" Borne asked. "Are they . . . lights like in the Balcony Cliffs? Or . . . electrical lights? Who turned them on?" So whatever he'd seen in books hadn't explained stars. At all.

"No one turned them on," I said, realizing after I'd said it that I'd just discounted thousands of years of religion. But it was too late to turn back.

"No one?"

"We're on a *world*," I told him, not knowing what gaps existed from his reading. "We're on a world that revolves around a star, which is a giant ball of fire. So enormous that if it weren't so distant we would all be dead—burned up. We call it the sun—and the sun is what you thought wasn't nice when it shone so bright on you the other day. But all of those points of light above are also suns, even farther away, and they all have worlds, too."

My eyesight had gotten blurry telling Borne this, the aftershock of our ordeal hitting me.

"All of them? Every single one? But that's like hundreds."

"Thousands. Maybe millions."

Across the star fields of Borne's body there coalesced one great sun in the center, also atop a stalk. Heretical was his astronomy at this point. He'd become metaphorical or metaphysical or just silly.

"But that's incredible," Borne said, quietly. "That's amazing. That's devastating."

Then something began to blot out the stars, to turn that glittering, shining brilliance into a great and final darkness.

"And what is that?" Borne asked, as if it was something normal, something else he didn't know about yet, and he trusted me to tell him, to let him know what to think about it.

I was speechless, because for an instant I thought the world was ending, that fate had conspired to put us on that roof to watch the end of . . . everything.

Then I realized what we were seeing, and I couldn't help a stifled chuckle. Oh, this was rich! Because it was the end of the world.

"What's so funny, Rachel?" An edge to that voice as Borne withdrew from the edge of my toes, drew himself up into his normal form, still sagging, still wounded.

"That's Mord," I said.

Yes, it was Mord—floating and diving across the night sky, high up, so huge that even from a distance he blotted out the stars. Across the night sky the giant bear Mord glided, seething, and we could hear faint rasps and roaring from the stratosphere, the choking gasps of his rage. Snuffing out first this constellation then that one, his form as it occluded the stars making me aware of them again. His was the greater darkness, and although I feared him and hated him and despised him, Mord was still, in that moment, the purest reflection of the city.

"Moooooordddddddddddd," Borne said in a kind of hissing way, and I saw even in the reflected light that every inch of Borne's unscarred surface had become sharp, jagged, pointed like spears and spikes, and the eyes now revolving tracked Mord's obliterating progress like gun emplacements tracking aircraft. Strafed Mord's position with analytics and calculations and trajectories.

"He's very far away," I said, in a soothing tone. "He can't hurt you." Neither statement was entirely true.

"That is what you mean by Mord proxy," Borne said. "This is the *source*."

"Yes."

"They are his children."

"In a way, yes."

"Why would he let his *children* do that to other *children*?"

I didn't have a good answer for him, but I was sure that Borne had absorbed enough about Mord from me and from Wick that he had an idea of what he was looking at. We had turned Mord into the boogieman in his imagination, the monster under the bed. Don't go outside, don't do this, don't do that because: Mord. But now Borne had been mauled by one of Mord's emissaries, and he was trying to understand Mord. The real Mord.

Mord continued to dip and glide and wheel and drop across the sky like a god.

"Mord is beautiful," Borne said with disdain. "Mord is strong. Mord is not nice." From his tone, I believe Borne was beginning to parody his own innocence.

"Mostly not nice. Remember the not-nice part. Avoid him."

"He kills the stars," Borne said. "He kills the stars and brings darkness."

"The stars all come back, though."

"But not the people down below."

You killed four of them yourself, back at the Balcony Cliffs, I wanted to say. But didn't.

WHAT WE BROUGHT BACK TO WICK

Escaping death made me giddy as we snuck back into the Balcony Cliffs, and Borne giddy because he saw me being that word and because I was trying to distract him from his pain. If pain he felt; he wouldn't tell me if it hurt.

Life took on a bright and shining glow after being so newly almost dead. I was also giddy with a kind of don't-care anger because I had stumbled upon a secret when we had finally gone down to the factory floor, one I had to bring back to Wick because it belonged to him.

Down those drab corridors we walked tall and then would be bent over with guffaws—which is how I knew I was my father's daughter, for that was his way, too. To be "doubled over" with his laughter or his grief. For during the trek back, Mord had gone in our estimation from "spectacular" to "buffoonish," his star-blotting the work of a clumsy, maniacal *floating* bear.

"Whoever heard of a floating bear?" I told Borne. "That'd be like finding a plant that was actually a talking octopus."

Borne latched on to a word he hadn't heard before. "Buffoon!" he said with enthusiasm. "Foon buff! Buffalo balloon!" I knew that word would distract him, that he would be turning it over in his head for a few minutes at least, wouldn't be thinking about the bears, just mutating "buffoon" until it was unrecognizable.

"Yes," I said. "Buffoon." Sobering a bit. Joking around with my friend Borne, who seemed no different after having moved out. Who had saved my life and his own, and suffered in the process.

"Buffaloon."

It's not that Borne wasn't genuine. No, he was always genuine. But he took his cues from me, had been learning how to *react* from me primary, and the world and books secondary. And I was determined that, for a few hours at least, Borne being hurt wouldn't mean being defeated.

If I hadn't been giddy, Borne wouldn't have expressed a "headlong happiness." He wouldn't have danced up to Wick by the swimming pool, danced around Wick on that nimble set of cilia— or taken it into his head to "get shallow," as he put it, and spread out his body weight before surging up the wall and halfway up the cathedral-like ceiling, there to peer down through star eyes, as he replicated the night sky once more.

"Hello, Wick," Borne said from the ceiling. "Hello, Wick. I brought you a present. Rachel had me bring you a present. Hello, Wick."

We had burst in on Wick with such bravado that I hadn't noticed how drunk Wick was, either on minnows or the more banal rotgut moonshine he traded for. But he was giddier than we were, and though I sensed danger in that, I was also too wired to care. We had made it back to the Balcony Cliffs. We were safe.

"Wick, this is Borne. Borne, this is Wick," I said.

I had some stupid idea in the back of my head that Wick could look at Borne's wounds. But what was Wick? A doctor? A veterinarian?

"We've met," Wick said. "We've talked. We're practically brothers now." A hint of something dark and self-deprecating in his tone.

"Yes, Rachel! I know Wick. Wick knows me. I went over and was neighborly. I went over and said hi to him after I moved into my new apartment."

That brought me up short, Borne much too pleased about being neighborly.

"In fact, Rachel," Wick said, "Borne already seemed to know a lot about me *before* we even talked."

"Yes, Rachel talks about you all the time, Wick."

"So I gathered."

My giddiness was evaporating.

I was just standing there, unable to believe that one of the things I'd covered with my giddiness—the anxiousness of two un-alike chemical compounds coming into contact for the first time—wasn't the first time.

Wick and Borne knew each other. Wick and Borne had talked. It felt like a betrayal, as if Wick had done something behind my back—even worse, that Borne had, though that was ridiculous.

What could I have wanted more than for Wick and Borne to talk to each other, to find a way to get along?

"What've you brought me, my friend?" Wick said, staring up at Borne and ignoring my surprise. "Have you brought me a very late lunch? Have you brought me spare parts? Have you brought me something else from the Company?" Wick was wearing mismatched flip-flops too large for him and plaid shorts and a white undershirt with a green smudge on it. He had probably been about to go to sleep.

"Claaaaaaaaaaaw," Borne said. "I bring claaaaaaaaaaaaaaaw." With a showman's flourish, a pseudopod sproinged out from his flat body, much to Wick's discomfort—he started, took a step back—while the stars withdrew and Borne's normal eyes dotted his surface. The tentacle thus extended did indeed offer up to Wick: claw.

Wick just looked at the proffered claw and I shuddered, seeing the blood-splashed factory floor all over again. Claw was almost as long as someone's forearm and fearsomely curved and ended in a point both broad and sharp.

"What. Is this?" Wick asked, wobbly. "Something from the holding ponds?"

"You know what it is, Wick," I said. I didn't like this version of drunk Wick.

"Claaaaaaw! Glorious claaaaaaaw. From a Mordbear," Borne said, and let the claw fall to the stone floor. Pseudopod retracted. Eyes alight with, brimming with, a kind of amusement, or was he bright with pain? "Now I want to expedition the ceiling."

" 'Explore,' not 'expedition,' Borne."

There came a smell from him like the salt edge of a wave: clean, crisp, pure. Borne got even "shallower" until he couldn't have been more than a quarter-inch thick and covered the ceiling.

"Are you marrying the ceiling, Borne?" I asked.

"I'm not married! I'm never getting married!"

"Sure looks like you're getting married."

"No! Just tasting. I'm getting tasted today. A lot."

"Tested."

"Toasted."

I knew he was recovering, that somehow going shallow helped, that tasting helped. I could see the scars, the mark of Mord upon him, realized all over again how traumatic the rooftop had been for him, despite his protests that he "would be fine."

Wick had picked up the claw, was turning it over in his hands as he stumbled to a chair next to his vat of swampy elixirs. The pool was dark tonight, a kind of mumbled bubbling close to its surface, a subdued green glow. Our light came from the fireflies and the lichen on the ceiling, most of which Borne now covered, although all during his exploration he thoughtfully turned on lights in his "face" to compensate.

I pulled up a chair next to Wick. "We had a run-in today. With Mord proxies. It's why we're late."

"I guessed as much—from the claw." Said as harsh as it sounded, preoccupied.

I took a good long look at Wick, slumped there in the chair, holding the claw. Oh gaunt skeleton, oh drawn cheekbones and hooded, shadowy quality to the eyes. Seeing him that way, distracted and concerned and so thin, I couldn't tell him that his first thought should have been to ask if we were okay. That his second should have been to hug me. That his third, if he was smart, was to know from the look on my face that we needed to talk.

"Can't you find out a lot from the claw?" My grasp of biotech and Wick's abilities would always be fuzzy, but I had been imagining stupid things, like making a clone of Mord, but a good Mord, a responsible Mord, a Mord that helped us.

"Yes, it's a claw. From a bear—a Mord proxy. I can do a lot with it. Thanks."

"What's wrong, Wick?"

"Do you think it's a good idea, bringing Borne in here?" He looked up at the ceiling, where Borne was expeditioning some texture, exploring some fireflies, and enveloping a nest of (non-biotech) spiders. "Leave the fireflies alone," he told Borne.

"You should know," I said. "You've already talked. You're already friends."

"Not friends. We talked in the corridor. If I had no choice about him being here, then I should at least get a sense of what he's up to. I've never let him in here before. Have you?"

"Yes, actually," I admitted. "And Borne and I have walked through all of the corridors and all the secret places, and there have even been places Borne could squeeze into and I couldn't." Rubbing our stink on everything, I wanted to say, rebellious. Making sure to rub our stink on everything. "Which means that not only is your question too late but Borne could help us to uncover more of our home. With his help we might find more supplies hidden away under all that trash."

"Borne this, Borne that," Wick said, tapping the point of the claw against the side of the swimming pool. "It was bad enough before and now you tell me this. Rachel: There is not now in the entire Balcony Cliffs, except this room, a single living creature other than you, me, and Borne. Doesn't that tell you anything? I asked you to have him out of here. I—"

"For all I know he's been bringing the lizards to you, Wick."

"No, he hasn't. He's been bringing them to the mouth he doesn't need."

"And neither Borne nor I are listening, Wick," I said, because I wasn't. Pests, vermin. Borne was just keeping the place clean. "Because we live here, too. We live here with you. Borne and me. Me and Borne and you. And isn't he amazing? Can you deny he's amazing?"

Borne was currently using competing tentacle puppet heads to have an argument above us about the uses of "expeditioning" versus "exploring" and the differences between them, clearly for my benefit.

"A work of art," Wick said. "A genius."

Before that I hoped Wick hadn't noticed Borne muttering about how Wick wasn't as much of a "stick in the mud" as I'd said. That the swimming pool from above was "really cool but kinda hot, A-OK." Had he discovered the remains of a treasure trove of teen heartthrob mags in the Balcony Cliffs?

"So I say again, *What's wrong?*"

"Send Borne out of here first," Wick said. "Get him out of here."

"No," I said. He hadn't realized it yet, but I was at the limits of my patience. In addition to being giddy and angry, I was exhausted and feeling the aches of our misadventure, and I needed sleep soon, to come down from the high of escape.

Wick considered that, astonished me by tossing the claw into the swimming pool as if it meant nothing, had no value at all.

"Okay, the hell with it," he said, sounding so unlike Wick. "Why not?"

He rummaged through a metal box and took out a fistful of alcohol minnows. Now I felt maybe he wasn't so much drunk as in distress.

"Here, Borne, have a minnow," he said, and tossed a half dozen up into the air. Not nearly high enough, but it didn't matter—Borne-bits reached down to pluck them out of the air anyway.

"Ooooh, minnows for a claaaawww!"

"Yes, Borne," Wick said. "Minnows for a claw. You *are* generous."

Borne began to feast with what for him were polite gobbling

noises meant to thank us. His slobbering made him sound like an old circus seal, and that annoyed me, too.

"So now you know Borne so well you're getting him drunk?"

Wick spun his chair around so he was facing me. "They don't have the same effect on old Borney-o. They just don't. Biotech's not the same as you. Most biotech's *unpredictable*—more than you realize. Borney-o biotech becomes blotto . . . some other way. Here, have some," and he threw a few minnows at me.

The minnows were really more like salted sardines, but when you bit into them a soft minty coolness crept through your mouth, and then the alcohol, or alcohol equivalent, slid in behind, with a real chill to it, and the cold and the tart aftertaste were good. On a hot day, it felt great.

"What didn't you want to tell me with Borne here?" I asked after I'd crunched down on a couple of minnows. "Just spit it out."

Another pause, and then he began to launch into it, but in a Wick way: through a side door, through a maze.

"Rachel, it's too dangerous here now. At the Balcony Cliffs. Too dangerous on our own. You know that yourself from tonight."

"But you didn't even ask what happened. You didn't even ask." I couldn't keep the hurt from my voice, though it made me seem like a child.

He winced. "Maybe because you're safe. Maybe because you're here and you made it back. Maybe because the Magician just sent me a message."

The chill of the alcohol couldn't compete with the chill at the back of my neck, the way that news made me feel claustrophobic and itchy and not-right.

"What did the Magician want?"

"What we get is protection," Wick said, ignoring my question.

"We get supplies, food, water, more and better biotech. I work with her against Mord."

I was giddy all over again, but it was the giddiness of feeling your stomach drop as you plunged over an abyss, the wild, terrible thrill of everything going the wrong way up or down.

"What does the Magician want in return?"

Wick winced, looked down at his hands. "You won't like it."

"Of course I won't like it, Wick. *You* don't even like it."

"She wants the Balcony Cliffs. And probably Borne-Borney-o up there. Because she'll want access to all the biotech. Every last bit."

The Balcony Cliffs. Borne.

The Magician wanted everything, including our souls.

HOW I FIRST MET THE MAGICIAN AND
WHAT SHE MEANT NOW

The rumors about the Magician up to that point had come to me vast and unsubstantiated, because Wick was terse on the subject and I had few other sources. Some said she was homegrown, rising from the broken communities in the west, and that she had made the Company's business her long area of study. That she had, early on, begun to gather up memories from anyone who could give her something useful—not just to sell but for any intel that might help her see what was going on inside the Company. She planned to use whatever she could glean against the Company. Until recently, that had seemed an idle threat. But when the time came, she knew enough to extort and bribe more tools and biotech off the last Company personnel holed up in the building, abandoned, eking out their existence complying with Mord's demands.

But others said the Magician had once worked for the Company or that she came from beyond the mountains that didn't exist because they were so far away or that she came here because her ancestors had ruled the inland sea that was now salt and desert and next to nothing. They said she was cruel and just, that she was tall and short. They said whatever they wanted, because the elusive Magician so rarely showed her face.

I had seen the Magician only once. She did not like to be out in the open, and, as she became more powerful, made herself visible mostly through the ragtag army of people she had made into allies. She worked her power, Wick said, from the way she could reimagine parts of the city as hers, and we had no competing vision with which to fight back. Those places only had form and substance and boundaries because of her efforts, lacked structure otherwise. We gained our power, or at least survived, by rejecting those boundaries and those spaces. By ignoring her control. From wanting to live apart, in the Balcony Cliffs.

The time I saw her I'd been driven to the far south to avoid a psychopathic scavenger. It was a day when I'd planned to take up my familiar position at Mord's flank, had tracked him far to the west, once again into territory I'd not visited much, with the cracked skull of the observatory to my right as a landmark. But I lacked the nerve that day to latch on, to pull myself up into that besotted fur, and my adversary had taken that as a sign of weakness.

To the south lay only the desolate plain and the Company building beyond it. On the edge before the plain, I veered to take refuge amongst some circular ruins on a ridge of hills. I had my binoculars in my pack and searched for evidence of my pursuer.

Soon my attention was drawn to the hill opposite, where there was a similar circular ruin. Perhaps both had been cisterns, or both had been sentinel strongholds, but against that brown-gray stone shot through with lichen and yellow vines, for a moment only, I saw the outline of a tall figure gliding across the ancient stone wall. It was gone so fast I doubted, put it down to being overly alert for signs of the other scavenger.

Not more than ten minutes later, I heard a kind of rustle or unfolding, and a voice came from beside me.

"Hello, Rachel."

I had my knife out, cast about me, stabbing, turned in a circle but was alone. My blade passed through nothing and no one. The attack beetle I'd readied floated out and, whirring, fell harmless to the ground.

"Put your knife away," the voice said, husky, deep, but a woman's voice. "Put it away. I'm not here to hurt you. If I was, you'd be dead."

I sent another attack beetle toward the direction of the voice. It divebombed the ground, landed on its back, circled there with its wings buzzing.

"That's a waste, Rachel," the voice said. "I never took you as the wasteful sort."

"Who are you?" I kept my knife out, but I didn't use another beetle.

"They call me the Magician. Maybe you've heard of me." The voice echoed, came from everywhere and nowhere.

At that time, she was nothing special to me—just another pretender, another grifter, another person deluded into thinking they mattered. A name that would be forgotten soon enough.

"What do you want?"

"You're direct—good. Just like me," she said. There was a hint again of the rustling, of the being-in-plain-sight. But I couldn't see her.

"Say whatever you want to say and leave." I still had the psychotic scavenger, Charlie X, to worry about.

"Are you happy now, Rachel?" the Magician asked.

Happy? Now? What a strange question. What a self-indulgent,

unanswerable question. I wanted to stab the air again because of that question, send my beetles spinning out from me toward all points of the compass.

"What business is that of yours?"

A low, deep chuckle. "You couldn't know this, but it *is* my business. So I ask again, are you happy? At the Balcony Cliffs? With Wick?" The smugness there, the hint of secret knowledge, of intimacy, made me hate her.

"Show yourself," I said. "Show yourself if you want to talk to me."

"You're a good scavenger. You have a good mind. I've watched you for a while now. Long enough to feel like I already know you."

"I don't know you." The light dulled and brightened over the desolate plains below, as clouds gathered and moved swift. Nothing else moved there. Nothing gave itself away. Charlie X was somewhere out there, wanting to kill me.

"But you could. You could join me."

"Join you in *what*?"

"Something more than *this*." She gestured at the sky, the sun, the land, as if we had the choice to leave it all behind.

"Why would I want to?"

"Maybe because I'm not like Charlie X," she said, surprising me. "I'm not stupid. I'm not mad. I'm not living day to day. I'm actually trying to build something here—a coalition, a way forward."

"What do you know about Charlie X?"

"I know he's dead, and that I killed him. Just the other side of that cistern, on the hill opposite."

Relief and suspicion and fear pulled at me.

"You're lying."

"I believe he was on your trail. I believe he meant to sneak up on you and take your life. I believe that won't happen now."

"You're lying."

"After we're done here, you can find out for yourself. And, you're welcome." An incorruptible assurance in her tone, and I did believe her although I didn't want to.

"What are you planning?"

"A way to defeat Mord. A way to bring us all into the future."

Such bitter, mocking laughter the Magician might never have heard before. "If you could do that, you wouldn't be here now."

"Did you know the Company made abominations much worse than Mord, Rachel? Did you know they've meddled in so many things they shouldn't have? Things that affect your life, too."

I spat into the dirt. "The rumor is you're beginning to modify people, and maybe not asking them first."

The Magician laughed. "Oh, I always ask first. But you should ask Wick for his opinion on that before you judge me. Wick just wants to be left alone. I want to change the city. Bring back what we had before."

"You want leverage over Wick."

"I already have plenty of leverage over Wick."

I thought that might be a lie, but her confident tone rattled me.

"But just not enough to get *him* to ask *me* to do work for you on the side, is that it?"

"You know, Rachel," the Magician said, "being blunt, being direct, is fine sometimes. Other times that quality leads right to the boneyard."

"I'm going to ask you one more time to leave," I said.

"Or what? You've got one attack beetle left, a spider, and no gun. And you didn't even know where I was until right this moment."

In front of me, a person appeared, just far enough away to make stabbing her risky. It was almost as startling as if a tiger had appeared before me—as rare and surreal and mesmerizing.

The cowl to her robes was down or I would have paid more attention to the fact her robes weren't clothing but a kind of biotech. She had thick dark hair and deep bronze skin and features that were lionesque or in some way regal, but for a scar that ran down her right cheek, hooking into her upper lip. If I was honest, the Magician resembled me more than she should, even down to the glittering eyes and her build. But my skin was much darker, I had no scar, my hair was short, and I had never been animated by that look of being born to command.

Mord could have hurtled down from the sky to devour her right then and she would still have kept her composure, even while finding some way to thwart his appetite.

"Now you can see me," she said. "What do you think?"

I stuck to my resolve. "I think, one last time, that you need to leave."

The Magician smiled, and it was as if the rays of the sun burst forth from her features—a radiance I couldn't deny, and still that dangerous sense of self-regard.

"You're a valuable commodity," the Magician said. "You should have happiness, boldness, *purpose*. You shouldn't huddle somewhere like a rat in a cage. But I can tell you aren't convinced. So goodbye for now, Rachel."

The cowl rose over her head like the living creature it was, and in a kind of glittering dissolve—a whisper, a hint of a flurry of movement—the Magician disappeared while I just watched with my mouth open. A lucky find, perhaps, that biotech, some kind of camouflage that reflected its surroundings, gave to that disguise depth, breadth, so she wouldn't move like a cardboard cutout across the landscape.

How could I know she was gone? The hilltop felt deserted, even with me still standing there. An *absence*. In the next few days, when I was paranoid she might still be tracking me, I strained to recover that sense of no-one-there, to know for sure that I was right. She had gone on to other things, other plans, other people. Yet even though I didn't like the Magician there arose, from the way she stared at me, the uncomfortable and mysterious thought that she *did* know me, even if I didn't know how.

I found Charlie X dead where she'd said he'd be, not a wound on him. Just horror splashed across his blurred features, as if he'd seen another side of the Magician. Or her true face.

✿

Three years later, the Magician's spirit had snuck right into the room with me, between me and Wick. She might make her head-quarters well to the west, in the ruined observatory, but she had found a way to make her influence felt from afar—because we were weak, because our supplies were running low and Wick could see no other way out. She had found a way in because she'd always been there.

Borne had gone quiet above us as our voices had gotten louder, and Wick had gotten more defensive.

"We are *not* giving up the Balcony Cliffs," I said. We were not giving up Borne, either. I was tired and drunk, drunk, drunk, but this I knew.

"We wouldn't be giving them up," Wick said, with little enthusiasm. "People would move in here, help us fortify it. We live here *alone*. How long do you think that can last?"

"It's lasted pretty long already, Wick."

I crammed another minnow in my mouth. Probably my fifth. We were both acting like if we finished off every alcohol minnow in the land tonight we wouldn't care.

"We're *lucky* we held out this long."

"Why now? Tell me why she's asking now?"

"I think she is planning something big. I think her plans are almost set." Wick's voice had lowered to a whisper, as if the Magician were listening, which only made me madder.

"And how did she reach out? Did she capture you on one of your drug runs? Did she give you all kinds of promises you know she can't keep? And if she did, how did you make it back here? Why didn't she just hold on to you?"

"The Magician's not *asking*. The Magician's telling. That's what she does these days—tells people things, and people do them."

The Magician on one hill and Wick on the other, communicating via hand signals or semaphore.

"*Who* reached out, Wick? Her or you?"

He mumbled something, stood, wrapped his hands around the sides of his chair, tapped its legs against the floor a couple of times.

"He said he reached out, Rachel," Borne said helpfully from the ceiling.

"Borne, stay out of this!" we both shouted at him.

"But you said you didn't hear him and I thought you'd want to know."

"Go back to my apartment and I'll come check to make sure you're all right before you go to bed," I said.

"Sure, Rachel. I can go back to your apartment."

Borne sounded dejected, or maybe I just expected he would. Slowly, he slid down the wall, congealed into an upright Borne position, resuscitated his eyes, and left us. If there was a whiff of indignant spider fart left behind, I tried to ignore it, just as I tried to ignore putting Wick's revelation before Borne's injuries.

"I wanted nothing except to be left alone," Wick said. "That's all I wanted, all I've ever wanted."

Familiar refrain. I'd never asked why he wanted to be left alone, though. That's Wick, I always thought. Wick likes to be left alone.

"It will destroy us, Wick. How can you trust her?"

"How am I supposed to trust *you*?" he said. "*You* brought Borne in here. *You* won't get rid of him. The proxies are getting worse—everything is getting worse. *We have no choice.*"

"You know what will happen to Borne when she takes over."

Wick shrugged, a shrug that said it wouldn't be his problem then, and maybe he even hoped once Borne became someone else's responsibility I would come to my senses, and we would be the "us" and Borne would be one of "them."

"But that's not even the worst thing, Wick, and you know it."

Wick looked puzzled. "What do you mean?"

"The feral children I saw tonight are the *same* as the ones who attacked me here in the Balcony Cliffs."

"There are many terrible people in the city," Wick said. "Lots of terrible people."

"The ones tonight acted like a patrol, as if they were working for someone. Do you know who? I think you know who." I wanted badly to say it.

"You should get some rest," Wick said. "You should go to bed." He wouldn't look at me, even when I shoved myself in front of him. Yet it didn't matter. The perverse thing was I knew Wick so well, and he knew me so well, that we both understood what I meant. It was almost the least of what we were conveying to each other in that moment. But still I pushed, because it had to be said out loud.

"That night the Magician's people snuck in and attacked me. It wasn't something random. They attacked because the Magician was sending *you* a message—and *you* knew that, and you didn't tell me."

"I never knew," Wick protested. "I never knew she would do that. Everything I did was so nothing would happen to you. Can you look me in the eye and say you think I *wanted* that to happen to you? No, never."

"Wick, you withheld information. You were in trouble with her and you didn't tell me." To his credit, he wasn't trying to deny it now.

"Would you have done anything different in my place?" Wick asked, shouting. "And would you have been *extra*-extra careful instead of extra-careful coming back that night? No and no. And we'd be in the same place right now. No matter what I did—unless I just handed over the Balcony Cliffs."

"You didn't trust me!" I shouted back. "You don't fucking trust me."

"It has *nothing* to do with trust," Wick said, exasperated, pained. "Nothing at all to do with trust." He said *trust* like it was a corrosion.

"If I had known, Wick, it would have helped. You would have been more open with me, you wouldn't have seemed so closed off, secretive. Don't you see that the Magician drove a wedge between us, that she wanted you to protect me from her demands? To cut you off from me?"

"*You* cut *yourself* off from me. *You* did that all on your own—by bringing Borne into our lives and not letting go of him. By clinging to him. You did that. You did that!"

"Did you know the Magician tried to recruit me three years ago?" I asked. "Did you know that, Wick? Of course you didn't. I kept that from you because I didn't want the Magician to have more leverage over you than she already has."

A cry of frustration from Wick. "How in the name of fuck is that different than me trying to protect you by not telling you things? It's not different at all! No difference! And I don't even care!"

We were screaming at each other, pointing at each other, but we couldn't stop.

"The difference is, Wick, you're hiding other things from me. You're hiding *why* the Magician has leverage over you in the first place. You're hiding secrets in your apartment you think I don't know about."

That brought him up short, but then he realized I couldn't know his secrets—I just had clues—because he'd been so careful.

"I don't have secrets!" he lied. "I don't have any secrets you need to know about."

"You don't have any secrets I need to know about," I repeated. "Do you know how stupid that sounds? Well, maybe in the morning you'll remember some secrets I do need to know about. Like the fish project. Like a broken telescope or a metal box full of biotech. Like not ever telling me about your family. Maybe in the morning you'll realize just how much I might need to know if we're going to live together."

Wick got up, started furiously stirring the crap in his swimming pool with a long piece of wood, his back to me.

"Isn't there somewhere else you need to be? Someone else you need to be with?" Accusing, stabbing, but also hurt. I could tell he was hurt, too.

We were locked into these positions from the beginning. Wick trying to shield me and do the right thing, conflicted about what that meant . . . and me naïve enough to think I could believe in Wick and Borne at the same time. Corrupted by that. Both of us aware, from some remote position looking down on ourselves, that regret, guilt, even arguing distracted us from getting on with the business of trying to survive.

I stalked out, intending to join Borne like I'd promised.

HOW I LET BORNE DOWN

Yet my attention was in the wrong place, focused on the wrong things, and in my anger I didn't go right to my apartment to check on Borne. My world had gotten smaller and smaller, seemed set on the borders of the Balcony Cliffs and holding on to territory I had thought was already hard-won and secured. It didn't strike me until later how Borne might feel, what he might be experiencing under his upbeat exterior. What it might have felt like to be told to go back to my apartment alone after being wounded, when he had sat vigil by my bedside while I recovered from my attack.

Borne's world had expanded in one day to encompass his own mortality, the horrors of the world, and the great expanse that existed beyond us. He had watched Mord rage and roar. He had been told that the Earth revolved around the sun and that the lights he saw in that black sky were all distant stars, around which revolved still other Earths with their own monsters, their own destroyed cities. No explorer in far-distant times had ever traveled so far, so fast. No astronaut circling the Earth had ever had to acclimate to more. None living or dead had had to experience that while also learning to speak and to think and to feel. Was it too much? Had he been built to withstand the weight of such great pressure? Just how much could he absorb?

On our way down from the roof that night—Mord now gone from the night sky—we had lingered on the factory floor amid the carnage because I still needed intel. I had to know more about the mutant children, who in their feralness seemed chaotic but in their discipline had acted like a patrol. I also wanted a sample from a Mord proxy if I could get one, and it was Borne who found the torn-off paw, who "tasted" the paw so severely that all he left for Wick was the claw. I tried to convey to Borne that he should be mortified but dropped it when I realized I was admonishing someone who might be in shock.

But I found something else. A smashed and slaughtered feral, with a jacket not so ripped I couldn't rifle through it looking for papers, for identification, for anything.

What I found was the insignia of the Magician. What I found was her seal and symbol. And with that evidence, the near-certainty that it was Wick's rival who had snuck ferals into the Balcony Cliffs to attack me, it all felt too close to home, like a way of sending a message.

Even my conversation with Borne on the way back to the Balcony Cliffs had seemed to converge, to have significance to my own situation, in mysterious ways. The words grew large in the night air, kept expanding, until I felt they were important beyond measure.

"How did the world get this way?"

"I don't know. Because of people, Borne. We did this to ourselves." We were still doing it to ourselves.

"Was it always this way?"

"Not always. There were more people and it was better." But not because there were more people.

"More people," Borne said, musing on that.

"Yes. And there were cities all over the world where people lived in peace." There had never been a time when all the people everywhere lived in peace. No one had ever had a lasting peace without ignoring atrocity or history, which meant it wasn't lasting at all. Which meant we were an irrational species.

"Cities everywhere," Borne said, as if he didn't quite know what I meant.

We were almost to the concealed door back at the Balcony Cliffs when Borne spoke again.

"Am I alone, like Mord?"

"Mord has proxies now."

"He's still alone."

"You have me, Borne."

"I mean, are there more like me? Or am I alone? Like Mord."

"I'm alone, too, Borne," I said, a little self-pitying. But was I alone because I'd made myself alone, or . . .

I had no real answer to that question. But I remember I didn't like Borne comparing himself to Mord. I didn't know what that meant or where that could lead.

ロ

I meant to join Borne at my apartment, but halfway there I changed direction and decided to go up to Wick's apartment and search it one more time. Given he was down at the swimming pool drunk out of his mind, it didn't seem like much of a risk, but that might have been my own drunkenness talking. It *was* my own drunkenness talking, my own sense of what I was entitled to after the trauma of that night. I wanted to inflict damage on Wick, find a way to punish him.

But after I'd disabled the couple of defense worms in the door and had turned to the more prosaic defense of the lock, I felt a presence at my back and turned and started—and there was Wick, behind me, in the amorphous darkness of the corridor.

I was tumbling over excuses or explanations as I pulled out the picklock, but when I looked again the corridor behind me was empty. Where had he gotten to? The drunk me decided it didn't matter and went to work again. Only, as the door opened, as I pushed it open, there was a tap at my shoulder, and there was Wick, reappearing like a practical joke.

This time I jumped up and cursed and fell back into the corridor.

"Oh-ho! Oh-ho!" Wick exclaimed, pointing a finger at me, drunk enough to do a shuffling dance of triumph. "I know what you're trying to do. Again. You're trying to break into my apartment.

Again." Smugness broke some illusion or spell, pushed aside his drunkenness to make his thin charm cadaverous or needle-sharp, the angular planes of his face harsh.

"Don't *sneak up* on me," I said, mounting my best defense.

"You know how boring it is when you try to sneak into my apartment without me knowing? So boring. Because I always know. Why wouldn't I know?"

"Maybe I forgot something I wanted to tell you and maybe I thought you might be in here. And asleep. And couldn't hear me knock so I, you know . . ." Motioning at the door, and making the nonuniversal sign for lock-picking.

Wick didn't understand.

"What's that? What are you doing? Driving a corkscrew into someone?"

I started laughing at that. For some reason I found that the funniest thing I'd ever heard, maybe because in my mind I was the sneakiest human being on the planet, and Wick was telling me I was more like a cartoon character taking extra-big sneak steps up to a door while the eyes on some painting on the wall moved and saw me.

"Yes, I'm sneaky that way. I'm sneaky. Sneak."

Wick rewarded me with his own little dry laugh, pushed past me into his apartment. But left the door open.

"Borne showed you sneaky tonight," Wick said as I followed him into his apartment. "He took on a Mord proxy and survived. Borne can do whatever he wants now. How can you stop him? Claaaaaaw! Claaaaaaw! Claaaaaaw!" Mocking me.

"Shut up."

Wick jumped onto his bed and lay there propped up on one elbow. I joined him, although with a distance between us.

"Maybe they wouldn't have lived long anyway," Wick said. "The Magician's children. Her charges. Her little people. Whatever they are. Besides being fucked up, because they're definitely fucked up." Some of that slurred, so I had to piece it together.

"You shouldn't talk about that." I felt cold, exposed, angry all over again.

"I told you—I never thought that the Magician would come after me."

"And she didn't! She came after *me*!"

I hit him in the side, hard. He flinched, wincing, said, "That hurt."

"It was supposed to hurt."

Wick turned away from me, staring at the wall. The taut quality, the armor that almost physically sheathed him when he didn't want to confront something.

I sighed, more like a deep convulsion that relaxed my tight chest, my tensed shoulders. I looked at the ceiling with the firefly lights. So pretty, so like living constellations. But one by one they were going out, at the average rate of two per day, and even with hundreds of clusters stuck there, Wick's place had become noticeably dimmer. Another few months and it would be dark, but by then we'd be in the thrall of the Magician or forced out by her.

Wick kept too many secrets. It was getting too difficult—occupying the same space but traveling through separate universes of need, of want.

"You owe me," I said, not angry anymore. "You need to tell me something, anything, about what's going on. And if you can't, then this is a lie. If you can't, then we have nothing."

"You hit me, remember?" he said. "Just now."

"You deserved it."

For a long time, Wick was quiet and very still. When he spoke, it was in a tone that told me not to ask questions about what he was going to tell me.

"The Magician found me because of the fish project," Wick

said. "She's not from the city. She's from the Company—last generation before it all began to fall apart. I knew her when I worked on the fish project, and that's how she knew who I was when she abandoned the Company.

"When she first came to me, we struck a deal. She had access to vast quantities of raw materials. What I stole from the Company had already run out. What she sold me saved me. Since, I pay her off in biotech and salvage. But now she wants everything . . ."

"What else does she know?"

"Too much. But there's one thing she doesn't know." Wick reached across me into the drawer beside the bed, pulled out the metal box full of the biotech that looked like nautiluses, handed it to me. "I think you've already seen these."

"What are they?"

"I used to get them from the Company," Wick said. "Now I make them here."

"But what are they?"

"Medicine. A very specialized medicine that I have to take. I have a condition."

"What happens if you don't?"

"You understand why I'm telling you? You are the only person who knows." I knew what he was saying: I still have secrets, but now you have power over me.

"*What happens* if you don't, Wick?"

"I'll die."

I stayed with Wick for several hours, my arm over his chest, in part because I was exhausted, wrung out because of our argument. Not just because we had argued, but relief. That we'd come back, again, from the precipice. That some of the frustration we'd inflicted on each other had come from the knowledge that, in the end, as long as we were shouting at each other we weren't done, we weren't over, and thus the sense that even though we weren't playacting in our disagreement . . . we were playacting in our disagreement. Where could I go? Where could he go?

I kept turning the new facts over in my head. Wick was sick, evidence of which had been right in front of me all this time, in his thinness, his translucent quality, his need for having diagnostic worms vigilant in his arm at all times. The Magician had been helping keep us alive in the Balcony Cliffs, and Wick had been more dependent than I knew. Our situation remained just as bad as before, maybe worse.

By the time I went back to my apartment to find Borne, he wasn't waiting for me. Nor was he in his apartment, and after searching everywhere, I realized Borne had gone back out into the night while Wick and I were arguing.

It was clear that what Wick had said was true: I couldn't control Borne anymore, if I'd ever had that power. Borne would roam the city whenever he liked from now on.

HOW BORNE TAUGHT ME NOT TO TEACH HIM

My parents took me to a fancy restaurant when I was twelve, as a reward for good grades, in our final sanctuary before the end. We had come to that city almost miraculous out of a landscape of lawlessness, fleeing a mad dictator who had taken to cannibalism and random amputations. We had made it through the outer fortifications and barricades, the quarantine of endless questions, because they needed teachers and doctors, and for eighteen months our new home had provided a measure of stability. My mother had a job as a nurse in a clinic and my father used his skills working for a builder.

The restaurant had spotless silverware and bone-white napkins and a server who started each sentence with "sir" or "madam." They even had hot towels and china finger bowls so you could wash your hands between courses. The walls projected images of the most calming and peaceful nature, from a rippling surf at the edge of a black-sand beach to a mountain view of a forested valley so fresh and clear you could almost feel the wind. Little biotech creatures that looked like fluffy baby birds mixed with adorable hamsters gamboled and chittered and put on shows on the wide window frame. Through the window, past the cute biotech: an ordinary evening scene, with streetlamps, a paved avenue, and even a few cars grumbling along.

My mother loved the biotech, wondered where it came from; something so advanced had to come from a place that had security, that could feed and house people. Biotech, she had come to believe, created a trail—became a kind of clue as to where might be safe.

This was just as things began to fall apart in that city, too, so the question of safety was on our minds. Even as everyone was trying to ignore the situation by attending with ever more vigilance to the finer things in life. I still was going to school, for the first time in ages. I worked hard for good grades. I was treated with no more than the average distrust of strangers. I fit in just enough to avoid most teasing about my frizzy hair and odd accent. What teasing I got came with a good-natured smile because so many children in the schools had come from somewhere else, too. I was proud of my effort, I was proud that I'd managed to adjust, to make my mind leave behind the horrors we had experienced before reaching that place.

My parents gave me a present: a biology book with foldouts showing cross-sections of different environments drawn in detail and in vivid but realistic colors. Jungles came wreathed in vines with tiny monkeys with huge eyes and poison frogs and ridiculously fancy birds. Deserts came with burrows under the sand that held solemn-looking mice and, above them, scaly monsters with flickering tongues and vistas broken by gnarled cactus. It looked new, but I knew my mother had been hoarding it for more than a year, wrapped in a brown paper bag. I'd snuck short reads a few times when my parents were asleep. I didn't know they'd meant it for me.

The food, when it finally came, was so perfect . . . it melted on the tongue, the meat like butter, the vegetables cooked just right, the bread rustic and silky inside the wonderfully burnt crust. Dessert was heavier, a sweet and tangy and spongy tower of something, with vanilla ice cream alongside. For dessert, too, the pratfalling biotech came tumbling off the windowsill and did a little dance around my dessert while singing "Congratulations!" I looked at these two creatures with delight, but a year earlier, in the wilderness, we would have caught them, cooked them, and eaten them.

By the time we left and walked home, my parents were agreeably drunk and we sat in the living room talking and laughing until midnight. I had no idea that I would someday lose them, that I would become a scavenger in a nameless city. That I would have dreams of drowning, that I would be a parent to pratfalling biotech that talked back, that challenged and pushed me in so many ways.

I often wished we had just stayed home, skipped the restaurant, because in memory the meal overpowers the evening afterward. No matter how hard I try, I can't remember what I said to my parents or what they said to me, yet I can still remember the taste of the ice cream.

"The world is so big, Rachel," Borne had said to me on the way back to the Balcony Cliffs, after we left the rooftop. "It just keeps going and going."

"It ends eventually." I almost said, "It gets smaller," but bit my tongue.

I didn't know if my world was getting bigger again after Wick's revelations. I didn't know which direction was down and which was up. But I did know I had broken my word to Borne that night and gone through a miserable day pining for him and putting up with a lightness to Wick's step, even a whistle at times that I resented, attributed to his happiness that Borne was gone, and blunted my sympathy for Wick's condition.

I don't know where Borne went the day he was missing, or in what disguise. I don't know if it even matters other than the stress it put on me, a mother's worry, or if that was the moment—the moment of inattention that caused all of the rest to go off course. All I know is he came back safe, and greeted me like nothing had happened and he had just stepped out for an hour.

But I wanted to make it up to Borne, and I wanted to do it by teaching him things more formally, so that he would know what stars were and what the sun was—the way my parents used to teach me even when there was no school, no dinner, no fancy restaurant. Because I still had what they had given me—rituals, values, knowledge—their way of preparing me for a hopeful future.

I'd lost all my possessions when I came to the city, but in my scavenging I'd found another biology book. It didn't have foldouts and there were fewer illustrations, but some of the art reminded me of the book I'd loved. I thought I'd give it to Borne, along with books on other topics. But the other books were camouflage, really, for what was personal to me.

Borne had locked the door of his new apartment, but why I tried to turn the knob rather than knock first, I don't know. Maybe because it seemed to have no biotech defending it. When I did knock, Borne didn't answer right away, and I thought maybe he was out, and I had a startled moment imagining him back out in the city before I heard a muffled "Coming!" and "I'll be right with you," and then the door swung open and he hustled me in with a curling tentacle, and him so familiar to me I didn't mind the strength around my waist, reeling me in.

So there I was in his apartment, a place he'd "made" himself, me clutching my books and trying to fend off images conjured up by Wick's words two nights ago. It was a single room, very large, though, as if he'd torn out a dividing wall, even if I could see no evidence of such destruction. I smelled fresh paint, though that was nearly impossible, and an underlying scent of lilac that he had no doubt wanted to be the overlying scent.

"Sit down," he said. "Sit down."

But he had no furniture, just an empty space, a bare floor, a huge globe of the world in one corner, like you used to find in old libraries, and a closet in the other corner, a cache of little plastic children's records spilling out from under it. He played them by forming a needle from his cilia and rotating the record. I could never hear anything, but apparently he did.

I sat on a stool made of him and between us was a carpet made of him that felt like the underneath of a bath mat . . . with a turret of him facing me so I'd feel comfortable. The turret wore a huge smile and had a big, goofy blue eye right in the top of it.

Although I had come to educate him, I also wished I could help him decorate his apartment, because the only things on the walls were the three "dead astronauts" we'd happened across our first time out, hanging from hooks.

The sight got our conversation off on the wrong foot. It made me cold all over, seeing those dead skull faces through the smashed glass. As if Borne had brought something deadly into our home.

"What are those doing there, Borne?" They did loll, they did sag, the faces looking down at the floor. Those were three *dead bodies* on the wall, three skeleton corpses.

"Oh, the dead astronauts? The fox said I needed to jazz up the place. I needed to give it some pizzazz, some oomph."

I was rendered speechless by so many parts of what he'd said. Foxes. Dead astronauts. Least of all, jazz, pizzazz, oomph—three words he never should have used outside of the books he found them in. But that wasn't the point.

"They're not dead astronauts. The fox told you *what*?"

"Never mind," Borne said. "It was a joke. I was joking. Now, what did you come over for? How can I help you."

How can I help you?

"Those are three dead skeletons on the wall, Borne."

"Yes, Rachel. I took them from the crossroads. I thought they would look nice in here."

Gaping, gaunt, one torn suit for each of us. When had he taken them? What traps had he set off and how had he survived them?

"They're dead people, Borne."

"I know. They're definitely not living in there anymore. The dead astronauts have gone away. There's nothing to read in them." The big eye in the turret had gotten small, intensely focused, growing out on the end of a delicate tendril to wander and wisp in front of me. I could have reached out and patted Borne on the eyeball if I'd wanted to.

"It's ghoulish," I said.

"Ghoulish," he said, savoring, making it sound like *goulash*. "You mean like ghosts? Like being haunted?"

"No."

"I promise you, there's no one here," Borne said, touching the suits, making them rock a little in their harnesses. ". . . Have I done something wrong, Rachel?"

I tried to adjust to the dead astronauts on the wall. Borne would not stop calling them dead astronauts, which means I must have called them that around him, and so their history was set. But the straight-up unimportant truth was that it irritated me that Borne had moved the dead astronauts to decorate his apartment, because that meant the intersection would be so much harder to identify next time.

"No, you haven't done anything wrong. But I know that some people might be offended by you hanging dead people on the wall." As if the Balcony Cliffs was full of other tenants.

"They look peaceful to me, Rachel. They seemed lonely. I think someone had put them at the crossroads, Rachel. I think some bad people had put them there. Now I have rescued them. Now they're safe, I think."

Safe and still dead.

"Borne, I hate to ask, but can you promise me you'll put them away at least, in the closet?"

"The closet is full." But something he read in the expression on my face made him volunteer to get rid of the astronauts, so he added, "I'm sure I can find something better."

I didn't inquire as to what "better" meant, and he never did remove the dead astronauts.

I could give Borne no semblance of a standard education because we had only what I could find in the Balcony Cliffs because who would risk salvage time to bring back books? So I showed him the biology text. I lied and told him that I had gotten it from my parents, and I wanted him to have it. That maybe we could go through the book together.

The tendril had withdrawn and the big eye floated above the big smile once more. Borne was a kind of sibilant blue-green, seemed almost to reflect the waves of a sea he'd never seen, as if the water and surf were washing over him.

"That's kind, Rachel," Borne said. "I do appreciate it—so much. But I've already read all of the books in the Balcony Cliffs. I've read them all and I think that might be enough for me to have read rather than to have lived."

"I don't see much of a library in here." A vaguely hurt comment, because I felt wrong-footed once more. I had already promised myself I wouldn't ask him where he'd disappeared to, that to do so was somehow dangerous, but I felt a distance between us I associated with the intermittent beacon that was Wick, not me and Borne. Not the me and Borne that had run up and down the hallways of the Balcony Cliffs when I'd been recovering.

"Oh, the stacks and stacks and stacks. No one needs the clutter. So much clutter. So many things to trip over. I have remembered it all. I read it all. I read everything."

I tried to think like Borne then: A very large invertebrate only getting larger, who needed room to stretch out. With skin that was more intelligent than mine. He wasn't human, even if he was a person. He didn't need what we needed. Which is why he had no furniture. Had it caused him mental anguish to be around so much clutter in my apartment?

"But you must have questions."

I meant "in general," but Borne merrily launched into specific questions.

"Oh, yes, questions! How long have humans lived on this planet? And what have they accomplished? I can't tell. You mentioned ghosts before. Do you believe in ghosts? Do you know if there is still a spaceship somewhere on Earth? There must be a spaceship somewhere, or two or three. Do you ever feel haunted? Do you ever find anything 'spooky'? Who are 'we' and who are 'them'? Did human beings ever colonize any other planets? How many human beings are still alive on Earth?"

"Those are a lot of questions, Borne," I said. I wasn't sure which to answer first, or what my answers might be. The books I'd brought him were of little help, not appropriate for what Borne needed—or needed from me.

"I've been haunted by them." Hauntings came up a lot with Borne once he wasn't a "child" any longer. I would come to realize a haunting meant something different to him. The landscapes he traversed looked nothing like what I saw, might to me seem like a bombardment of senses I couldn't even imagine.

"Who?"

Borne swiveled his turret toward the dead men on the wall, shone a mist-like magenta light upon them. "Them. But not as ghosts . . . I see it, I taste it. All the contamination. The low-level radiation, the storage sites, the runoff. Every place is sick—there's *sick* everywhere. I estimate I expend eighteen lizards a day keeping it off of me. It makes me be sure of *my self* every moment and keep track of *my self*."

I had looked forward to having adult conversations with Borne, and now I didn't want them. I didn't even quite understand what conversation we were having, and I didn't want to be reminded of the ways my body was being tested every day in the city.

But I tried twice more. First, I shared a schedule I had come up with, a schedule that, day by day, turned from one subject to the next. Basic math, language arts, hard science, soft science. It even included music and philosophy.

Borne examined the piece of paper in his nub of a pseudopod; he hadn't even done me the courtesy of extending a full tentacle but made me get up and hand it to him.

"Hmmph," Borne said. "Hmmph." Outsize, hammy acting.

Satirical sounds. He also hadn't made any effort to appear to be reading the sheet, but I knew he had. This was Borne being rude on purpose.

"What's wrong?"

"Borne plays the piano. Borne dances. Borne sings. Borne recites poetry. Is that what you want? While I'm doing other, more important things, I guess part of me could do that for you. I guess I could find a way if it's something you want." Said in a flat, irritated tone that must have been as much an attempt at learning the inflections of my language as the words themselves.

"But it's for you! It's something for you, so you can learn." Not for me. Never for me. Not even for the memory of a schoolgirl in a far-distant city, in music class, in a fancy restaurant, playing on a real playground and dreaming of being a writer.

"I'm learning *every day*, Rachel," Borne said in exasperation, as if I could not see the most obvious things. "I read and sample and observe every day. It is what I do."

It is what I do.

I pointed to the globe of the world, tried one last time. "Can I at least teach you about that?"

This caught his interest, and he pulled the globe over, held it up in his muscular tentacles, hoisting it like it was a paper mobile. For the first time I thought of him as not just strong but formidable.

"This place looks rocky, and I'd like to climb a mountain someday, and then down here are all of these lakes. Can you imagine it, Rachel? So many lakes. We have no lakes here at all. No lakes. I'd like to see a lake. Even a lake as a lark. I'd like to see a lark, too."

He began to excitedly ask specific questions about cities, about countries, about regions. But those places, most all of them, didn't exist anymore with those boundaries, or those countries had been absorbed by other countries and then those larger countries had dissolved into anarchy and lawlessness and become smaller cells once again. Most of the cities had burned, in my recollection— were the kinds of places my parents never taught me about because it cost them too much to do so.

Borne acted as if he'd been trying to solve a problem that had already been solved for us long ago, and I couldn't help him with that, didn't want to revisit it.

Finally, I stopped. I just stopped. The more I tried, the more Borne was becoming distant, disengaged, and the more I began to be taken aback by his stubborn refusal and on some level insulted by it. I had come here to educate Borne, but if I was honest I wanted to make sure I stayed close to him.

Yet I also wanted Borne to be "normal," to fit in, to be like a normal "boy." I wanted this desperately, especially after the events of the past few days. And it struck me, too, that maybe I hadn't kept up, that maybe it wasn't just Borne's physical growth that had accelerated but his mental growth, too. That, with no time to adjust, I still saw him as a child. That giant eye. That silly turret.

Which led to my surrender, which led to my next question: "What *can* I do for you then, Borne? There must be something."

No more turret, but once again the upside-down vase design, the Borne Classic. He contracted so that my stool was pulled closer and closer to the ring of eyes, and his skin was like an electric storm at twilight, with shocks of lightning manifesting as silver cracks in his skin and a mottled darkness of deep, deep green sliding into black but also a startling glimpse of blue, as of a boat floating over clear water. The smell of him was sickly sweet then, like brandy mixed with crispy waffles lathered in butter and syrup.

"There is one thing, Rachel," he said. "One thing you said

you'd do. Something you promised you would do." There was a pleading quality to his tone.

"Yes?" I nudged.

"You could check the places I can't feel anymore. You could tell me what's happening there."

And I was struck dumb by the depths of my thoughtlessness.

So that's what I did—check the places Borne couldn't feel anymore—setting aside my books, shelving my thought of "educating" Borne, because it's not what he needed. Doing what I'd promised to do the night the Mord proxy had attacked him. I felt awful.

That's the problem with people who are not human. You can't tell how badly they're hurt, or how much they need your help, and until you ask, they don't always know how to tell you.

What to say about Borne's body, or my inspection of it. He was all the things he could be—rough in places, smooth in others, bumpy and sandpapery in one area and as worn as river stone in another. The quadrants of Borne, the logic that held his body together and animated him, had a deep awareness of the tactile, and it was through touch that I began to understand his complexity—the circular tension of the suckers he could create, the waving stubby toughness of the cilia, which looked so delicate but were not, the utter indestructibility where he formed ridges, the glassy imperviousness of those eyes, which had a film over them that hardened as soon as the eye appeared and left only a millisecond before the eye was subsumed in the skin.

Everywhere he felt like one thick muscle with no hint of fat, but also he could be diaphanous in places that spread like fans or webbing. Articulated there I found patterns that seemed too filigreed and ornamental to have purpose, and yet they did have purpose.

With each new unfurling, Borne was letting me get closer to the heart of him, while he spoke not a word but let me find the wounds first myself. Nor did he change his scent, left all neutral but the touch of him, and the light . . . he changed the light so that it streamed from the top of his head like a fountain and sprayed across the ceiling and back down upon us, that I might better see him. Was this what it was like to touch something that no one had ever touched before, or rarely? Like a blue whale or an elephant? To understand that beyond the seeing eye, the knowing eye, there was such a wealth of unique touch? Such a different way to experience what came across in photos as wondrous enough?

I found the defects easily but kept going to ensure that I missed nothing, that I uncovered each broken place. When I was done, I had discovered three hardened areas—a roughness with no give, a stubborn thickness that slashed through areas of rippling motion, paralyzed Borne's normal functioning. When I had identified them, Borne confirmed they matched the areas he could not feel, and he changed the color around them to a deep burgundy, which leeched the color away from the places where he hurt. This left Borne almost unbearably white across those sections: a stretch of tentacle, a part of the side of his "face," and then another patch far off on the periphery, on what I would call a skirt of his flesh.

The imprint of Mord proxy fang, Mord proxy claw was clear to see there. The mark of Mord, like a brand. Less clear was the nature of the injury.

"Borne, now I need you to answer two questions. The first is, do you know if that affected flesh is dead?" I meant "necrotic" but didn't know if he knew the word. "And the second is whether there has been a spreading of the numbness since you were bitten."

Splayed out like that, fully exposed, under the fountain of light,

Borne looked more human than he ever had, for reasons I can't explain, despite the tentacles spraying out in one direction and the skirt in another and the central column of his presence and also various hunched-over assemblages of flesh under which the cilia writhed. It was in that mode that he felt the most familiar to me, in that moment when I knew him best.

"The flesh is dead. I receive nothing from it. The numbness spread at first, but I sealed off the dead flesh. I sense no other contamination."

"Borne, do you understand the concept of 'poison,' of being poisoned?"

"Yes, Rachel."

"Do you know if this substance, the contamination, came into your body when the Mord proxy bit you?"

"Yes—it was then and no other time. I was alert to environmental contaminants, sealing them out. But I thought a bite was just dead or lost cells."

"You've been poisoned. I think the Mord proxy's fangs or claws, or both, were coated in something poisonous."

As it turned out, I was right, and I had discovered another hazard to take note of in negotiating the world outside: Mord proxies were venomous as snakes. This poison had aided the Mord proxies in their fight with the Magician's patrol, helped hasten the utter annihilation of the mods and homegrowns.

"What should I do, Rachel? Am I in trouble? Am I going to die?"

"No, you're not going to die. But you may be in discomfort for a while. If you're like other animals, it will become scar tissue and go away. But infection could occur, so you need to watch them, and let me know if those areas change."

"Infected? Change?"

"Become inflamed."

"Inflamed?"

"You know—like, see this scab." I extended my forearm. I had gotten the bruises from stumbling on the stairs the night we'd been stuck on the factory rooftop. "See how it's red and there's some pus."

"Pus. Scab. Pussssssssscaaaaaabbbbbuh." Such not-nice words.

"Some pus is okay, but not a lot of pus. And you need to clean a wound if there's pus in it, because it means the wound is infected. But you won't die. But keep an eye on it."

"Not too much pus," Borne said, and three tiny stalks extended near each wound and three tiny eyes budded from each to keep watch. Which, from past experience, meant Borne was making a little joke about sentry duty.

"Something like that."

"Thanks, Rachel. Thank you."

"You're welcome, Borne. Anytime."

I would worry about him now. I would worry about his safety, because I had no control over it anymore, with no guarantee I could keep him safer if I had control anyway. I would worry about his naïve sense of trust. I would worry about the gaps, "forget" to take my books back with me because I believed he still had so much to learn.

Before I left, Borne said, "I can't stop, Rachel."

"Can't stop what?"

"Reading. Learning. Changing. That's why I don't need your books, Rachel. I'm learning too much too fast already. I feel it filling me up, and I can't stop. So when you want me to learn more, it makes me . . . makes me . . ."

"Stressed?"

"Yes! That's the word. Stressed. There is stress."

The Magician couldn't stop what she was doing, I couldn't

stop what I was doing, Wick neither, and now Borne was telling me he couldn't stop.

"It's okay," I said, too relieved that I was back in Borne's good graces to examine what he was saying. "It will be fine. I won't force you to learn. But get rid of the dead astronauts."

"They're burrowing, but we're in no danger," Borne replied.

"What?"

"Mord proxies. I can hear them."

I could hear nothing, and no one attacked the Balcony Cliffs that day, or the next, or the week after. But that didn't mean he hadn't heard them.

HOW THE MAGICIAN MADE THINGS WORSE

Perhaps I had hoped that if I ignored the Magician's ultimatum, if I kept avoiding Wick's attempts to discuss it with me, that both the ultimatum and the Magician would cease to exist, be driven from the city as if neither had ever existed, and some new path would shine out before us, showing us a way to keep the Balcony Cliffs and keep ourselves safe in the process.

But the Magician had other plans.

Ten days after I learned of the Magician's ultimatum, Wick took me to a secret vantage near the top of the Balcony Cliffs, one that required climbing up an unstable wrought-iron spiral staircase, one so looped and tight it felt a bit like being a contortionist to ascend. But near the top, you came up into a shallow buried pillbox with enough room to stand. Vents in the ceiling led to the surface maybe twenty feet above. A trough of a passageway at our feet headed due west.

It smelled pungent, like mold and earthworms, but a faint light bled out from the far end. We had to inch our way through it, narrow enough that our elbows clashed and the friction against our clothing made us sweat. The passageway led to a blind atop a high bluff, looking out from the eastern edge toward the rest of the city. A tight rectangle of a view so as not to be visible from below or above, but panoramic.

Wick had intel, gleaned from someone who badly needed his memory beetles. I thought perhaps that information was false and Wick just needed a break from his swimming-pool vat, wanted a panoramic view to clear his head. But I went along.

From our vantage there, peering through my binoculars, I can tell you these things were true: The crazy golden gleam of the sun off the cracked dome of the observatory to the northeast, the Magician's stronghold, was almost blinding—and no longer alone. Below that artificial promontory and somewhat south the gleam had been joined by smaller glints that signified gun emplacements. They hadn't been there three days ago.

To the southwest lay the Company building, a bloated white oval, the vast egg that had spawned so much discontent and chaos, and yet still fed us at varying rates and in a variety of ways, even if we did not always like the feeding.

At dead center from our vantage sat Mord, at a cleared intersection, cleaning his fur. Even dull or blood-covered or matted, that fur shone in the sun, and moving around that muted god-beacon in a rough arc we saw the burly shapes of Mord proxies, standing guard. Done cleaning his fur, Mord pulled a slender tree out of the ground, grasped the branches, and used the roots to scratch his back. Then he abandoned his sitting position to roll in the dirt. The earth-shattering roars and yawns that emanated from him then were all about scratching a good itch. Who knew how many skeletons lay crushed beneath his dust bath.

Between, the contested ground, the low country: a wide expanse of buildings, courtyards, former commercial structures, museums, business districts, a scattering of trees and bushes, and the telltale muted orange-and-green veins of Company lichen that covered so much of the stone there. There you could see both the blueprint for a return of civilization, of the rule of law, of culture . . . and how much work that would take.

No dwelling now cleared five stories, as Mord liked to be able to see when he went on a stroll and had brought much around him into compliance with his deranged building code. Some of this jumbled riot, which in places looked like a giant had picked it up and then rolled it across the plain, was broken and stacked while other structures revealed little of the trauma, the level of injury, that must lie within.

That ground wasn't simple, wasn't dead or alive, but contested between the animate and the inanimate. Not just communities and scavengers invisible to us from the blind, but waiting there in the sandy soil: the Company life that had been discarded and dispersed like dandelion tufts. It waited for a touch—a drop of water or blood, say—to germinate and to be counted on the battlefield as loot. No one could say where this might happen or when, and so even a derelict, abandoned lot toxic with oil pools and black mold might in a week or a year or a century blossom into strange life.

The sky above *was* simple, though: It belonged, all the fierce blue of it, to Mord, and wherever he alit and bestrode the ground, he owned that, too, even as he destroyed it. Belowground . . . well, the proxies now roamed there, wherever they could fit, but otherwise it was a reflection of the allies and enemies above, depending on the extent of tunnels and old subway systems and the basements of buildings now leveled and unremembered by the surface.

The Magician's growing influence led us to believe that there was an invisible wave rising from below that might in time wash us all away.

Seeing the map revealed so nakedly made naked, too, the thought of a growing conflict—to rule the city—and what choices! We were so lucky, after such strife, to be able to choose between a homegrown tyrant in the Magician, who strove to win by any means, and a Company-grown tyrant in Mord, who held the city in stasis, us unable to do more than react to his whims. Neither imagined as rulers could long be tolerated. Yet we could not imagine what lay beyond them except, with a shudder, the specter of the Company itself rising once again from its own ashes.

As we watched there came a sound deep and sonorous, and then the sound again, and a third time. Mord raised his broad head, upon which we could almost have built another Balcony Cliffs, muzzle pointed toward the sun, that he might better scent the air, in that swaying, singsong way of ursines.

Was this the sound of delicious protein being reckless enough to announce itself? Whatever Mord believed, he went from scenting to standing at full extent on two stout legs—so tall and so massive—until he'd identified the sound as coming from the observatory. Then, too light to be believed, Mord sprang up into the air while his proxy lieutenants stood on their hind legs as well and scented the air and huffed their approval. Up, up, he flew, until he was but a distant shadow in the heavens, a miraculous traveler, a psychotic inkblot, and then down, down with a plummeting certainty toward the source of the sound, the greatness of his bulk ever more solid.

But as Mord's dive straightened out, as he swooped in a curve toward the observatory, there came a ragged gout of flame from the gun emplacements. A stuttering fire and a roar not like a bear but like a mighty engine.

The Magician had launched a missile at Mord. The missile came out of the ground corkscrewing and shrieking, incredibly fast, spewing black smoke out behind.

Mord performed a maneuver I can only describe as *skidding* to a stop in midair, using his weight to reverse his position from headfirst attack to buttfirst scramble, now more vertical than horizontal. The missile adjusted, but with only a split second until impact, Mord's maneuver was enough. The missile spiraled whistling past Mord's head.

We thought it had missed because the missile kept going and gouged the ground on the desolate plain facing the Company building, exploding in a spray of flames and smoke. A sparkle of stars that quickly became a spreading fire.

But then we saw the side of Mord's head burning, too, and realized the missile had grazed the side of his skull, the damage hard to gauge at that distance.

Mord let out a howl of agony, an almost-human scream of rage, but the Magician's second and third missiles were already headed toward him, and Mord accelerated straight up, toward the sun. Up and up he went, and the missiles veered toward his heat signature, despite a creaking resistance from gravity, at a ninety-degree angle.

Would Mord reach the sun before the missiles found him? We watched, holding our breath. It struck me that the Magician might have succeeded in killing Mord. That Mord might die right now, right here, in front of us. And as much as we had all hoped for that day, some part of me, deeply perverse, was rooting for Mord to outwit the missiles, that it was too soon, we were not ready, none of us were ready.

Still Mord blistered up toward the sun until he was again just a dot, a satellite hovering above the Earth—and still the missiles followed, but at a slower and slower speed.

Until they faltered.

Until gravity began to weigh upon them, take a greater and greater toll.

Until they reached the moment of their greatest ascension, and fell off the trail.

Fell back, inert, to Earth.

That was an excruciating slow fall, too, trying to guess where they might land, these now-tumbling bombs, hoping and praying it would be nowhere near us. Thankfully, terribly, into that contested ground they smashed, exploded, and sent shock waves of flames shooting out to all sides. Some were extinguished immediately, but other fires crackled on and would for several hours, laying waste to what had already been half devastated, driving out those who had taken refuge and burning the rest.

The Magician's forces had no more missiles, and soon no missile launchers, for Mord came down again, this time more cautious, in silence from a position over the desert beyond the city. Low and silent, claws scraping and sparking the tops of desert rocks.

Those still defending the observatory, the gun emplacements, could not have seen what we saw from our vantage. They might even have thought Mord had been killed by a missile high above, for from their position he must have seemed to disappear.

At speed, fur buffeted by his acceleration so that he looked furiously in motion across his entire body, Mord approached from behind the observatory—came up and lunged over, and with a guttural battle cry, crushed the gun emplacements to dust, and to pulp any who still manned them. Then he demolished the observatory so that no glass at all remained and the solid bands of steel that ringed it were left contorted and deranged as if by a meteorite or the warping of extreme time, but in fact only because of Mord.

Already the Mord proxies had begun to close in on the observatory, which did not bode well for the Magician's future, and we could see their solid dark shapes clambering up the sides and tumbling inside as if to fill it up and render it down. I had an image in my head of that globe filling with blood until the Magician's entire force had been reduced to a more essential form.

But Mord was not finished. The crackling flame at his cheek had been snuffed out by his accelerations, but his fur there was singed and bloody and blackened, and the mute openings of his muzzle, the agony in one frantic paw held to his face, made it clear he now sought sanctuary to heal it. As the Mord proxies poured into the observatory district, their leader flew south, and at the wide ponds of runoff and offal and abandoned biotech next to the Company building, Mord laid down his head, put out the pain with water, and remained there long enough for an evil mud to form over the wound.

But as he did so, some relic of the Company defenses lurking in the holding ponds, a leviathan gray with age and be-gilled and scaled, pulled itself up out of that murky water and attacked Mord from the side. It resembled more an iguana than a fish, with a gaping bite, an off-center lunge that seemed to admit to missing limbs. From our vantage it was a scene in some aquarium, a fight between random creatures that had been placed there by a god who had wanted to see if a shark could defeat a bear. But a brief fight, for Mord swatted the thing senseless with his paws and then ripped out the leviathan's brain, and it slumped in the sand like something that had never been alive.

This was a scene that seemed scarcely believable, and yet I have not told you the most miraculous true thing, how the day progressed from myth to mythic, which no retellings can embellish. For Mord, thwarted it seemed by the derelict condition of the observatory and the poor fight put up by the leviathan, and still smoldering with rage and in search of an easier revenge, *turned his anger on the Company building.*

We watched in a shock I can barely describe as Mord tore open the top of the Company building like it was a sleek beehive and tossed the upper floors off to the far west, into the desert beyond the city. Now he was scooping out the contents and slurping his huge tongue through the maze of stone and plastic to get at the sweetness of flesh and blood, spitting out the rest. There was nothing human in his gaze in that moment, just the kind of hunger that could never truly be satiated. It was awful. People and creatures were jumping out of that exposed honeycomb to their deaths in the holding ponds, and he ignored them.

A desperate squadron of helicopters, long-hidden and clearly in bad repair, tried to rise from the upper levels, but Mord rose with them and swatted them out of the sky. Some of their broken remains, wings crumpled, lay around Mord and others became embedded in the surrounding desert, the desolate plains, as if they had always been there.

Then came, last defense, a swarm of flying biotech like locusts or wasps, so thick and dark it formed a vast cloud, but Mord only gave out a bellowing, huffing laugh and flew through that cloud again and again, with his mouth wide open like a whale filling its belly with krill, until almost none were left and the rest reduced to less than the sad comradery of tiny clusters on the horizon.

There was a joyous aspect to Mord in those moments, some sense of liberation to the way he moved that made me wonder if the Magician's attack, the reflexive action of the leviathan, had given Mord the pretext to maul the Company building. To do what he wanted to do anyway.

Defenses gone, the Company lay open to him and Mord dug deeper, and wrenched his claws through metal, stone, wood, and people alike, every once in a while finding a true treasure trove, and raising his muzzle to let a bolus of screaming, bloody morsels slide down his throat, the better to devour them. Even from our distance, you could now see the red smeared across his muzzle.

We watched, mesmerized and horrified by the torment suffered until, finally, all lay still and, sated, Mord gathered up the leviathan and flung its viscera and spine atop the mess he'd created of the building, a final insult, and flew away.

We could not escape the yowling and moaning of Mord in the aftermath, the way it permeated the air—how it made the blackest night seem to ignite with sparks of a grief and rage the depths of which we could never understand. Seether's flank. Seether. Mord. The great bear that might once have been human, who would return at dusk to the ruins of the Company for many nights, to sleep fitfully atop its remains, tormented by visions that would turn our own attempts at sleep into squint-eyed insomniac rovings.

While from all over the city Mord's proxies responded with their own growling, their own "Drrrrrk!"

And it was too much. It overwhelmed. The odds. The odds we'd be alive in a month, or a day. How I dithered in my wishes, thinking that perhaps the Magician's ultimatum would have been preferable, that if only the missile had hit its mark the chaos in the city would have remained manageable, of a kind we recognized.

The fires from the missiles lasted well into the night. By the next morning the rumor in the city was that the Magician was dead, dragged from her underground stronghold, disemboweled by the Mord proxies, and then eaten by them so that no trace of her should ever again appear upon the Earth.

But I did not believe it.

✿

I have tried to do justice to the vast scale of these events in this account, but at the time I was so scared I almost lost my shit watching from the blind, with Wick offering up a muttered commentary the whole time—and for minutes after.

"Is he really going to attack the Company? He is he is.

"How did she acquire missile launchers or missiles? That was clever. All those excavations underground.

"Now will this mean she comes after us sooner or much later? Is she damaged or is she fatal?

"The Company building goes down several levels below the surface—he's just cut off the head. The body's still down there. There's still life down there. Maybe.

"The Company has no control over Mord. None whatsoever. But at least now he's cut off his supply of Mord proxies. There is no other source. Unless they can breed."

I had no words with which to reply, not even the words to tell him I had no answers or to dispute the answers he provided. The only person he could reassure was himself. All I knew was that the Magician had proved a dangerous, reckless fool to have set all of this in motion but to have failed, with no evidence of a backup plan, and we would all pay for it in some way. Even if she was dead, her mutant children still roamed the city, and we did not know what might come out of the Company's now-exposed lower levels.

But we were very close and intimate in the blind, me and my poor sick Wick. I could smell the sweet bone-salt tang of alcohol minnows on his breath again. I didn't mind, and his hair smelled cleaner than it should have, and my hip was up against his, and my arm against his arm, and it was impossible to just see Wick as sickly or an enemy or an obstacle, not with all the lines and networks and traps radiating out from the Balcony Cliffs—still in place despite what we had witnessed.

"Where do we go if we have to leave the Balcony Cliffs?" I asked.

A naked question, and I could feel his heart beat faster against my skin. He was like a giant tree frog, eyes large, remaining motionless but for the heartbeat that trembled out of him. It confused some instinct in me, some default, that Wick didn't change color or shape, I had been hanging out with Borne so much.

He did not move, and so I leaned over and kissed him on the lips as his reward for contemplating the abyss. Or maybe because he was still not Mord nor Magician nor proxy, but only himself.

Then I wrestled his wiry form until I was on top of him and there was a severe question or concern in his eyes about what I meant to do, where we had left things after our epic argument. What I meant to do was to huff like a Mord proxy. What I meant to do was huff and growl and paw at Wick. To nip at him and breathe on him, and in all ways be a bear. Except for the kissing.

Maybe I'd gone a little crazy in the aftermath of slaughter. Or maybe I was trying to break out of my skin, thinking about how my parents had been actors in roles and the roles were to be my father and mother—and the reason I could see those as roles was that in such extremes, in private, they must have let down their guard and expressed their doubts, their fears, the extent of their despair or hopelessness as our situation worsened and the world revealed the outlines of its true harshness. But because of me, there were whole eternities of hours each day when they had to pretend otherwise, and how I wish I could go back and tell them not to do that. That all I wanted was to see their true selves, remember their true selves. These were my thoughts as I looked down at Wick, wanting us revealed each to the other, forgetting that Wick, too, was playing a role. And Borne, too. Our lives were rapidly becoming impossible.

"Mord's proxies are going to hear you and eat us both," Wick whispered in my ear after a while, after he'd figured out I wasn't going to eat him. We were close, so very close.

"You'd like that."

"No, you'd like that!"

And then giggling—out of humor, out of stress.

He stopped struggling, let me kiss him again and again, let me smell him like a bear. So this was what it was like to be Mord or a Mord proxy. The snuffling, the great strength, the prey that could not get away.

Crouched there on top of Wick, every point of my body against every point of his, I realized, as if for the first time, that happiness never came easy to Wick. I don't mean happiness in general but moments of happiness. Happiness in the moment eluded him without his alcohol minnows, his memory beetles; he carried too much weight, a weight he was always mindful of, that must be present in his life at all times.

But I could tell me on top of him was a stress, too, because he was so much thinner, and after a time, while outside trails of black smoke rose from the Company building and people in the low country with no shelter tried panic-stricken to find shelter, I dismounted, lay beside him, my arm around his side, my hand on his chest. Such a fragile heart for such a hardened man.

"How do we get out of this, Rachel?" Wick said after a moment. "I can't see how to get out of this. Anymore."

"Keep fortifying the Balcony Cliffs. Wait things out," I said.

I didn't have any more traps and the only other plan I could think of in the aftershock of watching Mord attack the Company was for someone to come along to save us. But no one would ever come along to save us.

We held each other for a time in that hideaway, that unexpected sanctuary, while the city smoldered and the world went on changing without us.

HOW I TRIED TO COPE

Although we did not know if the Magician was dead or alive, chief among our ills now seemed Mord's proxies, reeling across the city in the aftermath of the missile attack. I had so many terrible dreams connected to the proxies, terrible thoughts, in those times, and couldn't distinguish which were mine and which were imposed from some other source. For that's the way I felt: that I was not entirely myself. It seemed for a time that the Mord proxies forced all action and everything came out of their machinations. Even Borne's rejection of my books became part of the proxies' plan, because I had lost my mind. I was haunted by dreams of the proxies in which they now flew as well, and that the space in the roof above the swimming pool had opened up into a yawning chasm and the Mord proxies had swooped down into that space to talk to Wick, and that Wick plotted with the proxies to take over the Balcony Cliffs from me and Borne.

Drunk-stumbling in their own blood-murder, Mord proxies growled from fang-filled snouts a language that none had ever heard before, articulated even as they slaughtered, thoughts and desires that had never been expressed in the city, that were beyond even Mord. From the entrails left behind we tried in vain to divine what they meant, what sense could be made of . . . any of it.

Mord had never spoken except to roar or rage, had said no intelligible word. Yet these emissaries in his image—breaking down walls, smashing through doors to get to the live flesh-meat beyond— they spoke continually. They would not or could not stop speaking. Sometimes muttered. Sometimes huffed out or choral, together, from deep in their throats. We knew of their passage through the world by this entangled, glottal speech that we could not interpret. No translation existed, and there was no intermediary to explain. So since we could not understand anything but their actions, we resolved to snuff out these proxies, to halt their stream of speech as they desired to halt our own, did not care what phase in Mord's rough dominion they might mark.

But, mostly, we hid from them, avoided them, tried not to be killed by them. We disguised our scent, disguised our home even more. Ventured out less. With most of his clients dead or gone into hiding, it took little to convince Wick to remain behind our barricades.

During this time, I would wake in the middle of the night, startled from sleep, with the memory of Mord's giant carious eye, shining like an evil sun, replacing the real sun, and shining over my bed, only to find Borne instead, watching me, in need of comfort I believed, of someone to talk to.

I gave Borne what I had to give, even when exhausted, because I never wanted to lose track of him again. I feared that more than anything. I feared that he would slowly merge with the background, as the background became my primary concern: to shore up walls, to place a new barricade at the end of a corridor I now thought might be a security risk, and a pit below. We were afraid of people coming up on us from below, having seen the feral children pop up out of their lair. We could hear sometimes a lazy inquiry, a random digging *here* and then *there* that I thought must be the Mord proxies, perhaps even at rest, not giving a second thought to the likes of us. But not for long, not for long, Wick thought.

During Borne's visits, he would be in what he called travel mode about half the time, and he glowed a deep icy blue flecked with patches of gold that created star-shaped patterns on the wall. My fireflies had fallen below a level he deemed acceptable. His eyes were only two in number in that mode and had an odd intensity to them.

Sometimes Borne would adopt a kind of a new "bloat" position that made him look like a huge, fleshy eggplant on its side, his tentacles pulled down over his torso to provide stability. But, with more and more frequency, Borne would also change shape and color so often during a visit that it was hard to look at him, as if there were some things the human eye was not adapted to see. I didn't know if he was losing control of himself or entering some new phase.

I learned not to mind that he just appeared inside my apartment, even though I had to make an appointment to visit him. Even if he surprised me while I was untying my shoes after a long day or walking around in my underwear. We couldn't afford to use biotech to secure our apartment doors anymore; there was nothing that valuable for Borne to eat.

"How was it out there?" I would ask, rather than, "Why, why were you out there again?" Yet he always came back unscathed. Yet he always told me about his day, or some version of it.

"What happened in this city?" Borne asked once, in a voice like a world-weary old man.

I had no answer for him, thinking: I don't know, it just happened. Everything everywhere collapsed. We didn't try hard enough. We were preyed upon. We had no discipline. We didn't try the right things at the right time. We cared but we didn't act. Too many people, too little space. Weighted down, unable to see the way

Borne saw. Maybe the Mord proxies weren't an aberration but the end product of it all.

"It's dead. It's all in ruins. Everyone is . . . defeated."

I know a responsible parent would have pushed back, told him that wasn't true. But I'd had yet another hard day on the back of several more, with little sleep, and I couldn't help but laugh, scathing, at that. So he'd finally noticed. Some petty part of me rejoiced that he was becoming more like us. Or more like me in that moment.

"That's just the way it is, Borne. Survival isn't pretty. We're trying to survive. Do you know what I mean?" An honest question. Despite my worries, Borne seemed to have it easier than we did in some ways. We could starve away in the Balcony Cliffs and he'd just absorb a chair or something to keep on living.

"Yes, I know what you mean," he said impatiently. "But it doesn't need to be this way."

"So what are you going to do about it?" I meant that almost as a joke, or a provocation, but I must admit I was curious.

"I'm not sure yet."

"Let me know when you've figured it out."

"I met an old man today. He was digging a hole."

"Yes?"

"He was digging a hole and talking to me."

"Did he notice what you looked like?" And had he been real or a character in a book?

"No. But he told me he wasn't from here."

"No surprise there." Hardly anyone over thirty was from here.

"The old man told me he was digging for food, but all I saw were roots down there."

"Maybe he was too old." Maybe he was digging his own grave, had the dignity to sense his future and plan for it.

"He also told me you have to give up something to get

somewhere. That's what he told me. So that's what I'll have to do. If I want to get somewhere."

"Haven't you noticed? Everyone is out there trying to create their better future. Especially old men digging holes."

"Sarcasm?" he asked.

"Yes."

He asked that one-word question now, and so I wasn't sarcastic very often.

"Come help me, Borne," I said, sobering up, remembering who I was to him, and because I didn't like his jaded tone. "You should help me with the Balcony Cliffs."

"I guess I could spare an hour here and there," Borne said, as if his social calendar was full of appointments.

I just had to come up with a task for him that might keep him occupied and help us at the same time. Maybe keep him out of the clutches of old men digging holes.

Most nights now there was some kind of cacophony and a rawness, and such a sense of covert movement. So much noise out there— and echoes of noise—and a keening or growling or the sound of something or someone being killed. That was the sound of a city that no longer believed in one ruler or one version of the future. And, indeed, Mord at times would growl in a kind of disgust at this new version of events, and above us the proxy bears would dig where Mord had laid his head or maybe it was the Magician's men pretending—and that was the other confusion: one side trying to make their kills look like the work of the other side.

Although the Magician had more luck in this regard; the proxies were not dainty. Another sound in the night: the strangled agony of people dying on the street who had escaped the proxies but not the poison of their bite. Soon, too, the Magician's mutants not only came with harder carapaces but with their own poison, which shot out through their fingernails in a vain hope of piercing thick bear fur. With these "improvements" came a shorter but more intense life, their speed unnerving.

Borne coined the term *Nocturnalia*, for the way that life now welled up in unexpected ways whenever darkness slid over the city. There had always been a life out there in the blackness that did not include us and that moved to its own rhythm. But added to that now, what made the night both opportunistic and perilous, were the others lurking, so many out in it, thinking the night gave them cover. We couldn't interpret these others, hardly knew where they had come from, could not grasp, either, their allegiances, or the eruption of those who worshipped Mord in the aftermath of the Magician's failure, who sided with the great bear and chose to give their fealty and foolishly thought this made them immune.

Gunfire in the night was the barometer of our desperation— bullets so scarce in the city that each single shot that rang out, whether near or far, signaled a last stand. On nights when we heard more than a dozen, it was difficult to believe we would not be swept away by some inexhaustible wave of slaughter. Lights at night were traps, too, in a way they weren't before. Little pools and points of life, and nothing good could come from investigating.

The Magician had not returned, but her innovations were a tell, I thought. In her absence, too, myths had grown up around her, new stories, as if she had become a martyr. Borne brought one back to me as if it were valuable salvage. In this story, a strange bird with beautiful plumage had found its way to the city. A very strange bird that had come from far away. It flew around, lost and disoriented, trying to figure out the city. Where it was, exactly. What it was supposed to do.

But it wasn't supposed to do anything. On the second day, someone tried to catch it and broke its wing. The bird got away, kept flying as best as it could. Then a bit of walking biotech caught it, killed it, ate it. Then the Magician killed the biotech and used it for parts, and once again the strange bird flew in the city, but now at the Magician's behest, and no one would touch it, for it was the emissary of the Magician, and it was clear to everyone why the strange bird had come to the city.

Because the Magician had willed it.

And even if the Magician died, her strange bird would live on.

The stories about the Company building weren't much better. The Mord proxies patrolled the perimeter, and Mord had dug out a place to sleep on its flank, and a kind of refugee stream of bizarre biotech still came out of the damaged places to join the Nocturnalia. I did not like to glimpse these half-dead things, most gobbled up by Mord proxies, that crawled when they should have walked, or rolled or hobbled . . .

Nor could I stop thinking of the perfect little biotech slaves that had paraded themselves around my special cake in the fancy restaurant. In my mind, they kept spiraling that cake for years, as it decayed into black mold and then nothing, and they had to keep trudging around that cake, around and around, singing, until they died in mid-step and their flesh rotted and then faded away, revealing their sad, delicate skeletons.

Which kept dancing.

The way I tried to keep Borne out of trouble was to enlist his help exploring more of the Balcony Cliffs. I would have him along to punch a tentacle through the exterior walls of apartments and rooms we couldn't reach through the rock slides and other impediments. With my ability to scavenge outside severely curtailed, this was the only way to bolster our supplies.

Trying to break through in a normal way was nearly impossible with a hand-cranked drill, and more dangerous. But Borne had a knack for it using his own body, because when necessary his tentacle could become either diamond-hard or more vinelike, negotiate existing cracks, and then pulverize that part of the wall necessary to peer in. I had created a very long, narrow telescope out of the parts of three or four telescopes, so if Borne could make a fairly regular hole of a certain diameter, I could push the makeshift telescope through and take a look for useful salvage. Or, if it was a thin wall, I'd just eyeball the contents.

When that didn't work, Borne grew an eyeball on the end of a tentacle and told me what he saw. If there was something valuable, we'd widen the hole or risk blasting through enough of a doorway to retrieve the contents of the room. Borne and I played a game where we tried to predict what was in the room before we tunneled into it. Borne got them all right at first, and then started to get them wrong, on purpose I thought, sometimes ridiculously so.

"Spatula, kitchen table, bowls, dead fridge, some chairs, a sculpture of a giant bird."

Squinting through my pirate telescope, I'd laugh and reply, "Storage room, ladders, barrels, paper supplies, coffee machine."

But two rooms later, what would we find but the sculpture of a giant bird. Again, I began to believe that Borne had some kind of radar or sensing organ that went beyond our five senses.

Once, we spied on a room full of useless dead cell phones. Lizards crawled over the heaps of phones, having gotten in from a crack above. But it didn't hold lizards for long.

Another time, I had a moment of dislocation when I put my eye to a hole Borne had made and was looking at an entire house . . . a dollhouse, which dominated the room. Nothing in that room but the dollhouse, the disrepair of its five levels mimicking the neglect of the Balcony Cliffs. In that moment we peered in on an entirely different world, one that belonged to a far-distant time and place. I scoured that dollhouse for longer than I should have, given it had no value to us whatsoever.

Bodies were everywhere, but you found those out in the city, too, and these weren't even dead astronauts, so far gone it was easy to ignore the few husks of bones, the disintegrating skulls, a strand of hair resting atop a rusted-out toy car.

Through our efforts, we gained food packets, a couple of axes for defense, fuel to burn, and even, once, a box in shrink-wrap of a dozen emerald Company-made beetles in crisp metallic rows. Wick cackled when he saw that prize, and maybe for a moment he relented in his disapproval.

A floor, when I spilled water on it accidentally, turned out to be full of writhing alcohol minnows under the surface—much to Borne's delight, although I had to stop him from gobbling them all up. After that, I would bring along a tiny canteen of water just to moisten surfaces and coax out what lay hidden. Warn Borne to hang back a bit, first, because of his mighty appetite.

Borne liked this "game," but it was still slow work, because Borne wouldn't do it continuously for more than a couple of hours at a time, made excuses why he couldn't work longer—why he had to retreat to his apartment. None of his excuses seemed genuine, but I was too distracted by the chaos beyond our walls. It was like a constant dark spiral in my thoughts, pulling me away from the moment, from whatever I was doing.

Sometimes we talked as we worked, and that made me forget the pressure in my head.

"The first people I saw when I went out yesterday I said hello to and then they threw rocks at me and ran," Borne told me once. "The next person, a little girl, tried to stab me with a rusty knife and started screaming. After that, I adjusted my disguise again."

"They might have done the same to me or anyone." I said it calm, but was trying to push aside my worry for him. I could not mind that Borne now ventured out by himself. I had so very little control over him. Except I could still get him to bore a hole in a wall.

"They're all afraid of everything," Borne said. "Especially Mord. But Mord is just a very big bear and the Mord proxies are just bears that are smaller than Mord." He said this with disdain.

"That's a dangerous way to think about it," I said.

"Would they be afraid of me?"

"They're already afraid of you," I said. I meant it as a joke, but it came out wrong.

"I know," Borne said, sad. "That's the first thing I have to take away—and Wick, he doesn't say it, but he thinks I'm a freak. A monster. I pass him in the hall and say hello and he says nothing back. He's no better than the people in the city. Didn't you give him my salvage?"

I had, dutiful, and said, "These are from Borne," and it would always be something precious from beyond the walls, something that made flare up within me a momentary gratitude that Borne was foraging in the city. And Wick might say, "Thank Borne for me," but he wouldn't be smiling. There were limits to him with Borne, and he'd become paranoid again.

"He knows all our traps, all the passageways," Wick had said to me. "I had him show me yesterday. He knows everything, Rachel." Of course he did—that way Borne couldn't betray us entering or leaving the Balcony Cliffs, but Wick didn't see it that way.

He didn't remind me again, but it was in my head: Borne had stripped the Balcony Cliffs of every lizard, every spider, every cockroach, and thus now every extra source of protein that didn't require foraging outside. So what if his gifts made up for that— they didn't put us in his debt, by Wick's reasoning.

"I had an argument with Wick," Borne said. "He was probably in a bad mood. Then I went back later and tried to tell him I wasn't what he thought I was."

"An argument?" I never liked the idea of Wick talking to Borne, or Borne talking to Wick.

"Yes, it's when two people—"

"I know what an argument is. About what?"

"Oh—things. Lots of things. It's okay, Rachel. It's really okay now. I'm making it okay."

A moment later, he was telling me about nightmares he'd had and asking what they meant. A moment after that, he had become a pair of eyes floating in midair, but that was just him sidling up the wall while changing his skin to the color and texture of the ceiling, to perch there and ask, "Can you see me? Or am I invisible?"

At least I had found something new for Borne and me to do together, something useful, and I rejoiced in that, felt forgiven for trying earlier to educate him with my books.

Wick admired my ingenuity, but not the means. He didn't like Borne's involvement, didn't like how our excavations messed up his floor plan, because inevitably this meant the Balcony Cliffs changed, with some corridors we'd left buried now exposed. Any deviation from the floor plan in his mind caused a kind of trauma I didn't understand.

Yet other times, late at night, Wick would reverse himself, come by my apartment and when we talked show weakness, express admiration for Borne. He seemed in flux, truly conflicted, unwilling to resolve, and he lost focus for me. I found I hated his weakness more than I resented his former resolve, and during these times it was as if he recognized the fact, because he would leave before we could have sex.

He could die, he'd said, without his nautilus pills. But I still didn't know what the broken telescope meant, or the woman's face drawn across the head of a giant fish.

Would I ever know?

HOW WE LOST EACH OTHER

Then came a day that felt like a victory and a defeat—the day when Wick and I reached a lull. We had been working on fortifying the Balcony Cliffs with such all-consuming purpose that we could not now see any way to do more. Our muscles always ached and our minds were sore from trying to see the gaps in our thinking. With each hour of preparation, Wick was telling me that he rejected the Magician's hold over him—the evidence of his labor, his time, his effort.

We were done, but suspicious of being done, and now truly we had a siege mentality. I felt like I was waiting for a great force, a great pressure to burst down the doors, scale the walls, or to give up and go away. Perhaps the real reason Wick and I believed we were finished is that we both, on some subconscious level, understood that the quest to make the Balcony Cliffs safe was futile. There would always be a way in.

Still, we had done everything right—secured our inner ramparts, hoarded supplies, anticipated angles of attack—and yet no attack came. No zone or layer we could monitor with Wick's beetles and spiders or his informants registered any rumor of attack. Had we overestimated our worth with the city in turmoil? Were we, perverse thought, forgotten? Was this already a kind of aftermath and we would die of starvation or thirst rather than a knife to the gut or our throats ripped out? Our ironic new source of panic was that, in the event, there would be no one to surrender to.

It seemed preternaturally quiet on our borders most days.

"That just means they're biding their time," Wick said, not realizing how much Borne had done on his own to "clear out our perimeter," as Wick put it.

"Not even a lizard left," Borne had told me, and with nothing in that stretch of land, no scavengers waiting to glean.

But to feel under siege, even with an undercurrent of futility, was better than *being* under siege, or under outright assault. It could be stuffy and close in our refuge; we had plugged up the hole in Wick's laboratory ceiling for fear of Mord proxies peering in; and I never went out on the balcony anymore because I envisioned some homemade arrow through the throat or someone climbing up the wall and surprising me. Yet we still held on to what was ours, and celebrated the fact. Four weeks in, and no sign of the Magician, or her ultimatum. Clearly, she had more pressing problems, like being hunted by Mord, or being dead.

The night of the lull, I left Wick at his swimming pool, still reflexively obsessing over how to get the most out of his remaining biotech, and went to bed.

But I woke up with a start less than an hour later.

Wick had appeared at the foot of my bed. There was a moment of panic until I recognized him, and then I relaxed, although unhappy with his abruptness and the late hour. I didn't like how Borne and now Wick had taken to coming in without knocking or asking permission. It conjured up the past in a way I didn't want to think about.

"I locked the door, Wick. How did you get in? Why are you here?"

Wick shrugged, an awkward, rough motion. "The same way you get into my apartment."

Something about Wick's voice was off. In the bad light, my bleary state, his white skin seemed patchy, there pale and here translucent and in a few places ice-blue, as if he'd had an accident with his chemicals.

"What do you want that couldn't wait until morning?" I asked, sitting up in bed. Truth be told, I wanted him gone.

"Nothing much. I just wanted to know if you love me, Rachel."

"Oh for fuck's sake," I said, exploding. "You wake me up to ask if I love you?" Irritation was the least of it. I wanted to really turn into a Mord proxy and maul Wick. After all we'd done, all that had been done to us, to get our relationship back to some kind of normal, he asked me this.

"But do you love me?"

I did growl, then. "Go get some sleep, Wick." Sleep it off. "Go back to your apartment." He'd been suffering insomnia from stress, but I needed my sleep, too.

Wick didn't hear me or was ignoring me or didn't care, and, listless, sat down on my bed.

"What about Borne? Do you love Borne? How much do you love Borne?"

We'd come to the edge of this before, the way Wick's view of

Borne bordered on jealousy, but I'd never been asked to state my position quite so baldly.

"I'm like a mother to Borne," I said with patience. "He's like my child." I tried to be calm about Borne with Wick for fear I'd say something reckless and drive more of a wedge between them.

A wry grin, a sad one. "Is that what Borne still is to you? A child?"

"Yes," I said, lying a little.

What was the word for raising an orphaned intelligent creature? Maybe the word didn't exist yet. For the first time I dared to imagine if Borne had real parents, and a kind of despair overtook me. This idea that Borne had parents out there, somewhere, in a night that popped with distant gunfire.

"Thank you for telling me, Rachel," Wick said, and then he left.

I bolted the door behind him.

Yet an hour later, in the middle of the night, I hadn't fallen back to sleep. I kept thinking about the weirdness of Wick's visit, the way he had looked wrong. I couldn't let go of that. He'd been like a ghost. Not ghostlike but a ghost.

I put on some clothes, went to Wick's apartment, knocked, no answer. I knocked again, loud. Still no answer. Either he was in a deep sleep or out. So I walked down to the swimming pool, just in case.

As I approached the doorway, I heard voices. Borne must be in the room with Wick, I thought. Borne and Wick must be having a conversation. Great. I quickened my pace.

I rounded the corner, burst through the doorway into Wick's laboratory.

I came in on Rachel talking to Wick.

I came in on myself talking to Wick.

It was a clever fake, a good likeness, and it shook me to the core, to see myself like that. To see me having a conversation with Wick as if my body had been stolen and I was just a wraith.

Wick looked over at me, looked back at the other Rachel, flinched, with defensive beetles now raging across his arm. Apparently he could tell the original from the mimic.

"What are you?" he was shouting at the other Rachel. "*What are you?*"

But I knew what the other Rachel was.

The other Rachel was Borne.

Once upon a time there was a woman who found a creature on the flank of a giant bear. Once upon a time there was a piece of biotech that grew and grew until it had its own apartment. And once upon a time a person named Borne put on the skins of two people he admired and pretended to be those people. Maybe his cause was just, maybe his reasons were sound. Maybe he thought he was doing something right for a change. Maybe.

"Borne," I said. "Borne."

At the sound of my disappointment and horror, the other Rachel collapsed into Borne. A spasmodic ripple, a sigh that came from everywhere, echoed in the cavern, and soon: the Borne I knew, but more like a vast whirlpool full of eyes, narrow end attached to the wall behind him, the vortex spinning like a hypnotic illusion.

Where I had stood. Where Rachel had stood.

But that magician's trick came with a cost. "Rachel" had extended her hand, arm outstretched toward Wick's wrist, and as she looked at me in alarm, as her features dissolved into the vortex, as I watched myself fall to pieces, and as the eyes multiplied, and as the tentacles grew, they extended toward Wick's arm—touched his arm.

Wick cried out, stumbled back against the edge of the swimming pool, burned or in some way injured by that touch. As he did so, a sweeping gesture of his other arm, frantic to keep away from Borne's questing tentacles—and Wick released the beetles swarming around his body. They flew toward Borne in their dozens, meant to burrow into flesh, drill damage into him.

But they never reached Borne. Instead, they met Borne's surface and melted into him and he let out a great cry, surged out toward Wick like a darkly glittering tidal wave.

Except I was there, then, between them—Borne to the left and Wick on my right, mortal combatants.

"Stop! Stop!" I screamed.

I could have been caught in a crossfire. Either one could have ignored me and given in to impulse.

But, instead, Borne fell back even as he became even more huge and ominous, blotting out the light from Wick's remaining fireflies because he surged out across the ceiling like an angry surf. While I watched, as frozen as if I were the other Rachel.

Wick's remaining battle beetles swarmed over his body in defense against the next attack, and there came the slap and croak of creatures in the swimming pool behind him that suggested reinforcements.

But there was no further attack.

There was just Borne, rearing back and rearing back, as if he meant to dissolve into and through the ceiling, all of his surface wide eyes and tentacles that branched off and dissolved like slow-motion water droplets. And an attitude of cringing for forgiveness that became mixed with something still defiant in his posture until I could not read him at all. A stench of burnt butter, rancid liver, fading into nothing.

I play those first few moments over and over in my mind even now. I keep searching for what Borne was thinking, how he was thinking it. I want to stop time. I want time to stop and for Wick to leave and for me to talk to Borne without Wick there. And then I want Borne to leave so I can talk to Wick without Borne there. I need to know that I understood those moments correctly, that I made the right decisions. But I can never know that.

All I know is that I had put my body in front of Wick, in defense of Wick, and I was staring up at Borne, who covered the whole ceiling now and who could like a tsunami thunder down upon us and drown us in his flesh if he wanted to. As I looked up at Borne there were no constellations bright enough to blind me to him as a monster.

I was so close to Wick that I could feel the nervous thumping beat of his pulse against my body and his shaking against my shoulder as he stared off into nowhere. The screaming had stopped. The diagnostic worms were threading through the surface of his skin, doing the best they could against the shock of whatever wound Borne had inflicted, which meant Wick was semiconscious. We hadn't been able to feed the worms much for weeks, so I worried they'd die before healing him. But there was no blood, just bruising and the shock.

"I didn't mean to, Rachel," Borne said, pleading. "I didn't mean to hurt him. I wasn't going to hurt him. You startled me, Rachel. You made me."

"Did I *make* you pretend to be me and talk to Wick? Did I make you pretend to be Wick and talk to me?"

I was shouting at Borne. I was shouting and screaming at him because I couldn't do anything else. How stupid I'd been, how careless he'd been, and now everything was ruined. I could see that even if Borne couldn't.

"I wanted to help," Borne said. "I wanted to help. I wanted you both to be *nice* to each other." *Nice, not nice.* But he wasn't a child anymore. "I didn't want you to argue about me all the time."

"That wasn't for you to decide," I croaked, done shouting, my throat raw. "That wasn't right for you to decide."

I was scared as well as angry. Because something I'd known had been revealed to me. Something niggling at the back of my mind. The times Wick or I had said to the other "I never said that" and put it down to miscommunication or mishearing, or anything other than that the person we were talking to or not talking to was someone or something else. The way that had corroded my relationship with Wick, brought a special kind of insane distrust into our lives. Now we would have to verify every moment of our recent past, piece together our time together and apart, determine what was real.

Borne pleading, Borne trying to explain, and me not really listening.

Had it been Borne I got on top of in the blind and growled at like a Mord proxy the morning the Magician fired her missiles? Had it been with Borne not Wick that I'd planned the defense of the Balcony Cliffs? Had he been Wick when we'd slept together?—

No, that was a violation of trust I couldn't contemplate. Could not be true. I had to believe I knew the real Wick's body, that in tracing every scar and every imperfection, in having him inside of me, that there had never been a lie that monstrous.

But I had to ask the question.

"Borne, how many times have you been us? *Have you been in my bed, in Wick's?*"

It took a moment, but when he understood the question, Borne recoiled, took on a gray color as he said, "No. Never. How could you think that!"

"Why wouldn't I?"

"You're scared of me right now," Borne said. "But all I did is what you both do."

"We don't do that."

"You went into his apartment, sneaking around. He went into your apartment, sneaking and spying."

"Borne . . ." I looked up at him. He looked down at us, a ton of alien flesh with hundreds of eyes.

"I love you," Borne said in my voice. "But I'm scared of you and can't trust you."

"You *hurt* Wick."

"He was going to hurt me," Borne said. "I know he was. No matter how I tried, he was always going to hate me."

A cold, practical mood came over me, Wick so warm and febrile behind me, reminding me of the truth of some things.

"Should I have let Wick take you for parts, Borne? *What are you?*"

"Rachel, it's Borne. Your child. You love me like a child. You said you love me like a child." And I'd disappointed him, saying that, so why should it save him now?

"You're not human," Wick said, in a gasp like he was taking a breath for the first time. And I knew he'd stabilized, begun to recover from whatever Borne had done to him.

"But I am a person," Borne said. "Rachel told me—I'm a person!"

"A person who pretends to be other people," Wick said.

"Do you know me the way you know one of those lizards you ate?" I asked.

"No!" Borne protested.

"Then how can you pretend to be me."

"I can look like you, but I couldn't be you without—"

"Without killing you," Wick said. He stood beside me now, and from his stillness I knew he was ready to attack Borne again.

"I would never hurt you, Rachel," Borne said.

"Borne understands," Wick said. "Borne knows what he is. He's a killer. We have to take him apart."

Borne had turned stormy and midnight blue and black. A caustic smell of ink and seared moss. His voice when it came was troubled, uncertain.

"I won't let you. I didn't. I wouldn't. I haven't."

"I don't understand," I insisted. But I understood now. I really, deeply understood although I didn't want to. Perhaps I had known all along. What Borne had been doing out in the city, his acts disguised by the carnage of Mord proxy against Magician mutants. These people he had told me about, the old man, the others—what had those conversations been like? Had they ended abruptly? *Sampling.*

"He must have been doing it a long time," Wick said. "To have learned so quickly. To have grown so quickly." Across his features some reaction I couldn't recognize or fathom, a look so alien and wild and yet mechanical that it frightened me, made me feel caught between two monsters.

"Ask him, Rachel," Wick said. "Ask him. Nothing comes out of him, everything goes in."

Borne had attained his full expanse across that rough ceiling, head peering down from that expanse like a swimmer in an upside-down ocean. The full, impressive, frightening extent of him. I could see now that the Rachel doppelgänger still lived as an impression in the middle of him, as if he could always bring her out of storage, like a puppet, and that an impression of Wick lay beside her.

"There is a cost," Borne said. "A cost for what I am. For what I do. But I love you, Rachel. I love you and I can do better. I can stop."

I wavered, I'm ashamed to say, and Wick saw it.

"Prove it. Tell the truth. Be honest," Wick said. "Do you kill people? Do you?"

"I don't kill," Borne said. "I absorb. Digest. It is all alive. In me."

"Kills them," Wick insisted. "Ransacks their memories. Ransacks their knowledge of the world. Agree. Agree, Borne. It's for the best. Let me take you apart. You know it. Otherwise, someday you'll be worse than Mord."

Didn't it matter that Borne was conflicted, that he didn't want to kill? Maybe not. But the fear stole over me, from some almost imperceptible change in Borne's aspect, that we couldn't make him agree to die. That he would never agree to be taken apart, and that I would have such a difficult choice then, and Wick would never understand, even though it was about our survival.

"Leave," I said. "You have to leave and never come back. You have to."

Banishment. It just came out. But was there ever any other choice? Anything else betrayed Wick, betrayed the Balcony Cliffs, and Borne had made the decision easy. Yet it was one of the hardest things I ever did. *The* hardest.

Borne became sea-green, and all soft, diaphanous surfaces and reflected light.

"But I love you," Borne said. "You're my family."

"I love you, too, Borne," I said, and it was true. "But that doesn't change things." Maybe the memory of love was enough, maybe the time we'd had together would be enough. Yet, inside, I was panicking already, screaming at the thought of it.

"I'll have no home," Borne said.

"I know, Borne."

"I'll have no one to talk to."

I almost couldn't bear it, but I had to bear it.

"Borne," I said. "Borne, you have to do this for us. If you love us. I know it's hard, but it's not safe for us."

Why else had Borne moved out? Why else had he told me he

couldn't stop? Why else had he only spent one or two hours at a time with us the past few weeks? He knew. He knew all too well. And he was a murderer.

"I won't ever know another person like you," Borne said, and I felt that in my bones, in my heart and my head.

I would never know anyone like Borne ever again, and even if I saw Borne again it would never be the same as when we lived together in the Balcony Cliffs, the way we'd run down the corridors and punched holes in the walls and joked and laughed and I'd taught him new words that he'd held there in his mind like jewels, and repeated over and over until he knew them better than I did.

"You'll be better off," I lied. "It won't be as bad as you think," I lied.

Wick was silent. Wick wasn't part of this and knew better than to speak.

"Will I ever see you again, Rachel?" Borne asked.

"I'm sure we will see each other again, Borne. Of course we will."

There came another change in Borne's aspect, something only I could see and could not communicate to anyone else, but it read like stoicism, it read like acceptance. He came down off the ceiling, he became in shape more like the Borne I knew, the Borne that had lived in my apartment and that I had once thought was a plant.

Borne came close. Borne stood next to me, and I didn't flinch. He reached down to touch my face with one thick, soft tentacle. The orbiting circle of eyes. The body so much like a vase or a squid. The colors strobing there now were confident, bold, but I knew he was just trying to reassure me, and that shook my resolve, left me with doubt. Wouldn't a true monster, a true killer, have absorbed us or given an ultimatum, murdered us and taken over the Balcony Cliffs?

"I'll go," Borne said. "I'll be better off. Don't worry about me. I'll be fine. I won't forget you, Rachel. I won't ever forget you."

Then he was surging past me, out of the cavern, and I dropped to my knees, and wouldn't let Wick near me, heartbroken and unable to accept what had just happened. The siege from within was over. Everything seemed like it was over.

Borne was gone.

WHAT I FOUND IN BORNE'S APARTMENT

After Borne left, I was a wreck. I was a wreck that couldn't see, couldn't feel, that stumbled around smashing into things. Into walls. Into furniture. Everything a blur. I wanted to punish myself for what had happened. I wanted to punish myself and I wanted to go search for Borne and tell him I hadn't meant it and we could reform him, that we could stop his impulses, that he could fight them, that everything would be all right.

But I didn't. Instead, I lay in my bed in my apartment, doubled over and sobbing until I hurt from it, wanted to hurt from it. I didn't care what happened to me. Mord could have dug me up and swallowed me whole as a morsel and some part of me would have been grateful. And yet there was another part of Rachel, the part that had lasted six years in the city, who waited patiently behind the scenes, saying, *Get it out, get it all out now so it doesn't kill you later.*

When I woke after however many hours, days, or centuries, I checked on Wick. We found only the least number of words to say to each other, we made the least connection, and I couldn't look at him, because it was as if we were different people who had had different conversations, and I didn't know who I was talking to, had to begin to inventory all our many meetups the past months, to gauge which had been him and which Borne as Wick. Later we might tally them as requiem, claim those we had no right to claim so as to tell the other person that we wanted whatever supported a story that told of our love, our friendship, and nothing but those things.

Then, after a time, instinct took me back, the instinct for traps and avoiding them. Instinct took me to Borne's apartment—both to make sure he had truly left and to search it. I entered soft, slow, so hollowed-out that I felt nothing, but also half expecting to find Borne there, in the apartment.

But Borne was gone, and Borne had not left much behind. He hadn't had much to begin with. The three dead astronauts still hung from hooks on the wall, but they had no power over me; they were almost old friends now, so thoroughly had Borne acclimated me to their skeletons.

I found only what was in the closet—so many clothes, other people's clothes, in all sizes and styles, most of it ragged, worn, or bloodstained. Some of it I recognized as salvage from other parts of the Balcony Cliffs, and some I did not and of these most must have come from those he had "absorbed." There were fifty or sixty shirts in the closet. At least.

Hidden at the bottom, under mounds of pants, I found a thick journal with a *B* written on the front. It looked like nothing at all—tattered and foxed, something he'd rescued for reuse. It was locked, but the tiny key had been placed in the lock. I looked at it for a long time before I opened it. I stared and stared. I couldn't stop staring until the words blurred into oblivion. I guess that means I didn't want to read it. But I was Rachel the scavenger, and this was salvage of a particular type, and I was empty and searching for answers.

Much of the journal was in languages I couldn't read. But on the first page was his first, stuttering attempt to write.

My name is Borne.
—My name is not Borne. That is just something Rachel calls me. It means to carry something you don't want to carry.

My name is not-Borne and I came here on Mord's body, no matter what Rachel says.
—I did not come here on Mord's body.
—I became entangled in Mord's fur. (Who entangled me?)
—Where did I come from before that?

My name is not-Borne. I did not come here on Mord's body, but I am human.
—I am not human. I am not human. I am not human.
—Rachel says I am a "he." Am I he, she, or both or neither?
—I am a person.

Not nice. Not nice.
Beautiful.

I came here from a distant star.
I came here from the moon, like the dead astronauts.
I was made by the Company.
I was made by someone.
I am not actually alive.
I am a robot.
I am a person.

I am a weapon.
I am not/intelligent.

I have nine senses and Rachel only has five. I can make eyes anytime I want and Rachel can't. If she lost her eyes, she'd be blind. If I lost my eyes, I could still see.

I do not know when I am being what they want me to be and when I am myself. It is better when I am "cute." It is safer.

Not nice. NOT NICE.

Borne traveled from a distant star. Borne traveled from a distant Company. Borne could not stop eating. Borne could not stop killing. Borne doesn't think of it that way, but it must be. It must be killing.

BORNE MUST STOP KILLING. BORNE MUST STOP TASTING. BORNE MUST STOP BEING BORNE. BORNE MUST EAT WHAT IS ALREADY DEAD, LIKE NORMAL PERSONS.

What if I am the only one?
What if I cannot die?
What if no one made me?

Everything was in there. Everything I'd done to help him and everything I'd done that hadn't. Everything I'd made him into and everything I hadn't made him into. As he'd said, Borne had snuck into our apartments because he'd seen me sneak into Wick's apartment. He'd pretended to be me and pretended to be Wick because he didn't want us to argue, wanted us to be nice. Had seen us playing out roles, with all our baggage, and thought: What's the harm in doing the same?

I'd been teaching him the whole time, with every last little thing I did, even when I didn't realize I was teaching him. With every last little thing I did, not just those things I tried to teach him. Every moment I had been teaching him, and how I wanted now to take back some of those moments. How I wanted now not to have snuck into Wick's apartment. How I wished I had been a better person.

Rachel can't protect me from Mord, and I can't protect her from me.

In so many ways, Borne had told me, "I can't stop." *I can't stop growing. I can't stop who I am. I can't stop killing people*, and I had shut him out, ignored him, tried to pretend he was something other than what he was, and in doing so I had betrayed him. Because Borne knew what he was.

I didn't want to move out of Rachel's apartment. But I had to. Otherwise, I don't know what will happen to her. I keep eating lizards, but it isn't enough. On my own, maybe things will be better. Maybe I can be the one in control.

Days and moments noted when he'd gone out and "been able to resist" and "not able to resist." Charting patterns. Trying to understand himself. Experimenting with substitution. But the worst substitution was when he knew it was wrong but couldn't stop, couldn't ever stop, would never stop, and killed people so he wouldn't kill me. Getting desperate, at his wit's end and unable to talk to anyone about it.

The number of shirts in his closet multiplying as Borne grew larger.

Becoming . . . what? Originating . . . where?

He'd been more alone than I could have imagined. More desperate. There was no other way to describe it.

Worse still were the entries where Borne felt "grateful" to me. How kind I'd been to him, how much I'd taught him, how much he'd learned, how he would "never forget" me, as if he knew already when writing that someday he would be driven out of the Balcony Cliffs.

Nothing I found in Borne's apartment gave me comfort. But I did not believe I deserved comfort.

◘

A week or so later I saw Borne again, from afar. It was twilight. We still held the Balcony Cliffs and I'd come out to the balcony to look down on the polluted, beautiful river and all the shadows created by it. I was in a quiet mood. Wick had healed well enough, although not completely.

Far below, down below, I saw myself running along the river. I was running free, so fluid and lithe, over that rocky terrain. And I was not quite me, and, anyway, I was standing on the balcony, so I knew it was Borne below.

I hadn't known I was so fragile, so delicate in motion. I didn't know Borne had loved me quite so much.

The sight nearly broke my heart all over again, I can't lie, and there was an indelible, floating moment when I felt as if I was down there, looking out through Borne's eyes, and not up on the balcony in my own skin.

The feeling faded, and Borne, as if he knew I was watching, became himself again, free to be himself again, in that moment, and I saw that strange animals followed in his wake again. The little foxes and the rabbits and the things that looked like foxes and rabbits but were not.

He was just another part of the city now, I tried to tell myself, but the loss was too raw to think of him as just another obstacle, threat, or opportunity. That I could never do.

I thought the animals might be chasing after him, but, no, it became clear soon enough: Borne was leading them. Borne was somehow leading them. All the forgotten and outcast creatures, beneath the notice of the city.

While the river continued on its course, carrying all of us with it.

PART THREE

WHAT THEY TOOK FROM MORD AND FROM US

few days after we cast Borne out, Mord lost the power to fly. Whoever had taken that away from Mord must have hoped it would happen in mid-glide over the city, and that he would plummet from a great height and die in an ocean of his own blood. But it did not happen that way. He just woke up one morning and could not fly. Was this a relief? It should have been, but somehow it seemed foreboding, a sign along with all the other signs that the things we depended on were changing.

Mord sat in the apocalyptic splendor of his own fur across the cement of an empty parking lot, surrounded by his huffing, grunting, snorting proxies, and he could not fly. He could not float or soar or hover, though he tried. Such puzzlement in Mord's snarls, these snarls like hissed-out question marks, and then the titanic bellow to follow, that expressed in heavy breath his rage and his outrage. Mord could not fly and a dozen cults across the city must have collapsed and their followers fled in confusion or disbanded or killed themselves. God was God no longer. God would have to walk the Earth like the rest of us. He had lost something he had come to believe he would always have and relied on to be there, and its absence came as a shock.

Still, Mord tried to become a god again. He hurled himself at the sky, only to lurch and stumble and catch his balance with his front paws smashing against pavement. Drawing himself up to full height, a tension to his body as if with every muscle tightened he could will himself into the air . . . he stood there while the Mord proxies milled underfoot in a chorusing "Drrk-drrk" of confusion.

Mord tried again and again, offering himself to the sky—each time, rejected, no matter the method. A full running start, on all fours, a cautious expedition from the top of a three-story building crumbling beneath him even as he jumped from it. Another run, this time on his hind legs, but to no avail. Half a morning spent by the great bear, launching himself, seeking to recapture the magic, to restore the Company tech that had allowed him to ease his great bulk through the sky. He took to what came instinctual again: bounding on all fours through new wreckage and old, smashing everything in his path, splintering houses, collapsing smokestacks that fell out to the side like paltry straws.

No matter. Mord was trying to achieve an escape velocity he'd never had, or needed, and came rough-tumbling back down after a handful of breath-catching moments when it appeared he had once more achieved separation from the ground, when there could be seen a space between his belly and the earth, his paws and the earth . . . only for it to prove an illusion, and he fell, sometimes heavily, to bruise bones and muscles, with an impact that leveled a courtyard or apartment complex.

From the dust clouds of such destruction, Mord would rise, staring toward the horizon as if it held some answer. But mostly, as he came to accept this new limitation on his powers, Mord sat. Mord sat and pondered. Mord sat and pondered and swiveled his great head from side to side, surveying his domain, curious as to who would be the first to challenge him in his reduced condition. Mord looked as if his brain was full of murder, because he recognized what was to come—and he was ready. But he also looked like a bear cub, left to fend for himself amid the huge pile of bones that was the city.

I had seen Mord hungry and thirsty. I had seen him possessed of a secret anguish. I had seen him injured, favoring a paw or a muscled shoulder, but I had not seen him with his back to the wall or desperate or mortal. No one had, and yet we were about to, a fear and opportunity both. The perverse question in that city, for all of us, was what would bind us together were Mord ever to die.

"The Magician's back," Wick told me. "The Magician must be back."

"Is that it?" I replied, although I had little interest.

Wick still had a nose for information, even as his contacts thinned. Among the rumors that came to us in the days after: that some of the Magician's people had infiltrated the Company building, had gotten through the gauntlet of proxies, had flipped a switch or destroyed a mechanism, and this was the source of Mord's diminishment. Others believed Mord's earthbound status was a time-delayed effect of his mauling of the Company building, which had damaged a mechanism that had finally given out—or a sign that his cult within the Company had lost faith in him.

Whatever the truth, what did I care now whether Mord did or did not fly? I had suffered a terrible shock and an absence that could never be made right. This was the city, and we had to go on like it didn't matter, could not show weakness or we were lost. All that mattered, like Mord on a smaller scale, was making the effort to look around me to see what might next come at me in my new weakness, my time without Borne.

As the days passed and it became clear that Mord would never fly again, a sound we did not know we had been hearing removed itself from the city. A sound like a secret manipulation of the air, something that left so little trace I find it hard to describe. Because it had been a sound so invisible, so smooth, so without texture or taste or smell that all we knew was that we missed it now, even if we could not recall its nature. But this I knew in my gut: It had been the sound, the underlying subliminal hum, that meant Mord could fly.

I thought of Borne and his extra senses. I thought of the Company and Mord, and I wondered what else in this city we could not hear, would only hear when it was taken from us.

Faint but powerful evidence of the Magician's rebirth came to us much closer to home. With a regretful look, Wick told me to go to the northernmost Balcony Cliffs exit and see what now lay beyond it. I knew Wick wanted to distract me, to relieve the ache of Borne's absence, and to force me out of the emptiness in my head, or otherwise he would have just told me. But I went anyway.

Outside the northern exit, the Magician, or someone, had gathered the three dead astronauts Wick had discarded there, dug them open graves, put one body in each, and put a name on a piece of wood by each: Wick, Rachel, Borne.

Along with a word scraped out in the dirt with a stick: LEAVE.

The Magician's intel was out-of-date, if she was back and this wasn't the doing of her underlings or some third party. There were only two of us now in the Balcony Cliffs, and it seemed far emptier than that. But mostly when I saw the graves, I decided the Magician was not a serious person. Until then, even though we were enemies, I think I had at times given her too much credit—taken comfort in the idea that she represented some kind of hope for the future of the city and that after bloodshed and despicable acts might come peace or stability.

As I stood there, a familiar fox appeared from behind a pile of cinder blocks nesting in the moss nearby. But she wasn't really a fox. In that clear light, she looked like clever abandoned biotech. I thought I could see tiny vestigial arms beneath the fur of her chest. The darting of her gaze was too human.

"Tell the Magician she can fuck off," I told the fox, although I did not believe the fox came from the Magician. If anything, the fox came from Borne. Or I hoped the fox came from Borne.

The fox gave me a look I suppose I was meant to interpret, but signs and symbols did not interest me.

"Go away," I said.

The fox cocked her head, appraised me, let out a yip.

"Go away," I said again.

The fox did something with fur that clearly wasn't fur but some trick of bioluminescence to resemble fur . . . and slowly faded, bit by bit, until she had indeed gone away. But only by disappearing in front of me. I thought I heard the pitter-patter of paws receding.

Had she always known how to do that or had Borne taught her?

Something in me was tired of how the dead astronauts kept switching their allegiance, of the way these bodies kept being disrespected, had no fixed address or location. In truth, I didn't want to ever see them again.

So I took the time. I went back inside, found a rusty shovel, came back out, and buried them in those graves, tossed the placards away, rubbed out with my boot the word LEAVE, and said a few words over the ground, which I tried, with moss and pine needles, to make as anonymous as possible so no one would know anyone had been buried there.

"Be at peace," I told them. "Be at peace now and let no one recruit you for their stupid games."

When I had first heard the story of the Magician and the strange bird, it had struck me as somehow impressive or important—that it meant something. But it meant nothing.

Especially to a ghost, and that's what I was then. I was a ghost. I was a ghost. The lines had begun to fray and snap. The fireflies went out in my apartment. The toilet wouldn't work. We were down to two meals a day. I moved into Wick's apartment to conserve resources, but eventually his fireflies would go out, too.

Wrote Borne in his journal: "I met a kind fox today. She was following me and I meant to eat her, but she wouldn't let me, although she apologized nicely. After we had talked for a while, I decided I didn't want to eat her anyway."

Wrote Borne in his journal: "My earliest memory is of a lizard pooping on me and ever since I have hated lizards for ruining my first memory. But I also love them because they are delicious."

Wrote Borne in his journal: "The river isn't beautiful. It's toxic. It's full of poison. I sampled it, tested it. I'll never swim there, although I think I would like to swim. This entire city seems made to not let me swim anywhere. The river is poison, the wells are mostly dry, the Company ponds are also toxic, no matter what the fox says, and the sea underneath us all dried up hundreds of years ago. I should like a real bath, like children get in books. In an old bathtub with the feet like creatures. What I need is a big bath. A long bath. Bath. Born to bathe. Borne to bath."

Wrote Borne in his journal: "I know that Rachel says killing is bad. And I know that means I must be bad because what I do sometimes is 'killing.' But I cannot stop it, and it feels right, like breathing, and not like killing must feel, and I still can see them inside of me, and talk to them, and they are still who or what they were before, even the lizards, so how can that really be 'killing'?"

Wrote Borne in his journal: "It is hard to feel as if I am two or three places at once and have to concentrate on talking. It makes me sound like I don't know the meaning of my words."

Wrote Borne in his journal: "The world is broken and I don't know how to fix it."

When I could not find Borne's journal after a time, I knew Wick had hidden it from me, and I did not mind—was almost grateful. I had memorized everything I could understand, everything in a language I knew. The journal itself did not matter. It could be taken away from me at any time, by anyone. What mattered is what I chose to remember.

Borne's absence had simplified something in the Balcony Cliffs. It simplified me and Wick, and this made everyday life duller or leeched of some essential, stormy spectrum of color, made me think of myself as not quite alive. I often felt chastened and small and useless. But there was also the moment-to-moment relief of life being closer to what it actually was, with less pretense. Even this might have been an illusion, but everything is a kind of illusion in the end.

We had to create passwords for our identities, because of Borne, that we changed every day, every time we woke up or met each other in the corridor—any time we were parted by sleep or the demands of work. We lived in fear for a while of Borne returning and taking up a disguise once more.

They were silly things, the passwords, the only bright words amongst all the dull words, most of them suggested by Wick—who made it like an extension of the games we played when I brought biotech to him. That I sometimes laughed because of these passwords only made the rest of my days duller.

"Cheese please," I would say to Wick.

"Goddamn oyster," he would reply.

"Roosterhead."

"Mudskipper."

"Bear-crap bear-print bear-bear."

"Magician fester cloak."

Silly, very silly, but by these words we knew we were real—that who we spoke to was real. Even if I didn't feel real.

Maybe I laughed because the passwords sounded like things Borne would have said.

✿

Wick no longer talked about giving in to the Magician's demands, even after the discovery of the graves. Something had changed in Wick with Borne's absence and our togetherness despite Borne's absence, so that now her demands made Wick think more and more of the Balcony Cliffs as a fortress or redoubt against her. While, for me, I would just do what Wick said and make the words come out of my mouth that supported Wick's vision, because I had no vision of my own.

Work consumed us—thankfully. It drove most other thoughts from my head, and we welcomed that and we rejoiced, or at least I did. We could not predict the city, but we still had the Balcony Cliffs. We still had them, and we toiled once more to make the

Balcony Cliffs ever more impervious to the scenting of random murder-bears, labored unspeaking side by side at that hard work.

The most ingenious was rigging the fireflies in our apartment, using pheromones. It had a time delay of about thirty seconds, but if anyone other than us tripped the bioreceptors at the entrances into the Balcony Cliffs, the fireflies on the ceiling would start to die out in clusters. Least ingenious: clearing the air duct above the bed as an escape of last resort.

We were preparing for some catastrophe, the form of which we couldn't see. Because the networks and hierarchies had yet to become clear, and we had no real allies. Because the Mord proxies had learned to use tools, and Mord, vulnerable now, had become cunning and deployed them more like a general ordering his troops. We took stock of food packets, even though I'd rather have eaten live insects than the runny, goopy, long-expired lumps in those packets. Chicken salad congealing. Beef-carrot stew. We had twenty-three, which meant in terms of days we had about fourteen. Rainfall had been intermittent and largely toxic, so our water supply extended a meager week beyond our thirst. From what Wick jury-rigged to collect from the morning condensation, we could potentially keep that week in reserve. From what Wick could cannibalize from the swimming pool, we could gain ourselves another week or two of food. If we included the remaining memory beetles, which had a particular crunch and a sourness that made them another food of last resort.

"Food packet or memory beetle?" Wick asked me, holding up one of each.

"Food beetle?"

"Not on the menu."

Other things were back on the menu, though. The lizards had already crept back in, and the spiders, and I had witnessed three huge silverfish careening across a corridor floor, leaving a trail in the dust as if having a race. Every time I saw a living creature inside the Balcony Cliffs, I thought of Borne.

In our "spare" time, Wick and I sat side by side in a tunnel, in a room, in a corridor, shoulders touching, password-protected. Was this you? Was that you? Was that Borne? We were still reconstructing what we had actually said to each other, what he had not said, when I had not been there. As we removed the falsehood, as we built up the truth, damaged places became restored, whole rooms inside flickered with at least a semblance of light, and we cast the intruder farther out into the cold.

But I was not ready to cast out the intruder for good.

WHAT I TOOK FROM THE NOCTURNALIA

I began to walk out into the night a month after we lost Borne—several times. I told myself I was still a ghost, and no one would be able to see me because I was a ghost. Or I told myself it was recon to help out the Balcony Cliffs, or I told myself whatever lie would work. Because I needed a lie. Because Mord had become a more deadly predator and the Magician was resurgent. The Magician had found more recruits to join her medicated army; the Mord proxies had discovered their venomous breath could set fires, given the right accelerant. Mord vulnerable had lost a measure of awe, of dread, but that had not ended his rule. He had just become a more fearsome predator, adopted ruthless tactics.

Now, too, patterns began to emerge. There were people who seemed to just disappear, and the city had no answer for this except rumors—murmurs of an invisible killer from the tattered remnants of Wick's contacts and my contact with a handful of fellow scavengers. At first these disappearances had not registered as unique. Already the city lay open like a treasure for psychopaths. People disappeared all the time. People were dying with some frequency.

Yet, exchanging rumors with an old woman on a street corner, or a young boy at the places Mord proxies had just abandoned . . . it became clear something new was happening. Mord was terrible and horrifying and frightening, but this new thing could become shadow. It became what it ate. It could be your neighbor or your friend, some said. Rumors pinned the blame on various sources. One theory went that this was some new tactic on the part of the proxies—that to spread even more fear, they had taken to burying their kills instead of leaving them as a bloody warning. Or that just one Mord proxy, cleverer than the rest, had become psychotic and was acting like a serial killer rather than a bear.

Another theory held that the Magician, injured and deranged from Mord's assault on her strongholds, roamed the city at night, garroting the unwary and hiding (or eating) their bodies. Or, worse, that she had begun to use them for her biotech creations. But by far the worst rumor was that the Company had done the disappearing—that Mord's destruction of the upper levels of the Company had caused mysterious rulers in the lower levels to begin kidnapping people at night and brainwashing them and making them into zombified, deranged biotech.

I knew the truth.

I said nothing to Wick about my roaming, not even that I would be gone, and once outside I imagined Wick in the halls of the Balcony Cliffs calling out the name of a ghost, but no ghost would appear, and I would sustain myself with this meager hope: Every time I thought there could be no further breach of trust that our relationship could withstand, that Wick and I would be driven apart never to come back together, we discovered our limits were elastic, that we had so much more room to mistrust each other the worse it got out in the city.

But underneath my excuses, this ghost wanted to see Borne, no matter what the danger. Or perhaps because of it. The ghost wanted to see Borne and find some way to fix it. The ghost was confused, and the ghost knew that if Wick knew, he would not understand, so he could never find out. The ghost believed that she had put in the work being responsible and helping out around the Balcony Cliffs, and that she was only risking herself. Perhaps the ghost didn't care what harm might come to her. Perhaps deep down the ghost thought that without Borne there, Wick had no right to say where she wandered or did not wander.

Yet for any of this to work, for it to make any sense, the ghost had to think back to a simpler time, to travel into the past, through parts of Borne's journal, and in that past Borne had just been out for longer than was safe. Borne was a lost child who needed looking after. So I searched that nocturnal night—Nocturnalia, as he'd called it—treading wraithlike and anonymous down the ruined streets of our fucked-up city.

This ghost conducted a subtle search, making use of veteran survival skills. No ghost would wander half crazed, shouting out Borne's name. No ghost would walk up to a Mord proxy and ask if it had seen Borne, because, deep down, the ghost didn't really want to die—just maybe come right up to the edge, so that the entire spectrum of colors would click back into place behind her eyes.

Evidence of prudence: Once, at the heart of what had been the city's commercial district, the ghost peeked around a corner and saw two Mord proxies in the middle distance. They were tearing at a human corpse. The ghost turned back and detoured several blocks, then course-corrected again when encountering a handful of skeletal people at a street corner drinking homemade alcohol out of old bottles. Their eyes were looking out somewhere else and nothing about them even mimicked the idea of "kind" or "reasonable." The ghost believed the people would be ghosts soon enough, and she could talk to them then.

No, the ghost channeled anger and grief in another way: through controlled, bloodless, clinical searching. First, the ghost searched the perimeter of the Balcony Cliffs, and then, starting to the south, clearing those areas where *he* might have been most likely to go. While inside the ghost's heart raged, but what could a ghost's heart rage about? That the ghost hadn't been able to protect Borne from the world or the world from Borne, or frustration with herself at the impulse to still seek him out?

As the ghost immersed herself in the night, became steeped in it and more comfortable, the ghost's search became more and more meaningless. The ghost's purpose changed and the ghost became a chronicler in her head of a damaged city, a city that could not go on like this forever, torn between foes and monsters, before it, too, became a ghost. The body still gasped and drew breath and reanimated itself—contained the capacity to be rejuvenated, even now. But not forever. Eventually the collective memory would fail, and travelers, if travelers ever came again, would find a stretch of desert that had once been a vast ocean and hardly a sign that a city had ever been here.

Yet, despite this, people still cared. As the ghost wandered, she could see that people still cared, and there was a kind of dangerous ecstasy in that—a kind of displaced passion and recklessness from seeing the way people could still care about something dying, dead.

I might have snuck out until someone did kill me, if the ghost hadn't eventually found what she was looking for. Even a ghost could sicken of combing through a place populated by the fearful and dangerous, even if this particular ghost often snuck around with a confidant's stride, had become an actor steadied by sadness and self-loathing, making others leery of asking questions.

A man I could not see, a stranger recessed into an alcove, the ground in front seeded with broken glass and worse, gave the ghost the tip.

"Something strange? Something strange? Past the burning bear. Past the playground. Foraging. You'll find something strange all right. Then, maybe, you'll wish you hadn't."

Was the something strange enough? The ghost would have to discover that for herself.

"What about something familiar?" the voice said, cackling, proud of his joke, as the ghost drifted away. "Are you sure you wouldn't prefer something familiar?"

The burnt bear lay beneath the faded pink archway for an arcade long destroyed, paint peeling like a disease of the skin to reveal cracked stone and a latticework of exposed steel bars beneath. It was a landmark the ghost had used before, about half a mile from the neighborhood formerly graced by dead astronauts. Something had gone wrong with the proxy's breathing of fire and the flames had washed back over it, so swift that in death the bear remained on its haunches, blackened and hairless, looking like a huge half-demonic bat or rat. The skull was black and glistening and narrow without the fur, the torso all fused bones and withered meat and ash. The claws on the broad feet were an astonishing, threatening white, and no one would touch the corpse, fearing a trap. Every time I saw it, the corpse looked more like a statue: a memorial sent back in time from a future where Mord ruled the city unopposed and all worshipped him. We would go from the Age of the Company to the Age of the Bears, unless the Magician had her way.

I used the bear corpse to orient myself, venturing ever farther out on sweeps to check first for the Magician's patrols. It was safer on this side, in territory held by either the Magician or no one, as Mord pressed his advantage to the west and the Magician changed tactics.

Down through a darkened courtyard strode the ghost that night, past a handful of muttering specters, headed for an abandoned, long-looted department store, so old no one could read the sign. I climbed a ladder up the building's side. The ladder was new and shiny, which made the ghost smirk. Such an obvious trap must be a kind of joke left behind by whoever had killed or captured the trap-setters. As expected, nothing waited for me on the roof but safe passage and a slight breeze. The moon had gone to sleep or died and I couldn't look at the stars without thinking of Borne.

On the other side I found the fossilized remains of a public park centered around a rotting fountain. Despite evidence of attempts to resurrect that space, the swing set had become deformed and crumpled into the earth, and there was a faint smell of carrion and sour marrow. I would not set foot there, experienced ghost that I was, and I sidled along the edge, careful and slow, as if the playground dirt might be toxic or was actually a vast and horrific swimming pool that went deep and was full of monsters.

Beyond the park, I came across the exposed ground level of a skating rink or storage hangar and watched from the threshold as five scavengers sorted through a rich mélange of probably worthless debris. They had a glowworm trapped in an hourglass to see by, and when the sand ran out I assumed they'd move on. Their quarry included filthy plastic bags filled with nothing, old barrels, boxes sagging from water damage and mold, and a few piles of upended garbage that had been there long enough to have already been gone through and to have stopped stinking. But each generation lowered its expectations.

The two women looked a little like me, but one was bald and the other had darker skin. The teenage boy was white and, head down, ignored me. The last two were anomalies: a hulking giant of a man and a girl who couldn't have been older than twelve. Together and yet apart, silent but for grunts or nods, we stepped around the mummified husks of dead dogs and the dried-out shit of some large mammal, and looked for treasures. Curiously, I had noticed the big man last, which made me wonder if he'd stepped out of the shadows just after I'd arrived.

I knew nothing of these people, except that as scavengers went they had some sense of honor or integrity, for they did not set upon me or drive me out, although I was competition. Most turned to look suspiciously at me and then went back to their searching, which meant my powers as a ghost must be fading. I gave them a hard nod and a lingering stare and hoped both came across in the dim light.

From long experience I knew that they would get around to the dead dogs and the shit, but taking either apart was messy and would come last. Investigating death and shit also would release foul smells into the air, long dormant and locked in place. You could tell a seasoned scavenger by how numb their nose was, and yet also how agile their hands.

The girl found a couple of dried-out alcohol minnows by their dull glint and shoved them in her satchel. A few drops of water might revive them, but first she'd have to decide if those drops were more valuable to drink.

The hulking man wasn't nimble enough for this game and kept himself apart from the others. They picked the ground clean just as he began to bend over to examine those same surfaces. I wondered how he had survived this long, why he wasn't gaunt. Perhaps the hulking man had been hoarding a store of supplies and they'd run out, forcing him to scavenge. Perhaps he'd run with some crew or cult and been cast out or driven out by Mord proxies. Refugees who came to the city for sanctuary had often become refugees again.

"We have a hideout," the girl said, approaching me.

We have a hideout. It was a marvel to see a child not yet conscripted to the Magician's army of mutants. She was slight but steady, and she held my gaze even as, revenant, I circled her.

"We have food, supplies, and we're willing to trade."

Perhaps something remaining from my ghostliness, or the competence in how I held myself, had sparked that offer. Or some other impulse.

"Are you inviting me as a trading partner or as meat?" I asked. Maybe I also sought something as simple as a fight.

The girl laughed. It was so clear and tinkling a sound in that place that it seemed as if it came from the city's past, before Mord, before the Company. The kind of sound that could bring predators quick. None came, so she must have done a sweep of the perimeter.

"Neither," one of the women said. "We're not like that."

"I might be willing," I said.

The ghost felt a pull, an enticement. To become a vagabond, to descend to the street and stay there, to take my chances day-to-day, as I once had, and assure my safety by never having any expectation of it. Perhaps that was the best way to become a ghost.

"It's not far," the girl said.

I took it she was their leader. Perhaps because she was so rare, or because the Magician's shock troops had elevated the value of the young all across the city.

"I'll come if I can bring my partner." I pointed to the hulking man.

The ghost had noticed a few disconcerting things about the hulking man, chief among them that although he kept his shape well enough, the shape still changed at times. Not enough to be noticed in those shadows if you weren't looking for it.

"Him?" the girl said. "He's with you? We thought he was alone. He's always been alone before." I sensed in the girl's hesitation not just caution but miscalculation: Had she made an offer she thought I wouldn't accept?

The hulking man stood, was staring at the ghost even though he was the ghost.

"He's with me," I said.

"Are you with her?" one of the women asked the hulking man.

The hulking man nodded.

He must have wondered why he should follow a ghost, why I was doing this.

Through old damage—the twisted metal of collapsed machinery and tunnels dug through maelstroms of upended shopping carts and other inventions empty of purpose—we reached their sanctuary: a courtyard with half a roof, exposed to the elements but not, exposed to Mord but not. Seen from above, it would have looked like a ragged triangle of open space. A sliver they must hope Mord would never spy, because even earthbound he towered over almost everything.

They had makeshift tents arranged under the awning and sentries set at the single entrance. I hoped they were smart enough to have a secret exit. I counted twelve in all, most of them kids, none of them altered by the Magician. All of them were slim and the darkness slid through them, did not attach itself.

The group had found an impressive sluglike piece of biotech with no discernible head or tail and set it on fire. The creature didn't mind, let out a contented humming purr as it burned perpetual. The creature had a hypnotic allure, looked like a dancing, living skirt of flesh in the middle of that fire, a deep orange with ruffled lines of red and white running along the edges. It generated enough heat for them to cook food—and all it wanted in return was for them to set it on fire again and again.

I estimated from the ashes and the pile of fresh garbage that they had been in that spot for maybe three nights, and if they stayed three more they would become predictable and would all be dead. A Magician patrol might sweep them up; a Mord proxy would definitely sniff them out. But even the ghost had a fierce wish that they might survive.

Four huddled around the living fire, with the hulking man and me on the other side. The hulking man was sending quick glances my way, as if nervous. But what could he be nervous about?

"So what do you have for us?" the girl asked. I didn't like her smile now, like she had an ace card.

"Depends on what you're offering—are you offering that?" I pointed at the writhing fire creature.

The girl laughed and I couldn't help loving the sound. She looked like a fairy peering over that fire at me and the biotech a fire elemental she'd tamed. The ghost felt tired and old, staring at her.

"We need that," she said with an innocence I knew at her age must be false.

But I took pity on her, because she had to be nervous and

I knew the other eight waited in the shadows to jump us if we turned out to be dangerous.

"I have this," I said. I placed a battle beetle on my palm, close enough to the flames for her to see it.

My bulky friend bucked back on his haunches, but I put a hand on his shoulder. "Don't worry," I said. "It's not for you."

This battle beetle had seen better days. The iridescent carapace was cracked and the inner wings stuck out the back, couldn't fold properly. But the beetle could still burrow into flesh, compromise the well-being of an intruder, an enemy. It just couldn't fly very far.

"Good for close-in defense or combat," I told the girl.

"How many can you get?" she asked.

"This is the only one. But they're edible, too, and I can throw in a couple of alcohol minnows, depending on what you've got. Maybe more than a couple."

The girl's second spoke up, a scattered-looking, wild-eyed boy. "Your friend doesn't talk much. Why doesn't he talk?"

"Accident," I said, looking at my friend with a smile. "He doesn't talk much ever since."

"He makes me nervous," the boy said, not realizing he was making the girl nervous.

"He should."

And for a fair amount of time I stared at the boy and he stared at me while my friend tried to make himself look small and examined the ground.

"So," I said, switching my attention back to the girl. "What do you have on offer?"

The girl nodded to the boy, managing to toss in a scowl, and he nodded to someone else, and down the line.

What was on offer was more or less what I had expected. They brought forward the smallest and youngest person there. He was maybe eight or nine, bald against ticks and lice, dark brown skin, some haunting still of remembered baby fat, but his eyes were old and from the rigid set of his jaw, his folded arms over his ragged shirt, I knew he was afraid.

"For the battle beetle and the minnows, you can have Teems," the girl said.

"Why would I want Teems?"

Something in my tone must have seemed dangerous, or maybe it was how fast I replied. But either way, the girl was very careful in her reply.

"Because you know the Magician. Because if you take Teems to the Magician you'll get four or five beetles."

I was quiet, thinking about what she'd said, head bowed, with bad things crawling through my brain.

"Why do you think I know the Magician?"

"Because you're Rachel the scavenger. You work for Wick, and Wick knows the Magician."

The bad things in my head writhed harder, multiplied, and I tried to douse them in the flames created by the biotech, but it didn't work.

I'd been made by a little girl, someone who had only seen me for a few minutes, half cloaked in darkness. She knew enough about me to presume I would want to trade a human being to the Magician for biotech . . .

"What's the catch?" I asked. "You'd give Teems here away for one beetle and two minnows?"

"They're not giving me away," Teems said, arms still folded. A stern look made his face gaunt. "I want to go. I said I'd go."

I understood, of course. This group couldn't find enough food and water to live on, and Teems must be not just the youngest but the least-gifted scavenger, the weakest among them. Lose him, one less mouth to feed.

Teems's stake in this arrangement was not to just be cut loose and be on his own in a dangerous place but to be *given over* to someone else's patronage. And Teems wanted to own it, to construct a story about his life where he had control, where he had always wanted this to happen.

I knew I could get Teems for free. It wouldn't even take a beetle and two minnows. The girl wanted him gone, needed him gone. But Teems would have to take his chances some other way.

I held out the beetle to the girl and she took it with care from my palm.

"I don't want Teems," I said, "but you can have the beetle if you hold on to Teems another month."

Both Teems and the girl's second were looking at me with a kind of mixed hope, bewilderment, and disappointment. The girl was already trying to figure out what game I was playing, and what that meant to her.

"I don't know the Magician and I'm not this Rachel," said the ghost. "And you don't want to know Rachel or the Magician, either. Also, you shouldn't invite strangers to your campfire, pretty though it is, no matter how you want to show it off."

The girl had risen, as had I, and Teems retreated, and her boyfriend seemed conflicted, while the eight in the shadows had moved forward.

"Borne, you should show them as you really are." I stared at the bulky man, while I could sense the girl trying to decide whether to tell the others to attack us. The look on the girl's face was not what I would call charitable or forgiving.

Until she saw Borne in all his glory, for he had dissolved from bulky man to a glowing dragon-size version of their flaming biotech, an enormous fiery slug that loomed over their tents and gasped out flame, and because some part of Borne would always be a show-off, his version had a head and glowing eyes. It had been as easy as peeling a banana for Borne to shed his disguise.

All of them—the girl, her second, Teems, the others—drew back against the courtyard walls and after their initial gasp stayed very still and silent, as if maybe we couldn't find them that way. But their faces, touched by the light from Borne's flames, had a new tension and horror, a realization that the city still held secrets and surprises that could transfix them, strip them of the lie that they had survival instincts.

The girl held out the beetle and said, "You can take it. You can have it and anything else if you leave now."

"Keep it," I said. "And keep Teems. Don't follow us. Don't bring strangers to your sanctuary again. Don't stay here another night. Don't come looking for me. Don't seek out the Magician."

Then Borne made himself smaller and less fiery, and I led him out of that place.

I took Borne back past the playground to the roof of the department store, a few blocks from the burned bear. It had begun to snow, but the flakes were gray: ash from places to the west where the Mord proxies had put Magician strongholds to the torch. The ash wasn't hot to the touch. It wasn't anything. It was nothing, raining down from the black night sky.

There on the roof, out of view, Borne slopped over in relief, like someone who had been holding in his gut, streamed out over the ground, made a thick carpet of gentle neon eyes.

Now that Borne was there, in front of me, the ghost had receded, the urge to find him entangled in the reality. I asked him a question, but I can't remember what it was, whether it was important. It must not have been.

"Can I come home now?" Borne asked, ignoring my question. "Has Wick forgiven me?"

"No." Wick hadn't forgiven him. Nor had I.

"Then why did you come here?"

To see how he lived. To make sure he was okay. Some bond, an ancient affection. Inflicting self-damage. The reflexive twitching of a dead lizard tail.

"Did you see something new tonight, Borne?"

The shape in front of me seethed, frothed, rippled at the edges, retreated into solidarity with the idea of the human, became again the hulking man the girl and her group had known.

"Is this the start of some lesson, Rachel? You *made* me leave. You and Wick both. You don't have the right to tell me what to do now. Or to make me into a . . . a fireworks display."

"Do you see how people live? Don't add to their misery."

"I'd never been to their campfire before. I would have protected them. I would have tried."

"They're all Rachels," I said. "That girl. The other scavengers."

"I wouldn't hurt her," Borne said. "I didn't hurt her."

"But you had taken up with them. You'd been out scavenging with them before. Where do you think that would end?" Had I put that girl in danger by my own actions, even as I tried to help? The traps, the traps.

"I was trying to fit in," Borne said, hurt. "I was trying to make an honest go of it. To show you I can do that."

An honest go of it. Borne wasn't a patchwork creature, but his syntax always would be. I'd taken something away from Borne and not replaced it with anything useful. Now he was trying to fill that empty space.

"Who was he? Your body?"

"Just a scavenger, like yourself."

"And what did you do to him?"

"Nothing. Nothing much. When I came across him, he was dying. He had no family. He had no friends."

"Did you kill him?"

"Everything dies, Rachel. He was already dying. Would you rather I hadn't turned back into him? You seem upset."

"How 'dying' was he?"

"Pretty dying, I'd say."

"You haven't stopped killing."

"He was pretty dying," Borne repeated.

I said nothing. I did not move. The ghost was returning because the living, breathing person couldn't figure a way out. I still cared about Borne, still cared what happened to him, but I also felt a chill. I wondered what myths might grow up around Borne as they had once grown up around Mord, and how similar they might be.

Borne was too smart not to read some of that in my face, too naïve to remain silent.

"I have an idea, Rachel," Borne said. "Don't say no yet. Just listen."

"Borne . . ."

"I try to only kill evil people, Rachel, and people already dying. I'm getting it under control. I'm going to get it under control. And if I can stop, maybe I could come back to the Balcony Cliffs. Maybe you and Wick would let me? I would clean for you and I would make traps and even maybe help Wick with his biotech. I could come back with you now and we could try it. I promise I'll be good, Rachel."

Now it was my turn to ignore him.

"You can't use this disguise again, Borne. Your cover is blown. Someone told me about you. You weren't fitting in. People were beginning to guess."

"Okay, Rachel," Borne said, but his dour mask crumbled into

something more like contentment, as if I'd agreed to something. Maybe it was enough that I'd sought him out.

Borne in travel mode stood before me soon enough, but much bigger than before, and all I wanted was to have never gone out, to be back home, but once there I knew I would think about being out in the city again, talking to Borne.

"You can't come back yet," I said, and then wished I'd been firm and said, "Never. You can never come back." Why couldn't I? What held me back? That I couldn't suppress that last tiny bit of love for him? Of human sympathy? Of pity?

Borne went silent and there was a noticeable slump to him, and the ash kept falling from the sky onto both of us. I wiped at it, and it stained my shirt gray.

"Rachel . . . will I die someday?"

"Yes. Everything dies." He knew the answer already. Call-and-response. We had done this.

"What about the people inside of me? The animals?"

"They're already dead," I said. No matter how many times I said it, Borne would never understand.

"No, they're *not* dead, Rachel. I killed them but they're not dead. You're wrong. I don't think they will ever die."

"In whatever way was important to them, Borne, they are dead." But I didn't believe that when Borne said "dead" or "killed" he meant what I meant. To him, on some level I'd never understand, there was no death, no dying, and in the end we stood on opposite sides of a vast gulf of incomprehension. Because what was a human being without death?

"Do you still like lizards?" I asked, after a pause. There was no point in hammering him about the rest.

Borne made a sound like a chirp. "I still like lizards. But they don't like me."

"I can't imagine why."

"I like the Mord proxies more now, though," Borne said. "I'm hunting them down because they want to kill you. They're hard to kill, but I am trying. If they were all gone, the Balcony Cliffs would be safe again, Rachel. You wouldn't have to hide as much. Maybe I could see you more and we could talk more. You could come down with me to the river. You could go with me lots of places."

Borne, trying to find a back door leading into the Balcony Cliffs.

"It's dangerous to hunt the proxies. You shouldn't do it. There are too many of them."

I had to ignore the rest of what he kept pushing for. I had to. I had to be strong and snuff out the idea of clandestine meetings, of leading some kind of double life behind Wick's back. If I remained resolute, maybe this meeting would inoculate me, cure me.

"I have to do it," Borne said. "I have to. Everything will be better. You'll see. You'll see." Agitated, narrow of focus, a monster pledging his allegiance to my well-being.

"I have to go," I told him.

"Can't you stay longer? Just a little longer? Please?"

"I wish I could, but I can't."

Borne nodded in a way only Borne could nod. "I know. But it was so good to see you again, Rachel. So good. So good."

He extended a tentacle and I shook it like a hand with only a moment's hesitation. Smooth, soft. Like a person.

"I won't abandon you, Rachel," he said. "You think you've abandoned me, but I know you haven't. Not really. And I won't abandon you. Ever. You'll see. You'll understand."

The ghost was falling to pieces inside and wanting to be like mist or dew or anything but a creature able to receive what Borne was telling me.

Then Borne changed shape into something huge and tremulous, but also something long and low and streamlined and snakelike. He sped off at such a frightening pace that he was just a thick blurred black line zigzagging across the roof and then gone, over the side.

"I won't do anything to those people you saw tonight," Borne had told me. But I knew Borne's memory palace was vast and deep and full of skulls.

✪

Back by the dead, burned bear, someone waited for me. I had never seen him shine so bright, there in the darkness, in the rain of ash. Standing so tall and straight he eclipsed the bear completely. Perhaps I had never truly seen him before. His skin was radiant and his face like something beatific and resolute and ravaged that had been salvaged from the past. A likeness from an old painting, the light illuminating features too perfect to be real.

"Wick . . ."

"You can never do this again, Rachel. You can never do this *to me* again."

In his expression I could read such an extremity of loss and hurt and betrayal, so naked, as naked as anything I had ever seen in the city. I knew he had seen everything, listened to me talking to Borne, and I couldn't withstand it. I was ashamed. I couldn't stand there and be worthy of it.

But I wanted to. I wanted to be worthy of it, the way Wick shone so bright, for me.

I stood in front of Wick and I held his gaze as the girl had held mine in the courtyard. I nodded. I would never do that again. I would never seek out Borne again, no matter what. No matter how that hurt.

"Humdrum oracle," I said, to let him know I was real.

He seemed to vibrate there, his whole body, with the depth of the emotions he was feeling. So rigid and resolute. Standing on a precipice, needing to make a decision. Transfixed by a doubt shining out but also turned inward, as if he still hid something.

"Botanical garden eel," he said finally.

He was so utterly beautiful and so defiant and so *ready* that it was as if I had never truly seen him before, and even now when I think of my dear Wick, I think of him that way, standing by the dead bear as if he had conquered it himself, his eyes green-gold diamonds, his stance that of a man who believes he might lose everything but still willing to risk it all anyway.

HOW WE LOST WHAT WE HAD FOUGHT FOR

I had harbored a killer and could not shake free of that, kept turning it over in my mind, kept trying to rid myself of the residue. Borne wasn't even a killer as I was a killer, but someone who killed the innocent and tried to call them guilty. I thought I had been acting out of kindness, out of a sense of teaching Borne to be good. But would you make a wolf feel guilty for killing its prey? Would you make an eagle feel guilty for flying? The only salvation against the guilt, the only thing I could hold in my hands like something tiny and glittering found in the dirt that might be worthless, was the idea that I hadn't been able to cast aside my feelings because Borne meant something bigger. That I had continued to believe in Borne because my gut knew something my head did not.

Maybe that was a delusion, maybe that was wrong, but even as a ghost I hadn't been stripped of that feeling. Even as a ghost facing Borne in that desolate place in the city, I'd still come away thinking Borne was a decent person beset by a terrible affliction.

No matter how I tried to push beyond that to a place where Borne was evil, horrible, a psychopath, I couldn't do it.

I went home to the Balcony Cliffs with Wick, no longer a ghost. I went home into a sliver of time I count as happiness before the end, before we lost everything. Wick might recede from me again, or me from him, but in those few days I knew him with an intensity that could not have been prolonged without burning us both out.

In his apartment, I tore off my dusty, dirty clothes, and then his dusty, dirty clothes, and we fucked with a fury and oblivion that drove out everything else. I did not want Wick gentle, and he did not want to be gentle, and we took each other and kept on taking each other until we were sore and so tired we could sleep without dreams or nightmares—exhausted, and hungry, and with nothing solved but it didn't matter.

After, as we lay there, we talked as honest as we could. I told him about the scavengers I'd met and the Mord proxies at the intersection, and how numb and old I felt without Borne in the Balcony Cliffs. I was telling Wick this not to hurt him but to let the monsters out, to have a night without the monsters inside me. His body stiffened alongside me as I told him these things, and then relaxed again, and there was such relief in the ordinary.

In the aftermath, Wick's wiry arms around my shoulders, my waist, and then, as if we were addicts, sleep merged with wakefulness and Wick's hands were roving, busy, just where I wanted them, needed them. He grew hard against me once more, and we made love slowly, and I welcomed feeling diffuse and in pieces, everywhere and nowhere.

And, for those few days, it was almost normal again.

The fourth night after my return, I drifted off to dreams of the little foxes that followed Borne. They were in the dry ocean bed outside the city. They were playing in the sand and yapping and yipping and taking turns disappearing into the backdrop, only to reappear again somewhere else, as if it wasn't camouflage but instead *blinking* from place to place. Then one fox stopped to stare at me, and I knew it was the same one from the astronaut graves.

I woke several hours later to tiny meteorites hitting my face. I woke up to Wick's fireflies winking out, not one by one but in droves, swaths going dark, and the dead bodies falling onto the bed. Our alarm system.

I shook Wick awake.

"Wick—we need to go. Now."

He stared up at the ceiling bleary-eyed, and then he was reaching for his pants and we were putting on our clothes in a frenzy.

Thirty fireflies were left, then twenty, then ten, then we lived in darkness except for the faint pale glow from Wick and his remaining worms. The bed was covered in little dead dark bodies.

"Where are they coming from?" I asked, even though I knew. What we didn't know is who the intruders were.

"Everywhere." A preternatural calm from Wick as he pulled out his emergency pack, gave me mine.

My heart was a bludgeon trying to get out of my chest.

We had what we needed to survive. We knew our escape route. It had been maybe two minutes since I'd noticed the dying fireflies.

Wick threw open the door to his apartment.

The corridor was full of bears.

A wall of coarse, dull fur given depth by shadow. The glimpse of the massive head of another Mord proxy beyond the side and haunch of the one blocking our doorway. The smell of unconstrained savagery that close poured into the apartment: blood and mud and shit and rotting flesh. The traces of leaves and lichen, the hot, bitter aftertaste of Mord breath that filled up the corridor, finding our new air.

Half a second before I shut the door.

Two seconds before Wick fortified it with his last beetles, four seconds before Wick had pushed me up into the air duct, five seconds before I pulled him up into the air duct.

Ten seconds before the bears burst into the apartment and destroyed it. Swatted at the entrance to the air duct, Wick bringing his legs up to his chest, and then, as I pushed forward, surging almost on top of me to get away from those claws, those questing paws.

The bellowing and the terrible smell were right below us as we crawled through the air duct. A smashing, splintering sound was a paw punching up through the air duct behind us. Then another. More, following, ripping through the ceiling, clawing their way toward us, others trying to anticipate, get ahead of us.

We veered off at an intersection, both silent, feeling our bellies exposed as we crawled as fast as we could because the air duct still ran above the corridor. One well-timed swipe from below and the ceiling would cave in and our entrails pour out in a cascade of blood.

We were both like blind, dumb things burrowing in a panic so absolute that it came down like a dark, deep wall and became something like a great calm. Our packs were abandoned down below. Our minds were down below, being feasted on by the bears. Only our bodies had escaped, kept churning through the tunnel of the air duct reflexively, must soon come to a halt but kept going anyway. Our only urge was to get away, to get away, to get away, and we pushed forward heedless of harm, bruising our shins, scraping off the skin on our knees, because our devotion to escape from the place we had spent so much time defending was so mindless and absolute that nothing else mattered, nothing else registered.

At first I was in front of Wick, kicking him in the face without meaning to, and then he was in front and I was eating his kicks and yet there was no pain, not then. That came later, along with the lingering ache across our bodies, as if we'd been fish thrashing in a net, half in and half out of the water, unable to drown and unable to live.

Finally, though, the hot, raw pain of my bloody palm against the grit of a shallow mound of gravel and jagged pebbles brought me back out of my animal self.

"Wick! Stop!" I hissed, but Wick didn't hear me. "Wick!" But still he didn't hear me.

I caught Wick's foot, grappled with him, pulled him back into myself, pinned down his arms in that space and felt a shudder run through his body and with it a kind of resignation or surrender, and he went limp.

"Just listen," I said in his ear.

We listened. We could hear the bears in the distance, delivered to us via the acoustics of the air duct as a kind of tinny droning roar. A dim thick digging sound also sounded far away.

"Where are we?" Wick asked.

"I have no idea." If he didn't know, I definitely didn't know.

All I could see was air duct five feet ahead and air duct five feet behind.

"They destroyed it all. They're destroying it all," Wick whispered, thrust into a pain I knew wasn't all physical.

The attack had sprung all our traps, destroyed our biotech, had come from so many points of the compass at once that the snapping of those lines, the ease of it, traumatized us almost more than the physicality of the invasion. An intricate map, burned, with no copy. It made it hard to think. It made it hard to breathe. We could not even frame the questions that would come hurtling toward us later, like why and how.

And we were still in danger, we both knew that.

"How do we get out? They'll be watching all the exits."

"There's one way they might not know about. It leads out to the south."

"What?" Wick looked at me as if I had said something in gibberish.

I smiled. He wasn't the only one with secrets. "I had Borne make a tunnel through the old apartments when we were punching holes in the walls looking for extra supplies."

A flicker of hope in Wick's eyes, then a wince.

"But if Borne knows, *they* know."

"Borne didn't betray us," I said. "The Magician or someone else, but not Borne."

Wick wanted to protest that assumption, but another objection had occurred to him.

"But to the *south*?"

That was a problem. For more than a month we hadn't used the southern exits. The shifting lines of the conflict between the Magician and Mord meant the south was Mord country. To exit south meant we would be behind enemy lines and have to find our way back north to some more neutral territory, or even one in flux. Which meant encountering more Mord proxies.

"What choice do we have, Wick? We have no choice."

"We have no supplies," Wick pointed out. "We could try to circle back, slip into my laboratory, grab a few things."

"They'll kill us. They're not leaving. We're dead if we don't *get out*."

The bear sounds had only come closer as we talked, and proliferated, as if every room, every pocket of air, were in the process of being occupied by the proxies.

Wick, adjusting: "There's a safe place to the south. A hidden cistern. A little room next to a well."

"Then that's where we'll head," I said. "We have no choice."

It sounded like a last stand, but so be it. Soon we would know for sure if Borne had betrayed us. I thought of the twelve-year-old girl. I thought of the biotech burning blissful in the flames.

I kissed Wick on the mouth, pinned him with my gaze. "We're alive. We're still alive."

I didn't know how to interpret the guarded look on Wick's face. I didn't realize that leaving the Balcony Cliffs might be a death sentence for him.

¤

The way was clear. We managed to find the entrance to my secret exit without being seen, even as the sounds of pillage, the roars, and the "Drrk! Drrk!" echoed too loud for fear to leave us. But I didn't want to lose that fear.

Saving our lives became about passing through a series of large holes Borne had punched in the walls of the homes of those long dead. The holes were big enough for a hunched-over person to crab-walk through, or to crawl through on all fours. Many were consecutive, so you could look down through a row of irregular holes in rooms and have time to wonder what waited in ambush. Others I'd hidden, to confuse any intruder. So sometimes we had to move a table or broken-down dresser out of the way first. To find the mousehole to the next place, which might double back or surge forward only to double back. A convoluted path because I had determined to only use areas of the Balcony Cliffs that were not part of Wick's diagram.

The consecutive holes—their gaping emptiness, the frisson of unease—meant a commitment to scuttling through, putting our heads into a number of ragged guillotines and submitting to whatever evil might want to take us.

But the other rooms made us stop and realize what we were

losing, what we were leaving, all under the weight of so much personal history, the remnants of so many old, dead lives. I had been in these rooms—despite their number, I still remembered what they held that I hadn't scavenged. I was prepared to some extent. But it took a greater toll on Wick, to keep appearing in these rooms, to have to remain there, unable to escape other people's memories as we patiently prepared our escape to the next room, and the next and the next.

We were caked in dust and grime. Our hands blistered. Our joints sore, knees ever more scraped.

After a time, we could hear the Mord proxies barely at all, and despite the ghoulish mausoleum-like lurch and repetition of our progress, we could tell from a downward slant and a new, fresher quality to the air that we were headed in the right direction. There was the feeling, unspoken between us, that although hungry and thirsty, we would make it out. That though our hands shook from the aftershocks and when we sat to rest our minds were full of bears, we had a goal and a shelter waiting: Wick's safe place. Food and water awaited us. That was motivation enough. We were almost free.

The last doorway led to a stairwell heading down and I knew that at the bottom lay a disguised door and on the outside no hint at all but fallen rock, fallen branches, and a light covering of lichen.

We stood there teetering at the top of the stairs, far older than we had been just hours before. About to leave our home. About to be tossed out into the world we'd taken such pains to keep at arm's length, to only meet on our terms.

"Are you ready?" I asked Wick, his arm around me. The blood on his hand was smudging warm and moist onto my dusty shirt and I didn't care.

"We'll be like hermit crabs without their shells," Wick said.

"We'll find new shells."

A long, drawn-out, trembling sigh from Wick, an exhalation almost like a death rattle.

"I'm ready," he said.

Thus diminished, we left the Balcony Cliffs.

WHAT FREEDOM MEANT

Some landscapes in the city let you play pretend for at least a short time, and that is a good thing: to control in your thoughts what you can't yet control in reality. The terrain we emerged into, wincing and squinting from the harsh sunlight of midday, might in play-pretend land have resembled a slanted field of weeds that led down to a gentle ravine lined with pine trees and the tops of buried buildings. You might even have imagined the ravine had been formed by water erosion and that down in its glistening dark depths water still bubbled out, churned across jagged rocks, and then ran its course to a destination farther down, where the ravine flattened out to the desolate plain that defended the approaches to the Company building.

But there hadn't been water flowing for years and the trees were all dead and leafless and half fossilized, their lie exposed by the gnarled green cactus that had grown up around them. The weeds were fractious and yellow against the sandy ground and near the slope of the ravine had to burst up through a cracked asphalt so old, so dislodged and broken up, that in its blackened aspect that surface could as well have been the upsurge of some vast underground volcano.

Vultures circled above—a good sign. Something dead below meant too that things had lived, at least for a while, and broken tree trunks and a few mounds of refuse gathered around the nubs of old walls provided good cover if we wanted to try our luck down the ravine.

Wick's safe place lay to the west, a little to the north of our position. The ravine would take us out of our way, but otherwise to the immediate northwest there was little cover past the shadow of the Balcony Cliffs and we were fearful of being exposed to the Mord proxies.

My throat was parched. I had on my worst pair of shoes. In my pockets I'd found a dried-out alcohol minnow I split with Wick and not much else other than a pocketknife. Whatever Wick had he would not say, only that he would "hold it in reserve."

We started toward the ravine, scrambling down the incline to where it leveled out before a steeper descent, now walking on the field of asphalt and weeds. I looked back at the Balcony Cliffs, so overgrown with moss and grass at this angle it did look like a cliff top and not the edge of a vast building at all.

But as I stared, there came a glitch or stoppage in time, and the sound of Wick's voice as he screamed at me from some far distance and pulled at my arm, and I thought it odd that the sun had gone away and that there was a shadow across the Balcony Cliffs when there was no cloud in the sky.

A sun carious and bloodshot alongside the real sun. The Balcony Cliffs ripped away from me, a wall of dark brown between us. A counting out of my heartbeats so slow that each became like the drip of the last honey out of the jar onto a plate far, far below, and as elastic.

The world was full of noise and then full of silence, and in the silence all the air left my lungs and a great peace came over me and I was on my back on the ground as if I'd always been there.

A thunderous wave, a monstrous vibration through the earth, had flung me to the ground. I was falling away from Wick or he was falling away from me down the incline, come to rest tossed to the side, bleeding among the weeds, startling white against black asphalt. I could see him at the edge of my vision, but I had to force my gaze skyward, as if a weight already pressed down on me from those coordinates.

Mord rose above me, had been hiding or invisible, and the asphalt thrown into the air with the impact of him smashing his feet into the ground near us now rained down in clumps and I put up one hand to protect my face but could not stop staring. The blue sky, curiously calm, and the silence, and Mord, a huge golden-brown bear rearing up on hind legs to blot out the sky, to destroy everything from the dust motes to the sun . . . and me lying there looking up at that as his body extended higher still and the sky around that mass of fur burning and seething, a corona around the utter impossible smothering thickness of his fur, and there was his mighty foot raised and there his claws and above that the sight of a paw and at an impossible height up that golden length the muzzle, the fangs, the great yellow eye, the deranged beacon, as dangerous as in my dreams. And the eye saw me, I swear it saw me, locked onto me and worried at me and would not let go. I swear Mord *knew* me and yet I was still on my back, adrift in aftershocks, one of my eardrums burst and something moist and sticky running down the side of my head. I couldn't feel my arms or legs, those poor sad twigs.

With excruciating slowness, Mord grew larger and larger in my field of vision. Weeks passed as I lay there and Mord contrived in his infinite mercy and patience to remove the sky, remove the world, and become God of Nothing. Until one day, in harsh sunlight, Wick bleeding beside me, I could see the scarred black pads of his raised foot so close, every whorl and tuft of fur around the toes, the huge clods of dirt there dislodged and now lazily spiraling down with the foot while still waves of dust spilled off the sides.

He smelled of rich mud and subtle honeysuckle. He smelled of shit and, impossibly, of mint. The long, yellow claws were so very large, the tips curling over me so sharp, and I could see the fracture lines in them, the places where those claws had been split and repaired many times, how they were in their way as delicate and miraculous as they were deadly.

Less blue and more Mord, and I was about to be pulverized by our god, made into pulp beneath his tread, and then everything would be over and this stuttering, stilted attempt I had made at life would be over. All that effort relaxed into not-moving, not-thinking, my atoms released to become something else.

The pads of Mord's foot were cool and dark and comforting and very, very close.

But very close too was a word being shouted into my good ear, my own name: "Rachel! Rachel! Rachel!" It sounded ridiculous, like the cawing of a crow. With the word came a dragging sensation, a bumpy sliding drag, and I was moving over the ground fast as the foot continued to come down toward me.

The darkness spread but my face was in the light and I could see sky again. The darkness was very close. My chest was in the light, but my legs were in shadow. That seemed peculiar to me, as if it were raining on just one side of the street.

One final wrenching, jolting pull on my arms and I was flipped through the air by the impact of some monster stamping on the skin of the world and Rachel was set down again and was rolling downhill, rolling and rolling with some other creature attached to her back and still shouting the name of a ghost: "Rachel!"

The world went dark, but if I was dead at least I could hear again, and not just the voice in my head. The rumble and roar, screams, and imagined "Drrrk! Drrrk!" while a sack of flesh was dragged and thrown about.

Somewhere close was a river of fur that became a dark, dry river full of rocks and chemicals, and that's where I washed up, waiting for someone, anyone, to find me.

HOW WE FOUND TEMPORARY SHELTER

Once, as a bedtime story, though he never truly slept, I told Borne about my island of refuge, the place my parents brought me to when I was six or seven. There I had experienced a hard-won two years without upheaval, without war or refugee camps. On that island, I had begun to think I might live out my life. It had the same false sense of permanence as the Balcony Cliffs, only more so.

We lived in an apartment in the harbor capital, but I remembered with such vividness not our home or the buildings in the city but the botanical gardens and its decorative pond with a dead fountain in the center. Water lilies covered the surface with butter-yellow blossoms and round green lily pads with a raised edge that replicated the circular gray granite wall that surrounded the pond. The wall was just the right height that I could, on tiptoe, reach into the water and trail my hand there, tiny fish nibbling at my fingertips. In the silty water swam also carp, ponderous goldfish, and brown, mysterious eels with gills like explosions of lace. Fat ugly frogs stood sentinel on the lily pads and turtles the size of my thumb sunned themselves in that miniature world. Snails whose gray shells were transparent so you could see the darkness of their coiled bodies hid against the wall, and I had to be careful before leaning so I wouldn't crush them with my awkward, clumsy human body.

Nothing that had been altered lived there; biotech had been banned from the gardens, with the government set to classify artificial animals as akin to espionage. Malformed animals or rare ones could incite panic, and the newspapers ran articles about suspected biotech cornered and hacked to death by men with machetes.

But my mother would say at dinner, my father rolling his eyes, that biotech was already out in the world more than people knew. That it was *pretending*, trying to blend in, to escape notice.

After school, my friends and I would play at the gardens, overseen by one of the mothers or my father. We would climb the labyrinthine trees that overhung the pond, the ones with the intense strands of bright red blossoms that made me sneeze, the wind off the sea from across the road bringing a hint of salt and fresh coolness to our sweaty endeavors. Then we would be walked down the sea road to the harbor, and home. Along the way, when I had money from chores, we would run into the corner store and get salted plums and rice candy. The old lady behind the counter never smiled but would give me, free of charge, the little decorative umbrellas people used to put in drinks.

Most days, if it hadn't yet gotten dark, my parents would go down to the beach with me after dinner. We would look for shells or wade in the shallows with our shoes off. I liked to watch the grumpy-looking sand-colored fish sway back and forth under the surf. Then it was back home to do schoolwork, and before bed my father would read to me from a children's book or maybe even an adult book, or poetry with pictures alongside it. No one made printed books on the island anymore, and electricity was on-again, off-again. But I didn't notice that, didn't think anything of it. I was going to live on the island forever. Each day would be just like the last, and each night also, with the ocean breeze surging like the sea was surging, with wind crackling gentle through the palms and, sometimes, the little foot-patter of rats or mice that entranced me but sent my father into frenzies of mousetrap building.

In the mornings, a man who had grown up on the island and sold, among other items, boiled, filtered water in glass jars would keep an eye on me and the neighbor kids as we walked to school in our brown leather sandals and the badly made itchy gray uniforms the school recycled year after year. We'd do our language arts, our math, our science, and then be released into recess. The school was across the road from the beach, and we'd rove wider than was prudent, blunder, explore the very limits of our territory— to uncover a huge palm crab or some wayward crayfish taking a walk from the nearby river.

We rarely made it all the way to the sea without some adult calling us back. But I sometimes made it to the fence, to watch the mud flats where the river fed into the sea. I liked to observe the mudskippers—soft, slimy, puckish creatures with bulgy eyes and fins that doubled as a way to walk on land. I didn't even notice the marsh reek all that much, I liked the mudskippers so much—and the cautious fiddler crabs that would cover the mud when I was in the middle distance but then disappear down their holes leaving behind an empty ghost town when I was at the fence.

The mudskippers didn't even blink, though, remained behind like gray statues, unmoving but for a delicate flutter around their amphibious gills. Gulp, gulp, gulp they'd go, before, at their own pace, plopping back into the water. Some of them acted like sentries, and others seemed to enjoy goofing off. It was hard to tell the difference, though.

My mother asked a lot about the mudskippers, about whether any had strange eyes or acted differently. Or if I had ever seen anything else odd out there. No, I said, none of them did. No, I had not. She said she had heard a rumor about biotech seeking refuge on the mud flats. The biotech left a trail, she felt—and if you could track it to the source, that might be where safety lay. Which was when I guessed the truth: My parents didn't think that life would last. They thought the island was just a temporary shelter, that we would be moving on soon enough.

It astonishes me now that I could have ever led such an opulent life or had so much leisure time, or have looked at all that protein with a non-predatory eye. Any of that transported to the city I now lived in would have been ravaged and stripped down in half a day or less—the pond in the botanical gardens reduced to an empty pool of cloudy water, the mud flats just a barren plain.

When I had finished telling Borne about the island, he asked, "Is that from a story?"

"No, Borne. That was part of my childhood."

"So it was a story."

"No, it was real."

"Oh yes. From 'when I was a kid,'" he said, as if he'd been filing away some of what I said as a separate book of fairy tales. I was the old bore who couldn't shut up about the good old days that had never existed.

"It was real, Borne," I insisted.

"What's a dog?" he asked. Sometimes I also told him, if I was up to it, about the dog I'd fed on the island and had to abandon.

"You know what a dog is."

"A dog is a meal on four paws."

"Borne!"

"You said that."

"I said it as a joke." But there weren't any dogs left in the city, except on the fringes, distant and wary. No friendly dogs anywhere, because a friendly dog was a meal on four paws.

"Where's the island now?" Borne asked, as if islands could just float away, but mostly to change the subject.

"I don't know."

"Is it still the same?"

"I don't know."

"I think it's not the same now."

"It could be the same."

What did Borne know? I remembered thinking. His own brief childhood he'd spent rooted in place as a kind of glorified houseplant. He had never been anywhere.

But Borne had pressed on, not realizing how much it bothered me.

"How do you know it happened?" he asked. "Is it written down anywhere?"

How did I know it had happened? Because of its absence now, because I still felt the loss of it, but I didn't know how to convey that to Borne then, because he had never lost anything. Not back then. He just kept accumulating, sampling, tasting. He kept gaining parts of the world, while I kept losing them.

When I woke in Wick's safe place for the first time, or came to, Wick had propped me up against the stone wall next to him, facing the shallow water of a well. All was in shadow except the water, which emitted a light blue rippling glow. Above, the walls came in toward each other like a steeple, leaving just a small point of light at the apex. It smelled like moss and a clean sort of darkness.

Two of my fingers welcomed me back with a vicious, lancing throb, along with a shoulder laced with shooting pains like an electric spiderweb. My legs were scraped and bloodied through my ripped pants and my pelvis and left hip felt bruised, not right, hurt against the stone floor. A weakness in my ankle could be walked off, but the state of my left ear was more serious. That I might always have to listen out of the other ear, the sound coming to my left side muddy—always have to be alert. I could still feel in my bones the reverberations of Mord's weight striking the earth, and I was much too aware of my body to even pretend to be a ghost again.

Our shoes were dusty, dirty travesties, perched there defeated on the end of our legs, and I did not want to take mine off for fear of what I might find underneath.

Wick's wispy hair had become disheveled to mad-genius levels and his face had gotten so dusty it looked like a mask, through which his eyes shone wicked and intense. I didn't like the redness of Wick's face, his arms. I had thought him shaken but otherwise uninjured by our escape, but that redness made it seem as if he had been drinking or evoked certain algae when the water's been poisoned, a bloom that seeks contamination. It astonished me that despite this he was relaxed, lighter, less worried, giving me an impish look.

"Where are we?" I asked.

He told me.

Between us and the well he had overturned an empty crate. A single black kidney bean trembled atop that rough surface, served up on a little plate.

"Can you guess what that is?" he asked me. Playing our old games, except usually I brought the salvage to him.

"A bean."

"Correct! A bean."

"But is it really a bean? It could be something better?"

"No. Unfortunately, it is a bean. Of sorts."

"Where did you get the plate?"

"Never mind the plate."

"Are we going to eat the bean?"

Wick shook his head. "No, even though that is, technically, our last food. From my pocket."

Down to a single bean.

"A bean," I said. "Impressive. Prodigal. The bean returns."

"I just thought you should know how resourceful we were in our flight, before I open the pack I found here and see what else we have." He pulled a pack out from the shadows by his other side.

"Open the pack, then," I said. I was hungry.

"Wait, though. Wait a minute."

Before us, on the saucer, the trembling bean hatched and a tiny, moist insect emerged glittering, spread diaphanous wings that seemed etched from obsidian. It looked like a dragonfly but much more delicate. A damselfly that shook its wings once and took to the air, spiraled up above the well, and disappeared into the darkness of the stone walls. Maybe it went out the hole atop the cistern, or maybe it decided to live in the cistern. Either way, we never saw our "bean" again.

"What kind of biotech was that?"

"No kind of biotech at all," Wick said. "I have no idea how it got in my pocket. I have no idea how it got there. No one made it. It was an egg. Something laid it in my pocket. Isn't that amazing?"

"You let it go." Mock disapproval, still playing, but after Borne it wasn't the same.

Wick shrugged, fatalistic. "If there's nothing to eat in the pack, Rachel, it doesn't matter anyway. Let a bit of the Balcony Cliffs live on here. Why not?"

Our new shelter wasn't nearly as elaborate as our old shelter. The cistern looked from the outside like a sunken mound or slag heap of stones that must have fallen in and buried whoever had once lived inside. There was access through a movable stone where the mound had relaxed into the hillside and a trapdoor beside the well that led to a tunnel that led to a disguised exit a quarter mile away.

The circular well that occupied half of the flat stone floor enclosed brackish water recessed a few inches below floor level and perhaps once was contaminated. But biotech filters in the form of fat luminous blue slugs clung to the sides of the well, patrolling back and forth under the water's surface. That and the electric, burnt-match smell to the water were the best indicators that no one else had ever found this place. Otherwise, they would have been taken by someone long ago.

But it wasn't Wick's safe house—instead it was a safe house of the Magician's that Wick had discovered several months ago, and in that sense not safe at all. Besides, even broken and recessed, to the careful eye it still formed a visible landmark on the horizon.

I had only fragments in my head of what had happened after Mord's attack—glancing, stabbing memories of falling over, staggering up, of Wick dragging me, of sliding down into the ravine, of hiding there, while Mord strode inexorable past the ravine and into the distance as if he'd never meant to harm us, and maybe he hadn't. Maybe he hadn't even noticed us. Perhaps Mord had just been there as a shock to the system, to smash his feet into the ground, bring all the vermin out of hiding. But the Mord proxies prowled near, too, and soon enough we were running through the dead broken trees, through the peculiar gray-and-black rubble that made it seem like the surface of some alien planet. I'd run until I was too weak, whatever shock had suppressed my pain and animated me gone, and I hopped and shuffled and Wick led me along, encouraged me forward. Until I'd fallen unconscious not far from our temporary shelter.

The pack held the usual and no more than the usual: survival rations, a knife, a canteen for water, a couple of shirts, an ancient first-aid kit, a battered pair of binoculars, a gun without bullets, a compass, a few ancient protein bars I could tell already would be as hard as Mord's fangs.

Wick laid it out in a row like an offering to the god of the cistern.

"Food for a week," Wick said. "Water forever. Well, at least for a lot longer than the food."

I had to lean over and turn to hear him, my poor other ear torn and blistered, registering his speech as a faint, hollow clattering.

"Food for two weeks if we go down to one meal a day," I said.

"Dangerous. We're already weak."

"Can we carry this place around with us on our backs while we forage for food?"

"We can't stay here anyway. I can't stay here," Wick said.

"What do you mean you can't?"

"My medicine—those nautilus pills. I need them or I'll die."

I just stared at him; it was the most naked thing he'd said to me and until now his dependence had been an abstract thing, lodged only in my head. Mord's foot was falling again, about to crush me, and Wick alongside me.

"The only place that I might find more is in the Company building," Wick said. "You should head north, try to make it back to the city, while I head south."

"You'll go south and I'll go north. When did you decide this for us?"

"Or you could stay here and wait it out until I return."

I snorted at that. "Stay here and wait for the proxies to come and surround this place and kill me? Or the Magician to escape them and drop by? Or any old marauder who sniffs out the water?"

"Then north," Wick said.

"Stay here and die in the dark with the snails or try for the north and die in the light? Leave you to your fate? I don't think so."

But Wick wasn't done surprising me. He pulled an envelope out of his pants pocket. The envelope was the size of those that people used to send letters in and thick enough to hold five or six sheets of paper. It was filthy with dried sweat and stains and ground-in dirt, had been folded and unfolded several times. He had not written it here, at the cistern. He had written it well before we'd left the Balcony Cliffs and carried it around with him.

"I lied," Wick said. "I didn't just bring a bean out of the Balcony Cliffs. Here, take it."

But I didn't take it, looked at it suspicious. Nothing had ever seemed more like a trap to me.

"What is it?"

"A letter to you. From me."

"You forgot your medicine but you took *this*?"

"The letter was in my pocket. The medicine was in my pack."

"I don't want to read it," I said.

"That's a lie," Wick said in a teasing tone. He even smiled. "You do want to read it. Everything is in there, everything I never told you because I couldn't. But you need to know. If I don't come back from the Company, *read it*."

Wick was light, was making light, because he was: All the weight of him was in that letter, and he was putting it on me.

"There's only one problem with that, Wick—I'm coming with you. I'm not leaving you."

"Read the letter first, before you make that decision."

"No."

"Take the letter."

"No."

He held out the letter.

"No. What if you get sicker along the way? You'll never even reach the Company building."

"Why are you making things difficult again?"

"I'm not being difficult. I'm being clear. After you *just* saved my life, after everything else . . . you thought you could make me leave you. But it's not that easy, Wick. I won't make it that easy." I snatched the letter from his hand. "So I'll take your letter, but you can't stop me from going south with you."

Wick was quiet then, gathering himself. A quiver of some strong emotion passed through him. But I didn't reach out to him or acknowledge, knew that if I did confirm the weakness at the heart of him, he would break into fragments. That maybe, too, the letter was the best of him or the worst.

"If we go into the Company," Wick said, "you may see things you don't want to see. It won't be what you expect."

I laughed, but not without affection. "Oh, Wick, how would that be any different than *now*?" I was tired of talking things out. I wanted to be on our way, gone south, out of this temporary shelter that in the end would just betray us anyway.

"If we travel together, don't read the letter unless I'm dead."

"That doesn't give me much reason to keep you alive."

He snickered at that, and I nudged him in the ribs, and he dropped the subject.

But I think the trust Wick was looking for wasn't about when I might read the letter but something deeper. The truth was, I would never tell him if I read the letter. Wick would never know when I read the letter.

He would only know whether I stayed beside him or abandoned him.

In that temporary shelter, such simple things took on such significance. The way Wick held his head to the side, as if he lacked the strength, propped up against the wall, to sit straight. The many old scars on his hands and arms that came from the bites of his insect biotech. The exposed skin of his neck that had a tautness and a kind of naked honesty that made me want to kiss him there. The way he looked at me direct from that point on, as if we were only a few steps from the end of the world, and he wanted to fix me in memory.

I took off my clothes and used a rag dipped in the well water to clean myself. I washed out my clothes and let them dry on a rock jutting from the wall. Then I told Wick to take off his clothes and I cleaned him as well, washed the grime from his face, gently caressed the bruises and scratches on his body, ran my hands over his chest, his back, his legs.

When we were both clean, I laid my head on his lap there beside the shallow well, and looked up at the moss and cool stones above our heads, and for a long time I said nothing, did nothing, just listened as he talked about the Balcony Cliffs and how much he wished he had managed to hold on to his pack as we escaped through the air duct, how that would make our choices now so different, and how balanced against the fear and loss was the twinge of relief he felt, that without the Balcony Cliffs there was so much less the Magician could do to us, and how clever the Mord proxies must have been to overcome our defenses. This last was Wick trying to be optimistic, trying to hold on to a bit of self-respect, that absolved us in at least a small way.

"This place would've been easier to defend than the Balcony Cliffs," Wick said.

"And takes fewer bears to overrun," I pointed out.

Just a twinge, wondering what would happen if Borne went back to the Balcony Cliffs and discovered us gone, driven out.

"But there's nothing here worth overrunning."

Except the water. Almost anyone might kill for that.

"The Balcony Cliffs was too big for us anyway," I said.

"Yes, much too big, and full of bears."

"Infested with bears."

"Clogged and clotted with bears. This place is bear-free."

"So far."

"So far," Wick agreed.

The bears had been clever, smart, patient. They must have

been listening up top, buried in the moss, quiet and hibernating, and aware of our movements, to know where the traps lay, where our fortifications were strong and where weak. Even though this made little sense, even though we had been taken by blind fury and overwhelming speed and force of will, by a disrespect for casualties, and might never untangle just how thoroughly we had failed—and if we had been sold out by the Magician, one of Wick's clients, or someone else.

Yet there was more to it than that. It was hard for me not to relive the moment of impact—the initial smashing impact of Mord creating an earthquake with no warning, and then the way the air had been sucked away, while at the same time pushing out again to buffet me. The way the sky had spun and gone away and there was only Mord and the certain knowledge I'd be crushed to death.

But Wick was somewhere else, had been circling different memories of Mord, laying the groundwork, thinking the words that might get him to other words he didn't quite know how to let out of his mouth. Until they just came out, in a rush.

Wick had known Mord at the Company better than he'd let on; you could say they'd been friends. "He liked bird-watching and we ate lunches together and he read so many books. He was curious about so many things." And because of this, I gleaned from Wick's confession, Mord had done many different tasks for the Company, even leading a team that studied the chaos in the city—the dysfunction they'd created—and how to overcome it, how to rebuild. "But that was a joke—the Company was already failing and losing perspective. The people in charge, cut off from headquarters, began to get strange ideas."

There came through then, in Wick's need to speak, to get this out of his system, a cascade of grotesque images—of "strange ideas" more monstrous than Mord, some of which I had glimpsed in pictures back in his apartment. Digging gap-jawed leviathans that ate the soil and vomited it back out, transformed but also cleansed of whatever had lived there previous. Flying creatures with many wings that blotted out of the sun and patrolled the skies and killed anyone who opposed the Company. Among other ideas that seemed deranged and terrifying and more like someone's idea of how to torture the city.

But none of it had gotten past the planning stages . . . except Mord.

"When the fish project failed," Wick said, "they abandoned the city rebuild as well. They put Mord in an experimental division. As a kind of punishment." They blamed him for the fish project, even though it wasn't his fault, while the Magician suffered not at all. "None of us could have withstood what he was subjected to then, Rachel, what he was selected for." Was that true? Or was Mord always susceptible? I didn't think Wick had the perspective to know. "He could still speak and understand as they modified him and kept modifying him, until it drove him mad." The only outlet, the only relief: to keep a record, which Wick had smuggled out in a broken telescope through another employee after Wick left the Company. Along with the plans that had helped Wick become someone who "made" biotech, or at least modified it.

There was more, but no matter how Wick tried to articulate it, some things can only be understood when experienced, and I had not experienced what Wick had experienced inside the Company.

Today, Mord had tried to kill us by crushing us under his tread. Today, he was several stories tall and a monster. Wick was grappling with this, with the shock as much as I was, the wrenching dislocation of trying to make two separate worlds match up, the one that was normal and the one that was grotesque, the old and the new— the struggle to make the mundane and the impossible coexist just as it seemed impossible I had ever trailed my fingers through the water of a pond to let the little fish nibble or watched mudskippers through a school-yard fence or eaten at a fancy restaurant.

He could still speak and be understood.

The truth was, I didn't want Mord to be more like us. I wanted him to be less like us. To be able to say when he murdered, when he pillaged, that he was a psychotic beast, a creature without the possibility of redemption, with no humanity in him. I wanted something to be the same in the old world as in the new.

So I listened in silence and I nodded and made noises like I understood. Yet my attention was elsewhere. The letter burned. It was like a grenade, there in my pocket, and only I could determine when it would go off. Was Wick telling me this, allying himself with Mord, to prepare me for something in the letter? Or was he telling me this to lessen the impact of the letter? Or was this one last attempt to dissuade me from coming with him?

We did not discuss the letter again, or the plan to go south. That was already set, and Wick knew better than to bring it up again.

✿

That night, evidence came to us from near and far. In the middle of the night, I needed some air and I needed to piss, and we had no bucket. So I snuck out, a scrap of shadow, and squatted over a lucky clump of weeds near the ancient stones. A painful stance with all my bruising.

Way back in the direction of the Balcony Cliffs I could see cracklings of flame licking out over the tops of rocks and trees, and to the northeast and the west other fires had broken out—as if the action taken against us had been part of something larger. Much of the center of the city from that vantage seemed in dispute, but who fought, whose fortunes rose and fell, and in what neighborhoods, lay hidden from me.

I was finishing up when I noticed the perfect stillness of the night, which I had put down to my impaired hearing but might mean something more. I stood, quickly buttoned my pants, climbed up the cistern stones as best as I was able, and searched for hints of movement out in the night. It was all twisted bands of black: the branches of the dead, deformed forest at a slant down to the dead plain that preceded the Company building. Between the trees, for a long distance, patches of lighter shadow shone in the dim light, the clouds above almost blue-violet.

Nothing appeared, nothing moved, but I was patient, let my gaze drift. From the top of the cistern, so much territory spread out below that anything moving there would be in sight for quite some time.

Then, down through the forest, to where it leveled out before one last gentle slope—a rippling of invisible turbulence, a kind of rising through the air as of steam that manifested across those lighter patches. I could not be sure, but my instincts told me someone was running at great speed down the slope and had been visible from that angle for some time. Even if I couldn't see them. And you only ran like that if you were being pursued.

So I followed a line back from the flustered air, and maybe two hundred feet back up the slope, I found a coarse, moving river, too familiar. Too much like fur. A silent bounding and a wraithlike darkness, a surging, churning bloodlust, all bear in its reckless but joyful trajectory. At least three proxies, in pursuit of . . . what?

Their prey had lost a step on them, I saw, had stopped as if to think, that whirlpool of shadow, and then a swift turn on the heel toward new coordinates farther south. The shimmer against the trees reminded me of someone.

Then it was all just silence and movements I could not make sense of, and I went back inside.

To my surprise, Wick waited for me, standing as if he had never been asleep. The light from the well water washed over him in shades of electric blue.

"Mord proxies," I said.

Wick nodded.

I didn't tell him I thought the Magician might be out there, headed south like us. Even free of the Balcony Cliffs, I felt if he knew he might be influenced in a way bad for both of us.

As we packed, Wick said, "You need to figure out what you want to be after. Other than a scavenger."

"After what?" I asked.

But he never told me.

WHO WE MET ON THE DESOLATE PLAIN

We headed south, staking our hope on the idea of the Company building as our salvation. In our belief we were now no different than those acolytes who had worshipped Mord. Our rituals and our words were just different. Wick talked of his special knowledge of a side entrance near the two holding pools abutting the Company building. Wick assured me that with Mord now based in the north, the ruined levels would have already been picked clean and the scavengers moved on to other places. I humored him, although it felt less like a plan than the only thing we could do.

"Do you know how to get into the levels below?"

"Yes. Mord showed me, when he was still human."

"Isn't that old intel?"

"Nothing has changed."

Hadn't it? Wick spoke in such alchemies and distillations of hope that I couldn't pick out the facts from the fictions, or which he told me to reassure himself.

Deep, deep night we traveled through, in a no-man's-land between the city proper and the Company building, having exhausted the stretch of dead woods. This expanse had been seeded with biotech by the Company long ago, and over time abandonment had driven the traps deep; if we were lucky we would not set off any living land mines. For now, the buffer zone seemed lifeless except where precarious or perilous life emerged: a kind of mud flats without mud where the broken-up concrete foundations from dwellings long gone shifted beneath a cracked surface of salt and the miasma of pollutions far distant in time. Runoff seeped up through the ground from storage far below. If you were wise, you did not seek out the watering holes created by the runoff, or drink the essence of the once-living, expressed as spontaneous gouts of thick, oily liquid.

Still, it was better at night and better crossed at night, the ground in places faintly luminous from some memory of artificial microorganisms. In daylight, the plain was hotter and unpleasant and any predator could see you coming from miles away unless you had camouflage like the Magician. Cement foundations lurked beneath a sluice of crushed and useless things, with no landmarks for coordinates and even the vultures rarely hovered over the hinterlands. It stank of sour mud and chemicals, and depending on the wind we had to cover our mouths and noses.

The Company building through the ancient safe-house binoculars was a cracked egg well ahead of us—a flat white oval from the air, perhaps, and the damage spread out around it like Mord had been rummaging in the building's internal organs. But as Wick pointed out, the walls still disappeared into the ground, gave a suggestion of depth and of further layers preserved from damage.

To the southeast, huddled next to the building, we could make out the wide leaking ponds, more like lakes, that still held the dead and failing bodies of the Company's mistakes and the things that had escaped, or thought they had. I had escaped them for a time, too, but now I was coming back.

We had picked up hints of conflict during our trek across the plain. In the first hour, we could hear what sounded like Mord proxies distant on our trail, and as the light faded and sunset bore down on us in a searing bloodred flecked with gold, accompanied by a hot wind, there appeared two of the beasts in the middle distance.

By then we had already started our journey across the plain and felt exposed, hit the ground painfully behind a mound of gravel and surveilled the proxies with our binoculars. On my stomach, I felt as if the ground was going to curl up around me and devour me. I was hurting and knew I would have to get up soon, even if just to crawl, if I was to make my brain override my body.

The Mord proxies had been hunkered down like soldiers in trenches they'd dug and disguised, and as the last light used up the red and extinguished the gold, in the haze of blue-gray heat, we thought they'd peered out and spotted us walking hunched across that landscape, caught a glimpse of us in a shimmer or shadow.

But no: Their eruption and churning gallop from those trenches led them southwest, in a horizontal across our field of vision, kicking up dust behind. We could see no adversary, though, even when they seemed to have cornered their prey, blindly clawing and biting around an invisible source.

At a safe distance, the foxes that were not foxes mirrored the bears, mocked them with their own reversals of direction, their own snapping at the air—using their camouflage to disappear and then reappear in some other place, chasing their tails, and once a proxy stopped and stared at the foxes, as if unsure whether they were enemies.

"Someone's out there," I said.

"Someone's always out there," Wick replied.

"Rabies? Madness? Play?" I guessed.

"Or the Magician," Wick said.

"Biting flies?"

As we watched, whatever we couldn't see eluded what we could see, and the chase resumed far off onto the western reaches of the plain, although the invisible prey kept trying to dart south, dart south again, and as the light disappeared completely I thought I saw one of the proxies stumble, fall, as if receiving a blow, but then it was time to make our escape across the plain.

The foxes became burnt-umber flashes against the setting sun, then silhouettes sitting, watching. Then nothing at all.

So we strove on in darkness, across a plain less dead than we might have wished. There came lesser growls than those of bears—and the yap-yip of the foxes and the slither-rustle of what we hoped were snakes, a pitter-patter as of the pink starlike toes of burrowing mammals and even a quark-quark we avoided from a stand of cactus that might have only been a frog calling out for water. Blocks and slabs of black stymied any attempt to know what was threat and what was innocent.

"I don't remember it being this alive," Wick complained. But I doubted he had roamed here nocturnal in years.

The moon came out, muffled by clouds, and added a light purple wash to the sky, and with it came a hint of a more forgiving wind. We continued to trudge, then an hour before dawn we stopped in a place where the ground was darker and formed shallow ridges or gouges that carried sound to us undistorted. We made camp in the lee of a huge fallen pillar, as deep into the crevice as we could go, as far as we could override an irrational fear of the pillar rolling over and crushing us, or some midnight bear scooping us out like termites.

We did not know if the Mord proxies might now be headed our way, but tracking their intent had already slowed us, as had the way the night was more aware than expected. We would rest for an hour, and then, in the early morning, we would continue on to where the plain gave way to the holding ponds. Even wrapped, the ankle gave me problems on the uneven ground and Wick had to carry the pack most of the time while my shoulder recovered. I felt like some creaking, ancient creature, old before her time.

Wick and I shared a food packet in silence. After a sip of water from our meager supply, Wick slept while I kept watch, because I could not rest anyway. My hip ached and I felt as if I inhabited an exoskeleton that had been battered by hammers.

The moon from the recesses of the pillar looked dead, poisoned, a special kind of factory gray: the rounded head of a dead robot with the skull half exposed. But still I looked up at it because there was no other light in the sky that bright and nothing else in front of me.

I tried to conjure memories of nighttime on my island sanctuary, to convert the brisk wind into a tropical breeze and the shadows and sand into the play of surf, a fringe of dark palm trees. But I was surrounded by a landscape too dirty and yet antiseptic, and I was exhausted by my own obsession with the past.

My gaze wandered, drifted, and I suppose I almost fell asleep despite myself. I kept seeing the Mord proxies pursuing the invisible across the plain. I kept seeing the pads of Mord's giant foot descending to crush me, mingled with a peculiar feeling of self-annihilating awe.

When I started back into watchfulness, there was an overpowering smell to the air, like an ancient, waveless ocean buried in its own silt and salt and reflections. The darkness had arranged itself into something that resembled intent. The plain before me that had conveyed even in the murk the sense of its ridges now had smoothed out into a uniform glistening black layer. A kindness, really, a reminder, a memory to soothe: the tiny flashes and flickers of a thousand fireflies, like the ones on the ceiling at the Balcony Cliffs. A soft, golden blinking from the ground that wished for me to be calm.

The lip of this sea of dim twinkling light pushed up to the ledge of broken rock that flumed out from the pillar, peered in at me, inquisitive.

"Shhhhh, Rachel. It's me." A familiar voice, this illusionist's trick.

I went very still and resisted the urge to wake Wick.

"I scared the bears away," he said. "I sent them away, for a little while." But which bears?

"How did you find us, Borne?" That question seemed essential.

"Oh, a little fox told me you were here. I've been in the city, fighting Mord proxies."

"What do you want?" I kept my voice low and calm.

Now Wick stirred behind me, and I knew exactly what he would say, and he wouldn't be wrong.

"Hello, Wick, how are you?"

"Go away," Wick said.

"Or what, Wick?" Borne said, dismissive. "You'll toss some worms at me? You'll call me names? You'll banish me?"

I glanced back, put a hand on Wick's chest, whispered, "Let me talk to him. Trust me."

"I was sad you had to leave the Balcony Cliffs," Borne said. "That was such a nice place for all of us. Don't you want to go back to it?"

"Someday, Borne."

Despite the knife in my pocket, I was searching around for some weapon that might protect me, but I knew there was nothing. Only what would make me feel better in a false way. A rock. A piece of pipe.

He was so vast, covering the ground like an oil slick. I knew he'd been eating, he'd been sampling. If Borne's true nature came out and he killed us and Rachel and Wick only existed inside Borne, would we be truly dead or would we still exist in some altered state?

"You're going to the Company building," Borne said.

"Yes."

Borne made a clucking sound like he was disappointed in me. "But the Company building is *disgusting*. Just disgusting. I hate it. I don't want anything to do with the Company building."

Hiding an old fear of his, I knew from his journal.

Wick spoke then. There was even sympathy in his voice. "Borne, we're not going north. We're going south. And you can't help us."

Borne was quiet for longer than made me comfortable. In the silence I could hear a kind of quaking and gentle hissing and a querulous whimper—all from the field of fireflies that was Borne. Wick had receded into the darkness under the pillar, and I knew he was alert to attack, would rally his very last biotech against Borne should we need it. But that's not where my mind was.

"Are you all right, Borne?" I didn't mean to show concern, because then I would have to worry about how Wick felt about that concern . . . but I was tired and I'd raised him and couldn't help it. Even now, on this hellish plain under the dead moon, headed for an open grave, some part of me felt I owed Borne.

"Oh, Rachel," Borne said, sounding weary and, for the first time since I had known him, old. "I'm doing okay. I try hard. But the Mord proxies are clever. Even when I disguise myself as them, they eventually flush me out. I defeat them, I absorb them, but there are so many and their bites sting."

"Show me where you're hurt," I told him.

The fireflies faded and dull silver-gray patches glowed all across the broken plain that was Borne.

So many dead patches, so many places the venom had killed the tissue. Borne was too vast now and still growing too fast for it to hinder him much, but he'd suffered wounds, taken a toll. I could not tell looking at him who would win the war of attrition in the end.

"You should stop," I said, the old motherly concern coming out from under the armor. "You should find someplace safe to hide for a while and heal."

Borne laughed as if I'd said something ridiculous, ripples and whorls appearing across his surface. Such a human response from a creature that now manifested so inhuman. Borne laughed and the wounds disappeared and the fireflies reappeared, although not so many as before.

A small version of the old him manifested in front of me. The silly, looping vase with the ring of eyes, with the tentacles curving up out of the top.

"I'm too big to hide for long, Rachel. I can't compress myself into the right space. And I'm so hungry all the time, you know that, Rachel. You always knew that, and you told me and I didn't listen. Because I couldn't. The hunger only gets worse the more I eat."

So many eyes now, looking out at me with a knowing gleam, resignation. One weary veteran talking to another.

"Easier prey," I said, venturing into dangerous territory.

"No, Rachel, I've stopped trying to be good," Borne said. "It isn't in my nature. I was made to absorb. I was made to kill. I know that now. And it's no use."

"You must try."

Empty words that agitated him, made him flare up. "I'm telling you, Rachel, I can't anymore. I'm not *built* like you. I'm not human. I'm not a *person*."

Across the vast sea of him, in amongst the ripples, human heads appeared, like swimmers treading water. Animal heads, too, and the heads of mutant children and Mord proxies. A dozen proxies at least. These shiny, dark heads with holes where their eyes should be. Staring.

But there was no shocking me anymore.

"Stop, Borne," I said.

The heads withdrew, the sea became gentle and quiet. I smelled the sun on sand and the scent of the surf and all the things he knew lay in my past that I loved.

"You are a person," I said, because I had to say it. Even with the evidence before me, or perhaps because of it.

"Rachel, you can't see what I see. I can see *all* the connections," Borne said. "I can see where it's all headed, what it's headed toward. I just haven't been strong enough to see it through. I've lingered and I've delayed. I've thought maybe . . ."

I knew what he'd thought. I'd thought it, too, even after my promise to Wick. Wick was restless behind me. He believed Borne was going to attack us, but we were safe. We had always been safe, even if no one else had been.

"Do as I said and hide," I said. "Find a place. Disguise yourself."

But Borne had other ideas.

"Rachel, what happens when we die? Where do we go?"

"Borne—"

"*Where*, Rachel?"

"Nowhere, Borne. We go into the ground and we don't come back out."

"I don't think that's true, Rachel. I think we go somewhere. Not to heaven or to hell, but we go somewhere. I know we must go somewhere."

"Borne, why?"

"Because I came to you to say that I know how to make everything right again. I can see it so clearly, and I can do it now. I can do it. I'll make things right. You'll see—and you'll know I was telling the truth."

Just an infinitesimal pause then, and if I hadn't known him so well, I wouldn't have caught it, or known what it meant.

"And in the end everything will be okay again between us and you can live in the Balcony Cliffs again and I'll move back in with you and it'll be like the times we ran down the corridors laughing, or the time you dressed me up and took me out onto the balcony above the beautiful river. It'll be just like that."

"Borne."

All I could say was his name because I couldn't say anything that really told him how my instincts clashed with my reason. Not in front of Wick. And I thought, too, that Borne was gripped by the false power of remorse, which makes you think that by the strength of your convictions, your emotions, you can make everything right even when you can't. Remorse and a false vision made Borne say these crazy things, I thought.

"Goodbye, Rachel," Borne said.

"Goodbye, Borne."

How I misjudged that moment, and how I regret it. I believed I had to make my heart hard and not give in. I had to stand there and I had to say goodbye and I had to mean it.

"But we will see each other again. I know it," Borne said.

If I could go back, I would give him permission. I would let him leave having given him my approval, having told him I believed him, whether I did or not, to make him feel some form of happiness in his chosen path. Even given him the lie of a happy life in the Balcony Cliffs. I just hope that something in my face, my demeanor, told him that despite what he had done, I could never abandon him completely.

It happened very, very fast, then, with Wick scrambling up beside me in alarm.

Borne retracted and drew up into himself with fantastic speed as streaks of dawn light appeared across a muffled gray sky. For a split second he became thick and formless and dark, and from the thick stout stump that was the clay of him, Borne grew a massive golden-brown head of fur: a bear's head with kind eyes and an almost-smile about the muzzle, the wide pink tongue, so that I knew it was him looking out at me one last time.

Then the eyes grew yellow, carious, and the muzzle longer and sharper, the head bigger, so that Wick and I both retreated into the shadow of the pillar, and beneath the head a body expanded and spread out, vast and powerful, topped by that broad and beautiful head, and on that face for the longest time in the light of sunrise, an expression not of sadness or hatred or horror but of a kind of beatific certainty, an angelic beastliness, and fangs that were clean and white.

The body grew and grew and grew, shooting up toward the sky until the head of Borne as bear was so high above me and the massive, muscled body below it, those hind legs, the feet, wider than the pillar in front of us, and we shrank farther into refuge. The resemblance was uncanny and complete and yet based on absorbed Mord proxies, not Mord, and thus more inhumanly savage than Mord, the body more compact and less shambly than Mord.

This new Mord, new Borne, peered down at us from that great height, growled once, and then lurched off back north, back toward the city, while we sprang out of our sanctuary to watch.

Borne-Mord ran at first like a lizard, then a silverfish, and then staggered as if drunk, a huge swaying wobble that sent up clods of dirt and dust as he adjusted to being a bear. Then he caught himself, righted himself, and became ursine in the churning of his limbs, taking great strides on all fours as he roared out one word:

"Mord! *Mord!*" Calling out his opponent. Committed now. Leaving us behind. Striking out for uncharted territory.

Borne was set on his course and we on ours. There was nothing to say, nothing we could do but pack up our supplies, head south. Nothing I could do but turn away from that horizon, while in that distance biotech traps exploded underfoot, squirting out from beneath Borne's heavy weight, erupting in his wake, in the form of behemoths, leviathans, illusions of life that snapped impotently at the empty air and cast around for flesh to rend, and then fell back down into spasms of their own false dying.

Yet even as Borne receded, I could not help feeling he was still there, beside me, in some form, some disguise as subtle as the molecules of air I breathed.

The morning light revealed that the ridged ground around the pillar was the gouge in the earth created by the Magician's failed missile attack.

Coming off the plain, we spied a single duck with a broken wing near a filthy puddle. It waddled back and forth in front of the puddle, drank from it, stood sentry, drank again, stood silent. Waiting. A kind of mercy that no one had killed it, that it had escaped notice.

We moved on, toward the Company.

HOW WE FARED AT THE HOLDING PONDS

Dead fin and fluttering gill, the tremor disembodied, the slap-crawl of something meant for four legs that had two. Little curling shrimp creatures trapped in puddles that hatched and died, hatched and died perpetual, the same organism over and over, its own procreation. Toxic. A closed vessel. A piece of genetic material dove-tailing, perpetual and never ending, and never really living, either.

Across half the surface of the larger pond, a leaking of blood like a sightless eye, that had no origin, no source, but somewhere down below the blood kept pumping out diseased—drink of it and die—and perhaps it was one of the Company's more diabolical traps. Or perhaps it was beyond their control. No one there to turn it off so it kept spreading and wasn't their problem anymore, or their fault. Who would create such a place?

That was the nature of the holding ponds that abutted both the Company building and the desolate plain, those salt flats that weren't natural at all but ground-up plastic, glass, and metal. The waste produced that they could not burn or chose not to burn. It lay at the bottom of the holding ponds, too. It pushed up against the edges of the Company building like the sticky caviar of some industrial fish. It gushed out around our boots, clung there in clumps. It gave the lakes their color, so they reflected every hue that could be imagined, but, combined, made for us a dark green in a certain light, a pale blue or pink in others. That slight glow reso-nated in the curling wisps of mist that came off the flats, dissipated into nothing long before reaching knee height.

This was pollution and contamination at the source. This was where the biotech had been tossed to die or drown or be eaten by other discarded biotech, or scavenged by vultures or coyotes or people like me, who had the arrogance to think ourselves profes-sional scavengers of living tissue. Down there, too, more dead as-tronauts, a clump of them lashed to the bottom of the smaller pond, their contamination suits still bright orange, little or nothing left of their flesh or bones inside.

I had not hunted here for ages, but I knew the place, had al-ways hated it, found it mournful and diseased and the purest evi-dence of how much the Company must despise us. I did not like being part of its ecology, but I'd had no choice until Mord's rages, his unpredictable stance toward the Company, had made it off-limits. Then the conflict between the Magician and Mord, the Mord proxies, had kept it off-limits.

Wick had not been inside the building since he'd left the Company.

"As nice as you remember?" I asked Wick as we approached.

"Nicer."

It had never been nice, but now the side of the Company building along the length of the two lakes sagged inward and had become fire-blackened, and carrion spackled the white so that what had been pristine had become streaked red, green, and smudged charcoal with white peering through. Now, too, wall shards like thick eggshells, some two stories high, cut the artificial sand where they had fallen from Mord's rippage, some landing in the lakes. Along with the elongated lumps of fused-together helicopter like crumpled black dragonflies: the helicopters sent out to attack Mord. An oddly bloodless tableau, and not a pilot remained inside—not even a scrap of skeleton.

What had been less dealt with was Mord's shit, which lay at the approaches to the Company building in gently sloping piles like badly made bales of hay. It was dried and old and picked clean; thankful we were that Mord rarely came here now.

But we had to find the side door—camouflaged, there but not there, meant to open only to a careful, knowledgeable hand like Wick's. A place half underwater that few used or even knew about. It wouldn't have been possible before Mord ravaged the Company, and might not be possible now, but it was the first place to try.

Worse, there was a bear, and I say worse because at first it had run away from us across the dead plain, looking back over its massive shoulder as if confused as to its purpose.

Should it continue across the plain toward the horrible wonder of Borne-as-Mord, who had now reached a broken cluster of buildings and continued to dominate our line of sight? Or should it pursue us?

It slowed as if encountering a stiff wind. The beast turned, thoughtful, lingered there, then came back toward us, eating up the plains at a gallop. Looking through the binoculars, checking landmarks, estimating speed, I told Wick I couldn't be certain but thought the proxy would reach us in less than ten minutes.

Roughly, if we did not find the door within five minutes, we would have to abandon the attempt and be driven farther south, out into the desert. From there we would have little chance of curling back to the city through the devastated west. We'd join the dance of foxes for a time, out in the dust bowl of the ancient seabed. And then we'd die. Of thirst. Or predators. Or the bear would catch up to us.

In the near distance, the lake and all that tragedy of half-lives, of the mysteries of existence and why we did the things we did, to each other and to animals. And us, struggling through the difficult purchase of the artificial sand that we might make it to the side of the Company building, find a door, get inside before we became a bear's dinner.

In the middle distance, the dead plain and across it, the bear closing in, and then the living blot marks of bobbing, lumbering bears that had been drawn to Borne, stragglers who were still behind him in his disguise, but not very far. Some would succumb to the last of the buried biotech that had risen; those defenses appeared like smoke, like emerald-and-azure dust with purpose. Shimmering displays that disappeared into the wind at a thin angle, then reappeared as sheets of undulating microorganisms. We had seen a bear caught in that net buckle and fall, spasming, jaws spread wide, as if it could not breathe. But then the net broke, the bear rose, the old defenses revealed as ghosts, the Company without dominion.

In the far distance, things began to occur that we could not quite believe but could with the binoculars see well enough. Perhaps it was a mirage. Perhaps we thought it shouldn't be a thing you could glimpse in daylight, but for a long time we tried to deny it.

Wick laughed at the sight, and the sheer ridiculous intensity of the venomous bear approaching fast, the diaphanous beauty of the biotech over the plains. It did not go unnoticed between us, the irony of that—or that to escape the lesser threat we must take the greater risk. The oppression of that was like a heat on our necks, a knife at our throats. We had lost the Balcony Cliffs. We had given up our temporary shelter. We'd lost the city proper. And now we were about to lose the surface. Apparently we'd been richer than we thought, to suffer such continual diminishment and still be alive.

But what was endurance and shared diminishment if not devotion? For there was the care with which Wick guided me across the shallow part of the sand bridge between the two holding ponds, the ground-up shoals of refuse, the rotted plank some clever soul had laid down in shallow water, the uncertain route to the edge of sanctuary.

There was hope in that gesture, and a letter in my jacket pocket.

Funny what you remember and what you don't. I remember how the wet sand was engulfing my feet like it wanted to suck us under and I remember the unhinged look on the bear's face, the almost human disregard for its own safety as it careened through the sand at the far edge of the first holding pond, snarling with each step. I remember what Wick was saying but not why he was saying it, and I was caught in amber or was a ghost again. I was watching the bear as if transfixed by the sight of my own death approaching. All I could do was stand there, hoping a side door would open.

The bear bounding, full of life, full of fire, and us, alone and small, so small, next to it. And something true about that, something I couldn't quite see.

While down in the holding pond, almost at our feet, a large brown boulder down in the depths beneath the dead astronauts, covered with dead reeds, began to reveal itself, as huge bubbles quaked on the surface.

Wick found the door.

The door was jammed shut.

The door wouldn't save us.

The bear was almost there.

But there was a crack in the wall nearby. A crack big enough to form a passageway. A crack big enough for us but not for a bear.

It wasn't a dream. It wasn't a nightmare. This was the thing happening to us. I remember how tired we were, from lack of sleep and fatigue and rationing our water. We weren't prepared, not fit, not ready to meet our deaths with furious, desperate resistance. There were the pools we'd scavenged from and the Mord proxy rampaging toward us—and us clinging to the strip of land more like wet and porous sand, stuck between a bear and a crack in the wall. Bear or a crack, a seam.

We still had time. I thought we had time.

The Mord proxy's mask of anger and hatred and bloodlust, and maybe I had no argument with that. Maybe there was no real answer to that. But I was human, and I'd rather die lost in the dark than with my neck ripped open, face bitten off, entrails falling out.

The hidden bear, the one waiting for us, erupted from the holding pond as I grabbed Wick and pulled him into the crack with me, pulled Wick into that tiny chance at salvation—and that bear, silent in its intent, slammed into the wall outside, the impact so great dust welled up and the water from the bear's fur lashed me with wet, dirty drops.

Wick was inside the building. I could see that he was inside the building with me. But a rush of brown fur eclipsed the opening, the light, and there came a blast of carrion stench, and I knew it wasn't far enough. It wasn't far enough.

The static cry from Wick, the narrow stomach-churning claustrophobia as I ripped my way farther in, rough, raw rock against my cheek, Wick screaming, the bear swiping at him.

I grabbed Wick with one arm painful around his waist, and I wrenched him on top of me, and he stumbled, and fell backward into the crack and the great bear's claws swiped down and Wick shrieked again and then we were on the floor, pushing off blindly into the greater darkness.

I barely fit, my butt against one wall and my hands pushing out in front against the other, and sidling along crablike as fast as I could, so fast I was tearing my clothes, my skin, shoving our pack in front of us with my hand and then, when it fell, lodged below, the roar of the bear so close. The air close and thick, filled with dust and cobwebs.

Wick shoved in beside me, bumped up against me, a fast-shuffling push farther in. I wanted to run, to scramble, desperate to go in deeper, to go in so deep the fangs, the claws could not get at us, but there was no such thing as speed in that place. It was too narrow. You could not run. You could barely sidle.

"Come on, Wick! Faster!" Either I was saying that or I was just screaming or I was silent and focused on trapping myself farther in without tearing up my palms again.

"Pick one thing to concentrate on—the most important thing—and put all the rest aside," my mother was saying. On a ship. In a broken city. Through the long grass as we hid from men with guns.

"Are you hurt?" I was asking Wick. I couldn't see if he was hurt.

"My shoulder," Wick said. "Blood."

Venom.

We were mindless crustaceans dead-alive. Forever reduced to a force that tumbled forward away from the jaws snapping at the entrance. Not even autonomous, butting my pack with the top of my head to move it forward, it a terrible obstacle and behind us the sounds of the bear frantically tearing at the walls, pulling chunks away and scrabbling at the widening space while "Drrk! Drrk!" rattled around our skulls and sailed over us and rumbled from on ahead to put fresh fear in our reptile brains about phantom bears awaiting us.

Wick had gone silent and limp, and I didn't know if that meant he was dead or unconscious, but with a gasping lurch he reanimated and I think that meant his last diagnostic worm had done something to stop the bleeding. I reversed myself enough in that tight space to look back with Wick now inching right into me, up my body, about to crawl over me if I didn't inch forward, too, which I did. I could see in the light not taken from us by the bear's silhouette that Wick's shoulder had been shredded by the swipe: four claw marks stretched across, tearing away the fabric there, the welling of blood slower than it might have been, unable to see in that dim light how deep or shallow the damage might be. How seeded with dirt and the dead flesh of other prey.

The claws carried the same venom as the bite, but not every bear had venom. I could see that the last worm had died, forming a flowing white fringe around the wound. Had it died from encountering the venom or because it was weak and Wick had put too great a strain on its capacity?

The bear had ceased its demolition of the wall. The murderous eye held to the widened crack to pin us with its stare. Bloodshot, self-aware, taking our measure. I couldn't look away, even as I kept sidling, contorted. "Drrrk. Drrrk," and a kind of snarling sneer.

Then the eye was gone and the shadow of the bear's great weight removed itself from the crack.

Wick had regained his senses, come to rest there halfway across my lap, and I had stanched the last bleeding with a piece of cloth torn from the end of my undershirt.

"Fast," he said. "They are so fast."

"You're hurt. We need to get to someplace secure."

"Venom," Wick said, echoing my concern.

"You don't know that."

"I can feel it. The worm knew it. The worm always knows it," he said.

"You can survive the venom." People did. People had been known to. But not people already sick. Not people who had already gone through so much.

We were only twenty or thirty feet inside the passageway.

The bear had disappeared altogether. We could hear no sounds of growling. The strip of sky enticed us, a pure whitish blue. Such a hopeful glare, beckoning to us.

"I don't think he's gone," I said. "And I think there's a second one now."

"Throw a pebble," Wick said. "I can't."

But neither could I—even after eight tries in that cramped space, because I had to throw underhand. On the ninth try, the pebble flew true, and nothing swatted it from its trajectory. Nothing came roaring back to snuff out the light.

"The bears are still there," Wick said.

"How do you know?"

"I don't, but we can't risk it."

"This passageway is deeper than I thought," I admitted.

"What if it dead-ends?"

"We come back. Risk it. But you're hurt."

"I can get up. I can walk." Although "walk" was a laughable proposition in that fissure, that fault line.

"Crack of light or crack of darkness?" I asked.

"You build traps," Wick said. "What do you recommend?"

"That we wake up from this bad dream."

Wick laughed. It was the sound of a man resigned to whatever might come.

"Dark crack, then."

"Passageway."

"Crack."

"Crack-passage, because if I die I don't want my last words to be wasted on an argument about this."

Neither of us for a moment thought that hint of blue sky came without great cost.

Nor could we forget what we had seen in the far distance as we escaped the bears. For there, wreathed by smoke and fire, lamented by a chorus of distant screams and explosions, two behemoths had battled—mirror images—Mord versus Mord, and no doubt that Mord would win. And no doubt that Mord proxies milling bewildered at their feet must choose a side, and perhaps choose wrong. The two great bears up on their hind legs, grappling, drawing apart, chasing each other, then in reverse, and biting, swiping with massive paws armed with lethal claws, and most deafening even from here were their bellows and roars and exertions.

Borne fought Mord for the control of the city while we took our chances inside the Company building, and we did not know which god would be revealed victorious when we returned once more to the surface.

We headed into the darkness.

It was a miserable passage. The pack continued to be a misery even as we needed it—held out in front until my arm tired, or shoved along in what was like a kind of prison shuffle. The sky went from a thin line to a gray floating fissure and then was gone even as an optical illusion. I did not know how far up the crack extended, had no sense of a ceiling.

A sheen came off of Wick, an unhealthy angry red glow. But even this uncertain light helped me reassure myself by the pattern on the wall that Wick followed—that the slight hand in mine wasn't an illusion, as it sometimes seemed, when my hand went numb.

Sideways we advanced, and if the crack-passage had dead-ended I don't know what we would have done. We might have despaired and given up. At times the crack narrowed so that I was pushing against both walls to progress, afraid I'd get stuck. But it always eased up again, so that what I'd thought before was intolerable and narrow became a gift of generous space.

My eyes adjusted, but there was nothing to see. The walls harbored not a hint of biotech, not even Company moss. This emptiness pressed down on my chest, filled my lungs, and I fought off episodes of a scrabbling panic and nausea, a kind of succumbing to mindlessness that would have been so much easier than this continued condemned shuffle, one-two, one-two, one-two, push the pack, one-two, one-two, one-two, push the pack.

I talked to Wick as we pushed on, to keep his mind off his wound, and he would murmur back or squeeze my hand or make some other signal he had heard me.

"What was I like back then?" I asked him. "When you first met me?" A complicated question.

"Happy, distant, beautiful."

"Not like now. Unhappy. Accessible. Ugly."

"Just like now," Wick said. "Right now."

"I can't feel my hands," I said.

"I can't feel my feet . . . with your hands."

Hysterical laughter. Or just hysteria.

We sang songs. Stupid, ridiculous songs, in our terrible, ragged voices, which we made up on the spot. Or old tunes my parents had known, that I had to teach to Wick.

I told him stories because this made me forget, too, for whole minutes, the truth of our predicament, pushed out against the walls to give us more space. To be truly safe we should have been silent— we did not know what or who could hear us up ahead, or what might follow behind—but to be silent in that darkness seemed the final reduction of self and I would not accept that. I still had a voice. This was not some afterlife. I was not dead. Wick was not dead.

I told tales of improbable scavengers, of the best biotech finds. I told stories my parents had told me about the origins of the world, of how the earth had once been carried on the back of a sea turtle. I told the tale of shark deities and island men and women who became trees or birds to outwit monsters. I told stories of my adventures in the city, even though Wick had heard them all before. And when I faltered, when a gloom overtook me and I needed to stop, Wick would take up for me, in his worn, ethereal voice, telling me a legend about the city or some rumor he'd heard about the Magician or something he remembered about Mord.

We spoke between the deepest breaths we could manage, because the air only became staler and thicker, and we both felt as if it was hard to focus, experienced dizziness, and stumbled in our sideways lurch forward. There came, too, a sense of being trapped in a coffin that was moving with me, and only the scrape of our clothing, a snag of elbow against the walls, would remind me this was untrue.

Then came the moment I couldn't move forward any more, tripped over my pack, stubbed my toe, and came to rest there, legs half bent, hands on my thighs.

"Why have you stopped?" Wick's voice sounded weaker.

I didn't want to tell him. I didn't want him to know. That we'd failed, that we were done, and I didn't think I had the strength to go back. That it seemed as if we were trapped again in the air vent at the Balcony Cliffs, that we'd never escaped and everything else had been a delusion.

"There's a wall in front of me, Wick," I said.

I had wanted to be a ghost once, and now I might get that wish. Except I could feel all too much. I was grimy with sweat and the gravel from the wall and my legs were shaky, my hips so sore.

Wick had felt my trembling for some time, but he remained surprisingly steady.

"Climb," Wick said.

"There's no light up there. No hint of a draft. If we climb and nothing's there . . ."

We would fall, or worse, be embraced by the rock. The walls were so close you couldn't get the proper leverage to shimmy up them. Our effort would exhaust us, wring from our muscles any last effort, and at a certain point we wouldn't be able to control our legs, our arms. Then there would be no calamitous fall. Instead, we would drop in a slow simulation of mortal injury, buffeted and torn by the walls that held us close, lowered us in agony, would not allow us to just fall into the ground, dash out our brains. We would be so weak that even our meager chance of getting back out would become impossible. Who knew how long we would lie broken and dying in the dark?

"Climb," Wick said, and I knew he was admitting to me he didn't have the strength to turn back, either.

So we climbed into the darkness and did not look down because we could never return to *down*, and prayed to whatever gods we didn't believe in that there would be a light above. Any kind of light.

WHAT WE FOUND IN THE WRECKAGE OF THE COMPANY

I had told Wick a lie about Borne early on, because by the time it meant something . . . it didn't matter. This was before I had taken Borne out into the city for the first time. Wick and I had been arguing about whether Borne might be a weapon, and I had told Wick there were no indications that Borne was a weapon. But Borne had *said* that he might be a weapon, in another late-night conversation—the kind I initiated when I couldn't sleep or the kind that woke me up when I could.

Borne had been talking to himself again: "I don't feel like a weapon. I do not look like other weapons. Maybe I was meant to be a weapon, but I came out wrong. I don't even know where the word *weapon* came from. I did not have it before. Weapon weapon weapon. Weapon? Wea-pon. Wea. Pon. Weh. Apon." Digesting the word before it could colonize him.

His eyes morphed to spikes or ridges and he made himself into a miniature green-blue sea spread out across my floor, the ridges frozen waves.

"Rachel," Borne said, "I know you're not asleep."

Of course he knew. My eyes were open and he'd already proven to me more than once that he had preternatural night vision.

"Where did you learn the word *weapon*?" I asked. Borne was used to me asking where he'd learned something, even though he learned many things from me.

"Oh, you know," Borne said. "You know—the usual places."

"The usual places?"

"Here and there, hither and yon."

I decided that line of inquiry was useless because he was reverting to the language of children's books. I sincerely regretted gifting him so many children's books.

"I doubt you're a weapon," I said, drowsy. "You're too silly to be a weapon."

"A weapon can't be silly?"

"No," I confirmed. When I thought about it later, I realized most weapons were silly or silly-looking, just in a different way.

"But what if I am, Rachel?"

"Then I don't know," I said.

"You don't know *what*? How to stop me? If I am a weapon, won't you have to stop me? In the books, they're always stopping weapons."

That felt serious. What books? So I sat up in bed, and I became serious. As much as I influenced Borne, he influenced me, so raising myself up in bed and becoming serious felt like changing my shape and making my eyes different.

"You're being ridiculous," I said. Another trick I had was making Borne focus on key words—vocabulary I had introduced. Usually, Borne would enter a spiral of repeating the word in different contexts. But not this time.

"But how would you stop me?" Borne asked. "How?"

I didn't want to think about that question, not there in my apartment, in bed, right next to Borne.

"How do you stop other weapons?" Borne asked, pressing. "Have you killed people to stop them? How do you do that?"

"Let's assume you're not a weapon," I said. "You're not a weapon but something amazing and wonderful and useful instead. Discover what that amazing thing is, and then try to be that thing."

But I couldn't sleep after that, vaguely worried. Yet what did Borne *know*? We were all weapons of some kind. We were all weaponized in our way.

"Am I a person or a weapon?" Always, he wanted to know that he was a person. He just kept giving me different choices so one time I might slip up and say, "You're not a person."

"You are a person. But like a person, you can be a weapon, too."

Now, as Wick and I made our way up toward what we hoped was the light, I remembered that conversation, and part of hoping there was light was also hoping for what I never would have wished for in the past.

That Borne was a weapon. That no matter what happened to us in that moment of staring into the light, I wanted him not just to be a good weapon but a *great* weapon. The kind of weapon that could defeat Mord.

❖

But there was no light, because we had been stuck in the crack-passage until almost dusk. We found only a hole, as if left over from the Balcony Cliffs, and were glad for it, cackled to find it and the fresh air blowing out tepid there. Cackled and wiped our filthy faces of dirt and cobwebs, pushed up and out with our last strength to lie next to the huge yellowing vertebrae of some dead beast and, on the other side, a white plaster model of a bear's head, which made Wick giggle silently, holding his side.

"Oh, Rachel," he gasped. "Oh, Rachel."

The luxury of such space, of being able to stretch out, to

breathe such new air—it was too much oxygen at once, too much freedom.

We were looking up at a deep blue sky fading into gray, cloudless, with the dead moon coming into focus. There was a thin but pervasive briny stink that even the wind whipping across couldn't quite relieve. The smell came from the leviathan Mord had killed, whose vertebrae snaked through the wreckage around us.

Nothing moved in that place unless touched by the wind. The stillness of everything but us seemed unnatural, and yet nothing jumped out to attack us. It was just an abandoned building and every kind of debris lay around us, from twisted, broken equipment to the remnants of tents and other signs that the Company employees had been like squatters toward the end. All the makeshift last-stand minutia of their days.

What came to us with the wind was the only sound, as if brought to us from the past when Mord had destroyed the Company building. But Mord had moved on to hating Borne. We could hear him roaring, and the roaring of the other behemoth, and underlying one roar anger and underlying the other some sense of bewilderment, as if one participant still did not know the other's true nature. This sound—clear, distant, insistent—came from the north, and by this sign we knew that Mord and Borne still fought.

While we two sacks of flesh lived amid the damage Mord had inflicted on the Company. We were both so covered in grime that Wick looked to me like some cave creature exhumed and brought to the surface not after a day but after years and years. If Mord had still flown, could have observed from above, he would have seen two tiny scraps of meat not worth the effort of killing, lying amid a vast sea of upheaval and disorder bounded by walls that still stood high enough to block us from seeing out. Scraps of meat so delighted with our survival, so deliriously happy in our weakness.

But Wick was weaker than me. Every muscle in my body might

quiver and tingle, my side and back aflame from the friction with the crack-passage wall, but I hadn't been mauled by a bear.

I propped Wick up against that mighty vertebrae, rummaged through the pack for whatever aid I could find. Bandages, a pain-killer in pill form, some disinfectant.

"How do you feel?" I asked.

"Fine," he said, his voice a rasp pulled along a silver thread. "I'm fine."

But he wasn't fine. His hands trembled and his face had a look hooded by shadow that didn't come from dust, and neither did the yellowish cast under his eyes. The claw marks across his shoulder formed bloated gouges scabbing over but ripe. They bulged as if about to burst. I would have to clean the wounds and dress them, even if I couldn't take the poison from his system.

"This will hurt," I said—pointlessly from the way Wick looked at me. Good. He was alert enough to be annoyed.

Nor did he cry out as I did what I had to, even though I was ripping at his skin, then pouring fire over it, then wrapping up his shoulder, although not too tight so the skin wouldn't stick to the bandage. We did not speak about what the wound meant, the pos-sible phases of the venom working through him.

I gave him a sip of water from our canteen, took some myself, and we sat there for a long moment against the backbone of Mord's fallen enemy. I was too tired to interpret the stillness in any other way than that we were safe for the moment. But if I hadn't just come out of a crack in the floor, a place I'd expected to die in, I might have realized the stillness indicated control. The lack of scavengers indicated control. Someone or something ruled this place, despite the sense of abandonment.

"Do you know where to go from here?" I asked. We had no choice but to plunge on if we were able. My hope now was to find not just Wick's medicine here but something for the venom.

"Yes," Wick said. "If the door hasn't been buried beneath leviathan bones or girders."

There came again a hint of the bellowing from the city, the impression through the loud whisper of powerful voices that the outcome lay in doubt.

"Whenever you are able," I said, even though the idea of getting up was like reaching for a land remote and mythical while lying in quicksand.

"Now," Wick said, and, gritting his teeth, steadied himself with one hand on the ground and stood.

I followed, felt dizzy, almost fainted, recovered, the pack swaying like a heavy pendulum from my hand. Wick grabbed my wrist, pulled me the rest of the way up, wincing from the effort.

"We're almost there," he said. "I know the door will still be there."

All of our words, everything we said to each other in that place, was so functional, as if it was too late when you came this close to death, to an ending. That anything else we could have said to each other had needed to have been said in the past, before we knew the future.

We found so many signs of abandonment as Wick led me across that broken maze, those puzzle pieces of ripped-out walls and long-forgotten desks stacked like firewood, the spine and skeletal limbs of the leviathan lying over the top like an impotent guardian. The impromptu mounds of papers, covered in ash. The little tents dotting that landscape, with evidence of campfires nearby, and always centered around abandoned laboratories, open to the air, often crushed but with what lay around them undamaged as if Mord had wanted to pay them special attention. Every so often: the husks of dead bodies, under beams or just huddled in corners.

This place had been dysfunctional and half destroyed long before Mord had ripped the roof off. Not so much civil war between factions as a rising chaos.

Most unnerving: bears, everywhere. Photos and pictures of bears, ripped, water-worn, tacked to walls. Crude sculptures of bears, the busts of bears. Bears running, walking, on their haunches, diagrams of bears clearly meant to feed into creating the Mord proxies, all of them thankfully fading into shadow and gloom as night passed its dark hand over us. The extent to which the surviving Company employees had joined the cult of Mord was apparent—or the depths of their need to solve a problem that had no solution. They'd labored here using what knowledge they had left to serve Mord, desperate to serve Mord, and in the end he'd destroyed them anyway.

◘

In the end, too, there was no magic door, and seeking the lower levels was like being drunk on weakness and sickness and injury and holding each other up just long enough to keep on searching through collapsed ceilings and unstable supporting walls and all the choking dust, less and less concerned when we found yet another corpse.

For Wick it was like a homecoming to a place he had wanted to see destroyed—but only by him. That anyone else had destroyed it was intolerable, and I only cheered on this emotion in Wick because it lit a fire under him, made him burn purer, cleaner, for a while.

We went through the stages now of both our search and Wick coming to terms with the wreckage of the Company building. That the place he had been estranged from no longer existed as it had in his imagination, that the people who had lived so large in his mind had probably been dead for years. Lapsing into being mere employee once again, as if a place made the man instead of the man his place.

As we wandered purposeful, this realization that nothing was as he had hoped for fueled his search, which became a search for the familiar, for the thing changed from when he knew it. While the other knowledge, of passing time, of a clock ticking, came to us through Borne—Borne versus Mord, and how I knew that might make everything else meaningless, even as I helped Wick descend deeper into an unmoving, uncaring maelstrom of junk, of the useless and the mysterious and sad. Soon, we would no longer hear Mord's roaring, even faint, and we wouldn't know if it was because we'd buried ourselves too deep or because Mord had won.

"This was never here," Wick muttered. "Why did they do that?"

"This would have been useless," Wick ranted. "If they ate that instead of using it, they would have been better off!"

"Didn't they know such a barricade would not hold?"

Wick, teetering on the edge of being old, me getting a glimpse of a future him still trapped in the past. Neither of us had control over our monsters anymore.

When that time came, when we reached some threshold—some equation created by the haphazard combinations of girders, walls, collapse, some multiplication of wood or metal or plastic— Wick stopped walking, looked around as if he'd heard a sound. But it was the sound of something having been taken away. Mord and Borne fought on, or they didn't. But we could no longer hear them.

Losing that sound made Wick lose that burst of energy needed to complain, to heckle the ruins, and without my clock I was left only with the continued impression of someone or something watching from some hidden vantage. A wearying prickling of my senses, forever on alert. But Wick no longer cared, or under the venom's spell had lost that ability, and I had to tell him more than once to be quieter, to be slow not fast so we wouldn't stumble, our passage an echoing racket.

"It's near, it's near," Wick said a few minutes later, on the scent. At least he had that much left.

We reached the bottom of the collapse. When I looked up I could see a thickness, a depth to the maelstrom above us, which from that angle resembled a latticework created by a hurricane or earthquake. We had descended a tornado of debris. I can't say I liked the idea of climbing back up that artificial ravine, but then I didn't know if we'd get the chance.

Then Wick was banging his fist on a ruptured door, which led to a stairwell filled in with rubble, and slapping the sides, bashing his forehead into the doorway. I had to stop him, hold down his grasping, scrabbling hands without hurting his shoulder.

"What, Wick? What?"

Wick was burning up—I could feel his fever through his palms, and he was sweating, and his eyes had recessed farther into his sockets and I could see a light deep in those eyes like points of deep red flame—intense, alive, but much too bright. His gaze was too fixed, and I wondered if he was losing his ability to see. The atrophied worm stitched into his shoulder had gone from bone-white to black and begun to liquefy into an oily substance that stained his shirt. He stank of that oil.

"This was the place, Rachel," Wick said, a terrible panic in his voice. "This place. It was down there. But Mord's sealed it off. Mord's sealed it off so we can't get to it. He hates me. He wants to kill me. He wants to kill me. He wants to kill me."

Wick, delirious. Wick, head full of cotton and razor blades, speaking to me from the bottom of an old well. Imagining Mord taking a personal interest where nothing personal lurked. Peering down into that closed-off chasm, all I saw was a space too dark and cool and dusty.

"Listen to me, Wick," I said. "Mord didn't do that. Mord couldn't have done that. It's too precise and old. This doorway was blocked off a while back." With too much intent.

Wick slumped against the wall, head bowed, surrounded by all that useless salvage. "It doesn't make any difference."

I could see in the far-off flicker in his eyes the loss, the utter despair, at the idea of climbing back up, clawing our way through the crack-passage back to the holding ponds. He'd never make it in his condition. I didn't know if I could, either.

I splashed water in his face, even though we had so little. I made him take a sip from the canteen, open and eat an entire food packet, although only some of it stayed down.

Then I left him there, protecting our pack, looking emaciated and old, with the shadow of a beard. He was staring off into space as if he needed to not be in the world for a time.

While I looked for another way in. Because if the stairwell collapse was old, then perhaps with the shift of everything else, the piling on of catastrophe, some other entry point existed, might be revealed with a thorough search.

I pulled away a table from the wall. Nothing. I peeked in the space between a wall and a broken column that must have plummeted here from a higher level. Again, nothing.

Over and over again, nothing.

Wick ever more distant.

I thought of Borne, hiding things in closets. I ticked through

Wick's own hiding places, my preferences when I had to disguise some good salvage out in the field because it was too big to bring back without Wick's help. I came up with nothing.

"Wick," I muttered, "you have to come out of it. You have to help me here."

Then I noticed the head of a fox staring out at me from about twenty feet away, protruding from the wall as if a trophy. First thought: The fox is ghosting through the wall, the fox is uncanny. I'm dying. This is a hallucination. There will be a white light soon, following behind.

But then I realized I was looking at the fox peering out of a hole in the wall, and not so much the confirmation of fresh air below as air being pulled into that hole, and after the crack-passage, that hole would be more than sufficient . . . if it led the same place as the stairs.

The fox disappeared. But we would be going down into her den. We would be following those teeth, those jaws, that bright, animal-wary stare.

I considered that a moment.

"Wick—come over here. Bring the pack," I said.

No response. He wasn't far, but he'd sagged, as if sleeping, and when I went over I found he was barely conscious. Somehow I got him awake again, if delirious, made it clear we needed to go down into that hole. I told myself the nod he gave me meant he thought the hole might indeed lead to the same place as the stairs. I had a sick feeling in my stomach that wasn't just hunger. Because I couldn't know for sure. Because I don't think Wick would have known if fully alert.

But we weren't going to climb back up. We weren't going to stay where we were and wait to die. If I left Wick behind to explore, I couldn't be sure I would make it back up. If I left Wick behind, I might never see him again, and he might die alone.

"Wick, you understand, don't you?" I was just speaking to reassure myself. "We have no real choice. I know you're sick, but stay with me." Stay with me, Wick, a little longer.

Wick had to go first or I couldn't nudge him awake or push him forward if he became comatose. The pack had to go in front of both of us given the tight fit.

If we plummeted to the center of the earth, that might take care of all of our problems.

WHAT LAY WITHIN THE COMPANY BUILDING

We found the seventh level. The hole did lead there. We snuck in like mice, but in the dust the tracks of so many animals I would have guessed a menagerie or army had passed through there. Clandestine or not, that tunnel had been in use, but I saw no sign of the fox. We came out into a wide, high, featureless space with the blocked-off entrance behind us and an archway ahead leading to a warren of passageways and rooms.

A sense of abandonment infected the corridor, the archway, even as a faint white glow from the walls hinted at an illumination via microorganisms that had faded over the years. An antiseptic smell had faded, too, or been driven out by the musty-sharp scent of animal fur. The place had a sense to it of something about to reanimate but stuck—that it would never quite come back to life. Yet there was also a kind of thrum or hum or subtle fracture-like vibration in the background.

The room Wick hoped would help—with its stores of medicine—was only a corridor and a corner away. I propped Wick opposite the exit hole and followed his directions through the archway to the infirmary . . . only to find it ransacked. We had gotten there late. Whatever could be carted away had been taken—medical instruments, fixtures, chairs, even the tabletops.

But I was thorough. In a forgotten corner, I found four of the nautilus pills. They looked old and shriveled. I gently picked them up with shaking hands and dusted them off. As ever, we would limp along, we would endure but not thrive, but I was grateful for that small mercy. One per month. I had bought Wick four months, maybe five, if he survived the venom. I took them along with the other dregs, just in case Wick could use them, too.

I was only gone twenty minutes. When I returned, Wick still lay there. I got down on a knee and made him take the nautilus pill, which he reached for with gratitude, awareness, drawing in a deep breath.

"It's still down here. It's all still down here," he said, wheezing.

"But someone plugged up that stairwell for a reason," I said. That lost doorway, from this side, looked sealed with cement or stone. Someone had done a thorough job.

"Did they?"

Either he'd reclaimed a piece of his former self from the medicine or was more lucid because he had finally found an undamaged part of the Company, a place he recognized as home.

"Is there anything else down here, Wick?" I asked. "Something I should know about?"

"No," Wick said. "Take as many supplies as we can and leave."

But that's when I saw it—in the light. Over the animal tracks, over my boot prints and Wick's, in that same dust, another pair of boot tracks. And no one else there with us in the corridor.

"Who was here while I was gone, Wick?"

"No one."

"No one?"

"I didn't see anyone."

"Did you hear anyone?"

Wick shook his head.

There had been the sense of the level all around us as a vacuum bubble—no sound, so still and silent—and I had been lulled by the sudden generosity of air and space. But that feeling was gone now.

I had only a knife on me. We had a desperate need for more supplies—food, water, anything the place could offer. I couldn't take Wick with me, would be unable to drag him back to the hole if he lapsed again; he still had bear venom in him.

And I knew this place, I realized as I ventured farther. I'd walked these halls before—and I told myself it was because of the Balcony Cliffs. The way that Wick, due to some hidden impulse or nostalgia, had mapped our excavations of the Balcony Cliffs almost one-to-one to this level of the Company building.

Maybe I would never get to the bottom of Wick's secrets.

I left Wick the knife. I brought him to the infirmary, hid him in a corner so he couldn't be seen from the doorway. I put the pack beside him, made him put the remaining nautilus pills in his shirt pocket.

I told Wick I would return soon, and I went exploring. I went to see what that place's version of the swimming pool might look like. Would it be disgusting? But mostly I was following the boot prints in the places where the dust revealed them and the light caught on their tread. I didn't know if it was the right decision, but it was my decision.

As I went, I picked up the audience I had expected when I had gone to the infirmary. With each room I passed or looked into, I saw further evidence of their plans and their dominion. With each room, more of their furtive steps joined me. Two, then three, then six, keeping pace beside me, looking up at me in an unnerving way: the little fox that had followed Borne, or its twin. Mouth open, eyes glittering. And her companions, some of them in the guise of foxes and some not. All of these shadows in that shadowed land, and me feeling lucky I was just passing through. That they let me.

I slipped through those hallways as easily as they did—like I belonged or like I'd been here before.

But I couldn't have been here before, could I?

◻

I found her in what I will call the Hall of Mirrors. In another life, it would have held Wick's swimming pool, with all that fecundity of created life. Instead, there was just an artificial cavern almost like an amphitheater, with a dull metal floor and stone walls and a rounded ceiling that disappeared into murky heights.

At the far end: the half-light from a silvery wall. Alongside the wall a track for some kind of vehicle had been pried up and stacked to the side while in front lay a chaotic pile of upended plastic crates that had spilled open. Like everything on that level, the Hall of Mirrors had a smoothed-out feel, a generic quality as if all had been built out of a kit. How many other Halls existed in different Company facilities?

Off to the left side stood the Magician, contemplating that vision.

I teetered between fight and flight, managed to quell both instincts.

"Hello, Rachel," she said, not turning around.

I would never know if she meant to make herself visible to me or had no choice because her camouflage was dying. What had clothed her from the top of her head to the bottoms of her feet now lingered and leaked as a kind of living cloak. It shared attributes with moths and chameleons and bird feathers. It whirred and sighed and clicked there on the Magician's back, kept shifting and fluttering in a nervous way. It looked ragged and old and failing.

I stepped closer, but not too close, my boots clacking on the metal floor.

"Don't you speak anymore?" the Magician asked, with a familiar note of imperious irritation. "Don't you want to say something? Ask what this thing is, for example?" Gesturing at the silver wall.

I didn't want to look at the wall. I was afraid if I did, I'd lose sight of the Magician. I stepped closer, but still not too close. I could feel the lines of power, the traps waiting for me here, waiting for her here. I was well aware of the creatures at my back.

Slowly my eyes adjusted to the peculiar quality of that light and to the Magician's darkness. She stood straight as ever, but she looked rough, and there were smudges on the side of her face and her hair was wild. I wondered if she held herself so still because she was injured and didn't want me to know.

"I saw you on the plain," I said. "I saw you fighting off a Mord proxy. You probably injured your cloak then."

"They have it in their furry heads I took away Mord's wings," the Magician said.

"Didn't you?"

The Magician shrugged, weary, but with satisfaction in her voice. "Maybe Mord just didn't want to fly anymore. Maybe he was tired of it."

"You were a fool to attack Mord," I said.

A twisted smile in the gloom, a predatory look. "I almost got away with it. I may still get away with it."

"Yes, it must be going well, your war with the proxies, for you to come all this way in person," I said.

"You sound like someone who doesn't want Mord to die, Rachel."

"How long have you been following us?" I asked.

I didn't care about the answer; I only wanted to know what she planned to do. But I also wanted a little time to think about what I was going to do.

That's when she turned and I saw again her face, but now aged by a decade in just three years—hints of trauma, wear and tear, injuries. She had lost her bearings in some critical way, and I noticed, too, the trembling, the way she clenched her right hand as if making a fist against the pain. She was on the run—I knew the look by then. The Mord proxies had flushed her out around the time they'd attacked the Balcony Cliffs, I guessed, and things hadn't gone well for her.

"Long enough," she said. "Since the cistern, let's say. Since I gave the bears your scent over at the Balcony Cliffs, let's say. But that's not important. This," she pointed at the silver wall, "is very important, however. Something fabled, something precious, a thing they never talk about in the city, because they barely talked about it inside the Company."

I saw that with her other hand she clutched something like a wireless control panel. She pushed a button.

"So few memories that told me about this place," she said. "But still the hint. The hint of it was enough to want it to be real."

The wall of silver became a river of silver raindrops and then a frozen scene so real I couldn't accept I was looking at a kind of screen. It was like the holograms in the fancy restaurant from so long ago. But frozen on one scene, and one scene only.

"I have to hand it to your Wick," the Magician said. "He kept this from me, and I didn't think he'd have the nerve. Or that he'd know about it in the first place. I wonder if he kept it from you as well. Do you know how much he has kept from you, Rachel?"

The little foxes and their kin were slinking all around us by now and winking in and out of view as if slipping into and out of space, of time. She couldn't see that she was surrounded by a congregation, that she was surrounded by people, of a kind. I had almost missed it myself, had misunderstood for too long.

The Magician pointed to the screen again. "That's where it all went. What it was all for. They sent supplies through to us. They took and took from the city, and we sent products back. Not through a railway system or an underground tunnel but through *that*."

It was a pretty-enough scene, from a place undamaged by war, untouched by ruination by the Company. It kept flickering, stayed frozen but never came back into focus. But I could tell it was whole and functional and rich, and all of the other things our city was not and might never be. But it also wasn't real, and it wasn't going to save us. Any of us. And I refused to give it agency, allow it into my reality.

"Things haven't gone into it for a few years," the Magician said. "By the time I realized it might exist, this level was just a myth, a rumor. And might as well be now. Although they kept sending things through to us for a while, didn't they? Like those"— gesturing at the boxes, what had dribbled out of them.

I didn't think the Magician had peered into the other rooms. She hadn't seen even the little I'd seen, what else the fox and her companions had ransacked, brought out into the city or remade as their own. If she had seen all the tunnels dug into this level, from the base of walls, from ceilings, she had ignored that, too. Ways in too small for a human being but not for other beings.

"I used to dream that this was real," the Magician said. "I used to dream it was real and I would be able to pass through to the other side. But there is no other side now. What a terrible pity. I could have done even more over *there*. Still, studying it may be of some use."

No, the Magician had come right here. This was the treasure for her. She wanted another chance at resurrection, she wanted another chance. And that took more biotech, and here we were, standing in a cavern on a level that, even stripped of most things, still contained enough treasures for someone like the Magician to start over. With a little help.

"Who knows what will happen out in the city, Rachel," the Magician said. "No one can know what we'll return to. But I *know* you, Rachel. I know your life. We could make common cause. You could help me. I can protect you. I can make sure you want for nothing. You deserve that for leading me here."

Would she next ask me to abandon Wick? Was she that desperate? I couldn't tell you. She stood there before me in her tattered cloak and asked me to join the same cause that destroyed children, that experimented on children, and told the world that there was a good reason, the way the world always wanted to be reassured, because that was the easier path. And the terrible thing is that it wasn't such a bad choice for me, looking at it with the eyes of a scavenger, a cutthroat. It was what had gained her so much power— providing security, food, territory. It had made her a leader, no matter what you thought of who she led and how. No matter that she was on the run—she was still alive.

"And I could tell you much more about your past, Rachel, than you even know. Those blank spaces, what you don't know. I know what they should contain."

What would you have done, reader, who has been able to follow me like the Magician followed me, invisible and ever-watchful and without consequence?

✷

It is hard to explain how much I hated the Company when I saw that place with the frozen mirror. My hatred had grown all through the journey and Wick's faltering, and how he still paid fealty in his way. Now it had become like my own fear within me, or like a wave that kept running through me as if for the first time, with the intensity of the first time.

They had made us dependent on them. They had experimented on us. They had taken away our ability to govern ourselves. They had sent out to keep order a horrific judge grown ever more unmanageable and psychotic. They had dehumanized Wick. They had, in their way, created the Magician, because everything she did and everything she created was in opposition to the Company in some way. And, in the end, the remnants of the Company had walled themselves off from us when they were done with us, when it became too dangerous, leaving only remnants to fend for themselves and negotiate with Mord an increasingly dangerous and impossible cease-fire, one that would never hold.

All I would ever know of the heart of them was this fading, injustice of a place. Was it somehow the future exploiting the past, or the past exploiting the future? Was that mirror scene from some other, thriving part of the world? Was it another version of Earth? I don't know. All I know, or believe, is that it was a door to elsewhere—that the Company had come from some other place and been formed and deformed by it, and yet would always be embedded in *our* deepest history, against our will. Long after Mord died or was finally defeated. Long after I was ash or rotting meat or buried in one of the Magician's graves.

We were on our own. We had always been on our own. We had no recourse, and I cannot tell you how much some part of me had wished to not be on my own, had hoped there would be some person, someone, down in the depths of the Company who would have an answer, who still existed to explain it all, and who, if we asked them to, pleaded with them, would pull a lever or push a button to fix our situation, reset it, and bring forth everything afresh.

But there wasn't. There was only, after a time, the recognition that the Magician still stood beside me, that we were standing there, among all the animals that had gotten in through the cracks, had dug their way in, had come back into the place that had created their destroyed and destructible lives. The rats in the walls, who were in the process of rewiring everything, changing everything. They were the future, but the Magician hadn't realized it. She thought she was the future.

The cascading silver wall, this door that only worked one way, showed an enticing snow globe of a scene by a mighty river, with docks and piers and a dazzling blue sky with birds frozen in mid-flight amid the first signs of spring and bright, modern buildings on the land beyond that had never suffered war. A scene that would fill anyone from our ruined city with such yearning and, perhaps, recognition.

It was so obvious a trap.

The Magician was still talking. The Magician in that cavern was still trying to tell me things. Why I should join her. What this all meant. How the city could be saved from itself.

But I heard no more from her. I hit the Magician with a rock until she was dead, and the animals did nothing to stop me. Perhaps they would have done it themselves if I hadn't. But I did. There was no future for the city with the Magician still in it. I may have been at my limits when I decided that, but my mind was clear.

Funny, how the Magician thought she knew me, how careless she was around me because of that. But she didn't know me. She didn't know me at all, no matter how much she knew about me.

And she couldn't know one other secret: I had already read Wick's letter, so, really, you could say the Magician never had a chance.

But there was more than even Wick knew, and one thing he still hid from me, despite his letter. Wick had come here for a cure, for medicine. The Magician had come here for biotech, to once more launch herself into the ambition of ruling the city. And I had been here as Wick's ghost, the person who haunted him every day of his life.

We had all been too small in our thoughts, too small to realize what might be revealed to us if we really looked, if we really *saw*.

Those spilled-over crates from the Company contained a variety of items. Restocking of supplies to reassure the remnants. Raw material for creating more biotech to be shipped back. Food packets. Dead embryos to seed the city with more alcohol minnows.

But the last shipment from the Company had been Borne—many Bornes. Hundreds had spilled out from the containers in front of the slow mirror. Marked as children's toys, but the diagram on the side of the containers did not match what had rolled out of the crates. Borne pods. Dormant, trapped here by whoever among the remnants had had the foresight to close off the level.

Until the animals tunneled in.

After I killed the Magician as the fox watched and did nothing, I ran my hands over the delicate mechanism that once controlled the silver wall. There had been no future for the city with the Magician in it. But there also would have been no future if creatures from a secret shipment meant to absorb and "sample" had descended on the city in their hundreds.

Had the Company meant to destroy the city? Wipe it clean? Retrieve with the recon of what was absorbed? If so, it had failed. Everything that had spilled from those crates had been spiked, killed before it could live. There were only a handful that could have gotten out, and that could only have happened if the animals around me had wanted it to happen. If the fox had wanted it to happen. Had they tried more than once? Was Borne the first that had awoke? And had they modified him before setting him free? From what I had seen in the other rooms, the fox and her kind had been changing so very much. Those with hands had been helping those without. A quiet revolution sneaking up on us.

As for what Wick had held back, it was there in the letter to find, I suppose, but also in clues along the way.

Mord showed me what I was.

For in one of the rooms I had found what he had hid so ably and so well, lived with for so long: There was a mound of discarded diagrams and models for biotech. Boxes full of withered-away parts.

Each one had some version of Wick's face. Crushed. Cracked. Discarded. Tossed aside. Abandoned. Discontinued.

Wick had never been a person.

But he had always been a person to me.

WHAT I FOUND IN WICK'S LETTER

Dear Rachel,

I don't know how to write a letter like this one. This is the first letter I have written to anyone.

I told you I am sick, and that is true, but there is another sickness, and that is all the other secrets that lie hidden. One of these secrets you asked me to keep, and others I had to keep. But most of them originate from this fact: The first time you remember meeting me is not the first time we met. You didn't come here from the river.

You didn't come from the north. You came from inside the Company. I found you because you'd come from the Company.

Your parents died soon after you came here. They died in a terrible way and it left such a mark on you. I found you staggering near the holding ponds at the Company building on a day seven years ago, a few months before your memory of meeting me. You were distraught, far gone in your grief, and you hadn't eaten in days.

The holding ponds were a horror show back then, much worse than now. A cynical place that allowed the Company to think of itself as merciful because so much of what it dumped still lived, for a time. This abandonment of experiments occurred at a terrifying pace, and the feeding frenzy of scavengers and animals was murderous.

When I found you, you were walking through scenes of slaughter and desperation—a hell on Earth of Company discards. I don't know how long you would have survived there, how long before someone decided you were biotech, not human at all, and butchered you or captured you or took you and tried to modify you.

You were in shock. Your eyes didn't focus. Your clothing was torn and someone had already taken your shoes off of you.

You said something to me when I came up to you, as if whatever you were thinking you just said. But flat, disengaged, as if you came from another planet.

"You're beautiful. So beautiful. And someone beautiful wouldn't hurt me."

It was nothing like what I thought you would say, nothing like the person you are now, either, and it was the only thing you said for quite some time. I laughed when you said it. It was nonsense. It confirmed your dysfunction, your dislocation. It confirmed you as salvage.

And it wasn't true. I did hurt you, just not by leaving you there, and for a very long time I had no idea why. I could not understand why I saved you. I told myself it was because you were the only thing human in that landscape and I saw you so suddenly. Because I didn't expect you there. Because I didn't expect you to say that. Because, in a way, I had been discarded, too.

But back at the Balcony Cliffs, you did not get better, you did not stop being damaged, because of what had happened to you.

Some people come into the city from inside the Company, not from the outside. At least, they used to. Your parents had come from inside the Company—stowaways in crates, supplies being sent to the city from some other place. If I cannot tell you what that other place might be, it is because no one here in the city knows and most do not guess at its existence.

But if you came in a supply crate, you weren't human by Company rules. Instead, you were parts, or biotech. No exceptions. Just some small mercy that someone wouldn't kill you, a young woman, and they dumped you at the holding ponds instead, to let you die out of their sight.

But your parents died inside the Company building. They were killed coming out of the crates, murdered, and you had witnessed it, seen it all, and then been thrown out into a bloody wasteland at the edge of a city you did not know, that you had never seen before.

You couldn't get your bearings. Your parents had brought you here, so far from any sea, and then been killed in front of you, and it had broken something inside of you that you could not repair.

And one day just a month after I took you in, once you understood what I did, you sought me out and begged me to take your memories. You wanted your memories scattered to the four winds. You wanted them all gone—not buried or repressed or forgotten like a scar, but gone. Every last bit. You wanted to start fresh. "Fill me up with someone else's memories," you said. "I know you care about me, Wick, please do this for me."

It was the first time I had seen any emotion in you.

Because you wanted this, I knew you were out of your mind, but soon enough I also knew if I didn't give you what you wanted that you would find some other way, go to someone else for it, or worse.

You continued to be confusing to me. I had left the Company after the fish project, driven out, tossed to the holding ponds myself. Where they expected me to die, like others before me. Instead I made a life in the city. But I didn't consider myself a person. I didn't make decisions like a person. I felt, after all I had done and endured in the Company, that I didn't deserve that. I felt instead that I was lost and would remain lost and all I could expect was to survive. So I had made decisions like someone who wasn't a person, who just wanted to survive.

Yet I made decisions about you that didn't make sense. I should never have taken you from the holding ponds, never been involved. I should have left you to your fate, whatever that might be. It bothered me that I went through these motions of being a person, of letting you into my life. Only now, I had to cut you from my life if I was to give you what you wanted. You would have no memory of me, or anything in the city. For so many reasons, I told you I wouldn't do it.

Still you persisted—clung to this idea like it was the only thing that could save you, and I think you were wanting to punish yourself. I think you believed you deserved punishment—for being powerless. But you were also traumatized and hurt and lonely and confused. To have gone from the life you were living with your parents to being without them and in this place . . .

So, eventually, I did what you asked . . . or most of it. I took your memories of the city, your parents' death, the time right before. I took all of that away, but I left everything else.

I don't know if it will be harder for you, the Rachel now, to understand why you asked for that obliteration or to understand why I couldn't give you everything you asked for. You hadn't asked me to kill you; you had asked, instead, to become a different person, to be allowed to create a different life, from the ground up. And if I respected you—surely if I loved you—I should have done as you asked.

But the idea of making you less than a person, a cipher, was not possible for me. You could not know that, but it was the thing *least* possible for me. Nor could I imagine, except as atrocity, filling you back up with someone else's memories without your knowledge. So I told myself I would make it up to you, I would find a way, but, really, what I found was a selfishness: a way to still know you even though you no longer knew me.

After, I set you loose again, to be on your own again. Because what did I know about living with a person, being with a person, taking care of a person? Nothing.

When you woke, I had made sure it would be near the poisoned river, beneath the Balcony Cliffs, so I could watch you through my binoculars, make sure you regained consciousness and were still safe. I watched you get up, I watched you walk away.

And I thought that was it—that was the end of it.

But I kept thinking about you, what you were doing, if you felt better now. If what I had done was a good thing or a bad thing, or neither.

I could not help myself. I started to seek you in the city, and when I finally found you, for a time I just observed, thought that might be enough. But then, one day, the meeting you remember: back down by the river, where I sought you out and I lied to you. I pretended I didn't know you, offered you what I could offer.

I asked if you wanted memories of a better time. I could provide those. It's what I did. You said no. If you had said yes, I had resolved to do it, and then walk away and never seek you out again. In a way, you would have gotten what you wanted before.

I could never tell you what I had done. I was too afraid, and then, eventually, too much time had passed. I was living in the center of a lie. Even if, before, we had known each other such a short time, I felt ashamed of using what I knew of you to my advantage. Despite a terrible, unworthy elation beneath: that second chance, that moment, when you had stayed, and then we were partners, fortifying the Balcony Cliffs. Living there.

The Rachel without the Company, without her parents' death, was confused, yes, sad, yes. But you were also more sure of yourself, and you had lost that desperation, that agitation to the eyes that had told me of some deep wound. I began to wonder if I might be capable of being a person after all—there, at the moment of my greatest betrayal.

That is the most ironic thing; that I thought betraying you was a form of being trustworthy, as if the world were upside down.

But that is not the only thing I had done. Before we met again, before you began living again at the Balcony Cliffs, there was something else I never told you.

You wanted oblivion. You wanted not to exist. But there was a price for that. I sold your memories to the Magician. That was my price, the price you agreed to without knowing. The memories from inside the Company. The memories of me. Of your parents' death. How you had gotten to the access point.

The Magician had taken an interest in me, as she did in all creatures of the Company, especially people she had known in the Company. People she thought knew more than she did about the Company. She asked questions. She infiltrated. She discovered the survival of the fish project because I went to the holding ponds and she saw me there.

She used that information to figure out even more.

I did not really care about you when I first saw you. I did not care about you except as salvage. I did not care about anyone. Caring came later. And I didn't see the harm. I didn't think I would ever see you again. I thought the Magician would fade. That she would be one of those who got killed or was never heard from again. Nothing at that time except a certain ruthlessness, a coldness around the eyes, could have told anyone she would rise so far. Not given her opposition to the Company.

But the Magician knew about Mord from her other sources, and she was already using that to blackmail me, to extract. I gave her what I thought compromised me least, and in return she stayed silent and sold me the supplies I needed.

Because, it's true, what she found out: I helped create Mord. The Company used what we had learned from the fish project to build Mord. But the Company wasn't building him from scratch. Not putting a human face on an animal, as happened with the fish. No, they wanted to create an animal around a human being.

Maybe I didn't realize what the Company planned to do to him, but that is no excuse. I should have found a way out, or found a way to get Mord out. Except there was no choice. Not really. I was the one who did that, as the fish project wound down. I made the transition for him when asked to; I held his hand as it began, before he no longer really recognized me. At the start, I don't think he understood what was going to happen.

And then I was gone, discarded by the Company, and I could do nothing for Mord, not even comfort him.

I could not even save the fish—all I could do was put it out of its misery after it languished for a few months in the holding ponds. The only good thing it seemed that I'd done was salvaging you. I knew what you had really asked for, and what I had done, but I thought it would all go away, become nothing, not even history, but it didn't. It couldn't. It only lay submerged for a while.

The Magician had not just the knowledge of my role in creating Mord but then, when I brought you back into the Balcony Cliffs, that further knowledge of your history whenever she needed something. Until she asked for the Balcony Cliffs, and that was too much.

Then came Borne, and I couldn't take Borne from you because I had meddled in your life too much already. You kept asking me if Borne was a person. But I didn't believe I was a person, Rachel. So I couldn't tell you.

Because what you will learn, Rachel, is that I am not what you think I am. I am more like Borne, and every time you told me he was human, I felt less real, and I don't blame you for that, but that's how it is for me, and always will be.

You must understand that I have done nothing that was meant to hurt you. Everything I have done, for many years, has been for you and to keep the Balcony Cliffs safe. Please, I hope you will believe me.

✿

I had read Wick's letter while still in our temporary shelter. I struggled with it every moment of our journey into the Company building. I struggled with it every time I propped Wick up, gave him water, goaded him forward. Every time I looked at Wick, I saw something different, felt something different. He was like a mirror and a window, and the scene kept changing.

When I thought I could be reduced no further, when I thought nothing more could be taken from me, even what seemed to restore something to me became a further reduction. What if I had wanted to be lost? What if my earlier self had been the smartest, the wisest, to want to remove all of that from me? So I could survive. So maybe I could be happy. What if my unhappiness had always been from having remembered happiness?

We always have a choice, even if the choice is amnesia or your own death. But now, too, I finally understood the extent of the weight on Wick. That this was a secret that could kill him in a different way than his sickness. Something that would make many in the city hate him, even want to kill him. Or, among the Mord worshippers, lift him up in a way that would kill him just as surely.

Now I knew why Wick kept trying, forgave so much. Because he felt he had so much to be forgiven for.

But in the end, what it came down to was this: I did not *want* to remember. I did not need to remember. No one was less dead or more alive after Wick's letter. Whatever muddle had lived in my head that Wick hadn't taken away contained at least that knowledge. I had spent years not searching for them but mourning them, keeping their memory alive in my head. I did not want to remember more.

Wick's letter no longer exists. I destroyed it because it was dangerous. But I have not forgotten what he wrote.

There are parts of that letter I will never share with you.

THE WAY BACK AND WHAT I WITNESSED
ON THE HORIZON

The way back was no easier than the way there. The way back was harder, and no getting around that—no truth I learned struggling back, except that life is struggle. It placed me in some gray realm beyond, a landscape of exertion and anguish. I had nothing left to give, and yet still I had something left to give.

The little animals did not help; their purposes were so different from my own. They did not care that Wick was ill or that I was so very tired. They nosed around the Magician's dead body, and licked her hands and her face, and then left her alone and went on with their business. Perhaps she rotted away there, underground.

An attrition of steps I took with Wick, or could not take, in the moment, but had to take soon or the will would be gone. The worst thing was that I could not escape any of the passing seconds. Every moment came to me clear and distinct, and no one moment stood for anything but itself. I felt time ache in my body, in my need to get Wick back to some kind of temporary shelter. To fling myself free of the wreckage. I was thinking about my parents, of all the long, forced marches we had taken, how they'd helped me to endure, and how they'd been brave enough to get me here, and how I couldn't fail.

At a certain point, I could again hear the distant sound of conflict, and although still trapped in the Company building, I knew this meant the battle still raged between Mord and Borne. But when you can't escape the seconds, when you are sure you are going to die before you get free, some things don't mean very much anymore. The sounds I heard came to me through a murky sea of distance and memory.

I brought Wick back through the debris of the Company, up through that artificial tornado of junk and, sliding, torn skin and bruises being the best of me, back through the crack-passage—and even through the choked relief and gasp of our collapse onto the blood sands of the holding ponds, caressed by those shallow, dangerous waters—shambling our way into the light we thought might kill us, only to discover the guards had left their posts—the proxies gone, and on the horizon the mirage for which we had no conception, no compass.

Two great beasts fought amid the burning wreckage of a city. Smashed into each other, withdrew, engaged again—exhausted, exhausting, the brutality. Gray smoke drawn up into the sky to linger around the vultures gliding high above the behemoths' heads like ragged black halos.

Wick had had a relapse in the narrow space of the tunnel, would have fallen, become wedged there, unconscious and barely responsive, if I had not been vigilant—to prop him up, to push him forward, to hold his head when he vomited. The venom had worked deeper into him; his veins stood out black on the surface of his reddish skin, his lips stained black, his breaths shallow and foul. His eyes remained closed, but fluttered. I could feel his eyelids flutter against my fingertips in the darkness, and that is how I knew.

At the holding ponds, I gathered the last of my resolve and, staggering, carried Wick toward the desolate plain that was our reward for surviving this far. Toward a city torn apart by monsters.

There was nothing on that plain, or maybe there was but the sight of Mord doubled had startled them into hiding. We would have been easy prey, and yet, mercifully, nothing approached us. I had taken the Magician's camouflage biotech but could not bring myself to wear what was clearly in distress, placed it gently in the top of my pack before zipping it up. Maybe dangers lurked and waited but I could not see them.

"You're too valuable as salvage to leave behind," I told Wick.

"You're doing fine—you're getting better," I said to Wick.

"You just need to hang on a little longer," I pleaded with Wick.

So light, that body, so pliable, almost collapsible, as if the Company had made him that way, and so weak that I was stronger than him, stronger than I thought, his hands still able to grasp at me, involuntary, instinctual.

"We'll rebuild the Balcony Cliffs," I told him, though he could not hear me. "We'll live there again."

I did not say that thing just to comfort him but to comfort me. I meant it. But only if it was both of us. If it was just me, I would melt into the city. I would disappear and give up my name and my past and any hope of a home, and become no one.

At the edge of the plain, the dark dead forest waiting on the slope, I laid my burden gently on the ground amongst the sparse grass and dropped my pack. Wick's mouth was closed, his eyes were still closed, and he was cold. A terrible sense of drowning closed over me. Had he died as I carried him? Was he dead now?

I could not tell if he had a pulse, with my broken fingers, my hands that shook. There was a resting peace to his features I did not want to interpret. But he could not be dead. I would not let him be dead.

I put water to his lips, then mine. I kissed his filthy face and bathed it. I said his name again and again—and again. I paid no mind to anything but his slack, small body there in the yellowing grass. I could not even shake him or in any other way try to bring him back because I was sure the slightest tremor would do him damage.

I knelt there beside Wick feeling so very light and so very helpless. I was covered in dirt, in blood both mine and not mine. My stomach was a shriveled pebble in my belly, my body so dry I had no tears.

I calmed myself. I stopped the shaking by holding my right

arm in a vise with my left hand and taking Wick's wrist with my right hand—long enough to convince myself I felt a faint pulse of life there, that he would hold on if I just kept going, if I didn't give up on him.

I put my pack back on. I gathered Wick up. I got my legs underneath me, widened my stance, and lifted him.

Together, Wick and I started up the slope.

There comes a moment when you witness events so epic you don't know how to place them in the cosmos or in relation to the normal workings of a day. Worse, when these events recur, at an ever greater magnitude, in a cascade of what you have never seen before and do not know how to classify. Troubling because each time you acclimate, you move on, and, if this continues, there is a mundane grandeur to the scale that renders certain events beyond rebuke or judgment, horror or wonder, or even the grasp of history.

As I carried Wick up the slope, there came a sound from the city, a new sound. It was like the reverse of the sound that had left us when Mord lost the power to fly. A snap that kept snapping, as if it had moved through the ground, like an earthquake but not. A sound that made you look up.

Still far off, but clear above the trees, in the late-morning light, Mord no longer fought Mord. Instead, Mord fought Borne, for Borne had shed his disguise, had abandoned claws and fangs to become even more terrible and complete—like a true god, one who repudiated worship because he had been raised by a scavenger who had never learned religion. The monster I had helped raise fighting the monster Wick had helped create.

Such a shock, to see the fur instantly replaced with the Borne I knew, but much, much larger. A glowing purple vase shape, a silhouette rising that could have been some strange new building

311

but was instead a living creature. Borne was failing as Mord, so now he would try his luck as himself. He rose and rose to a full height a little taller than Mord, the familiar tentacles shooting out, while below, at his base, I knew that he was anchored by cilia now each grown as large as me.

Mord stumbled back, smashing walls of already crumbling buildings, great clouds of dust rising from his surprise. But only for a moment, and when the gouts and storms of dust had settled, I could see that Mord had surged forward to attack newly vulnerable flesh, while the proxies no doubt swarmed Borne's base.

There came from Mord's throat a chuffing roar of purest joy, as if blissful to no longer be fighting himself, to engage with a creature clarified and robbed of disguise.

For the cost to Borne was monumental, no matter how he altered himself, bristling with spikes and ridges—no matter how he battered Mord with tentacles that Mord tore off only for them to return. He could not stop the truest killer of the two—could not stop Mord from ripping into his flesh. Mord dug into Borne, tore off great curving slices, which shivered and quaked as they fell and as Borne screamed—a sound so piercing it buckled my knees on the hillside and I felt a deep fear, a rending, thinking of what should happen if Mord won, if Borne died.

Mord leapt again and again, brought Borne close, paws forcing the neck of Borne down as Borne strobed—as rings of eyes appeared and then disappeared, in his distress. Borne shook and flailed, pried at Mord with his tentacles, but Mord held on, trying to deliver a death bite. Ravaged Borne's throat and tore into him with his claws. Those fangs snapped through Borne with a terrible wrenching and crunching that laid my heart bare. The Mord proxies were dark smudges clambering up Borne's sides while Mord artfully runneled Borne's flesh as if it were wax and Mord's claws were made of flame. More of Borne came away, smashing wetly to the distant ground.

Borne now flailed in that embrace, being broken down in a way I had not known was possible, in a vision becoming so horrific I kept looking away as I stumbled forward with Wick. But it was no use evading. As Borne's life ebbed, I could feel his wounds through the gravity of my own.

Until Borne gave up.

Until Borne understood, I believe, just what he had to do. He would not win. He could not win. Weapon he might be, but Borne was not, in the end, hardened as Mord was hardened; Mord would keep devouring, would keep seeking the snap, the gurgle, the spray of blood that ended his prey, never retreat, never surrender, as if that meant death.

What happened next no one in the city could see all of, but all of us could see part of. Yet, in memory, it is complete.

As Mord feasted on Borne's flesh, Borne changed tactics. Instead of trying to become taller, he spread out, giving away his height, so that Mord was angled into Borne, tunneling through flesh, sloppy with it, seeking the heart of Borne, that he might tear it out and hold it up still beating for the city to see. But Borne kept flattening and widening the aperture at the top of his body until he resembled an enormous passionflower blossom. Complex and beautiful, with many levels.

To Mord it must have resembled surrender, as if Borne was dying and that is why the end came so quick, abrupt. Mord rose up, straight up, higher and higher on his hind legs, and then came down, straight down into Borne . . . but Borne was still opening up and opening up, and so Mord fell straight into Borne and kept falling and falling while the sides of Borne now rose, shot up with an elated speed, and tentacles formed over the top of Mord like bars.

Borne lunged toward the sky, closed like a trap, with the head of Mord still visible at the aperture.

There came a muffled whimpering and screaming, a howling, a roaring, a blustering, a snapping of mighty jaws. Mord punched out from his prison, still ripping through flesh, struggling to get free.

The air seemed to be sucked away, out of the sky, toward Borne. Sound left us.

There came a blinding silver-white light, a radiance that seared out across the landscape in a wave and threw me to the ground, Wick beneath me. A wave of light that emitted no heat. A thunderclap, very close, very loud. A word in my head, I swear, a word, just my name: "Rachel." Which meant something different than it had meant a moment before.

I lay there for a long moment, unsure of what I would see when I rose.

I got up. I looked back across the city. No bodies lay broken and giant across that landscape. No remains. No carcasses for scavengers to feed on.

Both Mord and Borne were gone, as if they had not existed, and the city was still and silent but for the grieving of the proxies and the sinuous smoke that still rose from all that had been destroyed.

But there was no space left in me. I was filled with the grief of that absence, could hardly breathe for it.

He was born, *but I had* borne *him.*

I knew Borne was terrified at the end. I knew that he had suffered, but that he had given us this gift of a better life anyway, and I mourned the child I had known who was kind and sweet and curious, and yet could not stop killing.

There is not much left to tell. So much of the rest is aftermath, the life I lead now.

At the cistern, our temporary shelter, I fed Wick as if he were a rare and fragile hummingbird, as the last of the venom worked its way through his system. I made him drink the water from the well. I dressed his wounds and cleaned them. I talked to him even though he still could not hear me. I held his hand. I kept watch for any enemy, but no enemy came.

As I worked, I told him I loved him, that he was a person. That he was a person. That I loved him. Because I meant it. Because I thought if he didn't hear it he might die, and, later, I might not be able to say it.

We were always finding each other and losing each other and finding each other again, and that was just the way of us. I don't know how else to say it. Perhaps only I could truly make Wick a person, by forgiving him, and if I forgave him, if I showed I forgave him, then maybe I could forgive myself and we could be people together.

Outside, it rained for three days and nights. That would have been strange by itself, an event, but this was no ordinary rain. All manner of creature dropped from the sky or, at the touch of this rain, sprouted up from the ground. Grass grew fast and wild outside the cistern, created paths of green, and on some of the dead blackened trees down the slopes I noticed new leaves. There were on certain avenues in the city, I would learn, new growths of vines and plants that had been gone for years. Birdsong came lyrical through the storms, and animals long-hidden emerged from sanctuary.

But most of it was biotech, uncanny. On the desolate plain the water triggered the last of the traps and up came vast clouds and explosions of life, even eruptions of bees, or things that looked like bees, out of the marsh, taken up by the wind and scattered. Elongated, elastic creatures dug themselves out from long slumber and, suspicious and almost in their stride apologetic, walked bandy-legged away to dig burrows.

At the holding ponds, the waters swelled and overflowed, and all that lay there flooded the Company building, spilled out across the plain, and even now we do not know how much of the new life among us comes from that moment. In the city itself, torrents of alcohol minnows came to slippery, wriggling life, joined by micro-organisms in the rain to populate broken streets and infiltrate cracks and grottoes. There came from across the city, to the astonishment of people used to poverty, such a sense, in that moment . . . of plenty.

On the third day the torrent ended, and the moisture evaporated or disappeared into the ground, and much of the greenery receded and the new animals died or hid or were eaten. To an observer fresh to the city, it might have looked as broken and useless as before. But it was not. Some new things remained, took root, became permanent. Some flourished. The city had been washed as clean as it could be, and what had been taken away was as important as what had been added.

On the fourth day, Wick's eyes opened and they were clear, and clean of pain, and he tottered to his feet, looked around the cistern with a weak smile on his face.

I had kept Wick alive. I had failed at so much else, but I kept Wick alive.

He gave me our last password in those first lucid moments, the word that told me he was real.

"We don't need them anymore," I told him.

A confusion spread across his face, until he understood.

A lesser person than Wick would have surrounded himself

with a fake past, with a personal history, constructed some pretense, handed out lies—or leaned on whatever fake memories the Company had given him. But Wick had not done that. Wick had kept himself apart, had preferred to be alone, to be lonely rather than to be held captive.

"You saved my life," Wick said, and kissed me, and I let him.

That night, we returned home to the Balcony Cliffs to sift through the wreckage and to begin again.

✿

The strange, forgotten animals abandoned by the Company live among us, along with their insatiable curiosity, like Bornes that want nothing from the old world. They need nothing from it. They are their own captains and lead their own lives, although there are still human beings who see them as food, as expendable. In their fearlessness, I find a kind of solace. In how they pursue their own plans, their own destiny, I find relief. They will outstrip all of us in time, and the story of the city will soon be their story, not ours.

The Mord proxies were still a terror for a time, but they had their own terror to face—that their master was dead. Many died within three or four years, and those left were both more dangerous and more civilized. They had their own intricate chirping, huffing language and have begun to develop their own customs. The cubs are far removed already from unthinking violence and act more like bears: wary and clever and more cautious, as if they understand better their place.

The feral children, the ones the Magician created, dissolved into the city. Some were too damaged, and these formed their own outlaw communities, entrenched deep below the factories, and at night the remnants come out to terrorize, to remind us they still exist. But they, too, are much reduced, and they can never again hold territory as they did under the Magician.

Others found their own way out—some could return to families and be forgiven and taken in, despite their physical deformity, despite their psychosis. Others had no such recourse but gave up their old ways and lived in the shadows under bridges and in abandoned buildings. They would never be entirely whole again, and there was nothing anyone could do to remedy that.

But I can stroll down an avenue lined with young trees now, visit a market where people under shelter of makeshift tents barter for goods. I can do that, even if there are still parts of the city I could never visit because too much violence lurks there. At times in the observatory district, we see regular lights, and some are electric, a part of the old world brought back to us. Wells dug or cleaned out, filtered, and communities growing up around them. The planting of vegetables. The rumors of an orchard or two.

There are fewer dead astronauts at the intersections to confuse us. There is only us now, and the monsters, who are both part of history and always with us. In this new-old city, I want no great power, no power at all, only power over my own life. All I wanted is for there to be no great power in the city at all. No Company. No Mord. No Magician. And, in the end, although I loved him, no Borne.

For a time, I saw the little fox outside the Balcony Cliffs. For a time, the fox followed me. The bright eyes, the alert ears, the quick gait. Did you pick me? I would ask her. Did you mean for me to find Borne? Or was it an accident, a mistake, chance? And did you know what might happen when I found him? I never expected an answer, and eventually the fox did not return.

Wick tells me we live in an alternate reality, but I tell him the Company is the alternate reality, was always the alternate reality. The real reality is something we create every moment of every day, that realities spin off from our decisions in every second we're alive.

I tell him the Company is the past preying on the future—that we are the future.

A *glittering reef of stars, spread out phosphorescent, and each one might have life on it, planets revolving around them. There might even be people like us, looking up at the night sky.*

Was there a world beyond? Is that what the shining wall of silver raindrops meant? A gateway? Or is that a delusion?

It doesn't matter. Because now we can make one here.

A world.

HOW I LIVE NOW

The Balcony Cliffs lay empty when we returned. We came in cautious, prepared to drive intruders out, but the bears had left and everyone else had been too scared to move in. The Mord proxies had destroyed so much, but what set us falling to the floor laughing was that at first we could not tell the parts they had destroyed from the parts they had left alone, except by the sign of their droppings. So many holes punched in walls by Borne. Seeing the Balcony Cliffs with fresh eyes, we realized we had lived in a tidied-up shithole that needed a more thorough airing than we had ever given it.

"What now, Rachel?" Wick asked me. "What do we do now?"

"Whatever we want to do," I said.

So we set to work.

Wick has never been the same physically, although he has some good days. The left side of his body has seized up and his left arm doesn't work right. His skin never became pale again but is crisscrossed with black vein lines. He sometimes has a distant look, as if listening to music I cannot hear. But most of the time he is not lost in fugue or memory, or wherever he goes during those episodes. We live, we stand by each other and make do with what we have. He fixed his swimming pool, still makes biotech, found ways to create his medicine before reaching the fourth month and the last nautilus pill.

I never told Wick I killed the Magician—she just never came back. If Wick could carry the heavy burden of his secret for so long, then I could hold on to mine and not burden him with it.

Nor did I tell Wick that I knew his secret, his final secret. We never talked about his letter, although he must know that I read it. To be together, Wick and I needed some secrets from each other, and some things we could not talk about—the talking was the trap. The things we say to each other, thinking they are so important to say, and yet later regret, that become a part of you no matter how hard you push them away, even as you can't stop thinking about them.

I prefer the old betrayals, the ones based on trust. My presence beside him tells him all he needs to know, and no matter what else he has done in his life, Wick has never killed anyone with a rock. Nor does Wick sell memories anymore.

Wick never believed he was a person, was continually being undone by that. Borne was always trying to be a person because I wanted him to be one, because he thought that was right. We all just want to be people, and none of us know what that really means.

Early on, I had thought Wick was reaching for a body across the bed. But, for a long time, he had been reaching for me—for the person called Rachel, who did indeed, in the end, love back the person named Wick.

Life is still hard, but it is fair, and there is more joy in it that doesn't feast on heartbreak.

There are also territories not worth holding on to, traps not worth setting.

Other people live at the Balcony Cliffs with us now. Other faces stare at me when I walk these corridors. Most of them we invited in, and many are children with no place to go. We do not ask anything of them except that they scavenge what they can and help maintain the Balcony Cliffs.

Wick creates things for the children, bits of biotech from odds and ends that make them laugh or astonish them. I like to watch Wick at play. I like to hear the children laugh. It is so much better than a fancy restaurant. It is more like the botanical garden on the island. It is almost like that.

Teems is one of the boys here and the closest to being my child. I had the fantasy of finding the girl, the leader, and raising her as my own, but I never found her. Instead, I found Teems, and I took him in. He was the first.

Teems is just an ordinary boy who likes playing catch and hates vegetables and reads my collection of books when I make him. Teems doesn't mind roughhousing in the mud, and the stubborn set to his jaw always makes him look as if he is objecting to something. But his eyes are large and wide and they take in everything, do not miss the smallest detail. He is honest and respectful and he has honor and courage as he is able.

I teach him only the useful things, the hopeful things. I teach him to be both the things I am and the things I can never be.

I am sure Teems thinks of me, of Wick, as old, as people who are too generous and not hardened enough. People who can no longer see the traps. But did we ever really see them? And we have had our adventures, Wick and I. We have had all the adventures one lifetime could endure, and it is fine that no one knows but us, that Wick and I hold on to those secrets together. There is so little of this account that anyone else in the city would understand or believe, and so little of it they need to understand.

✿

I have only one thing left to tell. How, on a sunny gunmetal day not long after we returned to the Balcony Cliffs, I went searching, as any scavenger would, near the place in the city where Borne and Mord had disappeared.

There, I found Borne again. I picked him out of the rubble. I brushed him off. He was weak, tiny—as small as the first time I found him. But it was him. He smelled like the ocean of my youth—the sea salt, and the surf, and the seaweed. But he might have smelled different to someone else.

I gathered Borne up as good salvage, and I took him back to the Balcony Cliffs. He did not speak, could not speak, but I felt as if he were still there, inside. He had killed so many people. He had done terrible things despite not wanting to do them. We had all done terrible things.

I put him on our balcony, right where Wick could see him, and promised myself that if Borne ever grew, if he ever spoke, I would end him. That if Wick wanted to take him, Wick should take him and use him for parts.

But none of those things happened. Wick did not take him. Borne did not move on his own; he was just a kind of plant, taking sustenance from the sun. Borne never spoke again, although I spoke to him and maybe I wished he could respond, but only a little. A lingering doubt, a lingering need, and I think you can forgive me that, at least.

We sit on the balcony on the good days, Wick and I, and we hold hands and look out at the light on the river at dusk. To those who know me, so many years later, I am just a middle-aged woman who lives in the Balcony Cliffs and takes care of children, a person who they see sometimes high above a river that is not as polluted as before, a river that one day may be truly beautiful.

BESTIARY

TEEMS'S BESTIARY
ILLUSTRATED BY ERIC NYQUIST

My adoptive mother told me many times when I was young that to reclaim our world we must know it better, and to that end she gave me an education I am unwilling to waste. Therefore, the descriptions below represent my initial attempt at beginning such a project of rediscovery, focused on the riches found in this very city. This bestiary is a work in progress that includes facts, folklore, and, possibly, outright lies. In general, I have chosen not to differentiate between what can be confirmed and what cannot because I have myself witnessed what to many would be considered miracles, not of this Earth, and therefore am unwilling to discount the miracles witnessed by others. Nor will I discard the playfulness of myth.

I have had help from several in compiling these entries, but in some cases I do not know the names of my sources and in other cases these individuals wish to remain anonymous. Distillations from Company lichen—still ongoing—have proven useful as well.

As is often written in the old books, "Any mistakes are my own and I welcome any corrections or additions."

—Teems the Scholar

 **ALCOHOL MINNOWS** (p. 25): Also known as "alkie sardines," these tiny silver fish were seeded throughout the City when the Company arrived—dropped in a torrent from helicopters into the polluted river. At first, this was seen as a friendly gesture, but in the ensuing decades it has become clear that this was the opening salvo in an effort to keep the population docile. These weird fish have survived and thrived ever since in the sand and dust. Because their fish genes are fused with the genes of succulents, alcohol minnows can burrow into very dry places for many years, living in a kind of suspended animation.

At times of sudden rain, they will appear in more abundance, but their reproductive cycle remains a closely guarded secret. The moisture that mimics liquor is actually a kind of resin or sap that serves the same purpose as blood in human beings. Some claim that the eating of an alcohol minnow changes the experience of shoving a memory beetle in your ear—that the two experiences exist in a symbiotic relationship—but there is no way to prove or disprove this theory. The taste of an alcohol minnow, however, is said to mimic the recipient's own best memory of having been drunk, and thus is different for every person. (See also *Memory Beetle*)

ANONYMOUS MEAT, PACKETS OF (p. 5): Due to the Company's decline, eyewitness reports of "packets of anonymous meat" are all we have to confirm the possible continued production of food items from the seemingly derelict Com-

pany building. Most later iterations seem inconsistent at best. One week, for example, people still remember that the "anonymous meat" writhed and bleated within its biodegradable packaging, and at other times the "anonymous meat" was actually tiny organisms made to resemble lions, tigers, bears, and other extinct creatures found in a product called Animal Crackers, which some of the older scavengers remember their parents recalling with nostalgia. Since the civil war with the Magician, the Company has fallen further into disrepair, with sightings of new food packets rare. (See also *Meat, Autonomous*)

COMPANY LICHEN (p. 154): Not to be confused with edible Company moss, this orange-and-green lichen roams feral throughout the City and has an unpleasant, acerbic taste. Created as a kind of organic surveillance tool, harvested Company lichen can yield photosynthetic images if immersed in the right kind of solvent. Long-lived and almost impossible to kill, certain patches of lichen doubtless carry a history of the City in submerged dermal images, since the lichen internalizes within its internal structures incredibly fine "rings," like a tree trunk. Since the collapse of the Company, this lichen serves no purpose, but for people in the City desperate for some kind of record of a barter exchange or other transaction, the custom is to conduct such business in front of active Company lichen; the resulting agreement is considered binding due to the photosynthetic "witness." (See also *Company Moss* and *Lichen, Not the Good Kind*)

COMPANY MOSS (p. 95): Although described as a "moss," Company moss is yet another animal-plant hybrid, with protein strands that resemble beef and an infusion of nutrients more commonly found in potatoes and beans. Company moss contains neurons in simple synaptic relationships, which means it can think in a very limited way. Company moss is edible, a dull but constant staple for many in the City. To further indoctrinate the population with the alcohol minnow, Company moss tastes better if you have eaten a minnow first. (See also *Company Lichen* and *Lichen, Not the Good Kind*)

COMPOST WORMS (p. 18): Worms need food, moisture, and oxygen, and in this way are not unlike human beings (no matter how you might complain about the comparison). Compost worms differ from "regular" worms in that they were made to live indoors and break down human waste. Some call them "shit worms" or "crap worms" or "turd worms." You may call them whatever you want in the privacy of your own bathroom. As might be expected, the spring celebration of turd worms practiced by some is largely an indoor, low-key affair.

It is largely the confluence of natural worms and unnatural worms in the soil that has sustained the City despite all of the problems. Most artificial worms have been altered to feed on dormant alcohol minnows. Most artificial worms have also been made edible, to be dual purpose in an emergency . . . with all that this implies. Other kinds of biotech worms include diagnostic worms (p. 32) and defense worms (p. 133). (See also *Earthworms*)

COYOTES (p. 265): Rumored, but existence may be apocryphal, even if tales are told of distant sightings in silhouette in the subterranean sections of the City that once held a subway system and underground mining facilities. If

coyotes exist, their lives must be so far removed from the life's blood of the City's commerce as to be considered a kind of haunting they inflict upon themselves. Legends surrounding coyotes speculate on a symbiotic relationship with Company-bred surgical mice that make them impervious to diseases, and that they have become the dominant intelligence outside of the City and we are simply too remote to observe this development. (See also *Doglike Animal, Brittle Remains of; Mice, Solemn-Looking*)

CRAYFISH, WAYWARD (p. 239): Although usually considered a nostalgic reference to a bygone time before the destruction of most of the world, the crayfish has adapted to desert conditions, aided by a high resistance to pollution and heavy metals. For this reason, the blotched crayfish, as it is sometimes called, has managed to survive in the City's harsh conditions. The crayfish can immerse itself even in the polluted river for brief periods of time without harm and retain moisture for up to a week. Adaptations that include pollutant-targeting echolocation and the ability to eat Company moss have helped its chances. This species is called "blotched" due to the unique pattern across its carapace, which helps in camouflage but also functions as a two-fold screening system for certain types of pollutants. When the blotched crayfish was more common, some scavengers would use changes in its coloration as a guide to the level of contaminants in any given part of the city. (See also *Fiddler Crabs* and *Mudskippers/Mudpuppies*)

DAMSELFLY (p. 243): Rare, the damselfly, with its diaphanous black wings, can exist only in certain temperatures below sea level. For this reason, remaining specimens in the City are usually found in hidden cisterns or wells, clinging to bits of moss and other  vegetation. And yet this species is not extinct, suggesting a toughness at odds with its delicate appearance and habitat requirements. Over time it has adapted by de-emphasizing eyesight in favor of other senses and has changed how it lays eggs to maximize dispersal to increase its range, if not its population. Unlike some species of insect that have been obliterated by Company versions that mate faster and live longer, the delicate look of the damselfly has made it an undesirable subject for biotech experimentation. Glimpsing a damselfly is considered good luck by inhabitants of the City, and this may also account for its survival.

DIGGING GAP-JAWED LEVIA-THAN (p. 250): A biotech beast modeled on both the mole and the basking shark that would have scooped up soil and spit it back out transformed, cleansed of any natural life, replaced with patented CompanyLife™. Such artificial life would have enacted Company feedback loops and other orders while serving as surveillance peeking up at the City's inhabitants. In effect, the Company could then claim that it owned the City, or at least the soil beneath every building. The practicality of such a claim, employed with efficiency and success in other locales, was never tested in the City, as both the City and the Company fell into chaos well before such a test could occur or the digging beast could even advance beyond the conceptual stages. (See also *Flying Creature with Many Wings* and *Leviathan*)

DOGLIKE ANIMAL, BRITTLE REMAINS OF (p. 13): Several "doglike animals" in mummified form litter the interior of the Balcony Cliffs, a vast complex of sunken and abandoned living quarters overlooking the City's polluted

river. The extreme age of these remains and where they are found suggest less that they served as pets than that feral dogs, possibly human-made, supplanted the original occupants in these apartments for a time. Rumors of an uplifted species of dog somewhat like a whippet—bred for aggression and used as guards in the apartment complex—are completely untrue. (See also *Coyotes*)

DUCK WITH A BROKEN WING (p. 264): Often sighted and also often misunderstood, the "duck with a broken wing" reported as living alone on the approaches to the Company building is in fact not a duck at all. But none who have approached it have ever lived long enough to report as to its true nature. As a result, ducks have flourished as a species in the City due to a general suspicion and caution. (See also *Elongated, Elastic Creatures*)

EARTHWORMS (p. 152): Good old-fashioned, durable non-biotech echinoderms who have adapted to the City's sandy soil and arid conditions. The salt of the Earth, but please do not salt their earth. The earthworm's ability to regenerate tissue and its rudimentary yet three-tiered nervous sys-

tem make it ideal raw material for biotech, simple enough even for amateurs to adapt. It is said, "Do not trust a bioengineer who cannot tell the difference between an earthworm and a compost worm any more than you would trust a plumber who doesn't know their ass from a hole in the ground." (See also *Compost Worms*)

EELLIKE THINGS (p. 54): Mysterious and often difficult to catch, the tough and hardy eels that inhabit the river and vestiges of underground reservoirs of the City may remain hidden for months before emerging into view. Unlike eels in the natural world, these "eellike things" are not just elusive but also very clever and go about their business with an intensity that makes it noteworthy when they do pop up. Rumor has it that the biotech signature on these creatures is three initials: "MCD." Who MCD is or what MCD's agenda is, not even the most astute scavenger can say. If few have seen the eels, then none have seen MCD or even know if MCD yet lives. Conjecture that MCD is Company-related or among the hidden masters who pull the levers of the world cannot be confirmed, for the obvious reasons. (See also *Elongated, Elastic Creatures*)

ELONGATED, ELASTIC CREATURES (p. 316): These being a new thing, and having popped out of the sand near the end of the world's story, they do not register in the normal way, and are often like shadow or mist to the naked eye, as if even

their atoms laugh at the scavengers who hunt them. These elusive creatures like to come out at dawn or dusk, when it is hard to look upon them directly. For they slink and slide past the senses, and are seen or experienced at the corner of vision. "There is no way," say wise women in the City, "for the past to truly see the future." (See also *Duck with a Broken Wing*)

FIDDLER CRABS (p. 239): Displaced persons from coasts of continents and from islands lost to rising seas displaced with them fiddler crabs, which they brought along as pets and as reminders of home. Fiddler crabs can live for three years, or longer under protected conditions. At one time, a handful of mud flats along the polluted river in the City became colonized by fiddler crabs

released as an intended act of mercy by refugees who had come to the City. The crabs breed rapidly and practice extreme caution in popping back into their holes. However, although used to estuaries, they are not a freshwater species and cannot survive forever in freshwater. Such colonies inevitably failed, and the only fiddler crabs still extant in the City are those that have not been released into the wild. (See also *Mudskippers/Mudpuppies*)

FIREFLIES (p. 21): Any fireflies in the City are artificial, the work of amateur bioengineers. Fashioned from gene splices between fireflies and bees, the City's fireflies are social creatures that like to congregate and pull sustenance from dew spots and by eating the

lice and mites that accumulate inside City buildings. In this respect, their predatory habits resemble certain types of wolf spiders. When encountered en masse of an evening, firefly swarms turn the dark to gold and in their pointillism rival the greatest of firework displays, suggesting that beauty can be inexhaustible. Most people in the City take pride in fireflies, as their particular contribution to the field of "made beasts." But as important, they love the social aspect of the fireflies, congregations and concentrations more possible than any human community in the dangerous City.

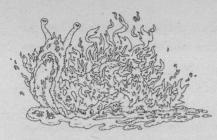

FIRE SLUG (p. 215): The terrestrial version of a sea slug, a repurposed Company invention, one meant to be sold instead of wood for fireplaces. But the fire slug loved fire too intensely and devotedly, and accidents occurred at an untoward rate. What is not understood is how the dance of foxes also seems to be mimicked by the handful of fire slugs that remain in the City—or why. Fire slugs can live to be more than a century old if left to their own devices. Made to flame and flame again by their oppressors, they will instead fade and desiccate within three to four years. But if even just an ember of their life remains within the gray dull remains, a fire slug can rise again in even greater splendor. Other kinds of slug include a fat, luminous variety (p. 244) that serves as a water filter, surgical slugs (p. 32) that cover and heal large wound areas in skin, and azure slugs (p. 19) that rejuvenate the soil through excretion of ground cover.

FLOUNDER CREATURE (p. 14): This dual-purpose fish and living map has a confused origin. Some claim the bioengineer Wick stole it from the Company, while others proudly  proclaim it is Wick's work, and thus proof of the mad skills of amateurs in the City. Regardless, the flounder has no parallel in the literature on biotech. The method by which Wick, or some unknown other, created a sensitivity to the architecture of the Balcony Cliffs demonstrates an almost preternatural ability and must be considered a myth of sorts. The Magician once introduced the slander that the flounder served no purpose whatsoever, had no agency of any kind, but that Wick would pretend, so as to convince his clients of his powers. In which case, the fish was merely a poor, confused flounder far from home, floating in a shallow pan, asymmetrical eyes peering up at all and sundry with something akin to a plea for help, or at least for honesty. (See also *Leviathan* and *Mudskippers/Mudpuppies*)

FLYING CREATURE WITH MANY WINGS (p. 250): Another of the Company's blueprints that was never created, perhaps rendered obsolete by the rise of Mord or simply by the Company's decline. According to a scavenger who once worked at the Company building, this bird would have been so large it would have blotted out the sun as it patrolled the skies, its fifty sets of wings both awe-inspiring and unwieldy. Sometimes the myths surrounding the strange bird become intertwined with those about the flying creature, and it is not unknown for those who worship the strange bird to come to blows with blasphemers attributing heroic struggles instead to a tool of the Company. (See also *Digging Gap-Jawed Leviathan*, *Strange Bird*, and *Vultures*)

FOXES (p. 10): Some residents recall their grandparents mentioning a time without foxes, which suggests they are not native to the City. Nor is there one kind of fox; nor can it be substantiated whether the Company created one or more of the several species or "versions" found in the City.

The desert fox, related to the fennec fox, is small and tan-colored but possessed of enormous ears. This type of fox tends to stick to the outskirts of the City, but often works in concert with other species, especially to coordinate attacks or initiate distractions to steal food. The desert fox burrows deep and furiously, using large front paws and powerful back legs. Scavengers who wander out into the desert looking for lost biotech have been known to break a leg falling through into a fox labyrinth.

The blue fox has been seen only three or four times, and none recently; it is rumored the blue fox was kidnapped by the Magician for her experiments. Scavengers tell the story that the blue fox was the secret leader of all the foxes and that the Magician kidnapped him out of spite because he was so beautiful and because she feared the foxes he led and worried that they might make common cause with the great bear Mord. But the blue fox, even held by the Magician's power and only a head upon a wall, could not be killed, for the blue fox did not truly live within our world. The blue fox had *slipped over* from elsewhere so that even if it should appear to die, it could never really die—not its heart, not its mind.

Once, it is whispered, the blue fox and Mord spoke together at dusk, the great ursine head bending low to peer down into the laughing face of the fox, and that some silent understanding passed between them, some moment of *seeing* beyond the comprehension of human beings, and that afterward the great bear rocked back on its haunches and was observed to roar with laughter . . . except that for a long time no one understood Mord had laughed because he had never laughed before. Afterward, too, the blue fox danced out in the desert until well after the moon came up, and the moon was blue too as if in on the joke, and all the other foxes joined in that dance.

"If you see a blue fox," people in the City tell their children, "you *must* laugh as if you have heard a joke—and then you must run, you must run for your life, for otherwise that blue fox will pull you over into his world."

Another one-off fox has been seen with tiny hands sprouting from its chest, a fox that in the dark teems with quiet bioluminescence. Both of these characteristics, sprouting hands and glow-effect, are trademarks of the earliest Company experiments in the City. For this reason, it is thought that the fox with the human hands must be very old indeed—a matriarch, whose origins and knowledge she has passed down to the others. That the human-hands fox and the blue fox traveled together for a time, trotting through the ruined buildings in the center of the City, must be a lie, the kind of fancy that a blue fox would spread just to be mischievous.

Certainly, foxes of all types have in the City exhibited atypical behavior or coordinated group behavior in stalking prey or they simply engaged in pranks—the pranks themselves indicative of higher-order brain functions and possible strategic analysis. According to legend, fox antics include foxes that gambol and seem to enact short plays out in the desert; foxes that leap over the narrow part of the poisoned river and back again, as if on a dare, for no particular reason except "why not?"; foxes that steal a scavenger's salvage and then return it later (perhaps changed in some subtle way), and just stand there, laughing with lolling pink tongues; foxes that appear to scrawl words with their paws in the desert sand; and foxes that at times warn scavengers of the approach of Mord, or appear to do so.

"The Lord loves a fox," goes the saying, "because no one else can understand their ways." (See also *Duck with a Broken Wing* and *Elongated, Elastic Creatures*)

LEVIATHAN (p. 158): Although some speculate that the leviathan that erupted from the holding ponds to fight Mord could be a version of the "fish project" that the bioengineer Wick would, when drunk, ramble on about to his clients or to some scavenger he hardly even knew . . . it was more likely some relic of the Company defenses. That some who witnessed the appearance of this leviathan reported that it "resembled an iguana more than a fish" would indicate it could not be Wick's "fish project." How long the leviathan had hidden in those murky waters and what it had eaten to survive cannot be determined.

Nor should we take the word of the old woman who lately likes to throw rocks at passersby outside the Balcony Cliffs, when she told one of her victims, "The leviathan was my brother! He was my brother from another mother and he cooked himself and tore off his own limbs to feed us and I miss him because that leviathan was not Company-made but had always lived there as I lived there until I assumed human form. Here, have a rock. And another." (See also *Flounder Creature* and *Mudskippers/Mudpuppies*)

LICHEN, NOT THE GOOD KIND (p. 59): A catchall term for vaguely hostile lichens that cannot be categorized as either Company lichen or Company moss yet are hard to tell apart due to similar patterns  or colors (such as green and red). Long-term scavengers in the City use this term for vegetative matter that seems aggressive in either

growth or locomotion—i.e., to identify a plant-animal hybrid that may be an unintentional mutation or a targeted enraged vector. The color blind are much more likely to be poisoned by hostile lichens, often serving as dispersal systems during certain disruptive lichen species' rather proactive breeding season. (See also *Company Lichen* and *Company Moss*)

MEAT, AUTONOMOUS (p. 59): Origins unknown, but definitely autonomous, with concern from some quarters that instances of such meat are not lab-grown, yet somehow authentic human and more mobile than one might wish. Nothing is more alarming than a sudden accumulation of autonomous meat, quivering in a semi-circle like a fleshy siege. As a defense mechanism, some autonomous meat will explode under threat. Speculation that it is "slab meat" refers to off-loaded meat from other biotech; in other words, synthetic animals that can grow edibles off of their bodies, but have done so too fast, creating anomalies and sometimes meat that burbles; also termed "sweat meat," as in "the newness sweated off the meat." (See also *Anonymous Meat, Packets of*)

MEMORY BEETLE (p. 6): One of the Company's more ingenious creations—both used to placate the local population and sold elsewhere—the memory beetle allows extraction of memory from one host to another or for a host to better access their own memories. This is a tactic used by unhappy residents of the City to forget their problems by

existing in the past. Memory beetles have also reportedly been created by rogue bioengineers, although the quality of these beetles may be poor and the memories thus thin or unsatisfying or unexpectedly banal.

Most "hacking" of Company biotech creates a mere echo of the original. But beetles function as excellent delivery systems for many different experiences, as their exoskeletons make them durable while their soft insides are ideal for housing certain kinds of genetic material. Their ability to fly increases their range, and it is easy to adjust beetle mating cycles to, in some cases, naturally create next-gen biotech. Other variants include the golden beetle (immediate obliteration of senses, good for escaping trauma, p. 12); the spy beetle (surveillance, p. 27); the diagnostic beetle (otherwise known as the medic beetle, p. 32); the defensive beetle (creating mist-screen and vectored noxious spray, p. 179); and the battle beetle (p. 180). This last variety was used by the Company as a solution to the problem of security. It functions as a kind of living bullet, as it tunnels into the flesh, seeking the heart or brain. (See also *Alcohol Minnows*)

MICE, SOLEMN-LOOKING (p. 139): As distinguished from ordinary mice found in the City, a "solemn-looking mouse" is slang in certain neighborhoods for mouse-based diagnostics and medical repair. Some species are small enough to live within the human throat, exuding a liquid through their paw pads that numbs the scratch. Such mice provide triage services. Developed as "in-house" medics for soldiers in foreign wars, a strain of "solemn-looking mouse" clings to a precarious existence in the City. Most scavengers revile these mice, consider them unclean or cursed, and recycle their parts for other biotech projects. A few revere the mice and actively participate in their use and trade these mice amongst their various throats to create the best medical combinations. But because these mice have regressive genetic markers, they often lose out to "real" mice for food and other resources when they fend for themselves sans human cohabitation. Thus, their range is limited to the boundaries of an unpredictable territory: the unnamed countries formed by the bodies of their hosts. (See also *Coyotes*)

MUDSKIPPERS/MUDPUPPIES (p. 239): These fascinating carnivores are a kind of fish with bulging eyes and strong fins that propel it across mudflats, its primary habitat. Although not found in the City, mudskippers are thought to be a partial influ-ence on two Company creations: the fish project worked on by Wick, the bioengineer, and the leviathan that, once discarded, lived in the holding ponds outside of the Company building. The mudskipper's amphibious nature and ability to walk on land like certain species of catfish make it a desirable subject for genetic manipulation, as does its tenacious toughness. Well into the Seventh Extinction initiated and sustained by human activity, the mudskipper, despite habitat loss, continued to maintain high population numbers and even population growth. It was also among the first subjects of the advanced biotech experiments that led to the growth of commercial biomimicry, of special interest to spy agencies and the surveillance sector. The introduction of these "fake" mudskippers into local environments on the mainland and on islands only strengthened the genome of the mudskipper in general—while also strengthening the paranoia of human populations in these places. (See also *Fiddler Crabs* and *Leviathan*)

PREDATOR COCKROACHES (p. 30): Most cockroaches are predators in some context, but for scavengers "predator" always suggests proactive attack. The predator cockroach is an aggressive, invasive species bred by the Company to coat the outer walls of its main building and to swarm in the case of a breach. However, these cockroaches are so aggressive that they swiftly resort to cannibalism when in close proximity to each other. Without culling and maintenance by the Company, they quickly ate each other into almost-extinction. Perhaps a couple hundred remain in the City, sequestered, and are of great value due to scarcity. Once used instead of currency, too few remain to form a stable monetary unit. Almost exclusively employed for intimidation and extortion, as their aspect is fearsome and their burrowing into flesh horrifying, if usually nonfatal. Q: "What are two predator cockroaches?" A: "One predator cockroach." Q: "What is one predator cockroach?" A: "Happy." (See also *Memory Beetle*)

RED SALAMANDERS (p. 16): Red is the color of caution or "stop," and when the red salamanders tumble from the sky, it signals that conditions in the City have faltered and contamination is heavy. For the  tiny amphibians sacrifice themselves to cleanse the City, dissipating in the heat, and are absorbed as liquid into the soil. The levels of poison in the air drop, taken in by their skin and then diffused through the medium of the fluid they become. And where they go as liquid is not known, except that like wraiths these very same creatures reform and are taken up by the sky and deposited again. These creatures are so very old and yet so very new, and take on our sins as their own, for which we should thank them. Or so say the elders in the City, such elders as they be, who also claim the salamanders are holy relics. For if you put your ear to the ground after the rain of their bodies, you can hear them singing for the joy of their service and the promise of resurrection. All of them soft in their singing, yet so beautiful.

SILVERFISH (p. 205): An ancient insect that existed on Earth before the dinosaur, the silverfish has thrived in the City, much as it has thrived everywhere for more than four hundred million years. Wingless, the silverfish depends on extreme speed and a nocturnal existence to pursue an advantage. The versions found in the City are much larger than the norm, live for decades, have become adroit at moisture extraction even in the driest conditions—sometimes existing on the bodily fluids found within its prey—and have been observed to be more social than their predecessors.

Silverfish will eat anything and, given the immense inventory of papers and books that housed the City's history, could be said by their devouring to have absorbed that history and made it their own to the extent that it now belongs to them. Inasmuch as an insect rules the City, it is the silverfish, as silverfish females produce up to one hundred eggs per day. A relative of the silverfish, the firebrat, has not fared as well in the City, for reasons too esoteric to relate here.

Impervious to pollution and poisons, the silverfish also tastes terrible, discouraging scavengers from harvesting it, and has a nasty bite that often becomes infected. Their molted scales, however, resembling the scales of a fish, are much prized by biotechs— or, at least, the properties of those scales when ground into glitter and reapplied to beetle carapaces.

The rantings of the old man named Ted-Ned, who stood outside the City's ruined observatory in better days, alluded to an empire of silverfish beyond the desert, where they have created their own complex society, with their own customs and their own ways of governance. Their cities are tiny but plentiful, forming sandy towers burrowing into the sky and extending far beneath the surface. Within these citadels, the silverfish have developed their own arts, based on speed and toughness, expressed in signs and symbols cut into the sand floor and flourishes cutting the air that fade as soon as made so that ever some members of the empire must replicate what will always disappear. The silverfish king sits upon a throne made from the cracked exoskeletons of a thousand locusts and holds a staff fashioned from the hardened horns of a dozen lashed-together rhinoceros beetle horns.

If you, a human, approach one of these silverfish cities, the melodious music from within will cease and they will appear ghostly and empty and you will think them merely the whims of some desert children, even as you marvel at the craftsmanship. Soon enough, though, you will not even notice this as you will have fallen into one of the main quicksand traps of the silverfish and you will be served up as a fine meal for two or maybe even three generations of young silverfish, contributing in your way to the culture of the silverfish empire.

The old man is crazy, of course, but there are children daft enough from staring into the flames of the fire slug all night to listen and repeat these things, and thus they perpetuate this nonsense, and thus silverfish have come to be revered in more ways than one. (See also *Damselfly* and *Memory Beetle*)

STRANGE BIRD (p. 169): Almost certainly apocryphal; no evidence of this bird exists in the City. For this reason, many believe the strange bird is a myth of freedom or imprisonment used as propaganda by the Magician. Possibly   this bird was unique biotech blown in from the desert by a storm and unable to find its way out, but if so the creature led a short and miserable existence in the City until scavengers tore it apart. Every sort of description has been given for the strange bird and every sort of story has been told about her, and this will continue until there is no City at all to speak of. (See also *Flying Creature with Many Wings* and *Vultures*)

TICK, WHITE ENGORGED (p. 26): Misunderstood by some as a real creature. In fact, simply a metaphor for the Company.

UNRECOGNIZABLE ANIMALS (p. 5): On occasion, scavengers find animals whose skulls seem "burst from internal pressure, eyes bright and bulging." Are these residual high-altitude experiments by the Company? The paranoid within the City specu-  late that there is another Company building hovering "above the sky," from which such things inevitably must fall. At times, this other Company building is conflated with the empire cities of the silverfish, especially among drunk storytellers late at night who should know better. (See also *Elongated, Elastic Creatures* and *Silverfish*)

VULTURES (p. 233): This kind of bird can be tricky and cunning, for some are actually automated cyborg drones, or "dark wings," programmed centuries ago to surveil or drop seed loads from now empty cargo bellies. The stomachs of real vultures can be strange enough, containing acids that dissolve anthrax, botulism, and cholera bacteria. They use their own vomit as a defensive mechanism, and the wizened boy down by the corner near the courtyard of dead astronauts swears that vultures in the air together are known as a "venue," while those congregated on the ground are a "kettle."

Alas, vultures tend to be shooed away and go distinctly undervalued in the City because in eating carcasses they clean up bits of biotech that might be valuable. Some vultures are colonized by the "dead" biotech they eat and thus become the eyes and ears of another organism entirely.

So you never really know *what* is hovering above you or who it reports to. But ever this was the way in the City and, really, the wider world as well . . . (See also *Flying Creature with Many Wings* and *Strange Bird*)

ACKNOWLEDGMENTS

My gratitude to bears for putting up with my nonsense about them. Bears are fascinating, intelligent, clever, awe-inspiring animals. They deserve our love and support. If you see one, please do not run. Instead, stand still. If necessary, fall to the ground, be still, and pretend you are a boulder.*

All bears are miraculous. Many humans are, too. Thank you to my first reader, my wife, Ann, and to Sean McDonald, my patient, brilliant editor at Farrar, Straus and Giroux, and everyone else at FSG for being patient and brilliant. Thanks to my UK, Canadian, Chinese, and German publishers for their early adoption of the novel. Thanks to my agent, Sally Harding, and the Cooke Agency—as well as Joe Veltre at Gersch. Thanks as well to Eli Bush, Scott Rudin, Alana Mayo, and Paramount Pictures for their enthusiasm and creativity.

Thanks to my stepdaughter, Erin Kennedy, and my grandson, Riley (Mr. R), for some of their thoughts on how Borne might speak. Special thanks to Erin for loaning me "long mice."

Thanks to one of my literary idols, Steve Erickson, for taking an early excerpt from *Borne* for his wonderful magazine, *Black Clock*, well before I had finished the novel. His edits and his support meant the world. Additional thanks to Elizabeth Hand for red salamanders, and to Scott Eagle for telescope scales.

Finally, thanks to our monster cat, Neo, otherwise known as Massive Attack, without whom certain aspects of both Borne's and Mord's personality would not exist. For instance, attitudes toward lizards.

---

*Please consult official bear-safety manuals prior to encountering bears.